THE DARK LADY

CAITEE COOPER

Copyright © [2024] by [Caitee Cooper]

All rights reserved.

No part of this publication may be reproduced, distributed, or transmitted in any form or by any means, including photocopying, recording, or other electronic or mechanical methods, without the prior written permission of the publisher, except as permitted by U.S. copyright law. For permission requests, contact Caitee Cooper.

The story, all names, characters, and incidents portrayed in this production are fictitious. No identification with actual persons (living or deceased), places, buildings, and products is intended or should be inferred.

Book Cover by Deranged Doctor Designs
Icon Design by Dallin Cooper
Edited/Proofread by Kayla Jackson

ISBN: 979-8-9877772-5-1 (eBook)
ISBN: 979-8-9877772-4-4 (Hardcover)
ISBN: 979-8-9877772-3-7 (Paperback)

Contents

For everyone who's ever fought Wormwood.

Part I: The Chase

Chapter One

Ellie eyed her magnificent, sprawling childhood home and tried to swallow the sick taste of fear gathering in the back of her throat. "I bet she knows we're here."

The silence in the truck thickened. Ellie squeezed the steering wheel, glancing at Oliver. He was sizing up her former sanctuary through narrowed eyes, the afternoon sun casting playful rays across his chiseled, soot-stained face. Ellie gave a tiny shake of her head. The day was far too beautiful for what had just happened.

Then again, she thought, *if the sun dimmed every time something terrible or unfair happened, the world would never see daylight.*

Oliver rubbed a hand over his face. "If she *is* here, she'll have a—"

Ellie flinched as he broke into hacking coughs. Hunching, he turned away, hiding his face in his elbow. She reached over and rubbed between his shoulder blades until his coughs subsided, then held out her water bottle.

"Thanks," he said.

"If only we had time to shower. The steam would probably help your lungs." Ellie wrinkled her nose at the smoke that still clung to both their bodies. It wasn't the sweet, comforting smell of woodsmoke—*that* she could tolerate, even enjoy. No, *this* was the harsh, acrid smell of a burning building, the stench of helplessness, horror, and despair. In short, all the things she'd felt when her brother Sam had run back into that hellscape to save his new sister-in-law's life. Then tenfold when Oliver had followed him. His mad dash back into the flames had been the bravest thing Ellie had ever seen.

And she was going to have nightmares about it for years.

"Sorry." Oliver cleared his throat. Or tried to; his voice was still raspy and hoarse. "At least she'll have a harder time sneaking up on us in broad daylight than she did last night."

"She floated right through a solid log wall," Ellie pointed out. "She doesn't have to sneak."

"True." Oliver eyed the cabin for a moment longer, then shook his head. "And I'm sure Wormwood's told her we were on our way back. The idea of them working together is …"

"Absolutely terrifying?"

"Yeah. I think we have to assume they're communicating, though." His voice lowered to a frustrated growl. "And since I can't seem to get Wormwood out of my head …"

Silence took the truck in a vise grip.

"We could just go," Ellie said softly.

"We could," Oliver said, "but if we end up road-tripping, I think we'll wish we had our stuff."

"That's true." Ellie scanned the windows, resolve hardening within her. Oliver was right. Even in the best-case scenario, where nothing was waiting for them inside, where they got on a plane and landed safely in Anchorage and were at Helen and Henry's house in Seldovia by this time tomorrow, *she* still needed clothes. And worst-case … Well, if the worst case happened, she'd be glad she hadn't unpacked very much during the last few days. At least she'd have clean underwear and a toothbrush. *If* they could get out without being killed by the Lady.

Though if that happens, she thought, *then I guess clean clothes are* really *a nonissue.*

Ellie threw the truck into park. "Let's go get it, then."

In seconds they were striding side-by-side up the walkway, the crisp scent of mountain sage thick in the air. They reached the porch, passing the swing where they'd sat the night before, which creaked in the afternoon breeze. Last night, it had been romantic. Now, even in broad daylight, it managed to look sinister.

Ellie stopped in front of the door, curling her fingers around its smooth silver knob, and hesitated. She loved this house so much. Through all the turmoil of the last few years of her life, it had always been there, solid, strong, and beautiful. But now it offered no refuge.

A warm hand twined into Ellie's free one, and then Oliver was at her shoulder. For a moment, his eyes—irrationally calm for the situation—met and held hers. Then, he reached for the door and eased it open.

Ellie tensed as she peered into the entryway, but nothing stirred. Oliver squeezed her hand, then let go and stepped inside, his calm expression undermined by the tense lift of his shoulders. Ellie followed him, her eyes darting into every corner, but there was only the usual: polished tile, knotty pinewood, and floor-to-ceiling picture windows that afforded expansive views of the mountains, the forest, and the Denver metro far below.

They made it through the entryway, the kitchen, and to the stairs with no trouble, the deep, soft carpet muting their footsteps as they climbed. They hadn't bothered to take off their shoes, but under the circumstances, Ellie was sure her mother would have understood. Oliver stopped at the top of the stairs and peeked into the long hallway. Ellie pressed against his side, craning her neck so she could see as well. If someone had come out of one of the rooms and seen them, they probably would have looked comical. Like two overgrown kids caught in a game of hide-and-seek.

Which, Ellie thought, *isn't that far from the truth.* It was just the worst game of hide-and-seek ever invented.

Ellie peered back down the stairway. From here she had a bird's-eye view of the entire kitchen and the formal living room. The house looked like several dozen friends and relatives had been in and out over the last few days: there was a dried spill on the granite bartop, the pillows and blankets on the couches and armchairs were rumpled and askew, and Ellie's music stand still sat in the corner with her concerto on it, which she hadn't touched in two days. Not since she'd played it for Oliver.

Ellie grimaced. Her violin teacher would *not* be thrilled that she was abandoning her rigorous practice schedule to run off to Alaska with some guy. But she'd worry about that when she made it back.

If she made it back.

"Still nothing," Oliver said, and Ellie seized upon his quiet baritone, letting it drive the morbid thought to the back of her mind.

"I don't see anything, either. But," she added as he made to move, "I think we should stay together. Just in case."

Ellie wasn't sure if she masked the fear in her eyes before Oliver looked at her. She wanted him to see her as brave. Hell, she wanted to *actually* be brave. She'd give anything for even a scrap of his courage. But, as always, her nervous system had other ideas, and she knew he could feel her hand trembling.

But Oliver just nodded and drew one thumb across her cheekbone in a light, comforting caress. "Okay."

Then he was tugging her after him, his steps quick and sure. Ellie clung to his hand and concentrated on breathing deeply as she followed, glancing into the rooms on either side. Empty. All of them. And when they arrived at the last one on the right—the one Oliver had spent two of the last three nights in—it, too, was empty.

Oliver released her and jogged toward the room's private bath, snatching some clothes out of his suitcase as he went.

"Is there anything you want me to grab while you're changing?" Ellie asked, edging toward his luggage. She'd been so focused on the Lady that she hadn't given a second's thought to the fact that they'd want to change their clothes. Her once-beautiful brides-maid dress—elegant, pink, and perfect until about three hours ago—swished around her calves, still breeze-light despite the ash all over it.

Oliver's muffled voice issued from around the door. "I think I've got most of it packed. Unless you want to check for loose socks."

"Depends. How badly do your feet smell?"

Oliver laughed. "Depends on the day. Yesterday and today, probably not too bad."

Ellie was already rounding the side of the neatly made bed closest to the window. There was nothing on the floor. And more importantly, nothing was flying across the tops of the trees with death in its pitiless black eyes.

The doorknob rattled behind Ellie and she turned in time to see Oliver step out, dressed in comfortable-looking hiking pants and a black T-shirt. He'd washed the soot off his face and was moving with purpose and grace. If Ellie hadn't known—and known *him*—she never would have suspected he'd nearly died in a structure fire only hours earlier.

"I couldn't find anything you missed," she said, hurrying toward him.

Oliver tossed his sooty clothes and toiletries bag into his suitcase and zipped it up. "Neatness is a habit you pick up quickly on a fishing boat."

He met her eyes and smiled, then fell into step beside her as they headed for the door, rolling his left shoulder awkwardly. Ellie didn't think much of it until he did it again; she was too busy peering into every room, just as she had last time. But the movement caught her eye, and when she noticed his strained expression, she frowned. "Is your shoulder okay?"

He looked away. "Yes."

"I'm ... not sure if I believe you."

"A falling board hit it when I was in the Luxembourg House. It's bruised. That's all."
He flexed it again.

"Well ..." Ellie hesitated as they stopped in front of her closed door. "*This* probably isn't
the place or time, but when we get ... wherever we're going ..." She swallowed. Butterflies
had joined the bats in her stomach, and she just wanted them all to calm down. "I know
my stomach isn't the strongest, but if you want me to look at it, I will."

"I checked it out in the bathroom, and I'll be okay."

Oliver stared at her bedroom door, his face a mask, his voice more brusque than she'd
ever heard it. Ellie felt a sharp pang of hurt before realizing she'd let her guard down; she
shook the feeling off and reached for the handle. It was perfectly reasonable for him to
not need her help for a superficial injury, and his sudden coldness was probably his nerves
finally breaking through.

And for good reason, she thought. So far, there had been no sign of the Lady—or any
other demon. But *her* room had been where the madness had started, where the Lady had
gone first. The creature knew. It was personal. What if the demon was in there waiting for
them, knowing they'd come back? Could she be that clever?

Ellie gulped. *I should've left the door open.*

Oliver let go of his suitcase and slipped a protective arm around her waist. "I doubt she
would've waited this long to attack us if she's here."

"That's probably true." Ellie's hand trembled on the doorknob, but she set her jaw,
turned the handle, and shoved.

The door creaked open to reveal an empty room.

All the same, both she and Oliver eyed every corner before stepping over the threshold.
It felt ... muted in here. Heavier. Like the room hadn't quite recovered from last night's
events, either. Oliver squeezed Ellie's shoulder before letting her go. She raced to her
walk-in closet, grabbing jeans and whatever shirts happened to be on top of the pile.

"I'm not sure how to be helpful here," Oliver said as she dumped the extra clothes in
her suitcase and hurried to the bathroom.

"Just keep watch," Ellie called over her shoulder. She shut the door and changed
quickly, then shoved her toiletries into her travel bag.

"Still nothing?" she asked as she pulled the door open. Oliver was standing by her
window, looking out over the mountains, his back to her rumpled bed and the neatly
rolled-up sleeping bag in the corner where he'd left it.

He shook his head. "Nothing."

"Okay." Ellie threw her sad, defeated-looking bridesmaid dress on the bed. It could wait until she got back—if Mandy, their housekeeper, didn't have it dry-cleaned first.

Oliver kept his back to Ellie as she threw in a few extra pairs of underwear, his keen eyes scanning the mountainside. Ellie was grateful for that, and not just because of his vigilance. Maybe someday they'd get to a point when packing her intimates in front of him wouldn't feel awkward, but today wasn't that day.

"Ellie."

The way Oliver said her name froze the blood in her veins. Slowly, Ellie raised her head. He'd gone taut as a bowstring, staring at something on the mountainside. For a second, neither of them moved.

Then, Oliver whirled. "We have to go."

Ellie fumbled the zipper shut on her suitcase and ripped it upright, adrenaline cutting its weight in half. "She's here?"

"Something is. It's coming from the northwest. Flying."

Panic turned Ellie's vision white. She stumbled over the threshold and into the hallway, and Oliver caught her by the shoulders.

"Stay with me, Ellie! We ran her off last night and we can do it again." He touched her cheek, then grabbed his suitcase and yanked it around the corner and down the first few stairs. "Come on!"

You ran her off, not me! Ellie bit down on the inside of her cheek and started after him, heedless of the jarring thud her suitcase made with each step. Oliver's eyes kept darting to the huge windows as they raced down the stairs and into the living room.

"Do you see it?" Ellie gasped.

"No." He hit the landing with Ellie hot on his heels. "I'm not sure if it was really there. It might've been an eagle or something. But we can't take chances."

Memories of those hateful black eyes filled Ellie's head and she gritted her teeth. "No, we can't." She skidded around the corner, nearly upending her suitcase, and cast one final look over her shoulder.

Outside, a skeletal figure wrapped in a ragged black dress skimmed over the trees. It was heading straight for them.

Ellie screamed, caught between freezing and running, but no, if she wanted to survive—if she wanted Oliver to survive—she had to control this fear, to beat it, to *own* it.

"ELLIE!"

Oliver was turning back for her, his expression desperate, fierce, the same one he'd worn the night before when he'd thrown himself between Ellie and the monster. But he was tired, worn out by his near-death in the fire. He couldn't fight. One or both of them would die if she didn't *move right now.*

Later, Ellie couldn't have said whether the force that erupted in her chest was raw, wild courage or fear of the highest magnitude. If it got her moving, what did it matter? She forced her feet forward, forced her mind to concentrate on the steps ahead of her, and suddenly she was free, moving, running.

For a second, Oliver looked like he might come back anyway, until his eyes focused on something over her shoulder. He paled. Then, he jerked into a run, reaching the door and wrenching it open. He hauled his suitcase through and down the front steps, then reached back for hers, but she'd already ripped it through the doorway and onto the porch, where it skittered madly across the concrete.

"I got it!" Ellie yelled. "Go!"

"Okay!" Oliver broke into a full-on sprint, reaching the truck seconds ahead of Ellie. He heaved his suitcase into the back and turned just as she reached him. "Start the truck! I've got it!"

Ellie tugged the keys out of her pocket and scrambled into the driver's seat. A bone-jarring shriek tore through her ears, obliterating Oliver's low grunt of effort. She whipped her head around in time to see the Dark Lady glide right through the cabin's wall. Effortlessly. As if the logs it was made out of were as insubstantial as Alaskan mist.

Whimpering, Ellie shoved the keys into the ignition. The engine turned over just as the passenger door flew open and Oliver landed in the seat next to her. "Drive!"

Ellie hit the gas. The truck's tires furrowed lines in the gravel as it rocketed forward. Oliver cried out, then Ellie heard the sound of his door slamming.

"Sorry!" she gasped.

"It's fine, just go!" He twisted, looking out the back window. "She's gaining, Ellie, you have to go faster!"

Ellie pressed harder on the gas, as hard as she dared on their private gravel road, watching the speedometer tick past thirty, thirty-five, forty— "We have to be losing her!"

"We are! Keep going!"

The main road was half a mile ahead, an asphalt snake winding its way through the gold-green Colorado wildlands. Ellie gritted her teeth as she barreled over a pothole, then slowed as she reached the intersection, where a big, red stop sign loomed.

Oliver glanced forward and his mouth fell open. "What are you doing?"

"There's a stop sign! I have to at least *look*—"

"She's catching up again! *Run the stop sign!*"

Ellie let out a screech, half of fear and half of defiant rage, and rushed through the intersection, sending the truck coursing down into the valley below.

"Yes! Good!" Oliver turned, watching their backs again, and Ellie stepped on the gas. They were approaching seventy miles per hour now, on a winding mountain road where the speed limit was forty for a reason.

"Where is she?" Ellie yelped, taking a turn so hard she could swear the truck's tires lifted off the ground.

Oliver braced his hand against her seat. "Falling behind! Don't slow down, though!"

"Don't slow—" *Have you seen this road?!*

But then Ellie narrowed her eyes. *She'd* seen this road a thousand times. She could do this.

"I can't see her anymore," Oliver said, "but don't slow down yet."

Ellie threw every ounce of energy she would have used to reply into staying on the road instead. They careened down the mountain at a speed that made her hope her guardian angels were both real and on duty, winding around corners and down steep sidehills until they reached the valley floor a thousand vertical feet below.

"I think we've lost her," Oliver said as Ellie negotiated the last turn. They dropped smoothly onto the plains, gliding through golden wheatfields that rolled out on either side of them.

"Good." Ellie took a deep, shaky breath, willing her core to relax. "I think I might have a heart attack."

Oliver put a hand on her shoulder. "You did great."

Ellie snorted.

"Seriously. Maybe you should street race."

"Not in a million years, Oliver."

He chuckled and let his arm drop, slumping against the seat and closing his eyes. "I'm glad there was no one coming at that stop sign."

"Me, too." Ellie's voice was trembling. *Everything* was trembling; her hands, her arms, her legs. She fought the urge to squeeze her eyes shut against the fog that threatened her vision. *Anxiety attack plus driving. Not a great combination.*

"The Lady—" Oliver broke into painful-sounding coughs again, hunching.

"Here, take ..." Ellie scrabbled for her water bottle with one hand. He could find it on his own, but she wanted—*needed*—to do something useful for someone else. "Take this."

"Thank you."

Ellie nodded. She glanced in the rearview mirror as he drank but saw only the familiar mountainscapes of home, steadily falling farther and farther behind. She swallowed, tears welling in her eyes as she remembered ... "I didn't close the front door."

Oliver lowered the water bottle. His head tilted sideways, and for a moment, Ellie was afraid he was going to call her out about how stupid it was to focus on *that*. But he just set the bottle in a cupholder, reached over, and began to rub her back. His touch was so soothing that Ellie let out an involuntary sigh, nearly closing her eyes again.

"I'm sure it'll be okay," was all he said.

For a moment, there was silence, and Ellie wondered if he was working up the courage to say the same thing she was thinking.

"Ellie, I don't think we can fly."

There it is. Ellie took another deep breath, trying to steady her voice, keep the tears from coming. "No. I don't think we can, either. She's too fast, and there's too much waiting. Security, boarding, flight checks ... she'll catch up to us." Ellie shuddered as she thought of Darien's words from the night before. "And I bet she'd bring down a whole plane just to stop us."

Oliver shook his head slowly, and when she glanced at him, he was staring at Boulder's tidy, chic outskirts with an expression that looked as bleak as Ellie felt. Then, his jaw tightened and he sat up straighter. "We'll just have to drive, then."

Cold fear grabbed Ellie by the spine. "I guess so."

They didn't speak again until they'd passed through the city and accelerated onto the Denver-Boulder Turnpike. Ellie couldn't help but glance in the direction of the Luxembourg House—or what was left of it. There was no smoke, no indication of the madness that had taken place there only hours earlier.

"I need to let Helen and Henry know," Oliver said, rubbing his eyes as if they were still sore from the smoke. "And while I'm at it, I might as well tell them the truth about closing the gate."

Ellie glanced at him. "They don't know?"

"I told them in general terms. But they don't know that I ... that someone's going to have to die."

Ellie's still-pounding heart sank to the bottom of her stomach. "There must be a way that no one has to die. And even if that *is* the only way, which I doubt, it doesn't have to be you."

In fact, she thought, *I won't let it be you.*

Oliver just put his free hand over hers, staring through red-rimmed eyes at the road ahead of them. For a moment, Ellie just let herself enjoy the feeling of his warm, callused fingers on hers. When they approached a turn, he reluctantly let go.

"I should tell Sam and Darien, too," Ellie said. "They need to know."

"Yeah—"

Another coughing fit seized Oliver, and Ellie waited for it to subside. The EMTs had said there would be no permanent damage. That as young and healthy as he was, rest, hydration, and relaxation should take care of it in a day or two.

Ellie watched out of the corner of her eye as Oliver pressed the water bottle to his lips again, and sighed. They had exactly *one* of those three things.

"Sorry. I agree," Oliver said. "Sam and Darien should know the Lady attacked us again. But ..." He gave her a small smile, "you might want to wait to send *that* text until they're already on their plane to Hawaii, or else they might run us down and demand to come."

"That's a fair point." Ellie frowned at the thought of what her brother and Darien would say when they found out. Darien would likely accept it with her usual levelheaded practicality, but Sam ... *Oh, Sam.*

Only when Oliver started chuckling did Ellie realize she'd said the last two words out loud.

"You know he'd try," he said.

Ellie shot him a look, a dry smile twisting her lips. "Yes, he would. I think Darien would prevail in the end, but we should spare the poor woman the stress."

"Yeah. While I have complete faith in the strength of their relationship, this isn't the kind of decision that needs to be dumped on two newlyweds. Especially after the day they've had."

"Your aunt and uncle, on the other hand ..." Ellie let the words fade as she guided the truck into thickening Denver traffic.

"I lied to them, Ellie. The sooner they know the truth, the better."

"What *did* you tell them?" Ellie asked. She felt for the Calls. Oliver hadn't told her someone needed to die for the gate to close, either, and when he'd pulled her into his room right before the wedding and finally let the truth spill out, it was like being slapped. Twice. Once because he'd decided not to tell her something vital about the problem they were trying to solve *together*, and then again by the raw pain and fear on his face. She could have helped with that. With *both* issues. But instead, he'd borne the burden alone.

Ellie still didn't know whether she was angry at him or touched. Maybe both.

"I told them the gate could only be closed at a solstice," Oliver said. "When I left, they were making plans to go up there in December."

Ellie set the cruise control, then poured every ounce of her exasperation into the sideways look she shot Oliver. "I assume you were trying to protect them, too?"

Oliver met her eyes, sheepish. "Now that I'm on this side of things, I realize how stupid it was, but yes. Them, you, the crew ... *everyone* I care about."

For a moment, the silence stretched.

"In my defense," Oliver finally said, "I was doing the best I could with the information I had."

Ellie's heart softened. "I know. And you had Wormwood in your head the whole time."

Her lip curled at the memory of that voice—the one that so closely resembled her own in her worst moments—whispering in her ear, magnifying her insecurities, taking her past mistakes and ballooning them until they were all she could see. In three short days, Wormwood had nearly destroyed not only her relationship with Sam and her extended family, but also the blooming affection between herself and Oliver. She still felt sick every time she thought about it. "I can't imagine he helped."

"No." Oliver's voice was a low growl. "He did not."

"Have you heard anything from him?"

"Not since the fire."

"Huh. Well, maybe we'll get lucky and outrun him, too."

Oliver didn't say anything for a moment.

"I don't think we will," he finally said.

Ellie bit her lip, taking the truck around a slow-moving semi that was parting traffic like a rock in a river. "They're all so different."

"Yeah. There doesn't seem to be a ... pattern to how they work, either. Wormwood can *literally* crawl inside someone's head, and followed me even on an airplane. The Lady can pass through walls and shapeshift, but we seem to always be able to see her, and she's clearly not as fast as Wormwood. Silverskin ..."

"He could just ... appear." Ellie shuddered, remembering her encounter with him at the Luxembourg House, and ... she frowned. In her room as well. "I'm still not sure why he didn't kill me in my room this morning. Unless ..." She put it together even as Oliver spoke.

"If we'd found you dead, there would've been an uproar. He was too smart, too disciplined for that."

"He wanted to make sure everyone who knew the whole truth was all in one place, so he could finish us all at once." Ellie shook her head. "That level of cleverness is scary, Oliver."

For a moment they were quiet, each lost in their own dark thoughts. Then a faint rustling reached Ellie's ears; Oliver was pulling his phone out of his pocket. "If you don't mind, I'd rather not put off this call any longer."

"I don't blame you. I think I'd rather fight a grizzly bear than Angry Helen."

A rueful, nearly silent chuckle escaped Oliver as he tapped the screen, then pressed the phone to his ear.

Chapter Two

"Sam, I need a hamburger."

Darien couldn't help but smile as her husband of less than a day looked back at her with those gunmetal gray eyes of his. A slow grin spread across his face and he turned, walking backward, his suitcase gliding almost soundlessly over the polished, gleaming floor. As she'd expected, the Four Seasons was gorgeous, and Sam—with his good looks, tanned skin, and white linen shirt—only completed the perfect scene in front of her.

Still, it wasn't quite enough to make her forget the madness their wedding had degenerated into, or the horror of nearly losing both him and her little sister, Ana, in the fire. Nor did it quell the worry she felt for those she cared about who were still recovering—her parents, both of Sam's grandfathers, Oliver, the surviving kitchen workers ...

But it certainly helped.

Sam waved his hand in an overly grandiose gesture at their surroundings, returning Darien to her gleaming reality with a grateful bump. "Darien, my dearest wife, I have brought you here so that for the next five days—and four nights—" he winked, and Darien smirked "—you can have whatever you want. And if what your heart wants right now is a hamburger, then a hamburger is what you'll get."

"You're the best husband in the whole world."

"Yes!" Sam pumped his fist. "Twelve hours in and you still like me!"

Darien laughed as he pressed the up button and the elevator doors slid open. "*Love you. Don't forget it.*"

She stepped inside and watched him pull their heavy suitcase in after him, letting her eyes wander happily over his muscled arms and shoulders. As the doors closed, he caught her admiring stare, and his eyes softened. "I feel the same way about you, you know."

Darien tilted her head up as he closed the distance between them. "Belly and all?"

She tried to keep her voice carefree, but a little thrill of nerves shot through her as she thought about the new life she'd bring into the world in a few short months. Sam—who she couldn't seem to hide *anything* from—must have seen it, because he searched her face, his eyes filling with gentle concern.

Then a smile tugged one corner of his mouth upward. "Yes. You look amazing."

Darien forced a smile onto her face, still trying to put down that nagging little flare of angst. "I'm excited, I really am. And I'm sure I'll recover just fine afterward. There'll just be … a lot of changes."

Darien's breath caught as Sam leaned down. "And you'll still be wonderfully …" He kissed her forehead. "… ravishingly …" He kissed her cheek. "… angelically beautiful, Darien. Through all of it. And I will love you through all of it."

He kissed her lips, slowly and passionately, and her pulse accelerated even as her knees went weak. Three years. *Three years* they'd been together, and he could still do that; in fact, he seemed to be getting better at it as time passed.

"I am *really* looking forward to spending the rest of my life with you," she whispered.

The elevator door slid open, so smoothly it was almost noiseless. Sam held her gaze for a moment longer, his eyes dark and gray and beautiful with open ardor. "Shall we go to our room?"

"Oh yes." Darien hitched their backpack higher on her shoulders as she stepped into the hallway. "But before we do too much more of that, I really, really need that hamburger."

Sam burst out laughing. "Seriously?"

"I'm dead serious. Our baby is eating me alive."

They stopped in front of their door, Sam still chuckling as he pulled the key card out of his pocket. "Do you think that means it's a girl or a boy?"

"I think that means it's hungry. Which means *I'm* hungry. So hurry up."

Sam pushed the door open. Darien stepped over the threshold and took in the spacious, casually elegant room with delight. Dropping the backpack onto the couch, she noted the wood furniture, the sprawling king bed scattered with rose petals, and the sliding door that opened onto their own private patio. The opulence, the luxury, the romance of it all …

Darien, you are one spoiled wife, she thought. And she was thrilled about it.

She moved to the patio and slid the door open. The ocean spread out underneath her like a vast, living thing, moving and dancing in the light of the full moon that refracted off its surface in a thousand little motes of silver. A gentle, salty breeze skimmed her dark hair back from her face and shoulders. She smiled, letting her eyes fall closed, and breathed in the smell of the ocean. Then another scent joined the first, sweeter, headier, and far more familiar and beloved: Sam's cologne. He wrapped his arms around her from behind and rested his chin on her shoulder. She leaned back against him with a sigh, and ...

Guilt pricked her as she thought about the loved ones—and the mess—they'd left in Colorado.

She did her best to ignore it. "This is so beautiful, Sam."

"You deserve it. You deserve everything good in the world." Brushing the hair away from her neck, Sam kissed her skin, and the feel of his lips finally drove the rest of Darien's guilt to the back of her mind. She turned in his arms and gazed up at him. His eyes were dusky, and the desire kindling in them made her blood warm. Reaching up, she kissed his lips. He returned it with slow, untroubled enthusiasm, twining his fingers through the ends of her hair. It was a long kiss, and she basked in its comforting joy and the perfection of the man she shared it with.

Then, her stomach growled.

Darien looked down, then helplessly back up at Sam. "It's not my fault you gave our child your appetite."

Sam let out something between a laugh and a groan, dropping his forehead to hers. "Better call for that hamburger."

He released Darien and she moved toward the phone. "You want anything?"

"Nah." He'd paused by the desk, examining what looked like some papers and a few brochures sitting on its dark, glossy top. "My motion sickness wasn't too bad this time but I'd better not push my luck. I'll wait until morning."

"Okay." Darien sat on the edge of their bed, dialed, and pressed the phone to her ear. "Sorry to be such a starving hyena."

Sam picked up several papers and flopped down next to her, crossing his long legs. "Hey, that's what vacations are for. We both slept on the plane and we're on Hawaii time now, so the night's still young." He shot her a grin. "And we can sleep in as long as we want in the morning."

"No kennel duty at 6 a.m., no calves being born at midnight—" Darien broke off as the operator answered the phone and she placed her order. Then she lay back, snuggling against Sam. "Did you find anything interesting on the desk?"

"General hotel info, the WiFi password, a local channel guide, the usual. But ..." He held up a little booklet and smiled when Darien perked up. "They also have a restaurant guide, and a couple little brochures about things we could go do."

"Let's take a look," Darien said. Other than tomorrow's visit to Oahu's famed Cultural Center and a luau later in the week, they'd kept their itinerary sparse. The best adventures always seemed to happen that way.

They perused a few leaflets about kayaking, snorkeling, waterfalls, and ancient Hawaiian cultural sites before Sam picked up a brochure with a dark cover. He grinned. "Hey, wanna go see a lava tube?"

Darien came up on her elbow. "Um, *yes*. I thought those were only on the Big Island, though."

"I thought so, too, but apparently not." Sam turned the paper over, glancing at the back side, then started to unfold it. "I guess—"

Movement out of the corner of her eye caught Darien's attention, weird and ... and *convulsive*. She whirled, heart in her throat, only to see a rose petal dancing across the floor. Another followed, blown by the gentle breeze drifting off the sea and through their still-open patio door. It was a beautiful sight; romantic, even. *Completely* innocuous, she told herself.

Sam sat. "You okay?"

"Um ..." Darien pressed a hand to her face. After last night, after seeing that ... *creature* in Ellie's room ... And after another one destroyed her wedding, killing people in the process ...

Well, she could understand why her brain had turned the flash of movement into a scuttling shape with claws.

"I guess I'm just a little jumpy after today."

"That's understandable." Sam looked away, but not before something vulnerable and uncertain flashed across his face. Just as quickly, it was gone. His arms stole around her waist and she let herself melt against the hard planes of his chest and stomach. He rested his head on hers and they simply sat there, gazing out at the ocean.

"Are *you* okay?" Darien finally asked.

He tensed. "Okay enough."

Frowning, Darien pulled away and looked up at Sam. His expression was troubled, his eyes more like storm clouds now than the liquid silver they'd been moments before. Gently, Darien took the lava tube brochure and set it on the bedside table. He watched her movements without saying anything as she sat cross-legged on the bed, facing him, and took his hands in hers. "Okay. I'm not a mind-reader, but I just *feel* like there's something bugging you, Sam."

Sam let out a deep sigh and looked down at their entwined hands. "I know it's our wedding night, and I *told* myself I wasn't going to do this, but are you okay if I try and call Ellie?"

Darien nodded, unsurprised. "Absolutely. I'm really worried about them, too."

Sam stood, went to the couch, and rummaged in the backpack for his phone. "It doesn't seem fair that we're here in this gorgeous place, able to do whatever we want, and they're out there being chased by the Lady and Wormwood and whatever *creep* lit the Luxembourg House on fire."

"I know," Darien said. "There's still a part of me that thinks we should have stayed."

But Sam jerked his head as he pulled his phone out. "No. My very first priority is making sure you and our baby are safe, and there's no safer place than an island in the middle of the ocean."

He crossed the room and settled on the bed next to her, looking stressed. Darien wondered if she looked the same way. After a moment, she laid a hand on his arm. "I'm sure they're okay."

Sam stared down at his phone. "What if their plane didn't make it? What if we made the wrong call?"

"You're her next of kin, right?"

Sam nodded.

"If the demons were going to crash their plane, they probably would have already done it, and you probably would have already gotten a call."

"Probably, but we don't know for sure."

"No, we don't, but it's a logical assumption."

Sam nodded slowly. "True. I just ..." He dropped his head again. "Even though everything in me screams to keep you safe, I can't help but wonder if I should've gone with them, too."

Darien raised her eyebrows. "What, so you and Oliver could have killed each other?"

He shook his head. "I don't think it would've come to that—"

"Sam." She paused, choosing her next words carefully. "You weren't … kind to him, there at the end."

"Ha. That's a very charitable way of putting it, my dear, and I appreciate it. Doesn't change the fact that I used his confidence in me against him. And basically accused him of trying to rape Ellie." Sam smacked his forehead. "Which I can't *believe* I said. In hindsight, that was such a stupid assumption. I know him better than that. I know his story. His *actual* story, not the thirty-thousand-foot version he tells people to get them off his back about it."

Darien blinked. "Really?" If Sam and Oliver had been that close of friends, it was no wonder Sam felt this guilty. She hadn't realized.

"Yeah. He told me when we were up in Portlock looking for my dad. We shared a tent with some other guys and, well, he tried to hide it but he's got … some scars … that I saw when he was changing once. I didn't ask him about it, but he saw that I'd noticed. Later that night, the other guys had fallen asleep, but neither of us could, so we ended up having a long talk. He opened up to me. Told me everything."

Self-disgust marred Sam's features. "The guy trusts me with that much, and *what* do I do? I turn around and spit it right back in his face."

Darien's heart squeezed; she reached a hand under his chin and lifted his face so his pained eyes met hers. "Hey, you stop. You were under the influence of a literal demon from an alternate dimension." She grimaced. "Or something like that, anyway. The point is, you weren't yourself."

"My actions and words were my fault, Darien. It doesn't matter what drove me to say them. The point was that I *said* them."

"It *does* matter. Yes, what you said hurt Oliver, and it was stupid. But you fought it, Sam, and you didn't let it win in the end. And Oliver gets it. He's been fighting Wormwood for weeks now. He knows what it's like."

Sam sighed. "He's a good guy. I'm glad Ellie's with him. I'd honestly be glad if she stayed with him long-term, too, after this is all over." He paused. "And I don't think the demon followed me here. There was … a weight, almost, that I felt I was carrying, and that's gone now."

"Good."

"I still feel so protective of Ellie, though." He looked up at her. "Maybe too protective?"

Darien smiled and took Sam's hand again. "Maybe a little. But I think that's just part of being an older brother. Plus, she's the only family you've got left." She shrugged. "It makes sense."

"Letting her run off on a dangerous trip while being chased by demons who want to kill her doesn't feel very good. I'm not feeling like that great of a brother right now."

Darien stared at him for a long moment. "Tell that to Ana."

Sam's eyes went wide; his mouth opened, then shut again. Darien pressed on. "My little sister's alive because you were willing to run into a burning building to save her." She reached up to touch his face. "You're a good brother. The four of us talked it over and made the best call we could. Both Ellie and Oliver are smart, competent, and capable, and they understand the risks. Now we just need to trust them."

Sam held her gaze, then let go of her hand and reached for his phone. "Darien, you're wise and comforting as always. I would be a basket case without you."

"Yes, you would."

He smiled. "Ten here is what…"

"One o'clock Mountain Time, I believe."

"Do you think that's too late?"

"No. If they're flying they won't pick up no matter what. And if they got grounded, I'll bet they're still driving and we'll be a welcome distraction."

"Okay." Sam paused, pinching the bridge of his nose. "I'm not sure what'll be worse: Ellie picking up or Ellie *not* picking up."

And before Darien could reply, he hit the call button.

Chapter Three

The sun had gone down hours ago, and the moonless night was blacker than the asphalt underneath the truck's wheels. Ellie squinted through puffy, red eyes at the clock on the dashboard. It was almost 1 a.m.

She stole a look over at where Oliver slept. He'd been great company for the first few hours, driving from dinnertime until well after the late-summer sun dipped below the horizon. But then, somewhere on the empty Wyoming prairie, his words had started slurring.

At that point, they'd switched drivers. And quickly.

Once they were settled, Ellie insisted he lean the seat back, close his eyes, and see if just *maybe*—on the wild, off chance that he was *tired*—he could nap. He'd fallen asleep as he was telling her he'd never been able to sleep in the car, and she'd smirked for nearly ten minutes afterward.

Now he rested against the rich leather with his arms folded loosely over his stomach, his face turned toward her. Those expressive blue eyes that always betrayed him were closed, the planes of his face peaceful. She'd never seen him this relaxed before. He always seemed to be in a state of casual alertness, attuned to his surroundings and ready to act—or react—at any moment. The fact that he'd fallen asleep was a powerful reminder of how harrowing the last twenty-four hours had been.

Ellie returned her gaze to the road, scanning the barrow ditch, the back seat, the shadowed truck bed ... but there was nothing out of the ordinary. No human figures in places they shouldn't be. It was just her and Oliver.

For now.

She changed lanes to go around a slow-moving truck, wincing as the tires hit a pothole she hadn't seen. Oliver stirred, then relaxed again, and Ellie breathed a sigh of relief. She'd done remarkably well these past few hours, but now she was starting to droop. And this godforsaken prairie just ... kept ... *going*.

A clamorous ringing burst through the truck's speakers and Ellie jumped. The truck swerved, and Oliver jerked upright. "*What*—?!"

"It's okay! It's just Sam calling." Ellie scrunched her eyes shut for the briefest of seconds. "Sorry. I forgot my phone was connected to the truck's Bluetooth."

She glared at her brother's name on the screen even as relief seeped through her—both at hearing from Sam and at Oliver's return to consciousness. He needed the sleep, and she regretted letting more be snatched from him, but at least now she wasn't alone.

Ellie pressed the accept button. "Hey. Status update."

"We're in Hawaii, safe and sound," Sam said. "And given that you're not on a plane, I'd much rather hear *your* update."

Oliver's seat droned upright as he rubbed the sleep out of his eyes.

Ellie shuddered. "It's not a happy update. The Lady attacked us at the Shack. We had enough time to change and get our stuff packed, but—"

"*Hell*, Ellie! Are you okay?"

"It was close, but we're both fine. And we've learned we can drive faster than she can fly, so that's reassuring at least."

Darien's voice joined Sam's. "Where are you now?"

"I don't know. Somewhere in northern Wyoming."

Light bloomed out of the corner of Ellie's eye; Oliver was squinting down at his phone screen. "Closest town is Sheridan. We're about fifteen minutes away. The next big one after that is ... Billings, in Montana."

"Holy ... you've made it clear to Montana?" Sam asked. "When did you leave the Shack?"

"Around three," Ellie said.

"No kidding," Sam said. "That's impressive. Good driving, you two. Have you seen any ..." He paused, and when he spoke again his voice sounded almost reluctant. "Any demons?"

"Nope," Ellie said. "Which is good, because we're exhausted and need to sleep. We might end up spending the night in Billings." She suppressed a sigh. "What's left of the night, anyway."

"Please do," Sam said. "I don't ever want to get a phone call about a family member being in a wreck again."

Ellie closed her mouth; there was nothing to say to that.

After a moment, Sam spoke again. "How're you doing, Oliver?"

"I'm okay." Oliver coughed, then cleared his throat. "Sorry. I sound worse than I am. How're you?"

"I've been better. But physically I'm bouncing back. I didn't spend as much time in the smoke as you did."

"It's amazing what a difference two minutes makes," Oliver muttered, leaning back against the seat. Then, louder, "Tell us what's going on on your end. What happened after the fire?"

"Well, Darien and I are all right, obviously, and we made it to Hawaii with no issues. The baby's threatening to eat Darien alive, so we're waiting on a hamburger."

Oliver chuckled. "I wondered why you were calling us on your wedding night. That makes more sense."

"The hamburger is part of it, yes," Darien said. "But it's also because Sam has been worrying like a mare with her first foal ever since we touched down and got your text. And honestly, so have I."

"The stars happened to align to favor you two with our presence," Sam said with a mock gravity that reminded Ellie suddenly and sharply of their father. "You should be grateful."

"Otherwise, yes, we would have been far too busy for you peasants," Darien said.

Oliver chuckled and Ellie smacked a hand over her reddening face. "Can you just tell us your update already?"

"*Your majesties*," Oliver added.

Ellie caught his eye, grinning, as Sam replied.

"Well, since you asked so nicely ..." He paused as if gathering his thoughts. "We stayed as long as we could to help pick up the pieces after the fire. We nearly canceled our flight—"

"Once we knew everyone was going to be okay, though, my parents wouldn't hear of us staying," Darien interjected. "Neither would your grandparents. And Grandpa Forth can be pretty hard to argue with. I think he would have marched us to the airport in straitjackets if he'd had to."

Ellie snorted. "Probably."

"You don't have to justify yourselves," Oliver said. "We would've shoved you out the door, too. In fact, I'd have tied the straitjackets' arms myself."

Sam sighed. "Thanks. It feels terrible being here in all this luxury when everyone else is—"

"Sam, stop," Ellie said firmly. "Just enjoy it. You deserve it. And we'll be a lot more effective now that we don't have to worry about you two being safe."

Darien's whispered "I told you" floated over the truck's speakers and Ellie cracked a tiny smile. "How's everyone doing? How are Ana and Carlos?"

"Ana and Dad are still in the hospital but the prognosis is good for both of them," Darien said. "They'll probably both be released sometime tomorrow." To Ellie's surprise, she chuckled. "Apparently she'd snuck back into the chapel to meet Matt because they have a thing."

Ellie smiled. "That's kind of cute."

"He's been keeping her company this whole time," Darien said. "Who knows? Maybe we'll end up having another De Leon/Forth wedding."

"Maybe we won't even blow everything up this time," Ellie muttered.

Sam chuckled. "Given our track record, that's a good goal to set."

"Any update on the kitchen workers?" Oliver asked.

"The ones that got out are all going to be fine eventually," Sam said. "Most need skin grafts and serious pain meds, and recovery will take a long time, but luckily there's a lot they can do for burns."

"Good," Oliver said.

Ellie gave an amazed little shake of her head. Was it only ten hours ago that they'd been in that gorgeous, lavish ballroom, looking forward to the promise of an afternoon spent celebrating with family and friends? What an incredible luxury. She couldn't believe it had taken a literal explosion for her to recognize it as such.

Sam's voice came over the speaker again. "There were three others in the kitchen who weren't so lucky."

Ellie's heart dropped. Oliver rubbed a hand over his eyes, resting his elbow against the windowsill. When neither of them said anything, Sam went on.

"The preliminary findings indicate that there was an explosion in the kitchen."

"That is *brilliant* detective work," Oliver muttered.

Sam laughed humorlessly. "The kitchen workers—the ones lucid enough to give accounts anyway—said that's exactly what happened. It was caused by a bag of flour."

Ellie frowned. "What? *Flour*?" The glance she shared with Oliver told her he was just as confused as she was.

"Yeah," Sam said. "I guess one of the workers was carrying an open bag and she tripped, and it poofed up everywhere just like when Ellie tries to bake brownies and turns the mixer on too high a setting. Only there were twenty pounds of it instead of a cup or two."

"And it's flammable?" Ellie asked, too baffled to acknowledge Sam's dig at her baking abilities.

"Flour is more combustible than gunpowder under the right conditions," Darien said. "And there *were* open flames: the commercial gas range was probably on, and we were having creme brulee for dessert. I made that once in my high school culinary class and it definitely involved a cooking torch."

Ellie shook her head. "Wow." She paused. "Do you think Silverskin was involved?"

"Wait," Sam interrupted. "Just so I can keep everything straight: this *isn't* the Lady or Wormwood we're talking about, this is the new one. The one you thought you saw in the ballroom, Ellie?"

"Yep. And we—well, Oliver—named him Silverskin."

"Why Silverskin?"

"Because he had silver skin?" Oliver caught Ellie's eye and shrugged, which she returned.

Sam grunted. "Makes sense. How do we know he wasn't the same demon that was trying to get me to rip Oliver limb from limb?"

Ellie glanced at Oliver. "You're the one who has the most experience with these things. Do you think Silverskin and Sam's demon were the same?"

Oliver considered for a moment. "Sam, did you ever see him?"

"I don't think so. I ... sometimes I thought I'd see ... like, a shadow out of the corner of my eye. Mostly at night, or when no one else was around. But I just chalked it up to pre-wedding stress."

Ellie looked over to see Oliver nodding thoughtfully. "I only encountered Silverskin once, during the fire. But—and Ellie and I actually talked about this earlier—he didn't seem like the 'hide in the background' type. He seemed too ... intelligent. Focused. He planned too well."

"Based on...?" Sam asked.

"Back in Seldovia, Slubgob and Wormwood and whatever was attacking Henry didn't seem to plan, they just fed. But everything about Silverskin implied forethought and focus. He was there to get the job done. He was going to ... rip my face off. Literally."

Ellie shuddered. "You didn't tell me that part."

"I'm sorry. I'm not sure I interpreted what he was saying correctly. I was in a stressful situation."

"You don't say," Sam said.

Oliver gave a wry chuckle. "Something about facing your own violent death makes it hard to think clearly. But his threat tracks. There were a couple stories that started circulating in Seldovia about wildlife that had been ... mutilated ..." He trailed off at the look on Ellie's face.

"Jeez," Sam said softly.

"Okay, I have a question," Darien broke in. "If Silverskin wanted us dead, and he was the driven type, then why didn't he just kill us all in our beds this morning?"

"Well," Ellie said slowly, "if he couldn't kill without ... mutilating ... and they don't want to draw attention to themselves, then he would have had to find another way, right?"

"I think most rational people would've just blamed a messed-up serial killer," Sam said.

"That's possible," Darien said, "but there are also plenty of people who think more ... supernaturally. For example, my family believes in spirits, and the afterlife, and demons. Murders like that would have made national news. Maybe someone in Alaska would've seen it and put it together."

"Specifically, maybe it would've given Helen and Henry enough evidence to convince Seldovia—and Homer and Nanwalek even—to fight," Oliver said. "And then the demons would've had three whole towns up there trying to close the gate. Their strength is in secrecy. That's what the Nantinaq said."

"And they've acted accordingly," Ellie said. "Even with the growing incentive they have to kill us."

"Do we know how many there are?" Sam asked. "Because if we've all successfully outrun the ones that are bugging us—"

"You think you left yours behind?" Ellie asked.

"Yes," Sam said. "I feel lighter than I have in days. He's for sure gone."

"Good," Ellie said.

"That is good," Oliver said quietly. He cleared his throat, his expression turning businesslike again. "We don't know how many of them there are. There could be only a handful, or there could be hundreds. Based on my experience in Alaska, though—and what the Nantinaq implied—my money is on there being lots of them."

"I think you're right," Ellie said. "I saw ..." She fought the urge to bury her face in her hands as that memory rose in her mind, focusing instead on the lights of the town in front of them—Sheridan—and the feel of the steering wheel's smooth leather under her fingers. "At the cave the ... the first time. With Dad. Before I passed out, I think I saw them come out. And there were *lots* of them, probably hundreds at least. They were still coming when I lost consciousness."

"Great," Sam grumbled.

"Well, I think we should use what we know instead of speculating too much," Darien said. "And we *know* the Lady was also around. You said she's a shape-shifter, Ellie?"

Ellie stared at the tar-black road, still fighting the memories. "Yep."

"So how can we rule out that Silverskin wasn't just her in disguise?"

"Oh," Oliver said, straightening. "I told Ellie but not you guys. I killed Silverskin. The reason we know the Lady and him aren't the same is because he's dead."

Ellie could practically hear Sam's jaw drop. "Are you *serious*?"

"What? How?" came Darien's voice at nearly the same time.

"I stabbed him with a board that had fallen from the ceiling. It had splintered and its end was all sharp. I think it might have still been on fire, actually—"

"That's hardcore," Sam said. "Oliver the demon slayer."

Ellie smiled at the embarrassed little grin that crossed Oliver's face. The lights of Sheridan, though the interstate skirted most of them, were a welcome change from the moonless, velvety darkness that blanketed everything outside the truck's headlights. It was nice to be able to see him better. It was nice to be able to see *everything* better.

"I just got lucky," Oliver said. "Anyway, he shriveled into a puddle of goo, which burned along with everything else in there."

"Except you, luckily," Ellie said.

He nodded. "Luckily."

"I'm just glad to hear they can be killed," Darien said.

"Me, too," Ellie said fervently. "And the fact that we haven't seen any since leaving the Shack is also encouraging."

Her eyes tracked a Comfort Inn that appeared on the side of the road until it fell behind them. *Billings,* she reminded herself. "I'm starting to let myself hope we can actually sleep tonight."

"Yeah ..." Oliver murmured, then hesitated, as if he really didn't want to say what was on his mind.

"Spit it out, Oliver," Ellie said.

He rubbed a hand over his eyes. "We've lost the Lady, yes, but Wormwood's still here."

Thick, heavy silence settled over the truck.

"You're sure?" Sam asked.

"Without a doubt. He's here, right now, in my head."

Ellie stared at Oliver as the last of the town's lights receded behind them. How could he look so *calm*?

Oliver flicked a finger toward the windshield. "You're swerving."

"Sorry." She corrected, feeling slightly sick. "And he's in cahoots with the Lady ..."

"As long as Wormwood's in my head, the Lady will be able to find us."

The four of them fell silent again.

"Well," Darien said slowly, "there's not a lot we can do from here, but if you need support, please call us."

"We'll keep our phones on," Sam said. "You can beat him, Oliver."

Ellie tapped the steering wheel, only half aware that she was beating out the rhythm and finger pattern of one of her violin exercises. "There has to be a way."

Oliver nodded slowly. "There's always a way, even if it's 'close the gate.' And if that's the case, we drive fast, take lots of car naps ... and if we can, we find a way to kill the Lady."

There was another beat of silence, which Darien broke. "I have so many questions. And thoughts."

"Don't we all," Ellie said. "Pick your favorite."

"Why hasn't Wormwood just killed you? *Both* of you. He's had plenty of chances."

"I've wondered that," Oliver said. "My best guess is that he can't. The Nantinaq said they were all individuals—"

"Which we've seen pretty hard proof of at this point," Sam said.

"Yeah," Oliver said. "So maybe, for whatever reason, he *can't* kill. Just play mind games."

"Ugh, he sounds like mine," Sam said. "Here's hoping that monster doesn't show up on our honeymoon. That could make things awkward."

Darien let out a little "urgh," and Ellie repressed a revolted shudder. "Okay, moving on. What other ones do we know about? What *was* yours like, Sam?"

"He just ... made me angry over silly things. Never at you, Darien, but people who try to mess with my loved ones—"

A muted series of thuds—like a knock—sounded through the speakers. Sam's voice was muffled when he spoke again, as if he'd turned his face away. "Darien, your burger's here."

"Yes!" Darien said.

Ellie smiled. "We can let you go."

"We'll stay if you want," Darien offered.

"No, it's okay," Ellie said. "You enjoy your hamburger and get some rest."

"You sure?" Sam asked.

"Yes," said Oliver firmly. "We've left the Lady behind for now, and we'll stop to sleep soon. It'll be okay."

"We'll update you tomorrow," Ellie added. "Thanks for checking in on us. Love you both."

"Love you, too," Darien said.

"Love ya, sis," Sam said. "And Oliver, you're all right I guess."

Oliver chuckled. "I'll take it."

After they hung up, Oliver yawned, rubbed a hand through his black hair, and coughed a couple of times. "Sorry I fell asleep. I didn't mean to—"

"I hoped you would. That's why I suggested you lean the seat back, you know."

"Well, it worked." He rubbed his eyes again. "I can't believe I'm still as tired as I am. Or that my eyes still feel like they've been sandblasted."

"I wish I could just tell you to go back to sleep, but ... I really need your company."

"It's all right. I honestly feel bad I left you alone for so long." He shook his head. "I've *never* slept that long in a car before."

"Hey, there's a first time for ev... ry... thi ..." The rest of Ellie's sentence drowned in a huge yawn, which turned into a low moan. She hadn't known she could feel this tired. Or, rather, she hadn't realized she could feel this tired and *still keep going*. But she was reaching her limits, and fast. "Oliver, even if we just stop to switch drivers, I think I need to call it quits in Billings. At the latest."

He put a hand on her shoulder and she let herself look at him again, long past being worried about the bags under her eyes or the messy remnants of her makeup. It was dark anyway.

"By the map, we're an hour away. Can you make it that far? I'm happy to switch with you now if you want."

Ellie glanced at him again, this time more shrewdly. The exhaustion was so clear on his face that she wanted to cry. "I got it, but thank you. The *real* question—that I'm not sure is actually a question—is whether we risk stopping for the night or just switch drivers and keep going."

Oliver drew a long breath in, then let it out just as slowly. "I think we need to stop. Sam and Darien made a great point: exhaustion could kill us as easily as the Lady."

Ellie didn't bother to hide her sigh of relief. "Excellent. Let's sleep in Billings."

Oliver propped his elbow against the windowsill and rested his chin in his palm, staring at the asphalt speeding underneath them. It was starting to look to Ellie like *it* was what was moving, and that the truck was just floating, suspended, above a yellow-striped treadmill thousands of miles long—

"Anything in particular you want to talk about?"

Oliver's voice jerked her out of her daze. She reached for the air conditioner and turned it up. "Um ..."

In the silence, Oliver let out a little chuckle. "Drawing a blank all the sudden?"

Ellie smiled. "After today? I'm trying to narrow it down." She thought for a minute, then swallowed as she remembered Sam's words about the people who hadn't survived the explosion. "I feel *really* awful for the ones who didn't make it out."

"I do, too."

For a moment they were silent, Oliver staring out the window. At what, Ellie had no idea.

"Anything else besides your survivor's guilt?" he finally asked.

Ellie sighed. "Lots of ... stuff. I might be too tired to unpack it all right now, though."

"No problem. We'll have plenty of time in the next few days. If you want."

"I'm sure I will." Ellie yawned again, then shook herself. Maybe they could do a little digging, figure out how to get Wormwood out of Oliver's head. But ... Ellie hesitated.

Based on her own experience, Wormwood attacked the most sensitive, painful territory possible. She wanted to be delicate, as compassionate and kind as Oliver himself had been when she had bared her soul the night before the wedding.

"What I'm curious about is *your* day," she said.

Oliver stared at her. Then he burst out laughing. "We sound *shockingly* domestic for the situation we're in."

Ellie was surprised by the chuckle that rolled out of her, and even more surprised at how natural it felt. "Yes, tell me about your day, honey. I hear you killed a demon by stabbing him through the chest with a broken board."

Oliver looked over at her. "Yes I did, dearest. Thanks for taking such an interest in my work life."

"Well, your work has just been so interesting lately, it's hard not to."

"Has it? I've hardly noticed."

Ellie giggled, reveling in the sound of Oliver's quiet laughter until both faded into companionate silence. She let it stretch, sure his face was shadowing like it always did when he was brooding.

"I wish we knew almost ... anything!" he finally said. "I *killed* Silverskin and still feel like we're sitting ducks."

Ellie chewed her lip, her frustration as keen as his. "Want to analyze it? See if we can find a pattern or something?"

"We might as well. It'll keep us awake."

"Okay." Ellie willed her tired mind to work. "Just so I can keep everything straight, Wormwood appeared right after you killed Silverskin?"

"Yeah. I tried to stab him, too, but the wood passed right through him. Just like when I tried to punch him back in Seldovia."

Ellie felt a pang and stole another glance at him. As she suspected, his eyes were brooding, his brow furrowed. She wanted nothing more than to reach out and smooth those lines, watch those eyes change as they looked into hers—

Oliver looked at her and his gaze softened, a half-grin raising one corner of his mouth. "If you keep swerving like this, you're going to get pulled over."

"Ha! By who?" Ellie jerked her eyes back to the empty interstate, correcting the truck's trajectory. "I'm concerned about you. I was really hoping to let you rest more and now you're over there worrying like Helen in a roomful of orphans."

"Aaahh Helen." When Ellie glanced over again, the expression on Oliver's face was somewhere between fond and sheepish. The Calls had taken the news of their road trip—*and* the truth about closing the gate, *and* Oliver's wild, impulsive plan to sacrifice himself to protect them all—just like Ellie had thought they would. Henry had rumbled a stern rebuke. Helen's ire, on the other hand, had struck like a hurricane made of pure, elemental anger, worry, and love. Oliver had been quite shamefaced when he'd finally hung up.

At least he'll probably never try something like that again, she thought.

"Was Silverskin *in* the fire?" Ellie asked.

Oliver thought for a long minute. When Ellie finally looked at him, his face was set in grim, haunted lines.

"I'm sorry," she said quickly. "I don't want to make you relive it—"

But he shook his head. "It's okay. It's ... not the worst thing I've ever been through."

Ellie's mouth fell open. What could be worse than nearly being burned alive?

"Anyway," Oliver said, "Silverskin was in the fire at first, but stepped out of it as he got closer to me. Wormwood *was* in the fire. Almost the whole time."

"So, it seems like fire isn't the answer," Ellie said. "What about wood?"

Oliver shrugged. "We tried wooden stakes back in Seldovia and they just went right through the demons, like everything else."

"Was there something special about *that* wood in particular?"

"I don't know much about construction or woodworking. I'm sure it'd been treated with something. Some ... chemical. And it was burning." Oliver paused. "Maybe that's it. A fire-weapon."

Ellie's eyebrows lifted. "Well, good thing I packed my flaming sword and all my fire arrows."

Oliver snorted, then cocked his head. "Actually ... I think there's something about flaming swords in the Bible. I can't remember, though. I was so young when my mom dragged me to church, I only remember fragments."

"Well, you know more than I do. We never went to church. And besides, these aren't Bible demons." Ellie leaned over the steering wheel, stretching her back. Though her thinking still felt sluggish and off-center, the conversation had perked her up. She no longer felt like her head was about to sway right off her shoulders.

"So a flaming weapon." She gave a bemused shrug. "Or a wooden weapon."

"Or something that was used to treat the wood."

Ellie nodded. "Those seem like reasonable guesses. I'll do some research on the wood thing tomorrow. While *you* drive."

"Deal."

Ellie and Oliver were quiet for a long moment as the dark road slid smoothly underneath them, uninterrupted by ... *anything*. The absence of people in this wild corner of the country was unnerving, and made even more noticeable by the lack of artificial lights along the roadside. It was just the two of them gliding along the black highway, kept company only by the stars and the cool, incessant wind.

"So ... what have you heard from Wormwood?" Ellie asked quietly, then realized how absurd that was. *As if lowering my voice could keep him from overhearing.*

When she stole another look at Oliver, he was frowning, considering her question. Despite their grim situation, Ellie felt an odd little burst of happiness that he was there beside her, that they were doing this together. She felt so at ease with him. So far, her worry that romance would somehow taint their friendship had proved unfounded. So far, it had been the best of both worlds.

But that "so far" had only been about twenty-four very strange hours. *And he hasn't even told you what he did.*

Ellie sobered immediately.

You know that's going to come up. And probably tonight.

Her hands tightened on the steering wheel. Had *that* been Wormwood? Or just her own fear talking?

"I hate this." She glared at the lights of the little town that emerged in front of them. *Wyola, Montana,* the green road sign read. *Population? Probably around seventeen, including the dogs.*

"You hate ... what?" Oliver said cautiously.

"I hate not being able to trust my own thoughts anymore. How have you survived the last month?"

She felt Oliver's eyes on her and met them briefly. They were grave, sympathetic. Then he half-smiled, the strong, angular lines of his face softening. "You had a lot to do with it."

"I really tried."

Oliver reached out and touched her cheek. "I can't overstate how much you helped. Helen and Henry, too, and Sam." He withdrew his hand, leaving her skin tingling. "Anyway, it's just been more of his usual little jabs. Has he attacked you at all?"

"I don't know," Ellie said. "I've had thoughts that *could* be from him, but they also could just be from ... me."

"Thoughts like ...?"

"At the moment, like how much I hate driving."

"I've been enjoying it, believe it or not."

"You're not the one driving."

"My offer stands. Say the word and I'm happy to take over."

A fresh wave of weariness crashed over Ellie; for a moment, she was tempted. But stopping would only delay them further. Plus, there was no guarantee she wouldn't flop into the passenger seat and immediately fall asleep, leaving a still-exhausted Oliver to drive these dark, deer-filled roads alone. "No. I'll get us there."

"And *I'll* drive the first leg tomorrow."

"Sounds great. I'll start my list of entertaining stories to tell to keep us both awake."

Oliver smiled. "Not that *I've* told many entertaining stories on this trip."

"Well, we still have forty-five minutes. Feel free to start any time."

Ellie snuck a quick look over at him again as the last lights of Wyola capered across his face, a face that was losing its smile, growing subdued again. Her own smile faded, and she wondered if his thoughts had gone where hers had: his real story. Whatever the specifics of that time spent with the gang had been, whatever was clearly still eating him up on the inside.

A thrill of foreboding shot through her. *Will I ever be ready to hear that?*

She hit the gas as the speed limit increased, her heart rate accelerating with it. Did she dare ask? Did she dare not? She wasn't a therapist; she couldn't help him work through whatever had damaged him so badly. But if he got it out in the open, and she could actually *support* him through it ...

She gave a tiny shake of her head. *That'd be a nice change.*

Ellie took a deep breath. "The other thoughts that I can't tell if they're mine or Wormwood's are ones about ... what you did."

After a short silence, Ellie snatched another look at Oliver.

He looked anguished.

Her heart thudded and she snapped her eyes forward again; she didn't have the social alacrity to deal with this right now. She should really just shut up. But it was weighing on her so heavily, and he'd seemed like he wanted to tell her that morning in his room, and a conversation like that would *definitely* keep her awake …

She swallowed. "I think it's reasonable that I'm concerned—"

"It is."

"But I can't tell … is Wormwood amplifying my fear? Is he …?" Ellie paused. It was incredibly frustrating trying to talk to him about something this important while driving in deer country at night. She wanted to see his face, read his eyes, comfort him if she could. But the opportunity was here, right now, and she found herself suddenly wanting to take it.

Oliver willing, of course.

"How scared should I be of you?" she asked.

For a moment, there was silence.

"Not very," he finally said.

She stole another look but Oliver was staring forward, the lights of the dash etching his profile in lines of luminous blue. There was steel in his gaze, the same look she'd seen just before he'd run into the burning Luxembourg House after Sam. Her heart pricked, a deep empathy stirring within her.

"What I was part of was disgusting," he finally said, his voice a whisper. "I learned skills that make me dangerous. How to fight, how to shoot, how to steal, and how to get away with all of it. And then I learned that I didn't have it in me to actually *use* any of them. At least, not in the ways the gang wanted me to. And that part I don't regret."

He paused and Ellie waited, unsure what to say, unsure what to feel. She was having such a hard time reconciling the Oliver she knew—her brave, hardworking, kind *fisherman*—with the man he was convinced he had been.

"Do you want me to tell you now, or do you want to wait until we can sit down and really talk?" he asked in that same resigned voice.

Ellie batted away the part of her that screamed for him to tell her *right now*. "What would make you more comfortable?"

He ran a hand through his hair, then reached for his phone. "Let me check how close we are."

Ellie waited, tapping her fingers in the rhythm and pattern of her violin concerto now.

"Thirty minutes," Oliver said softly. "I guess now's as good a time as any."

Ellie swallowed, her hands closing on the wheel. "Tell me your story, Oliver."

Chapter Four

Oliver was glad Ellie couldn't see him shaking.

Thanks to the good people in his life—the Calls, the crew, most of Seldovia now that he thought about it—he'd bounced back more spectacularly than he ever thought he would. While rotting in that miserable jail cell, being able to function at a more or less normal human level was all he'd hoped for. He'd surprised himself when he achieved that goal, and that success had led him to aim higher, to save for an education, to hope that maybe he could actually make something of himself.

He hadn't, however, let himself hope for someone like Ellie. Her grit, her courage, her beauty, the joy of hearing her laugh, her soft, intoxicating lips ... The way she *looked* at him, as if he'd hung all the stars and then thrown up an aurora for good measure ...

What he was about to say could change all of that. But she deserved to know.

Oliver closed his eyes against the memories starting to pound against the inside of his skull, vivid and terrible. More so than usual. A hot surge of anger forced his eyes open. If the choice was between two terribles—telling Ellie about his past or letting Wormwood win—he'd take the first option. It wasn't even a question.

"You know that the people I lived with right after moving out of my friend's house were part of an organized crime ring. A gang." He was relieved to hear that his voice was still steady.

"Yeah." Ellie stared down the road with grim eyes. For a moment, Oliver wished he were driving. At least then he'd have control over *something*.

"At first I thought they were just thieves," he heard himself say. "That they were like me: wronged by life, down on their luck, willing to skim a little off the profit margins of the rich just so they could have enough to eat. All my high school friends had gone their separate ways, my mom was dead, Dean had been gone for years ... I had no one. Then, suddenly, I had these guys. They took me in. They helped me when I was vulnerable. And all I had to do was help them in return."

He glanced out the window at the cold stars. They'd burned impassively down on him as he'd done all this, and would keep burning long after he was gone. The thought made him feel both smaller and, somehow, stronger.

"So I did," he said. "It started with shoplifting. A little food here, a pair of headphones there. The food we'd eat. The other stuff we'd sell. They gave me back most of what I ... *'earned.'* And it was surprisingly lucrative. Before long, I didn't have to worry about paying rent."

Oliver shook his head. "So that's how I spent the summer after *I* graduated from high school. I lost touch with my old friends—encouraged by my new friends, of course. There were three of them in the house with me, and they were always wanting me to prove myself, prove my loyalty.

"Three weeks in, me and the guy I was closest to—Philip was his name—stole a bunch of jewelry from a local shop. We made off with thousands of dollars worth of merchandise, and they opened up to me after that. They told me they were part of a gang. They said I was talented and wanted me in. They thought I could go places, rise in the ranks, they said they had a job for me ..."

Oliver dug his fingers into his itchy, tired eyes. "I didn't see any other way, Ellie. My past was bleak, so bleak that my mom had to sell herself just to keep food on the table."

He heard Ellie's sharp intake of breath but didn't want to see her face, so he kept talking to the dashboard.

"I drank for the first time when I was thirteen years old, at a house party. The first of many." It was spilling out of him now, much more than he'd intended, like he needed to justify himself. Like *anything* could justify it. "My mom was high a lot. She tried to hide it from me but I knew by then how weed smelled because I'd done it, too. Just not at home. She needed to escape, so I just ... I just let her. We were both lucky we didn't turn to harder drugs, lots of people in our situation do. But Mom was ... even living in what was basically Hell, she was still wise enough to retain *some* control over herself. She never lost hope, never quit trying.

"She finally landed a job—a *good* job—when I was about sixteen. I'd made a good friend at school—the same one I lived with after she died, actually." A strange combination of gratitude and shame pricked him; it was the same every time he thought about Kyler's family. "I confided in him, told him what was really going on. Within a few days, they had us over for dinner, and within a week, she had good, stable work and had attended her first addiction recovery meeting.

"Everything started to turn around. Life got so much better. Mom stabilized, our lives stabilized, I made better friends and quit doing all the things they tell teenagers not to do. It was wonderful. I finally understood how all the other kids could be so great at school, and sports, and ... and *life*. It was like that for almost two years."

Oliver bowed his head. "And then, in January of my senior year, Mom was diagnosed with cancer. Stage IV. She'd been really tired and achy, and it finally got so bad that she went to the doctor. They gave us the news and the prognosis, and told her to get her affairs in order. Two months later, she was dead. After all we'd been through, after all she'd overcome ..." He gritted his teeth against the emotions that were threatening to overwhelm him.

"I didn't believe there could be a future for me after that, after life had been so cruel to me," he finally said softly. "And to her. So when the gang said 'join up,' I said yes."

Ellie guided the truck around a corner that hugged the bottom of a hill and Billings burst across his field of vision, glittering. Oliver barely saw it.

"They took me to a club that night to meet the boss. Well, one of the bosses, anyway. He called himself Jag, I don't know why. Probably because he drove a Jaguar. And upgraded it every year. He was so proud of that stupid car." Oliver snorted in disgust. "He said there was a place for me but I needed to prove my loyalty *again* by beating up a member of a rival gang that had been encroaching on our turf.

"So the next day, I did. Philip and I went to the street corner where there'd been action. We saw these two young guys approaching. We flashed our signs and they took the bait. Philip ... he knew how to fight. He'd been born into the gang. And he'd been teaching me pretty much ever since I'd gotten there. Looking back I can see that it was one of the ways they used to earn my trust."

His mouth twisted in a grimace. "Anyway, we beat them. I ... they both lived, but I don't know ... the extent of their injuries. It's not like the movies make it out to be, fighting. Taking a beating. You break bones, cause internal injuries—"

He stopped as Ellie made a pained little noise.

"Sorry," he mumbled, addressing the road now. "I know you're sensitive to that kind of stuff, I ... I'm sorry. Do you want me to stop?"

"No. If we're going to do this, if we're going to succeed, we have to be able to trust each other." She glanced at him with searing, silvery-blue eyes and his heart nearly stopped. "I want everything. Your good, your bad, all of it."

Oliver forced himself to breathe. "It doesn't get better. I'll spare you the worst details but ... you're absolutely sure?"

"Yes."

"Okay." He took another deep breath, then continued.

"After the ... the beating ... I became one of their little foot soldiers. I wasn't a full member yet but it was coming. I ran with them on two more robberies, beat up some rival gang members, got shot at, did some drugs." He blew out a long breath. "And I had a family. It wasn't a family like the one I'd just left. My friend's family, where there was a mom and a dad and four kids who spent weekends together and it was more or less peaceful and happy. Where the worst thing that happened was when Callie's rabbit got loose and we never found it again. But the gang was the only family I thought I deserved. I was so angry, so bitter. I felt so betrayed by life. I just wanted the adrenaline. I was convinced I ... I belonged with these broken people. And some of them even cared about me." He let out a mirthless laugh. "So I thought.

"About a month later, Philip came home and told me I was in. That they'd be jumping me in—initiating me—that night. By that time, I'd finally admitted to myself that I hated it all. I hated the meaninglessness of it. Most days we got up late and did nothing but drink and do drugs. Our nights were wasted with gambling and pointless games. The other guys paid for hookers. I never could bring myself to ... to pay for sex, though."

He put his face in his hands. "I just couldn't. I couldn't help but think of my poor mom. Philip and the others made fun of me for it and I think that's when I started to hate them, too. Maybe they didn't believe life could be different, maybe their moms never got the lucky break that mine did, if they were even in the picture at all. But I knew better. I'd been given a taste of better: those years when things were stable for us, and the time I spent at my friend's house after Mom died, watching how a real family actually worked. I realized I didn't want to be a gangbanger until I died violently in a gunfight or a knife fight. But by then it was too late. I didn't know how to get out without being killed.

"So that night I showed up for my jumping in. It happened at a nightclub that Jag and another one of the bosses co-owned. They'd cleared it all out for the night under the guise of holding a private party."

Oliver closed his eyes as the memories battered at him. *Jag sitting in a chair, facing him, a woman sitting on his lap wearing nearly nothing. She was watching him, too, with cold, disinterested eyes. Eyes that barely disguised her loathing. Another, younger woman—maybe a little younger than Oliver—stood behind them, also wearing almost nothing. She had been very attractive. And had looked very frightened.*

Oh Ellie, I tried to do the right thing, he thought. *If only I'd have done it sooner.*

"Jag set a timer on his wristwatch and they beat me for thirty seconds. They ... it ..." He shook his head, fighting against the images in his mind, so vivid he could feel the pain again. *He was on the ground, trying not to curl too hard into a ball, Philip laughing as a foot drove into his back, another into his ribs, the pain searing through him as they cracked—*

"Thirty seconds," he whispered to himself. "Amazing how long that can be."

"Oliver," Ellie said in a strangled whisper, "that's so horrible."

He looked over at her and saw a tear trailing down her cheek. He wanted to wipe it away; he was just about to reach up—

What makes you think she would want you to touch her? What makes you think she's ever going to want you to touch her again?

Oliver let his hand fall, blinked away the moisture in his own eyes. "It *was* horrible. But I survived. The truth is, what came next was worse."

"How? *How* could it be worse?"

Oliver couldn't tell if that was anger, disgust, or fear in her voice. *Probably all three.* "Ellie, really, I can stop— "

"No, Oliver! Tell me the rest!"

"Okay." He held up his hands. "Okay. Once time was up, they all stopped and stepped back. I felt terrible. I learned later that they'd cracked four ribs. I stood up anyway and faced them. Looked them in the eyes. I tried not to let them see how much I hated them, but I'm not sure I succeeded. Anyway, gangs mark their members. Lots do tattoos but Jag was ... wilder. And *weirder*. They branded me instead."

"They *branded* you?"

Oliver closed his eyes, trying to push away the stench of his own burning flesh, and nodded. "On my back. My left shoulder. So I don't plan to do a lot of swimming during all that leisure time we'll have on this trip, you know. It's not something I really enjoy showing off."

"I'd imagine not. So ... you have to be getting to the part where you get out, right? You said there was a mole ..." She paused, frowning. "When we went on that walk and you told me ... you said there was a mole on the team and that you'd had a robbery go wrong ..."

He waited.

"You were the mole. You brought them down."

Oliver nodded. "Yes."

Ellie breathed a huge sigh.

"It didn't happen exactly the way I told you," he said grimly. "It's not nearly as noble as it sounds."

"Tell me."

He paused, gathering his thoughts. *The fear in that girl's brown eyes...*

His body hurt. Breathing hurt. He'd been cut on the cheek during the beating and he could feel it bleeding down his face. His back hurt.

Burns ... burns, it turned out, were a special kind of hurt.

"She's yours, Big O," Jag said, grabbing the girl by the arm and shoving her forward. She stumbled; it was so clear that she wanted to hide, cover herself, run, but she couldn't. She was surrounded by men who only wanted her for one thing. She wasn't a person. She was a commodity. And she knew it.

Reflexively he caught her before she fell, pulling her to him, her soft skin nearly overwhelming against the battered nerve endings of his own bare torso. She didn't look at him. She was shaking.

"She's yours," Jag repeated. "And whatever others you can find out there, huh? That's gonna be your job, pretty boy. We just had to make sure you were serious about runnin' with us, and that you were tough behind that nice face of yours."

"What do you mean?" Oliver asked.

Jag settled back in his chair. "I mean, we sell people what they want ... drugs, jewelry, sex ... and we gotta get the goods from somewhere. Your job is gonna be getting that last one. You got the looks and the charm to be mighty persuasive, persuasive enough to make them want to stay. You can have it all: money, women, fast cars, whatever you want. Whatever makes you happy."

I'll never be happy like this, Oliver thought. In that moment, holding that poor girl against him, he realized he no longer cared if he lived or died. This wasn't living. This was Hell.

"So go on, take her," Jag said. He crossed his long legs, lips parting in a leer. "Give us a show."

Oliver stood there, trying to keep his revulsion from showing on his face. The girl trembled but reached for the buckle of his belt. He took her hand, and she froze.

"I think," he said quietly, "that I deserve some privacy."

Jag's smile slid off his face. "Excuse me?"

Oliver shrugged. "You've got one of your own. I think I've earned a private room with this one."

Silence enveloped the room, menacing as a storm front. They could beat him, kill him, right here right now. Simply for that request.

Then, Jag laughed. "I like you, Cole. You got balls." He sat back again, pulling the other woman back onto his lap. "Pick a room, they're all available. You have an hour."

Oliver nodded. "Come on," he said, pulling the girl after him.

"Oliver? You ... you were saying it wasn't as noble as it sounds ...?"

Ellie's uncertain voice cut into his mind and he realized he was shaking even harder now. He felt clammy, sick. The memories were as vivid as if they were playing on a screen in front of him; he could smell the alcohol and smoke with each unsteady breath, could *feel* the pain of the brand searing into his back, throbbing in time with his racing heart. He shrugged his shoulder; the pain wasn't real. The stench of alcohol wasn't real.

The smoke still lingered, though.

He put his face in one trembling hand and groaned. "Wormwood's definitely leveled up."

"Do *you* need to stop?"

"No." He dragged his eyes upward, forcing himself to draw air into his lungs with purpose, calming his ragged breathing. Ellie glanced at him and he forced himself to look back at her. Her eyes had darkened, the distress in them clear. They flicked back to the interstate and the thoughts slammed against him.

She hates you. As she should. You beat those boys, probably funded human trafficking, helped distribute drugs that kill people—

"I didn't know!" The words burst out of him and Ellie's grip tightened on the steering wheel.

"I'm sorry. Wormwood's here, in my head."

"I gathered. I should have known. Oliver—" She reached over and grabbed his hand. "We're in this together. I care about you. For both our sakes, for me to know I can trust you, you need to finish your story. At some point, at least. If you can't right now, I ... I understand. But I also think the sooner we get this all out in the open, the less Wormwood will be able to use it against us."

Oliver felt a spike of molten anger that shocked him before he realized that it wasn't his. "I agree, Ellie," he growled softly.

Ellie let go of his hand as they entered the Billings city limits, the streetlights sliding across her smooth, pale skin. She waited while Oliver gathered his thoughts.

"After they ... *marked* me—" beside him, Ellie winced, "—Jag threw a girl at me and basically told me to rape her. In front of all of them. He told me that my job in the gang now that I was a full member would be to lure girls in so that the gang could sell them." He shuddered in revulsion.

"So they were going to turn you into a pimp, basically."

Oliver nodded. "Basically. And I think that knowledge is what finally gave me the courage to leave. If it was a choice between being killed or becoming like the men who sold my mother ..." His voice hardened. "I chose death. I honestly thought I would die that night. And I didn't care."

"How ... how *did* you get out?"

"I ... I demanded privacy ..."

Oliver closed his eyes as the memories crashed over him again. *He scanned the layout, the rooms, there were several along the back hallway, and—yes! An exit, out of sight of the big dance hall—that room would do. He pulled her inside, closing the door behind them and locking it.*

"We're getting out," he said, staring wildly around the room, trying to ignore how much pain he was in. Breathing *hurt but he needed air ... somehow he needed to be able to run, to have some stamina—*

"W-what?" Her voice was soft, petrified. "You're not going to—?"

"No. We're getting the hell out of here. Right now."

"They'll kill us."

"They won't kill you. You're too valuable." Oliver gritted his teeth; his body was on a hair-trigger, torn with pain and fear and desire. He pushed them all away. It was Anchorage in September; it would be both cold and still light outside and she probably wouldn't leave unless they could find a way to cover her ...

The curtains.

Oliver was to them in seconds. He tore one of the heavy velvet panels off the hook, gasping at the pain in his ribs. Light streamed in through the window and he blinked rapidly as he turned back to her.

"Here, wrap this around yourself and follow me."

"Will they kill you?" she asked as she took the curtain and pulled it around her shoulders.

"Only if they catch us."

The girl shrank back, clutching the curtain more tightly around herself. She was shaking, tears trailing down her cheeks, terrified nearly to the point of immobility. Oliver grabbed her shoulders and she stiffened.

"Listen to me. I'm not going to hurt you. I'm not going to rape you. I want to save your life, and my life. There's an exit at the end of this hallway and you can't see it from the main room. We sneak out, and we run. Get out of this part of town and to a police station, fire station, anything."

"What if one of the members sees us run? One who wasn't here tonight?"

Oliver shook his head. "Most of them are here, and I know what places to avoid so we don't run into the rest of them." He released her. "If you stay, you'll be stuck in this life for who knows how long. Maybe until you die. You'll carry their drugs and their babies. Is that what you want?"

She shook her head, and he was relieved to see the tiniest spark of fight enter those dulled eyes.

"Then let's go."

He pushed the door open, adrenaline sharpening his senses, and peeked down the hallway toward the dance hall. If only he could help the other woman, too.

Maybe if they were fast enough, the police could.

"Come on," he whispered and snuck out. The girl followed on silent, bare feet and he winced as he looked down at them. There was nothing he could do about that.

Oliver pushed open the door to the outside; it squeaked and his heart started to pound in his throat. He motioned her through, closed it as silently as he could, and then turned, shivering in the chill, misty rain. A small groan escaped him; shivering hurt. What a sight the two of them must look: him battered, bleeding, and half-naked and her wrapped awkwardly in a smoke-stained velvet curtain.

"Follow me," he said and lurched into a shuffling run.

Oliver gritted his teeth, forcing his breathing to slow once again. "Where was I?"

"You asked for privacy," Ellie said in a quiet monotone.

"Okay. Sorry. Wormwood."

"I figured. Are you sure you can—?"

"Yes."

"... Okay. However ... fast or slow you need to go ... I'm here." Her hands fidgeted on the wheel and the expression on her face was taut, pained.

"It's almost over," he whispered, realizing he needed to hear those words as much as she did. "Things get better from here."

"Good. Past Oliver needs some good things to happen in his life."

Oliver almost smiled. "They do."

He took another deep breath. "So I asked for privacy, and—you have to understand that in a gang, you don't make demands like that, not unless you have a *lot* more power than I did. I fully expected to be beaten, maybe even killed for my audacity. I didn't care at that point. Like I said, I expected to die. But to my surprise, they granted my request. So I took that poor girl with me to a back room and we were able to sneak out.

"We made it to a firehouse, came bursting through the door, we looked absolutely awful. I told them there was gang activity happening at Jag's club right at that moment. Street drugs, prostitution, all of it. They mobilized law enforcement and they ... they got them." Oliver could hear the satisfaction in his own voice; he didn't try to hide it.

"Good," Ellie said. The low snarl in her voice made him look up. Her face was set, rigid, her eyes cold, her posture radiating righteous satisfaction. He blinked at the anger, the *intensity* he saw there, as if the core of strength that drove her fight against grief and fear had finally emerged into the outside world.

I wonder if Ellie even knows that part of her is in there. And he found that he wanted, so desperately wanted, to see more of it.

She sent the briefest glance his way and he shook off the thought.

"They didn't get everyone, unfortunately, but at least they got Jag off the streets. He was terrible."

Oliver paused for a moment. "It was clear to anyone who knew what was going on that I'd just been initiated. My injuries, the fresh brand on my back … They took me in for questioning, booked me, the works. I got a really good public defender, which would usually be an oxymoron. They're the walking definition of underpaid and overworked. But mine was excellent. He fought hard for me. I told him everything, told him I was willing to testify against all my former gang, give them any evidence I had …"

He took a deep breath as the tremors started coursing through his body again, like chills from a fever. *You're far away from all that. You've changed*, he reminded himself.

You think she sees it that way? Wormwood cackled. *She can barely look at you.*

The pain flared up in his shoulder again as *his shirt rubbed against the scorched skin of the fresh brand.*

"Do you have any idea how rare this is?" the police interrogator asked.

Oliver didn't look at him, just rested his forehead in his hand, elbow on the cold metal desk in front of him. His head hurt and he just wanted to lie down.

They said there'd be no lasting damage. All the same, four cracked ribs were no picnic.

"I've never seen a gangbanger get out and come running straight to the police. Never. You have a death wish, boy?"

"No," Oliver rasped. The room smelled like chemicals. It wasn't helping his headache.

"You have any idea how hard it is to get out of a gang?"

Oliver finally looked the officer in the eye. "Well yeah, seeing as I just did *it."*

The man scowled. "Don't get smart with me. They've marked you as one of their own. You'll never even be able to take a shower *in prison without being in danger from rival gangs. And if any of your old 'friends' find you, they'll put a bullet in your head so fast—"*

"Officer," Oliver said tiredly. To his surprise, the officer went quiet, staring down at him with inscrutable eyes. "Your scare tactics aren't going to work."

The officer arched an eyebrow. "Why's that?"

"Because I don't care what you do with me. I didn't care what they would *do to me if they caught me, and forgive me, but you're way less intimidating. I couldn't live that life and still live with myself. The only respectable option for me was to run for freedom or die trying.*

"So I'll help you. I'll give you every name I know. I'll testify against them, in court, to their faces if I have to. I'll tell you the location of every house, every apartment where members lived. I'll tell you where they sold their drugs, and their prostitutes, and which robberies we

were behind. You don't have to use scare tactics to get me to do it. I'll tell you right now just to get them off the streets. You got a notepad?"

The officer eyed Oliver, who put his face back in his hands as his weariness threatened to overwhelm him. "I've ruined my life, I know, but maybe I can still do some good before you lock me away. Then … I guess I'll take my chances in prison. At least there I'll be able to look myself in the mirror every morning and not hate what I see. Guess I just won't take my shirt off. And keep my back to the wall in the shower."

The room was silent except for the buzz of the fluorescent light overhead. Then, the officer nodded.

"Let me go get that notepad."

He swept out of the room, the door slamming behind him—

And the tremors were back; now Oliver felt clammy *and* nauseous.

Is this what PTSD feels like? he wondered.

"Sorry," he said hoarsely. "I've never experienced anything like this before. It's like Wormwood's pulling me into a flashback. It … it's so vivid it's like I'm experiencing it again." Oliver groaned, leaning forward. "That's *really* rude."

Ellie made a noise in her throat, something like a growl but more pained. "Oliver—"

"I'm not stopping. I won't let him win. The worst is behind us."

"Are you sure?"

"Yes." The trembling in Oliver's body was subsiding, his mind growing clearer. He clasped his hands in his lap and went on. "In the end, I took a plea deal, and somehow, amazingly, I was only charged with a single misdemeanor: petty theft."

"I'm sure it helped that you basically handed them an entire gang on a silver platter and saved a girl from being sold into sex slavery," Ellie said in that same muted tone.

"There were eight that were rescued from the gang in total," Oliver said softly. "It was hard … it was surprisingly hard to testify against the guys. Mostly against Philip. Even after what they'd done, even though I knew what they were, I'd still considered them family for a while." He shook his head. "I guess I get attached too easily."

He paused, then went on. "But yes, it was a combination of a great lawyer, the fifth amendment, a sympathetic judge, and sheer dumb luck. I wasn't knowingly involved in anything other than the thefts and beating up rival gang members, which didn't even come up and I let it lie. Aside from making me look and feel pretty stupid, my lack of knowledge about their plans for me ended up really helping my case. Beyond all hope, I got a second chance at life." He paused. "Though maybe it's just so I can die at the gate instead."

"No. There has to be a way where no one has to die."

Oliver sighed. "Maybe." When she didn't respond, he finally looked out at the outskirts of Billings: brightly lit industrial buildings, structures that looked distinctly barn-shaped, and dark homes that he hoped were peaceful. "So now you know. That's my story. You can ... you can do with it what you will. If you don't want to be with me anymore, I understand."

Ellie just nodded, her eyes fixed on the road, and said nothing. Oliver let his eyes linger on her profile for just one moment longer. Then, when Ellie hit the blinker, he tore his gaze forward.

I've lost her.

Chapter Five

They were silent until Ellie pulled into a well-lit gas station several long minutes later. She threw the truck into park and, after only a slight hesitation, met his eyes. Hers were still distressed, but beyond that, they gave away nothing.

Oliver couldn't hold her gaze, so he groped for the door handle instead. "I'll fill the tank."

"Wait."

He turned to see Ellie offering her card. For a moment, he thought about protesting, but a gas tank this large and a trip this long would quickly eat into his savings. And with how much they were raising tuition every year …

Hesitantly, Oliver took the thin strip of plastic, careful not to let his fingers brush Ellie's. His worries about finances aside, part of him registered her open display of trust. *That's got to be an encouraging sign, right?*

When he got back in the truck a few minutes later, Ellie was busy with her phone. "I found us a Marriott. It's right next to the highway, so if we have to make a fast escape, we can just go."

"Good thinking," Oliver said.

The ride to the hotel was short. And that was good, because Ellie had gone silent again and Oliver didn't break it. She still wore that grim, thoughtful expression, her eyes bloodshot, shadowed with fatigue and the remnants of her makeup. Wormwood, too, said nothing. He must have known Ellie's silence hurt Oliver far more than taunts ever could.

Ellie parked, staring at the softly-lit hotel entrance as the truck idled. Oliver dared not say anything. He just waited for the verdict.

"So just to make sure I've got this straight," Ellie said. Her voice was steady, and when she looked at him, her eyes flashed strangely.

See? See the disgust there?

Oliver dropped his gaze, rubbing his eyes with his hand. *I don't need your help to read Ellie, Wormwood. She's kind enough to tell me.*

You need all the help you can get, Ollie.

He gritted his teeth.

"Your mom's death gutted you. You tried to pick up the pieces but ended up with a gang because they took you in. Within a few months though, you realized you didn't want that life and were willing to die in a bid for freedom if that was what it took."

Oliver nodded and Ellie went on.

"And you did get out. And in the process, you saved eight women from a terrible fate and got a nasty, evil gang lord and most of his cronies off the streets."

"It sounds really good when you put it that way—"

"That's just the truth, Oliver."

When he met her gaze, her eyes were soft. There was still sadness in them, pity, and even fear, but none of the revulsion he'd expected to see. Hope raised its head from where it had nearly been smothered in his chest.

Ellie took his hand. "You made mistakes, yes. But you can't be blamed for what you didn't know."

He looked down as she intertwined her fingers with his, stunned that she was still here, that she hadn't run, that she was *touching* him.

"Look at me," she whispered.

Oliver did. Her wide, clear eyes bored into his, and his breath caught.

"You screwed up in a bigger way than most people. And then you made it right in a bigger way than most people. You trust the people who know you, right? Henry, Helen, Bill … me?"

"Of course."

"Then trust our opinion of you. Trust that you've done enough, and let it rest. Let *yourself* rest."

The air rushed out of Oliver's lungs in a sigh and he gripped Ellie's hand in his. She squeezed back, then leaned over and kissed him, softly and slowly, and something in his soul—some tight little snarl of anguish and doubt and shame—seemed to ease.

"You," he said hoarsely, "are incredible, Ellie. Incredible."

"It's true."

Oliver smiled. "What do you say we take this inside?"

To his dismay, Ellie's face shadowed again. She released his hand and reached for the door. "I think we definitely should go inside."

Oliver suppressed a sigh. *I could have worded that better.*

He opened the door and reached for his suitcase, glancing across to where Ellie tugged at her own luggage. The truck's artificial light spilled across her striking features. Her long, dark hair was still pulled up into the elegant hairstyle she'd worn at the wedding but wisps of it had escaped, falling around her face. For a moment, he couldn't help but stare at her.

"Um ... Oliver? You all right?"

"Sorry." He pulled his suitcase out onto the pavement. "You just looked really pretty."

Oliver smiled, and Ellie smiled back, but there was a tightness around her eyes that he suspected wasn't just from weariness. They trudged across the parking lot together, their suitcases clattering behind them. He could practically feel the tension within her, boiling toward an explosion—

"Okay, here's the thing," Ellie finally said as they approached the hotel's sliding door. Despite his exhaustion, Oliver had to hide a real smile as her cheeks reddened.

"I really like you, Oliver. Like, a lot. And that's still true even after what you've told me. But ..."

He waited; he was pretty sure he had a good idea where this was going.

"I'm not ready to ... to share a bed or anything. Please don't take that the wrong way, I just ... I don't want to move too fast and last time, with Vito ... but then *Noah* ..." She was full-on blushing, stammering, and he almost chuckled.

"It's okay. I'm not ready for that either, Ellie." His smile twisted into an expression of disgust. "Plus, Wormwood."

Ellie shuddered visibly. "Ugh. Okay, we're good, then."

The hotel door slid open and they stepped into the welcome warmth of the entryway. Though August nights weren't as cold in Montana as they were in Seldovia, the wind still carried a chill.

In what Oliver thought was a very optimistic move, Ellie checked them into a two-room suite. "Hey, you never know," she said as they rode the elevator up to the third floor. It hadn't taken her long to relax back to her usual self after their conversation, though that irresistible little blush hadn't completely faded. "I thought we could sleep with both our doors open. It'll basically be one big room but with more privacy."

The elevator door slid open and Oliver forced his sluggish feet forward. "Worth a try."

Ellie slid the key card into the slot, then pushed the door open, stepping into the room. Oliver followed, gazing around the suite, taking in the kitchenette, the fridge, the polished countertops and comfortable-looking couches.

This, he realized, *is what having money is like.* He'd never imagined being able to just *check in* to a room like this. He'd seen the bill; it had cost upwards of three hundred dollars. But to her, it was pocket change.

Ellie set her suitcase upright and turned to face him, barely stifling a huge yawn. "Do you care which room? One's a king and one's queen-sized."

He shrugged. "I'm happy to take the queen."

"Okay." Ellie grasped her suitcase's handle and pulled it toward the room on the right-hand side. "I don't know about you, but I'm *dying* for a shower."

"Me, too. You can go first if you want, though."

Her laughter echoed out the door, and she poked her head around its frame. "Each room has its own private bath, Oliver."

A bemused grin spread across Oliver's face and Ellie leaned against the doorframe, watching his reaction with evident enjoyment.

"This is so luxurious I hardly know what to do with myself," he said. "You definitely win the prize for best traveling companion I've ever had. For several reasons."

Ellie smirked. "That's what I like to hear."

"Tomorrow we'll have to work out what I can pay for—"

But Ellie turned, flapping her hand at him. "I'm not worried about it. Now I'm going to go shower before I collapse right here." And with one last magnetic smile, she closed the door.

Oliver stared at it for a minute, warmth glowing in his chest, before turning and dragging his suitcase into the other room and pushing the door shut behind him. He was so ready to wash the stench of smoke off his body.

***

Fifteen minutes later, Oliver opened his door to find Ellie curled on the couch in the living room, fast asleep with her phone in her hand. Its screen was tilted toward him, and he smiled when he made out the lines of her book, black against the dim white background.

He leaned against the doorjamb and surveyed her. Earlier in the day—yesterday, now—she'd been so stunningly beautiful that if he hadn't already believed in angels, he would have after seeing her in that ballroom. But *this* Ellie—just out of the shower, her wet hair tumbling down pale shoulders left bare by her black tank top—this was the Ellie he knew. The orphan who had battered through the tears and the nightmares to emerge, shaken but victorious, on the other side. The friend who had been there for him even through her own struggles. She transfixed him, captivated him.

Oliver crossed the room and sat down next to Ellie. When he put a hand on her shoulder, she stirred, her eyes fluttering open. She stared up at him for a second then smiled. "Hey."

"Hey." He brushed a few soft tendrils of hair out of her eyes. "Feel better?"

"Yeah." Ellie pushed herself upright, then wrapped her arms around his waist, resting her head on his shoulder. "I feel like a whole new person. And I don't know about you, but I'm ready to fall into bed and not move for nine hours."

Oliver pulled her closer. "More if we can get it. Though somehow, I don't think we will." He wasn't fully aware that he'd lain back, half-reclining against the arm of the couch, until his muscles relaxed into the soft cushions beneath them. It was a mistake; as Ellie snuggled against him, Oliver realized it was going to be very hard to move away from this place. This *peace*. He had no doubt that the press of her body against his side and the ease with which he could run his fingers through her hair were more comforting than the big, empty bed in the other room.

Ellie nuzzled against his neck, and Oliver's eyes fell closed.

"How long do you think it'll take them to find us?" she mumbled.

"I wish I knew."

"How stupid are we if we don't set an alarm?"

"Pretty stupid."

"Probably." Ellie pulled back and squinted down at her phone. "It's two-fifteen. Is … do you think eight is too late?"

Oliver's tired mind grasped at all the straws it could find or make up, and came up with nothing. "Yeah. But we're not going to last long if we don't sleep. If we can get at least six hours in real beds, then take turns sleeping in the truck ..."

She gave one slow, determined nod. "Okay, then. Eight it is. And here's hoping we won't get woken up in the middle of the night by an evil banshee ... demon ... *thing* ... either."

Oliver's heart went out to Ellie; even her speech was beginning to unravel. He opened his arms, inviting her back, and was as happy as he could ever remember being when she took him up on it, resting her head on his chest again and draping her arm across his stomach.

"Here's hoping," he mumbled, and for a few precious, wonderful moments, they just held each other.

"What if we just stay here?" Ellie finally asked.

"We'll fall asleep."

"That's our goal, isn't it?"

The soft whisper of her breath on his skin made Oliver inclined to agree. "Yeah. But ... will you *stay* asleep?"

"Probably not," she admitted.

"I don't think I will, either. This won't stay comfortable for long."

"Mmmm. That's very sad."

Oliver turned his face into her sweet-smelling hair, half-formed replies trying and failing to take shape in his brain. For the moment, they were safe. His body was screaming at him to stay down, and his heart belonged to her anyway so why bother moving, and he was drifting, floating ...

"—*so* good at getting up—"

Oliver sucked in a sharp breath, sensation flooding his mind again, and a sense of loss prickled him as Ellie pulled away. She looked down at him with a soft smile, her long hair framing her face. "Were you asleep?"

"Yep."

Her smile widened, affection in her gray eyes. "Let's get you in bed."

Oliver suppressed a groan as he pushed himself up and rubbed his eyes. When he opened them again, Ellie's smile had faded and she was looking up at him with a gaze that could only be described as longing.

"If you have the energy for it," she whispered, "I would happily tell you a proper good-night."

Her lips curved up in a smile that was somehow both sensual and innocent, an invitation to share a stolen moment of joy in the middle of a nightmare. Oliver gazed down at her, wanting to fix this image in as sharp of clarity as his tired mind possibly could: the lamp casting her clear skin in honeyed tones of light, her warm eyes, framed by long brown lashes, bright with an affection that pierced his soul.

He leaned down and kissed her, his head still swimming with the fact that she was *here*, and not hiding from him in the other room, and ...

Ellie kissed him again, harder, and he wanted to stay right here in this moment of tender vulnerability and never leave, never do anything but this. He put his arms around her, drawing her loosely to him. A twinge of pain shot through his temple, but he ignored it as her fingers threaded their way into his hair. She tilted her head, letting his lips part hers as he deepened the kiss—

A second, harder bolt of pain lanced through Oliver's brain, right behind his eyes. It hurt enough to make him gasp, and Ellie broke away.

"Oliver?" Her fingertips brushed his cheek. When he opened his eyes, her face was right there, beautiful and ... *worried*. "Are you okay?"

He nodded. "Headache."

Ellie gazed at him for a moment longer before a tiny smile touched those perfect lips. "Go to bed. You really need it."

"I really ..." He did. He did need to rest. Desperately. But Ellie was so warm and soft, and gorgeous, and smart ...

"I really ..." His hands were going around her waist again.

"... need ..."

She was sighing, her eyes fluttering closed, her arms twining around his neck as she tilted her face up.

"... you," he whispered against her lips.

She let out a little sound as he tasted her again, and he was gone. Drunk. He was wrapping her in his arms and she was melting against him and her hands were in his hair and this was exquisite, *she* was exquisite—

Pain.

It hit him again like a punch to the temple, and he groaned, dropping his head onto Ellie's shoulder.

"A—again?"

Even through the pain, Oliver couldn't help but feel some gratification at how breathless she sounded. But his pride was short-lived. "Yeah."

"I have ibuprofen."

Of course you do. "You're brilliant. I'll take some." Oliver raised his head, then pressed his forehead to hers. Maybe it was the exhaustion, maybe it was the hormones, maybe it was the headache, but for a moment, he was too overcome, too utterly stunned by his feelings for her, to say anything.

"Thank you, Ellie," he finally whispered.

"You're welcome," she said smartly.

He let out a short laugh. "I mean, thank you for not ... hating me."

Ellie pulled away, searching his eyes. "I stand by what I said Sunday night, Oliver. I think you're a beautiful person, scars and all."

Her hand slid to his shoulder, and he stiffened as her fingers brushed the ugly, raised brand, palpable even through his shirt if someone knew what to look for. His head started to pound again.

"Is that it?"

Oliver nodded. She'd probably already felt it when they were dancing, but hadn't given it a second thought until now.

"I hate imagining what they did to you. It makes me so angry. It ... it ..." Ellie's eyes began to glisten and she clenched her jaw against the tears. "But I love what you did. How you reacted. Oliver, you saved people's lives. You deserve a good life, too."

"I do deserve a good life," he murmured. *And if nothing else, I can probably pull off a good death.*

He'd taken punches that hurt less than that thought, but he smiled at Ellie anyway.

"I'll help you believe it," she whispered.

He said nothing, just looked into her eyes, and what she'd said the first time she'd kissed him burst into his mind.

I just couldn't tell you with words.

And that was exactly it.

Oliver kissed her one more time, as slowly as he could. But the pounding in his head was becoming a roar, and despite himself, he groaned.

Ellie pulled away, rubbing her thumb across his cheek. "We should go to bed."

"We should."

She stood and offered her hands, which he took. Then, once he was on his feet, he hugged her. Twinges of pain sparked all along his scalp, but Ellie burrowed into him with a contented sigh and they swayed gently back and forth. It was so stupid of him to still be holding her; they should both have fallen into bed fifteen minutes ago. But some instinct told him that there would be few of these moments in the foreseeable future. And weren't these peaceful, transcendent moments what they were fighting for, anyway?

Raw pain bled through his head again, and he grimaced. *Relative peace, anyway.*

"Oliver ..." Ellie sighed, then released him. "Go to bed."

His hand went to his temple as the pain faded to a dull throb. "Yeah."

"Wait, let me get ..." Ellie was already moving, disappearing into her room. Seconds later, she came back with a massive bottle of ibuprofen. Mutely, she held it out and Oliver took it, his fingers brushing hers.

"Thanks."

"You're welcome." Ellie gave him a sleepy, sweet little smile that made his heartbeat wobble before she turned away.

"Door open?" he asked.

"Door open. I'll ..." Ellie let out a frustrated sigh, stopping on the threshold of her bedroom. "If the Lady does show up, I'll try to fight back this time. I'll try not to let her just wreck me."

"With luck, we'll have left her far enough behind that it won't be an issue."

"I hope so." For a moment, Oliver could see bone-deep terror in her face. But then she covered it up with a smile. "Good night, Oliver."

"'Night, Ellie. Sleep good."

At first, Wormwood raged. After all he'd done, after all his hard work ...

The wind played across his ... skin? His eyes fell closed; the sensation was subtle, but powerful. Intoxicating, even. He could understand why both Death and the humans clung to this place, the kind of existence it offered.

"You nearly lost him."

Wormwood opened his eyes. "I won't lose him. He hates himself too much. That kind of self-loathing isn't fixed in one night."

"You lost the girl."

"The Lady's better suited for her, anyway." Wormwood leaned against the warm metal of the car next to him, looking up at the hotel room where they slept. That little breeze kept fluctuating. He never knew what it was going to do, how it was going to feel from moment to moment. "How close is she?"

"Close."

Wormwood felt ... disappointed.

"Then make sure they die," the quiet, cold voice said. "Until they're taken care of, you must tail them. You're the only one who can. Currently, at least."

Something in the way Death said it both chafed and frightened Wormwood. The latter won. "I will."

Chapter Six

In the deep, silent darkness of the early morning, Ellie awoke. It was a sudden awakening, the kind she rarely experienced without an alarm clock. Given her phone's silence and the fact that the hairs on the back of her neck were slowly prickling to attention …

Her heartbeat accelerated.

She turned her head a fraction and scanned the room. The Lady had come through the ceiling last time, gliding down like a hideous carrion bird come to feast on her terror and despair. But there was nothing there. She scanned the corners, what she could see of the bathroom …

Nothing.

Ellie lay still, trying to get a grip on her breathing. Willing her fear not to turn into a ribcage-squeezing, mind-killing anxiety attack, she glanced at the digital clock on her bedside table.

Five-thirty. She'd been asleep for three hours.

Silently, she lay her head back down on the pillow and waited. One minute. Three minutes. Still nothing. A ray of hope pierced the fear clouding her mind. *Maybe she's not here. Maybe I was just … being … paranoid …*

Voices.

Ellie's senses roared to such a high level of alertness that it was almost physically painful. She curled in on herself and looked toward her door, open to the shadowed living room, and beyond it, Oliver's room.

The voices were coming from that direction.

Ellie sat up, the soft sheets and warm comforter piling into her lap. It might be an illusion, a distraction to lure her out. But why would the Lady want to lure her *toward* Oliver when the two of them were stronger together? It didn't make any sense.

Oliver's voice drifted from the other room, tight and pained-sounding. "No."

Ellie snapped to a decision. Knowing what she now did about Oliver, he was probably having a nightmare. But nightmare or no, she didn't like it; didn't like how she felt. It was the same apprehension that had oozed into her veins before the Lady killed her father in Portlock. This time, she wouldn't be caught flat-footed.

Ellie swung her legs over the side of the bed, cursing the rustling of the sheets, then padded toward the open door.

***

In his dreams, Oliver was branded over and over, once for each of the gang members who had beaten him. They stood in a loose circle with him kneeling in the middle, and took turns searing the mark into his skin until his back was a charred, raw mess of burned flesh. He cried with the pain. They jeered.

"You ruined us, Cole." Philip spat in his face. "You betrayed your brothers."

Oliver tried to divert all the scorching heat in his back into the glare he leveled at his former friend. "You were never my brothers. And you deserved what you got."

Philip snarled and jabbed the hot iron into his chest, right over his heart. Oliver screamed and screamed, and ... and ...

The dream dissolved. His body relaxed into the soft mattress beneath him, the stench of burning skin blurring, sweet brown sugar wafting in to take its place. The sear of the brand on his chest was replaced by a cool hand, and he became aware of someone stretched out on top of the blankets beside him, and then a pair of lips met his, kissing him lightly.

"Ellie," he murmured. "I'm sorry. I was having a nightmare. I didn't mean to wake you up—"

She put a chilled finger to his lips. "It's okay. I'll take it all away. All the pain, and the fear ..."

She kissed him again, deeper, shifting her body so she lay across his chest and his pulse accelerated. Groggily, he kissed her back even as part of him ... wanted ... to pull away?

Oliver broke the kiss, blinking sleep-fogged eyes, and squinted up at Ellie. In light of their hasty conversation in the parking lot, he was a little surprised she was in here.

Especially doing *this*. Not that he was complaining, but it was out of character. And that concerned him.

"Thanks," he whispered uncertainly. "I think I can go back to sleep, or ..." He glanced at the clock. "If we're both awake, we ..."

She kissed the corner of his mouth.

"... probably should just ..."

Her lips moved across his cheek, up to his temple.

" ... we should go ..."

Ellie tangled her fingers into his hair, and Oliver stopped talking as her lips dropped to his neck. Involuntarily he closed his eyes, drawing in a sharp breath as her weight settled more fully on top of him and every nerve ending in his body erupted.

"Ellie," he said faintly. "Ellie, I thought we weren't ready for this yet."

"I know," she sighed against the spot where his collarbone peeked around the neck of his shirt. "You just sounded so ... anguished. I wanted to make you feel better."

Oliver gritted his teeth against the part of him that just wanted to surrender and pushed her off him. He sat up, staring at her silhouette. "Look, you know I care about you a lot, but I'm ... I'm just not ready. I'm insanely attracted to you, believe me, but I can't. Not yet, and especially not with Wormwood around—"

"You're thinking about this way too much." Ellie reached for the hem of his shirt and started tugging it upward.

Oliver grabbed her hand, which was—he frowned—*frigid*. He looked into her eyes, eyes that were a too-dark shade of gray. "No."

It was all wrong. The Ellie he knew *would* take no for an answer. In fact, the Ellie he knew wouldn't have been here in the first place. He ripped himself away and scooted back, a revolting suspicion beginning to form in the back of his mind. "Let's ... let's turn on the light and talk about this. Something's not right."

***

Ellie threw up her hand against the unexpected brightness as Oliver's lamp blazed to life, the light driving the gloom of night to pool in the corners of the living room. She squinted, then pressed forward, her shadow lengthening behind her as she approached the doorway. Oliver said her name, and Ellie stopped dead.

"Ellie, why are you so cold? What happened?"

Her chest began to constrict. He was talking to someone. And his *voice* ... it was low and husky and alluring, a tone reserved for tender touches and private rooms. Unless he either sleepwalked, or there was something he wasn't telling her, the person in there with him was ... *her*.

Ellie lurched forward. Still half-blinded by the light, she stumbled over Oliver's threshold and saw him sitting upright, half-covered by blankets. He was dazed-looking; his hair was tousled and his shirt rumpled and twisted around his middle. In that moment, Ellie knew exactly what was happening. So it was no surprise when the next person she saw was herself.

For a second, they all stared at each other. Then, the other Ellie sighed. "You just *had* to go ruin it."

She burst upward, her body shredding into a form that was both awful and familiar, the tassels of her ruined black dress writhing through the air like adders. The Dark Lady's black eyes blistered into Ellie's and she couldn't stop the scream that tore from her throat. In an instant, it all crashed back: her father walking away from her, arms held out for the grotesque specter in front of him, calling her mother's name. The terrible pressure on her throat, thrashing, dying as he drowned in front of her—

The Lady raised a bone-thin hand and squeezed, and for the second time in her life, Ellie was suffocating. She choked. Oliver's sharp cry pierced her ears as he sprang toward her. She fell against him, heaving uselessly for air, panicking, clutching at her neck.

"NO!" Oliver bellowed. He dropped Ellie and she fell, thrashing, to the floor. She rolled onto her side, tears blurring her view and streaking down her cheeks; her vision was going black at the edges—

Oliver lunged at the Lady, his hands outstretched, teeth bared in a snarl.

And slammed into her.

The force of his blow sent them both careening backward. They crashed into the wall with a bone-jarring *thud*, and the pressure on Ellie's throat released. Air flooded into her lungs; she gasped again and again as oxygen drove the buzzing terror of imminent death to the edges of her brain. Wheezing, she staggered upright, but her head started to spin and she collapsed onto her knees, draping her arms across the bed to stay upright. The sounds of Oliver's scuffle with the Lady faded in and out and she sucked in more air, willing herself not to faint.

He can't die he can't die he can't die—

Ellie forced her head up just in time to see Oliver punch the Lady.

The blow cracked the creature's head back into the wall. For a moment, she looked stunned, even fearful. Then she snapped her head upright with a sickening *crunch* and screamed, her jaw dislocating, her wasted maw inches from his face. Oliver yelled right back and drew his hand into a fist—

A sharp *pop* echoed through the room. Oliver jerked, tripping against the bed and landing flat on his back on the mattress, his blue eyes wide and staring at nothing.

An unbelievable surge of adrenaline jolted through Ellie. She didn't think, didn't plan, she just heaved herself upright and crawled over the top of the covers toward Oliver. He moaned and rolled onto his side, his body twitching oddly but at least he was alive, he was *alive—*

An earsplitting shriek shattered her relief. Ellie twisted to see the Lady advancing on them, and fear slammed into her like a physical blow. She shrank back, tears streaming down her cheeks. The Lady stopped feet from them, her jaw slack, her shoulders hunching as if from weariness. But her eyes ...

Ellie had never seen hatred like that.

"I can still break *you*," the creature hissed. "Once he's dead, I'll kill you *so* slowly."

Panic fogged Ellie's mind, leeching into her vision. The Lady raised her arm and Oliver went rigid. A choked cough tore from his chest and one hand flew up to his neck, and *still* he tried to push himself upright, to fight—

Ellie threw herself in front of him. Then she looked up into that ghastly face, clenching her teeth against the terror that threatened to rip her mind apart. "He's mine. You won't take someone else from me."

And for the first time in her life, Ellie threw a punch.

It was bad; she had no idea what she was doing, and when her fist connected with cold, spongy flesh, she screamed almost as loudly as the Lady. Ellie overbalanced, tumbling over Oliver's legs and nearly off the bed. *It's over. We're dead, she'll kill us both.* Still, somewhere within the fear-soaked darkness that coated Ellie's mind was a glimmer of ... *triumph*. The fear hadn't consumed her. She'd fought back.

If only she hadn't lost.

Ellie's heart nearly crumbled again at the thought of what was coming, but she looked up, determined not to give the Lady *all* her fear, to salvage what dignity—what *courage*—she could.

The demon was gone.

For a moment Ellie just crouched, frozen, hardly able to believe they'd somehow driven the demon away again. Then she collapsed into a sitting position, her breath coming in sharp gasps. Beside her, Oliver managed to come up onto his elbows. His head was bowed between his hands and he heaved in lungfuls of air.

Ellie dragged herself over to him, placing a hand on his shoulder. "Oliver?"

He groaned, raised his head. The muscles of his back were taut; veins stood out on his arms. "It's you." He tried to push himself up again but collapsed.

"Here ..." Ellie helped him roll onto his side, guiding his head into her lap. "What did she do to you? Do ... do I need to call an ambulance?"

"No. I ... I think the feeling's coming back. Give me a few minutes."

"The feeling in what?"

He clenched his teeth. "The left side of my body."

"What the ...?" Ellie's voice came out an octave too high. "*What did she do to you?*"

"It was like she ... *shocked* me. Like, an electric shock. She touched me, right here—" he dragged his working arm to his left side, right over the lower part of his ribcage. "And then there was a *pop* and my muscles seized up. I think I blacked out, and the next thing I knew I was on the bed and I couldn't sit up."

"Are you sure you don't need me to call?"

"I don't know. Maybe." He took a deep breath. "But not yet. The feeling's coming back. I can move my limbs. Sort of." He hesitated, then reached up with his good arm and brushed his fingers along her neck. "Besides, explaining these bruises would be hard."

Ellie winced. Oliver's hand fell to his side. "Sorry. I shouldn't have touched them."

"It's okay. They hurt, but it's a ... deeper hurt. I think they'd be painful no matter what."

"Maybe they'll heal quickly." Oliver's eyes fell closed, his voice becoming a low murmur. "Like last time."

"You remember that?"

"Of course I do." He cracked one eye open. "You were hurt. And I cared."

Ellie stared down at him, transfixed. She studied the strong lines of his face, his black hair still tousled from sleep, his unfairly long lashes laying against his cheek. Then, she leaned down and kissed him on the forehead. "I care, too. A lot."

Oliver's expression twisted; it was like he wanted to smile but could only wince instead. Ellie straightened, giving him space, half-aware of her own body shaking even as she tried to hold him together. For a moment, they were silent, Ellie stroking her fingers through his hair, watching the dim ring of light brighten around the curtains. The sun was coming for them. And with it, who knew what else?

When Ellie finally felt like she could control the tone of her voice again, she spoke. "So the Lady was impersonating me..."

Oliver's face clouded, though he didn't open his eyes.

"And she was in your room in the middle of the night," Ellie continued, "and was dressed pretty skimpily ... I feel like there's only one reason she would have shown up ... that ... way ...?"

Oliver opened his eyes, and the wry smile that twisted his mouth didn't quite dispel the lingering revulsion in them. "You're a way better kisser than she is."

A disgusted sound burst from Ellie's battered throat. "She seriously tried to seduce you?! I'm going to *kill* her. I'll tear those stupid bony limbs off and beat her to death with them—"

"I like it when you get feisty," Oliver chuckled. Then, he tensed, groaning, and Ellie realized he was trying to move. "Help me sit up."

Ellie pushed against his shoulder, steadying him as he rose into a sitting position. She let her hands hover next to him in case he toppled again, but her caution was unfounded. He was pale and still clearly shaken, but swung his legs over the side of the bed and leaned back on shaky arms. "Give me a second. Then I think I can stand."

Ellie eyed his still-spasming leg. "Yeah?"

Oliver began to swing it back and forth. When it jerked, his expression darkened. "Do we have a choice?"

"Probably not." For a second ... just *one* second ... Ellie let her eyes fall closed. When she forced them open again, light was leeching into the room in earnest. The promise of another exhausting, terrifying day.

"Why try to seduce you?" she asked. "Why not just kill us both and be done?"

For a moment, Oliver was silent. Then ...

"It would have broken me." His voice went hoarse. "*Completely* broken me. And I don't know how you would have felt if you'd have walked in and ... and seen ..."

A lump rose in Ellie's throat; she couldn't tell if she wanted to scream or throw up at the thought. She swallowed. "It would have broken me, too."

"They want to torture. Not kill." Oliver's voice trembled slightly. "And they're really good at it."

Ellie drew her knees up and wrapped her arms around them, as if curling into a ball would insulate her from the horror crawling through her veins. For a moment, she was too sickened for words.

"I wasn't going to do it," Oliver said.

"I know."

Silence settled over the room. For a moment they just sat, Ellie trying to hold herself together while Oliver's limbs twitched and jerked.

"I punched her," he finally said.

A little ray of hope penetrated Ellie's internal darkness. She uncurled, sitting cross-legged on the bed.

"So did I." She flexed her hand, grimacing. The feel of the demon's pulpous flesh giving under her knuckles ...

Oliver grinned. "Nice. I'm sad I missed that."

"Me, too. It was the fiestiest thing I've ever done." Ellie stood, shaking her hand. "And maybe the grossest. Do you care if I wash my hands in your sink?"

"No."

Ellie caught a glimpse of him rolling his shoulder as she walked away. It seemed less twitchy. Hopefully that wasn't just because of the distance.

"I've never been able to do that before," Oliver said over the sound of the running water. "Make physical contact, I mean. Other than Silverskin."

"Me neither. Not that I've really tried." Ellie picked up the jasmine-scented hotel soap and scrubbed the knuckles on her hand like she was a nurse going into surgery. She glanced up, meeting her own bloodshot eyes in the mirror. "What was different ...?"

Her mouth opened, and she touched one soapy hand to her purpling neck. "She was choking me. In the *act* of choking me! That's what was different!"

Oliver's eyes widened and he twisted to face her, twitching as he did. "Using her power on you made *her* vulnerable, too."

"And she seemed shocked!" Excitement flushed Ellie's cheeks; she turned off the water and trotted back to Oliver, plunking down on the bed with enough space between them that she didn't accidentally jar him. "I was barely conscious, but she looked like she wasn't expecting you to be able to hit her. And ..."

Venom surged in her heart, unexpected, caustic, and disturbingly gratifying.

"It looked like it hurt," she whispered.

Oliver's head turned. Ellie glanced at him; his expression was difficult to read but his eyes ... they had that look in them that seemed to strip her bare. Like he, too, had seen the change, the tiny but dark shift that had just happened in her soul.

She broke off their stare. "What was Silverskin doing right before you killed him?"

"Reaching for my face."

Ellie's stomach slithered into a knot; she swallowed. "Got it. So what if ...?"

Without warning, Oliver moved again, pushing himself awkwardly to the edge of the bed and settling his feet on the floor. Ellie was to his side in an instant. "Do you need help?"

She put a hand on his shoulder but withdrew it when he winced. "Sorry."

"It's okay. My head still hurts and it just ... flared ..." His brow creased and what seemed like fear passed over his face, but then he shook his head. "That's all it was. I'm sure being shocked would give anyone a headache."

He let out a short sigh. "Sorry, I know we need to get to the bottom of this." He looked down, swallowing, then shot Ellie a smile that was so clearly haunted that her heart twisted. "Talking about Silverskin and the fire is just easier if I'm moving."

"Understood," Ellie murmured. "And as much as I wish we could both rest more, the sooner we get out of here, the better. We can talk on the way."

"Yep." Oliver took a deep breath, then pushed up, as slow and shaky as a man four times his age, his jaw clenching with the effort. Ellie sprang to her feet and held her hands out. "Here ..."

He took them and grunted, pain spasming across his face. Ellie dropped them immediately. "Sorry!"

Oliver rubbed his temple with his good hand, his face pale. "Still not your fault."

Ellie blinked, and had just opened her mouth when he eased past and started limping around the bed.

"Anyway, Silverskin was going to kill me. His hand was ... was inches away from my face." Oliver lurched to a stop in front of the suitcase and started rummaging; his arm shook and twitched, and he dropped the shirt he'd picked up.

Ellie stepped to him, looking into his pale face. "Do you ... need any help?"

Oliver didn't look at her, nor did his taut expression change. "No. I got it."

Her stomach squeezed, but she took a step back, crossing her arms. "Okay. Back to the demons ... Are you seeing the pattern that I think I'm seeing?"

Oliver glanced up at her. "That when *they* try to touch *us* they're vulnerable?"

"Not only touch, but interact with us in *any* physical way?"

A grim smile lifted one corner of Oliver's mouth. "That's the pattern I'm seeing."

"Me, too." Ellie mirrored his grin. "Which means ..."

"We know how to fight back now." With effort, Oliver hefted a pair of jeans and the shirt he'd dropped earlier and headed toward the bathroom. As he passed, he met Ellie's eyes; in them she could see both simmering anger and renewed determination. Her heart leaped. Maybe it was their new realization, or maybe her lingering adrenaline, or maybe she just really liked him. Whatever the reason, she looped her arms around his waist in a loose hug and kissed him softly on the cheek.

He winced.

Ellie released him, rocking back. "Sorry. Again. I was trying to be gentle."

Her face started to burn, and guilt struck her as a visible tremor shook his frame.

"It's okay," he said through gritted teeth. "My body's just not being ... it's struggling."

"Okay. It's all right." She backed away, uncertain. "Do you want me to stay close? In case you ... I don't know, fall over or something?"

He laughed; it was a low, pained sound. "I think I'll be fine."

An awful thought rose to Ellie's mind: *Do you not want to touch me because the Lady stole my body?*

But she shook the thought away. Unwanted seduction aside, Oliver had just been shocked, strangled, *and* survived an attempted murder. She couldn't blame him for needing a minute, and it wasn't like they had time for him to hold her until all her stress and terror and anxiety were gone, anyway. At the rate things were going, that might take *weeks*.

She turned on her heel and started for the door, wrestling her anxiety into a tight little wad at the back of her brain. "Okay. Go change. I'll grab some clothes and ..."

She glanced back and paused, watching Oliver limp into the bathroom. His body had made visible progress; he walked like he was sixty now, not eighty. But …

Ellie swallowed. "Um … if you need help, will you let me know? I can help you … change if you need—"

Oliver's face closed off. "No."

Heat rose in Ellie's cheeks again; she meant to duck away but Oliver chose that moment to look over at her. His face softened. "Thank you for offering. I'm … just not ready for you to see my scar yet."

Ellie's mouth opened in a huge "o"; she snapped it closed just as quickly. "Right. Understood. Not a problem." She turned and crossed the living area to her room, caught between wishing she could be less awkward in these situations and hoping she'd never get the chance to practice again. "Let's leave doors open in case we're attacked again."

"Yep." Oliver's voice echoed into her room, only slightly muffled by distance. "Then we can continue our conversation, too."

"Which is good, because I've had a thought," Ellie called back as she pulled a pink tee shirt over her head.

"Shoot."

"I think that attack made it really obvious the Lady and Wormwood are working together." Ellie reached for her jeans. "It was so … *specifically* targeted on so many levels."

"Yeah. It was designed to destroy both of us if it had worked. Not just kill us, but give them what they wanted: our misery."

"But how does Wormwood fit?"

"What do you mean?"

Ellie threaded her thin belt through the loops of her pants, considering. "If his attacks are psychological … how does that work? How does he get inside your head? Why can he follow us at speed when it seems like even the Lady can't?"

"I have no idea." In Oliver's room, something *flumped*, and Ellie tensed before realizing it was probably just his toiletry bag landing in his suitcase or something. Still, she only relaxed when she heard his voice again. "I'm done changing, by the way."

"Me, too." She tossed her shorts and tank in her suitcase and headed for the bathroom. "Let me pack the rest of my stuff."

"Okay." From Oliver's room came the sound of a suitcase zipper. A second later, his voice grew closer. "In answer to your question, I think it goes back to what the Nantinaq told me: they're all so individual. Wormwood must have a ... quirk ... that allows him to do what he does."

Ellie shook her head at her own wan reflection. "These demons are insane." Swallowing, she winced and put a hand to her throat. Pain burned down into the bruised flesh, but a bizarre little part of her welcomed it. It meant she was still alive.

She examined the contusions, reaching up to probe them with her fingers. They were as ugly and awful as they'd been after Portlock. Worse, actually, because they hadn't had as much time to heal. She shook her head, then started snatching the stuff she'd gotten out the night before and throwing it into her bag. *I'll just wear my jacket and turn up the collar until we can find a place to get a scarf.*

Oliver's voice interrupted her thoughts; it sounded like he was standing outside her bedroom door. "Can I come in?"

Ellie almost smiled at his courtesy. "Of course." She was zipping her bag when Oliver appeared in the doorway. He stepped back to let her pass, and Ellie scrutinized him as she walked by. He was dressed in jeans and a nondescript, long-sleeved shirt; he even had his socks and shoes on. More color had returned to his cheeks, too, and his eyes, while tired, held less pain and more of their usual spark.

Ellie tossed the little bag into her suitcase and zipped it, her brow puckering even as relief eased through her at his appearance. "How long does it usually take a person to recover from an electric shock?"

"I'd bet much longer than I am. And your bruises already look different."

Ellie dropped her gaze to his neck, where his deep-purple bruises were already starting to green at the edges. "So are yours. How hard did she strangle you?"

"I don't know. I was hardly conscious, but ..." He frowned. "I never couldn't breathe."

"That's lucky," Ellie said, and she meant it. "When she was strangling me, it felt like she *literally* crushed my windpipe. Both times."

"Well, she'd already shape-shifted, strangled you, and electrocuted me by the time she got around to choking me. And she'd flown hundreds of miles to catch up to us." A wry smile crossed Oliver's face. "Maybe she was getting tired."

"I sure hope so. They *have* to have their limits." Another bud of hope bloomed in Ellie's heart; she hefted her suitcase to the floor and rolled it out to the living room, Oliver following her. "Maybe she pushed herself as hard as she could because she thought she'd be able to kill us, but then when she wasn't able to, she cut her losses and ran."

She turned back as they reached his suitcase, but stopped. He was reaching for his luggage, the expression on his face darker than she'd ever seen it.

"Oliver?"

He blinked, and she saw the moment when he realized she was watching him. His expression smoothed, but his eyes … he couldn't do anything about what they gave away, and for that, Ellie was grateful. Because now she was *sure* there was something eating at him, and she wasn't about to let him walk away without at least offering her help.

Ellie set her suitcase upright, one hand still on its handle. "Is there something else? Or is it just … general 'this morning' madness?"

Oliver stared at her for a moment, then let out a soft sigh and took a step toward her. "No, there's something else."

Ellie's heart fluttered as he approached; by the time he stopped less than a foot away from her, it was dancing.

"I've been trying to decide when the right time to tell you this is, but I think it's now." He smiled a sad smile. "Because secrets suck."

"*Thank* you."

Oliver's grin widened for a second, then disappeared as quickly as it had come. "I think Wormwood—or something—is causing me pain every time I touch you."

Ellie's heart stuttered to a stop. Immediately the gears in her head started turning. Last night he'd complained about a headache when they'd kissed.

No.

And to have it happen again? It was such specific timing. It was too consistent.

Please, no.

But the logic kept coming and she kept listening, just like her parents had taught her. "How long has it been going on?"

"I first noticed it last night, when we were on the couch."

Something in Ellie's stomach unclenched a little. "So … you haven't been stoically enduring pain every time you've touched me since landing in Denver, right?"

"No."

"Oh, good. I would've been furious if there was something *else* you were trying to struggle through on your own without telling me." She softened her words with a little smile, and he returned it briefly before going on.

"No, I'm done doing that. But anyway, I figure there's one sure way to test it, and we need to know."

He opened his arms. Ellie hesitated, but he was right; there was really only one way to know. Tentatively, she stepped into his embrace and wrapped her arms around his waist, hoping she—Wormwood—wasn't hurting him.

And at first, nothing seemed wrong at all. In fact, it was the opposite. Oliver held Ellie against him, loosely at first. Then, when a few uneventful seconds had passed, his arms tightened around her, his sigh wisping across her skin as he buried his face in the curve of her neck. Relief hit Ellie then, so dramatic that it nearly made her dizzy. She relaxed into his arms, turning her face into his shoulder, inhaling his crisp scent.

At least we still have this. At least they could still share these pure, uncomplicated moments when the world melted away and all that was left was the two of them, their affection, their struggles, their friendship—

Ellie felt it when the pain hit.

Oliver shuddered and rocked back, pressing his hands against his eyes. A low moan escaped him as he leaned forward, cradling his head. Ellie took a hasty step away so he didn't accidentally touch her again, helplessness and rage curdling within her.

"Well, there's *that* answer," Oliver muttered.

"Oliver ..."

He put up a hand. "It's okay."

"It's not. We can survive for a few days without touching, but ..." Ellie shuddered. "It's so invasive. He has no right."

"That's exactly what I told him." Oliver dropped his hand. "I was hoping I'd gotten rid of him last night, and the headache was just a normal headache." He grabbed his luggage by the handle and tugged it over to the door. "Guess I'll just have to find a different way to kick his butt."

Ellie sighed and pulled her suitcase up next to his, suddenly aware of the space between them in a way she hadn't been before. *Ironic, that instead of wanting the distance to disappear, you want to keep it there now.*

"If you think of anything I can do," she said, "please let me know."

Oliver looked at her; his eyes were calm on the surface, but underneath, something seethed. "I will. I'm beginning to think the only way I'll be rid of him is to close the gate.

And since that might be the case—" he put a hand on the doorknob "—you ready for another road trip?"

"As long as it's with you. And as long as we find a place to buy some weapons on the way."

Oliver grinned and opened the door, the light from the hallway spilling across his face. "I knew there was a reason I liked you."

A low simmer of wrath burned in Death, but he held it in check. He would deal with the Lady presently. "What weapons are they acquiring?"

"I don't know yet," Wormwood responded. "I'll tell you when I do. He's thinking a lot about fire and wood, though. In fact, they're going through a list of chemicals humans use to treat wood right now."

As Death read Wormwood's thoughts, he didn't miss the the other demon's flash of apprehension. It was unsettling that it was directed at the humans, and not at Death. And that little undercurrent of jealousy...

Death rocked back. Wormwood was resentful. He was bitter toward other demons who didn't have an assignment, who were free to roam, to go to cities, to find new prey...

He schooled his emotions, and his voice. "Keep me updated. I should have plenty of time to—"

On the very horizon of his perception, almost too distant to make out, something pulsed. Something young, fresh, new. A strange feeling, perhaps something akin to what the humans called wonder, stole over Death. He smiled.

"Wormwood, I must go. Another is Awakening."

"How many does that make?"

"In the last night? Thirteen that I am aware of, and I'm sure many more who are outside my reach."

A thrill passed through Wormwood; Death felt it like it was his own.

"Can I ask where before you go?"

Death just smiled. "Exactly where I need him to be."

Chapter Seven

S am ducked into the huge, luxurious shower, his tired muscles relaxing as the warm water spilled over his shoulders, and pulled Darien into his arms. "Hey, beautiful."

She grinned up at him. "Hey, babe. How was your workout?"

"Good. Hopefully enough for Coach to forgive me for running off to Hawaii during peak practice season."

Darien's nose wrinkled. "It's me he'll need to forgive."

"Nah. Your job at the clinic had spoken. We did what we could to accommodate everyone."

"That's the truth," Darien pulled away and tilted her head back, closing her eyes as the water ran through her long hair. Sam stared. She was the picture of grace and serenity; she looked like a mermaid, like a princess straight out of a Disney movie. And she'd chosen him.

A little jolt of pure joy shot through him at the thought.

"The ocean is nice," Darien murmured, "but there's nothing in the world like a hot shower."

"Mmm-hmm. Especially with my hot wife."

Darien grinned. "Am I the hottest on the whole beach?"

"Uh, yes."

Darien smoothed her hair back one more time, then stepped forward and looped her arms around his neck. "Convince me."

Sam didn't need to be told twice. He brought his hands up to encircle her waist and kissed her. She responded with enthusiasm, her hands making slow, soft circles through his hair, down the back of his neck. When they finally broke the kiss, Sam's heart was pounding.

He leaned down, brushing his lips against hers again. "How about that?" He nibbled at her neck, right under her ear. "Or do you need more convincing?"

Darien giggled as he kissed across her shoulder, down to her collarbone. A swell of emotion crashed into Sam: admiration, passion, joy—he felt so alive here, so strong, more even than when he was on the football field. How she could do that to him, he didn't know if he'd ever understand. It left him in awe.

"Oh!" Darien gasped. And not the good kind.

"What? You okay?"

"You stepped on my foot."

Sam blinked. "No, I didn't."

"Well something hurt it, and we're the only ones in here." Darien gave him a reproachful look, then leaned against the shower wall, caught her ankle, and lifted it. Sam bent and examined her skin but there wasn't a mark on it. Shrugging, she let her foot go, rolling and flexing it before lowering it gingerly to the floor.

He watched her, baffled. "I'm sorry, Darien. I really don't think I stepped on you."

"It's okay." She winced as she settled her full weight onto it. "It didn't hurt that bad."

Sam opened his mouth, then shut it again. Clearly, it had. But he also didn't think he'd *done* it. Years of training had pounded an absolute awareness of where his feet were at all times into his head. Sure, he'd been distracted, but not enough to have accidentally stepped on his pregnant wife's foot.

Had he?

An awful suspicion crept into Sam's mind. He peered around Darien into the corners of the huge shower, then beyond the glass doors into the bathroom itself. But there was nothing out of the ordinary. Just clean tile floors and shining marble countertops.

"Huh," he grunted. *Maybe I* was *that distracted*. And, as embarrassing as the thought was, it was accompanied by an amount of relief that was almost pathetic. "I'm sorry, Darien."

"It's okay."

Sam reached for the soap and started mechanically rubbing it into a lather. "It's not, but ..."

He sighed. He was still trying to wrap his mind around the fact that demons existed. That creatures like Bigfoot, which he'd joked about all his life, actually wandered around out there, apparently defending the world from even worse things. What was next? The Tooth Fairy? Santa Claus? The Chupacabra?

And then—Sam suppressed his shudder—there was *his* demon. Realizing it not only existed but was actively feeding on him had been almost as terrifying as encountering the Lady, because there had been no escaping it. The thing was just ... *there*, inside his head, preying on his fear that he would lose everyone else he loved.

And manipulating him accordingly.

Sam turned away from Darien, rubbing the rich soap onto his skin. She rolled with life's punches like she'd seen them all coming from ten miles away and already had a contingency plan. Normally, he admired that. Now, though? He grimaced. His world had been turned upside down, the sure foundation of his own rationality blown to bits. And the people around him who also knew the truth? Ellie, Oliver ... even Helen and Henry? While they were all clearly rocked, none of them seemed as off-balance and adrift as he felt.

Sam let out a long, silent breath and reached for more soap, staring at the shower's slate-grey tile wall. What else was real? What else wasn't? If his parents and Lily were still out there, were they okay? Were they happy? Suffering? Were they still ... themselves?

His jaw tightened. *Snap out of it, Sam.* The last thing any of them needed was for him to give in to the constant, low-grade panic that had licked at the back of his mind for nearly forty-eight hours now. He could shoulder it. He could move forward into this new, much weirder, much scarier world.

"Hey." Darien's soft hand slid over his soapy shoulder, and he let her turn him to face her. Her expression was grim, and the wariness behind her eyes suggested he wasn't the only one whose thoughts had jumped straight to those interdimensional freaks. "We're safe here."

"We think."

She lifted one shoulder in a shrug. "It's true, we can't know for sure." Something changed in her expression, and it took a moment before Sam realized it was mischief. "But come on. Can you imagine a demon that only goes around grabbing people's ankles?"

Sam stared for a second. Then, he started to laugh. "In light of our experiences with the Lady, my demon, Silverskin, and Wormwood? I think I'd rather deal with an ankle-grabber."

Darien let out a dry chuckle. "Ankle Tickler. The most fearsome demon of all time." Her expression turned painful as she shifted her weight, looking down again. "I'm not going to die. I've had way worse things step on my feet before."

Now it was Sam's turn to wince. "Like that cow." He still remembered the bruises it had left on her foot. She'd been lucky the stupid animal hadn't broken anything. And the stupid animal had been lucky Sam hadn't found it and turned it into steak.

Placing his feet very carefully, Sam pulled Darien against him again, dismissing his deep, nagging suspicion as he did. *There's no way the demons have made it this far. She's safe. We all are.* For a long, perfect moment, he just held her, rocking her back and forth and letting the warm water run over them both.

"I love you," he finally murmured. "I love you so much. I want to make you this happy for the rest of our lives." A chagrined smile touched his lips. "And I'll start by watching my feet better."

She snorted. "There are worse flaws to have as a husband." A pause. "But yes. Please."

Sam let out a quiet laugh, his embarrassment soothed by the smile in her voice.

After a few moments, Darien pulled back and reached for the shampoo.

Sam stopped her. "Can I?"

"Of course."

Sam took the bottle, dabbed some onto his hand, then started massaging the tropical-smelling bubbles into her hair, running his hands through its smooth, glossy length.

"I've been thinking a lot about what Oliver said about angels," Darien said softly.

For maybe the first time ever, Sam was glad she wasn't pressed against him. It was easier to hide the sudden tension he felt. "Yeah?"

"Yeah."

She went silent for a long time and Sam hesitated. He should say something.

But what?

Slowly, Darien turned to face him. She wrapped her arms around his neck and cocked her head. Sam tried to smile but could feel the moment when it failed on his face. Her expression softened, and for another long moment she just appraised him with those gentle, patient eyes.

"We'd better go if we want to make our program at the Cultural Center," she finally said.

Sam suppressed a sigh of relief, grateful Darien hadn't pushed the subject. "Yep. You rinse off. I'll shampoo and be right out." He reached for the little bottle, only too happy to let the sight of Darien rinsing her hair distract him.

***

Minutes later, Darien drifted to her suitcase, twisting her wet hair into a braid as she went. She tied her ponytail holder around it, then reached for the zipper, wincing a little as her injured ankle took the brunt of her weight.

Come on, she thought. It wasn't like it still hurt. In fact, it hadn't ever *really* hurt.

It was more the psychological implications than anything else.

Darien shook herself and started pulling on her clothes. Sam wouldn't take long to join her, and then they'd go—

Something moved in her peripheral vision, something over by the window. She whirled, heart in her throat, one hand clenching into a fist ... only to make eye contact with a massive raven that had just landed on the balcony.

She slumped, pressing a hand to her forehead. *You. Have got. To stop.*

Turning her back on the oblivious bird—now pecking happily at something on the patio—Darien finished dressing, then let the lid of her suitcase fall closed. She grabbed the stack of pamphlets she and Sam had glanced over the night before, then let herself collapse on the bed. Wiggling a little, she rolled onto her belly. By the doctor's best estimate, she was between six and seven weeks along, and though she wasn't showing, laying on her stomach was tougher than it used to be. Still, that wasn't going to stop her from enjoying it while she still had the chance.

Darien rifled through the pamphlets until she found the one that featured the lava tube, then started skimming it, enjoying the feeling of her heart calming down as much as—or maybe more than—the reading material itself. And the more she read, the more absorbed she became; the cave went deep under the mountains but, apparently, offered easy access for its first section. Perfect for someone who wanted a caving adventure with very little fall risk.

Darien flipped the last flap open and smiled. *And, as a bonus, petroglyphs!* She examined the little images more closely. Tribal designs, human figures holding spears with strange-looking tips, flowers ... and then several figures that *didn't* look quite human. Including ...

The hair on the back of Darien's neck stood straight up. Including a crude drawing of two cloaked figures. One was ragged, tattered, and skeletal, and the other was completely shrouded in black.

Darien's hand trembled as she brought the pamphlet closer, so close that her nose nearly touched the glossy paper. The second petroglyph had two green shells for eyes.

Behind her, the door opened, and she heard the rustling of clothing.

"Sam?" Her voice came out funny.

"Yeah?" Sam fell onto the bed beside her, fully clothed, and propped himself up on his elbows. "What's wrong?"

"Look at this." Darien tipped the brochure toward him.

Sam peered at it, then his eyes widened. He gestured to the picture. "I don't like that."

"I never saw Silverskin," Darien said. "Did you?"

"No. But that sure matches his description. And *that* sure looks a lot like the Lady." Sam frowned as he examined the picture, leaning close enough to rest the side of his head against hers. Then, he pulled out his phone and snapped a picture. "Let me send this to Ellie. She and Oliver might be able to tell us if we're just being paranoid or not."

"Good idea," Darien said. "Put all four of us in a group text while you're at it."

Sam tapped his phone screen, chewing on his tongue. "Done."

"Great," Darien said as her phone buzzed. She held up the pamphlet. "It says there are three more major petroglyphs in the cave that aren't pictured. I vote we go check it out as soon as we can."

Sam said nothing for a moment, his face pulling into a frown.

"I'm torn, Dar," he finally said.

"On whether we should go?"

"... Yeah. I ..." He sighed. "Actually, I do think we have to. If there are any clues there that could help Ellie and Oliver ..."

Darien kissed him on the cheek. "You're sweet, Sam. I think we'll be okay. The brochure says the petroglyph part of the cave is easily walkable, and like you said, if we can find *any* information ..."

"No, I agree. We need to go." He took a deep breath. "I only have two questions."

"And those are?"

Sam smiled. "Should we go tonight after the Cultural Center, or tomorrow?"

Darien grinned, then glanced at the clock. "It's what, ten-thirty?" She considered for a moment. "If what I've heard about the Cultural Center is true, we'll probably be there all day. Especially with the lunch program we've booked."

"Probably," Sam agreed. "So let's go tomorrow. Enjoy the Cultural Center today without worrying, have takeout on the beach just like you wanted ..."

"Then save most of the day tomorrow for exploring a lava tube. That sounds great." Darien grinned at the smile that cracked through the worry on Sam's face. "What's your second question?"

In answer, Sam pointed at the picture of the warriors. "What's with these spears?"

"I was wondering that, too." Darien squinted down at them again. "Because it looks like there's something bulky on their tips, and if they're right next to a picture of Silverskin—*if* that's Silverskin—that might be important."

"That's what I'm thinking," Sam said. "If ... Dar, these implications are crazy, though."

"They are. It would mean the demons were here in Hawaii at some point. Likely hundreds—if not thousands—of years ago."

"And it would also mean," Sam said quietly, "that the ancient Hawaiians beat them. If the gate's been closed before, that's hard proof we can succeed again."

Relief and hope welled in Darien's chest. "That's incredibly comforting." *And bittersweet, given that for the gate to close, someone had to die.* She cringed at the morbid thought, then rolled onto her side, facing Sam. "So here's an idea."

He mirrored her. "What?"

"While we're exploring the Cultural Center, we look for strange spears, weapons, petroglyphs, drawings ... anything that could give us a hint."

"I like it." Sam gathered his legs underneath him, then stood and clapped his hands together. "Let's do it."

"Great." Darien followed more slowly, grunting as she stood. "Soon I'm not going to be able to lay on my stomach like that."

"That'll be difficult for a tummy sleeper," Sam said, sympathy lining his eyes.

"I'll get through it." Darien reached for her shoes. "I think—"

Something touched—no, *slithered*—around her ankle and her words turned into a shriek.

Sam jumped toward her. "What? What is it?"

Darien peered at the floor around her feet, where there was … nothing. Well, nothing except the shoe she'd just dropped and her bikini, discarded after their impulsive midnight swim. She closed her eyes. *Of course* the top had somehow gotten wrapped around her leg. "It's just my swimsuit. I'm sorry to be so jumpy."

Sam took a step forward, his voice constricting in the way it did when he was trying to cheer her up. "That damn Ankle Tickler. I'm telling you."

Darien forced a smile as she bent to pick up her shoe again. "He's almost as bad as the morning sickness."

"That's it. Twitchy ankles. That's the strangest pregnancy symptom I've ever heard of."

Despite herself, Darien burst out laughing.

"And the poor guy looks just like your bikini," Sam added. "That's gotta be embarrassing for any self-respecting demon."

"Right?" Darien chuckled, then paused as a hazy image took shape in her mind. "I actually imagined him more like … What was the name of that thing we learned about in Animal Biology? With the crazy-looking hands? Do you remember?"

Sam screwed up his face. "I think I know what you're talking about. Can't remember what it's called, though—"

"An aye-aye! That's what it is."

Sam grunted. "I see it. But the creepy version, because it is still a demon. Or whatever they are."

"Whatever they are, indeed," Darien muttered, tugging on her other sandal. *She* sure didn't know. And Ellie and Oliver had been so vague about their descriptions. Whenever she tried to puzzle through it all, her brain automatically reverted to the demons of the Bible. But *that* wasn't right, not when Ellie and Oliver—and apparently, the Nantinaq, too—had been adamant they weren't.

No, these monsters had to be something else. Something new. And as to where they fit within her personal beliefs? Well, she'd work on that. The world was strange and wild, and Darien suspected there was a lot more to it than either science or religion professed to know.

She finished buckling her sandal and sat up, looking to where Sam stood with his arms crossed, a slight frown on his face. Immediately, her heart leaped. The bright Hawaiian sunlight softened when it bloomed through the window, and the effect it had on Sam's already good looks was breathtaking.

"Grappling with life's deep questions again?" she asked softly.

Sam appeared to shake himself. "Yeah. There are a lot more of them now than there were a few days ago."

"There are." Darien stood and offered him a hand. "But the most important things are still the same. We have each other. We have our life together. We have our families, even if they're kind of weird."

Sam he looked away. "And broken."

Darien's smile faded as she guessed where his mind had gone. She touched his cheek, making him look her in the eyes. "Sam. You're not evil for choosing to take our family out of danger. Ellie's smart, and she has Oliver, and he's smart. They'll be okay." She hesitated; while her family was together and reasonably happy, they had their baggage, too. Nothing as traumatic as what the Forths had been through, but ... "Besides. All families are a little broken."

Sam was still, his eyes deep, mercurial pools of heartache. For a moment, Darien was afraid she'd overstepped, trivialized his problems, even. But then her husband swallowed, leaned down, and kissed her lightly. "You've never had a hard time with faith. In other people, and in ..." he shifted uncomfortably, "a more metaphysical sense. I might have to lean on you while I try to process all this."

"You can. You always can."

Sam kissed her again, more deeply, then pulled away. "So about the Cultural Center ..."

Darien let every ounce of her excitement show on her face. "Let's do it."

Chapter Eight

"Okay, let's recap," Ellie said as they stumped out of the sporting goods store toward the truck. She carried a heavily laden plastic bag in one hand, an ax in the other, and had an empty leather quiver slung across her back, its strap a black slash across her chest. "First, let's celebrate that we've managed to both shop *and* make it to the truck without being attacked."

Oliver grinned as he lowered the tailgate of Sam's truck. "I didn't think we would be here."

"Yeah. There are too many people. And cameras. Plus, we're bristling with really weird weapons now." Ellie thumped the ax down in the bed of the truck and shrugged the quiver over her head, laying it beside the tool-weapon.

"Don't tell me you're disappointed," Oliver teased as he set the bow case—and the wicked-looking compound bow inside—next to the ax and quiver. Then, he placed the two boxes he held under his arm beside them. Both held a dozen pre-fletched arrows, one set each of carbon fiber and wood.

Ellie gave him a sideways look. "Part of me just *really* wanted to swing the ax at the Lady's head. Payback for stealing my beauty sleep."

Oliver chuckled. "That's fair. I assume you know how to use it?"

"Sort of. I've split a couple logs in my time. Only a few, though, so don't overestimate me."

"That's better than nothing. And I know you're pretty good with a bow, since we all shot at Helen and Henry's that one afternoon."

"True. I've never shot with wooden arrows, though."

Oliver raised one of the arrow boxes, examining the thin wooden shafts inside. "Me neither."

"Cool. This'll be fun, then." Ellie rustled through the bag, extracting a little roll of copper wire and setting it next to the arrows. "So, how do we want to do this?"

"Well, it's my turn to drive," Oliver said, folding his arms over his chest and leaning against the tailgate.

Ellie flashed him a brief smile. "Thankfully."

"So maybe you can wrap the copper wire around a couple arrows—both wood *and* carbon fiber ones—so we can have some options ready if we need them. At least, that's what I was thinking when I threw the wire in the cart."

"That sounds like a reasonable plan to me." Ellie chewed her lip for a moment, and Oliver instantly remembered what it was like to kiss her, as vivid and real as if it had been a movie waiting for someone to hit play. His hands curled into fists. *Get out, Wormwood. Those memories are mine.*

It's rude to not share, Ollie.

"It'll be all right," Oliver said. "It doesn't have to be perfect, just tight enough to stay on the arrow until it hits the Wormwood." He shook his head. "The demon, I mean. Whichever one is idiotic enough to show itself."

Ellie's expression darkened; she was getting better at picking up when he was struggling. *Not that my little slip helped.* Oliver swallowed. He wasn't trying to hide the fact that he was having a hard time; in their situation, with how close they were, there was no point. Plus, what he'd told her was true: he was inexpressibly thankful for her support, her presence.

That didn't, however, mean he wanted her to know how vicious and awful the war really was.

Ellie's voice was a soft snarl when she spoke. "Pretend it's Wormwood if it helps. *I* might pretend it's Wormwood." She brushed some hair out of her face, her expression changing to worry. "I'm just afraid ..."

"What are you worried about?" Oliver asked after she'd been quiet for a second.

She crossed her arms, frowning. "Of all the ingredients used to treat lumber, copper makes the most sense."

"It was in every preservative mixture we could find," Oliver pointed out.

"Yeah, but what if ...?" Ellie worried her lip some more.

Yummy.

Disgust and resentment welled up in Oliver; he willed himself not to respond even as a little shard of longing, pure and tender, pierced him, too. Instead, he picked up the second box of arrows and moved around the truck to the passenger's side, setting them in the back with deliberate gentleness. "I don't think we can realistically get ahold of any of the other components in those mixtures. Unless you happen to have a lumber processor on speed dial."

The door opposite him opened and Ellie set the bow case gently on the other side. "I have many connections, but none are lumberjacks, no." She stepped back and glanced at the ax, lying lonely on the tailgate. "Should we just throw that in the backseat, too?"

"Might as well. Even with our luggage, we have room. You still have your knife?"

Ellie's hand dropped to her beltline, the movement seeming unfamiliar to her. "Yep. You?"

"Yep." He could feel its weight, solid and reassuring. If the Lady dared let him get within arm's reach of her again, he'd be ready.

Unless she sneaks up and electrocutes Ellie. Or you. I know it hurt. *I know* you're scared *of it happening again, you coward. You're not as strong as you think you are, Ollie.*

Oliver closed his eyes, the shame hitting him like a blow to the chest. He shoved it down as Ellie spoke again.

"And we've got first-aid stuff," she said as she strode to the tailgate and grabbed the ax.

Oliver fumbled with one of the boxes of arrows; his fingers still didn't work as well as he wanted them to, but given the circumstances, he was grateful they were working at all.

"And all Sam's survival stuff," he said. *A hatchet, matches, Sterno ...* That last one had been especially intriguing to Oliver. If fire killed the demons, having a few cans of flammable gel handy could only be a good thing.

Oliver's phone buzzed in his pocket, but he ignored it as Ellie reappeared across from him, settling the ax on the floor next to Sam's first-aid kit and the black tote that held his survival gear. She looked up, her gray eyes cool and calm and so, *so* tired. "Ready to go?"

"Yep." Oliver closed his door, then stepped around the front of the truck to the driver's side, crossing paths with Ellie on the way. "I've lined out all the stuff you need. It should be within easy reach."

"Thanks, Oliver."

"No problem." He settled in the driver's seat and pulled the door shut, then looked over at Ellie. She had one foot in the truck and was staring down at her phone with her head cocked and an odd expression on her face.

"Everything okay?" he asked.

"Um ..." Ellie eased herself into the seat and closed the door. "Did you get Sam's text?"

"I got *a* text. Hang on ..." Oliver pulled his phone out of his pocket and swiped it open, then clicked on the new message there. It was a group text: himself, Ellie, Sam, and a number he assumed was Darien. Oliver squinted down at the little picture Sam had sent, unable to make out much beyond a few humanoid figures carved into what looked like stone. His eyes went to the message below it.

Found this picture in a brochure. They look familiar to you?

An odd sense of foreboding came over Oliver. Feeling almost ... *reluctant*, he tapped the picture. It expanded to fill the screen, and he gasped.

Two figures stared out at him, far from detailed but what was there was enough. The skull-like planes of the Lady's face, her tattered dress—they were burned into his memories; he'd likely never be rid of them. And the figure next to her ...

Even in the full light of day, Oliver shuddered. It, too, was cloaked, and would have been nondescript except the artist had somehow affixed two earth-green shells to the figure's face, creating the impression of staring, emerald eyes.

His phone buzzed again and another picture appeared below the first. Oliver clicked it immediately. The gloss from the brochure cut a weird line across the image, but it looked like a line of stick figures. They carried what he assumed were spears, but instead of the points he'd expected to see, the weapons were tipped with what might have been ... flowers?

A suspicion started to form in Oliver's mind, just as a second text from Sam came through.

These look like warriors but their spear tips are weird. On fire? Connection there? We're visiting this cave tomorrow to see what we can find.

"This is crazy, Oliver."

He looked up, meeting Ellie's stunned eyes.

"If these are cave drawings of demons ..." she said, "that means they've escaped before. In *Hawaii.*"

He nodded, looking back down at the picture. "And it seems like they beat them."

For a moment, they were silent.

"Ready to go?" Oliver asked. According to the map, the country they were heading into was relatively rural. They likely wouldn't have cell service in between cities until Calgary.

"Yep," Ellie said.

Oliver started the truck, put it in gear, and trundled out of the parking lot.

"I don't want anyone I love to ever go in a cave again," Ellie muttered as they turned onto the highway.

"If they saw this in a brochure, then I assume it's well-traveled."

"Probably." Her voice was soft, worried. "It still scares me, though."

Oliver resisted the urge to take her hand. "They're smart. I'm sure they'll be fine."

"... Yeah."

After a moment, Ellie reached back and pulled both boxes of arrows and the copper wire onto her lap. "I'll get started on these."

Oliver nodded slowly, the suspicion that had formed earlier in his mind taking center stage again. "Ellie, I'm thinking fire might be what kills them."

She paused and cocked her head, one hand wrapped around the spool of wire. "Between the picture Sam just sent and your experience with Silverskin, I'm honestly leaning that way, too."

"We should probably still be prepared with fire, wood, and copper," Oliver said quickly.

"I agree. Hang on, let me text them back."

When Oliver glanced over at Ellie a few seconds later, a little smile had spread across her face. She set the phone in her lap and returned his gaze. "It's good to have a lead."

"It is." Oliver held her eyes for a few seconds longer than was safe, then made himself look back at the road.

"I'll get started," Ellie said.

"And when you've finished, take a nap."

Ellie didn't look up from the copper wire she was twisting around the tip of one of the wooden arrows, but she smiled again. "*That* I can do."

Chapter Nine

Some part of Ellie knew she was asleep. Unfortunately, that part wasn't smart enough to wake her before her dreams went from bad to worse.

The pool in the cave was as vivid as it had been that day in the canyon; Ellie could *feel* the mist on her skin, smell the wild, pine-scented air. She stood just inside the lip of the cave on the solid stone—

No. Not stood. Her feet were ... *buried*.

In the stone.

Even in a dream the panic attack that followed was real and raw, like a living, breathing force that sucked the air from Ellie's lungs and jolted her heartbeat into a frenzied staccato. Her body was a symphony gone mad. The fear was in her blood, in her bones, behind her eyes.

It was *everything*.

Footsteps.

Ellie froze as a second wave of panic smashed into her, icing her blood in her veins, numbing everything but the fear. The demons' world was empty; they were all somewhere behind her. She didn't know what was advancing over the rocks and it didn't matter; she was going to die here. Like her dad, just like him, and no one could help her, let alone save her—

A voice started to sing, a voice out of the past, when the world had been stable and beautiful and understandable.

Lily.

Ellie moaned as her little sister wandered into view, wearing her favorite pink leggings and a tee shirt and holding a freshly picked bouquet of wildflowers.

"Lily," she called hoarsely.

Her sister didn't respond; it was like she couldn't even hear Ellie. Instead, Lily looked up. Ellie watched those gray eyes widen in wonder as she saw the pool. Her lips parted. Then, she stepped toward it.

Ellie redoubled her efforts, and suddenly her pounding heart, racing blood, and frantic breathing were *gifts,* the anxiety lending her far more strength than she was capable of on her own.

It just wasn't enough.

"Wow, what a gorgeous color," Lily whispered, kneeling by the pool.

"Don't, Lily—!"

Lily stood, then splashed into the pool with reckless abandon, just like she'd done during their childhood days at the lake.

"NO! NO, LILY, IT'S—" Ellie's words dissolved into a senseless wail as the water closed over her sister's head. Her wavy, auburn hair was the last thing to disappear under the surface.

Ellie screamed again, crouching, scrabbling at the cruel rock encasing her feet, trying uselessly to find and break whatever invisible thing held her captive. She didn't know how long it took a person to drown but it might not be too late, she could still save her sister—

Another voice started to sing, *another* voice she never thought she'd hear again. And for the second time, this awful place turned what should have been joy at seeing her mother again into agony so acute she didn't know if she'd survive it.

Ellie started to sob as her mother strode into view, tall, beautiful, and unafraid. "Mom, no. Mom, don't, please..."

Her mother saw the pool, cocked her head, then walked straight into it. She never even said a word.

Ellie fell on all fours and heaved and heaved, but even her retching couldn't block out the sound of whistling that reached her ears. That old classic rock song her dad had liked, that he used to whistle without even realizing he was doing it. And just like his daughter and wife before him, he walked into view with a vacantly happy look on his face. When he saw the pool, his expression didn't change. He turned toward it.

Ellie couldn't watch this again; she was going to *die* if she didn't do something.

She gritted her teeth and struggled with everything she had; she was going to force her way out of this even if it broke her ankles. She pulled and twisted, her tendons and muscles popping and shredding. She ground her teeth against the pain, channeling it all into a shrill cry that she knew they couldn't hear.

But her feet remained rooted, and when she looked again, her father was stepping down into the pool.

"DAD, NO—" She gasped as one foot came free, pain searing all the way up her leg and into her hip. "Dad, I'm coming! Stop! PLEASE!"

It wasn't enough. He was gone, just like last time. She hadn't stopped it.

Ellie fell forward onto the frigid stone and started to sob from pain, fear, and utter helplessness. She cried and screamed like she'd gone insane, because she had, and there was no escape. The fear would always win; she'd never be rid of it, it was shaped like a corpse wearing a tattered black dress and would never, *ever* leave her alone again—

Another voice, one that made the blood drain from Ellie's face. Sam had a beautiful voice, he'd just never used it.

Her brother stepped into the cave, looked behind him, and held out a hand. A second hand took it, small and olive-skinned, and Sam smiled at Darien as she followed him. Ellie screamed, thrashed, pulled at her other leg. Her muscles were going to tear, and she'd never run again but she didn't care. With a strangled cry, she threw everything she had into breaking free.

The force holding her gave.

"Sam! Darien!" Ellie stumbled to her feet but screamed as her ankle gave out, twisting underneath her as if she'd broken every last little bone in it.

Sam took one step into the water, his gorgeous baritone filling the cave, his face still full of joy as he gazed at Darien, who followed him. Ellie dragged herself toward them but she was going to be too slow; her brother was waist-deep already and Darien had both feet in now.

Get up! She gritted her teeth so hard she was afraid they'd crack, and forced one foot underneath her. *Get up!*

"Sam!" she screamed as she straightened. She took one hobbling step toward the pool, where he'd led Darien farther into the water, and hope spiked in her chest. She could make it. Maybe she could *finally* save someone she loved.

Something clamped onto Ellie from behind, some force that was stronger than steel, strong as the bones of the earth. It locked her muscles, froze her into a living statue. She managed to roll her eyes downward and nearly threw up again.

Arms were around her middle, or something like arms. They looked raw, ropy, like they'd been skinned and left in the sun for a week. And they were too long, far too long to be human.

The dried-jerky muscles shifted, and what must have been a fist unfurled, revealing bladelike fingers a foot long each. Ellie gagged and closed her eyes, paralyzed by fear, waiting to die like a rabbit in a trap. This must be the Gatekeeper, must have been what Oliver had felt when he'd come up here alone, all alone. He was so brave, and so kind, and...

When Ellie heard the footsteps, she knew it was him. They were quiet, quick, and purposeful, and he didn't sing.

When she opened her eyes, he was looking at her.

"Oliver," she choked. If he could see her, maybe she could talk him down, because losing him ... she couldn't, it would *break* her—

The thing that held Ellie exhaled and a wave of freezing air hit her neck, flowed down her back as if her shirt wasn't even there. It was so cold it hurt, and she gasped, hot tears stinging her eyes and sliding down her cheeks.

"You are mine," the creature behind her rasped.

"Oliver," Ellie pleaded. "Don't."

He just gazed at her, his expression kind, sad, full of longing. Then the tiniest smile touched his full lips. "For you, Ellie."

Oliver turned and walked into the pool.

Ellie's heart ruptured.

"Yes," crooned the thing that held her. It could have her. There was no one left. She was alone, helpless, dying as blood gushed from the hole in her heart—

The world shattered into a jumble of rushing wind and discordant notes, and Ellie jerked upright so violently that she nearly hit her face on the dashboard of Sam's truck.

"Ellie!" Oliver's voice was frantic and sweeter than a serenade. "Ellie, it's okay! It's okay."

"Oliver," she croaked, and reached for him on instinct. *He's right there he's not dead and he's not going to die I won't let him die—*

Her fingertips were inches from his arm when she froze, remembering. Hesitantly, she looked up; his eyes were darting back and forth between her and the highway. He glanced down, saw her hand, and swallowed, frustration joining the alarm on his face.

"Are you okay?" he asked, fixing his eyes back on the road.

Ellie snatched her hand away and slumped in her seat, shaking, still panting like she'd run five miles. "I'm so sorry. I had a … a nightmare."

She jumped as Oliver's phone rang again. He scooped it up from where it sat in the center console and hit decline, muttering: "Helen's going to kill me, but you come first." He glanced at her. "You started twitching and muttering about five minutes ago. I've been trying to wake you up ever since."

Ellie sighed and closed her eyes, forcing her muscles to relax. She rolled her ankles, relieved at their strength and the lack of pain. "It was bad."

Oliver ran a hand through his hair—a hand Ellie now realized was trembling. The corded muscles of the arm that gripped the wheel stood out as if he'd been clenching his hands.

"You don't have to talk about it," he said. "But if you want to, I'll listen."

Ellie sighed again and closed her eyes. His voice was so soothing. She wanted to wrap her arms around him, bury her face in his chest, feel the gentle brush of his fingers through her hair. Her heart gave a throb of pain that was almost physical. *Later. Something to fight for.*

Ellie forced her eyes open and squinted at the dash. It was nearly noon; she'd slept for almost three hours. Bright, dazzling sunlight washed over her as Oliver turned a corner, warming her, relaxing her, and she looked out the window. Miles and miles of farmland sprawled on either side of the highway, colored a million shades of late-summer green. On Oliver's side, mountains rose, smooth and blue at this distance but no less imposing for it.

"Where are we?" she asked.

"According to the last road sign, we're getting close to a town called Shelby."

Ellie rubbed her eyes. "Shelby, huh?"

"That's right. Home of the finest cornfields on earth! Or …" Oliver squinted. "Is that corn? I'm not sure."

One corner of Ellie's mouth tugged upward. "Oliver, those are hayfields. Do you seriously not know what *corn* looks like?"

Oliver shrugged. "I know what it looks like on a plate. What more do you need?"

A tiny laugh escaped Ellie.

"We don't grow corn in Alaska." Oliver frowned. "Just really big bears."

She burst out laughing. Or was she crying? It didn't matter; she was so glad Oliver was here and alive and teasing her, but her heart still hurt from watching him walk into that pool. And apparently, *this* was how her body was going to deal with it.

"I'm so sorry." Ellie wiped her eyes, feeling her face redden.

"For what?"

"I don't know. Freaking you out by having a nightmare, then having a disproportionately emotional reaction to it?"

"You're fine, Ellie. You can't control your dreams." Oliver let out a quiet sigh. "I want to help you, but I don't know how. Is there ... anything I can do?"

"Other than making me laugh so hard I lose any dignity I had left?"

"As fun as that is—" he cast a sly grin her way, then looked back at the road "—yes. Other than that."

Ellie's mirth faded, and she pressed her palms to her face, gathering her thoughts. He'd trusted her last night with the darkest, ugliest part of his life, and they'd both come away stronger because of his courage. Maybe sharing this—as trivial as it seemed—could help her as well.

She let out a long, quiet breath, then raised her head, staring out at the road. "I dreamed I was trapped in the cave."

Oliver swallowed. He didn't have to ask which cave she meant.

"Everyone I love most died in front of me. Lily, Mom, Dad, Sam and Darien." The road blurred in front of her as tears pooled in her eyes again. "... You."

Ellie wiped her eyes on her forearms. When she peered at Oliver, he looked ... *stunned.*

"Ellie ..." He met her eyes, his own wide. Then, he seemed to shake himself. "That's awful. I'm sorry."

Ellie hesitated; she'd gotten the impression he'd wanted to say something else.

And do I? she wondered.

The fact that her subconscious had lumped Oliver in with her family was telling. As was the fact that his death—not her parents', not her siblings', but *his*—had been the final straw in pushing her over the edge. It could have just been because his was the last to occur in the dream. Recency bias, and all that. But still ...

Her heart started thumping, and she stole a glance over at Oliver only to find him looking back. He jerked his gaze to the road, but not before she saw how his eyes burned, intense and ardent, just like they always did before he kissed her.

Ellie turned and stared out her window, chewing her lip, heart thumping so hard now she wondered if she'd see her pulse through her tee shirt if she looked down. It was too soon for her to have it this bad for him. They'd only known each other for a month, and it had been the strangest, ugliest, most trying month of both their lives. Yes, she thought they could have a wonderful relationship—they already did. Yes, she wanted to be with him long-term. But the sheer *depth* of feelings her dream had evoked ...

It scared her. Still.

She sat up a little straighter. *No. I've beat this fear. I won't run from this.*

Ellie half-turned and had just opened her mouth when Oliver's phone started buzzing, the sound as jarring as an angry hornet trapped against glass. His eyes dropped to the screen and Ellie swallowed the words she'd been about to say. They literally had thousands of miles left to discuss feelings; this could wait. And ... well, she had to admit that calming down before having a discussion like that wouldn't be a bad thing, either.

"Is it Helen again?"

Oliver nodded. "I do need to talk to her, but I stand by what I said earlier. If you need to talk, she'd understand."

"No, there wasn't much more to it than what I've already told you, honestly." Ellie nodded at the phone. "Pick up. Helen's probably worried out of her mind."

"Okay." Oliver tapped the screen, then pressed the phone to his ear. "Hey, Helen."

Even over the rushing of the road underneath them, Ellie could hear the worry in Helen's voice. A mixture of affection and guilt surged in her heart; she looked out the window again, this time at a field of cows, their hides a mixture of glossy black and deep chestnut in the bright summer sun.

"I know, I'm sorry," Oliver said. "I texted you—"

More chatter that Ellie couldn't make out.

"Why don't I just put you on speaker? Hang on ..."

Oliver hit the button and set his phone down on the center console. Ellie leaned over, resting her elbow on the cushioned leather. "Hi, Helen."

"Ellie! Are you okay? Oliver said in his text that the Lady had caught up to you—"

"Helen, I'm okay! I'm okay." Ellie's hand drifted up to her throat and the bruises there, probing them gingerly. They ached less now than when she'd gone to sleep. "Oliver and ..." A little seed of confidence sprouted within Ellie at her actions that morning. For the first time, she'd managed to fight back. "... and I ... drove her off again. She put up a fight, but we're both doing a lot better—"

"Doing better? Did you get hurt?"

Ellie swallowed. "Not ... terribly. She tried to strangle me again but obviously didn't succeed." She glanced over at Oliver. "And Oliver's actually driving. He's pretty much back to normal—"

"Oliver! *Why* don't you tell me these things?"

"Because I don't want to *worry* you—"

"It's my damn *job* to worry about you! What happened?" Helen's tone was a motherly mix of love, anxiety, and rebuke. A lump rose in Ellie's throat; it had been years since the accident, but in that moment she would have given anything to hear her own mother speak to her that way. She looked out the window before Oliver could see the roiling emotion on her face. *Stupid dream.*

"It wasn't too bad, Helen—"

"You have a tendency to downplay these sorts of things, Oliver—"

"Helen!" Oliver's tone was exasperated; but the little grin on his face—half-indignant and half-affectionate—spoke volumes. There was light in his eyes that hadn't been there before the phone had started to ring, and in that moment, Ellie seemed to see him more clearly than she ever had before. A fatherless boy with a mother in an impossible situation, whose life had been turmoil ... and who now cherished the family he had with a love that was pure, simple, and beautiful. Gratitude welled within her for Helen and Henry and all they had done for him.

"Helen," Oliver said again. His voice was firm, but that little smile had snuck into it now, gentling its edge. "Remember you have a demon in your head, then take a deep breath. I'm fine. We're both fine. Though I guess I can't speak for you, Ellie."

"I'm fine, too. Remember how my bruises healed really quickly last time, Helen?" she asked.

"Yes! Are they doing that again?"

"Yes. We've both healed incredibly quickly."

"That's a relief. Now, Oliver." Helen's voice turned stern. "Don't think you've gotten out of telling me what happened to you. Spill."

"I got shocked. I've been trying to tell you, but you keep interrupting—"

"You got *shot*?"

"No, no, sho-CK-ed!"

"... *What?*"

Oliver scrubbed a hand over his eyes. "The Lady can shock people. Electrically. Or something."

Helen was silent. Ellie could practically feel her alarm radiating all the way from Seldovia.

"How?" she finally asked.

"We don't know," Oliver said. "It seems like we barely know anything about them. But apparently, the Lady can electrocute."

And shapeshift, and strangle ... Ellie clenched her jaw and forced the thought out of her head. They'd escaped three times now, four in her case. As Oliver had said earlier, the monster clearly wasn't infallible.

"The Nantinaq did say they would get stronger," Ellie said.

"He did," Oliver agreed. "I didn't realize it would happen this quickly."

"Or dramatically," Ellie said. "And now that Wormwood can—" She bit off the sentence, then glanced at Oliver, who glared at the road in front of them. The light in his eyes had dimmed, the lines of his face were as hard as granite.

"What can Wormwood do?" Helen asked.

Oliver gave a resigned sigh, and Ellie shifted uncomfortably. His was such an ugly, personal struggle, and the fact that it intersected with their budding relationship made it even worse. She should have known he wouldn't want to talk about it, should have thought before speaking. The more fatigued she got, the harder that was to do. But *still* ...

"Wormwood can cause headaches now," Oliver finally said. "More like migraines. Specifically when Ellie and I ... when we touch."

"Well, that would complicate a relationship."

Ellie looked up at the sound of Henry's gruff rumble; Helen must have put her phone on speaker, too. His voice was tinged with sympathy and a faint note of ... was that *amusement?*

"Yes," Oliver said stiffly. "It does."

To Ellie's shock, Helen started to chuckle.

Oliver's scowl deepened. "I fail to see how this is funny."

"Oh, that Wormwood's made a huge mistake," Helen said. "You two already had so much to fight for. Family, friends, revenge, the whole rest of your lives ..." Her laugh became quieter, almost sinister. "Throw love into the mix and you'll be unstoppable."

Oliver blinked, then met Ellie's eyes, and for a second there was nothing in her world but his searing gaze.

A harsh, grinding rumble jerked Ellie back to reality. "Whoa! Watch the road!"

"Sorry." Oliver jerked his eyes forward, his fingers bone-white on the steering wheel.

"It's okay," Ellie said, "I—"

"What's happening?" Helen's voice overrode Ellie's, with far more panic in it than Ellie felt the situation really warranted. "Are you two all right?"

"We're fine," Oliver said. "I just got distracted for a moment."

"Oliver," Henry's low bass rumbled, "if you've been injured, you need to rest."

"I know—"

"You'll be a lot safer if you do," Helen broke in. "We're really concerned about you. *Both* of you. Ellie, you're one of the family now, too, in case you didn't already know."

Despite her earlier flash of frustration with Helen, a calming warmth bloomed in Ellie's chest at her words, as if her heart had sunk into a hot bubble bath. The corners of her mouth lifted. "Thanks, Helen. I'm honored."

She looked over at Oliver again. He was staring out the windshield, his eyes soft. Smiling again.

"So are we," Helen said. "And that's all the more reason for you two not to run yourselves too hard."

"Helen ..." Oliver squeezed his eyes closed as if he were in pain, all traces of his too-brief smile gone, then opened them just as quickly. "We're being chased, remember? That's why I haven't been able to send you anything but the fastest updates."

Silence.

"Well, you damn well better tell us now," Helen growled.

"I've—" Oliver rubbed the bridge of his nose. "I'm doing my *best*."

Ellie frowned. "Really fast, can we just acknowledge that at least two of us are probably being emotionally manipulated?"

Silence filled the truck, broken only by the soft slap of Oliver's hand as it dropped back to the steering wheel.

Ellie felt a dull flush creep up her neck and into her cheeks. "I don't know if it helps to point out the elephant in the room in this situation, but I've also never seen you all fight, not really. That doesn't seem like ... well, *any* of you. So I thought ..."

"No, you're right, Ellie," Oliver said. "*Damn*, he's getting subtle."

Henry grunted. "A rare four-letter word from Oliver. Ellie, that's a red flag, in case you didn't already know. It means he needs extra TLC."

Ellie's eyebrows went up. Henry was right. That might have been the first time she'd ever heard Oliver swear. *Another question to add to the conversation list.*

"Slubgob is getting worse, too." Helen's voice dropped to a mutter. "You'd think I'd be better at this after a whole month."

At that, Oliver winced so hard that Ellie was surprised there wasn't a shockwave. Her heart wrenched at the look on his face, and she wondered if similar thoughts to the one Helen had just expressed were going through his mind.

"It's hard when the thoughts are your own to begin with," he said quietly.

"That's very true," Helen said, her voice as grim as his.

Silence yawned between the four of them. Ellie was afraid that if she kept looking at Oliver she'd start crying again. Instead, she squinted at the town in front of them, at its squat skyline that hugged the prairie as if it were afraid to climb more than three stories from the earth. That must be Shelby, the last town before the Canadian border.

Ellie let out a deep, silent breath. With luck, they could at least distract themselves with a couple of good sandwiches.

"We can outrun the Lady, at least enough to give us several hours to rest each night," Oliver said, his voice low and admirably composed now. "We can't seem to outrun Wormwood, though."

"Because that's just ... how he is?" Henry asked.

"If you mean 'that's one of his special abilities,' like the ... the Lady shapeshifting, then yes," Ellie said.

"The fact that they're all so different is making this real complicated," Henry grumbled.

It is. Ellie closed her eyes, hiding her face in her hand. Her eyelids felt like sandbags, her eyes themselves like they'd been shoved full of their contents. Even in the middle of this conversation, it would be so easy to let her exhaustion win, to fall back asleep.

"We have to find another way to get rid of him," Oliver said. "So, Helen, if you want to help, you can maybe do some field research on Slubgob. See what, if anything, gets rid of her."

"Well, unfortunately, the way I think I'll get rid of her is by not worrying. And given the situation you two are in, that's not likely."

"Try," Oliver said.

"And you try to ..." Helen went quiet. Then, "You're not still beating yourself up over the ... your past, are you, Oliver?"

Oliver let his head fall back against the headrest, exhaustion breaking through his purposeful, stoic mask. "I didn't *think* I was, but that's ..." His jaw clenched, as if the words were causing him physical pain. "That's the struggle, yes. And you can speak openly. Ellie knows everything."

"Good," Henry said. "That can't do anything *but* help."

"I try," Ellie said at the same time Oliver said, "It does." Then, he caught her eye and offered her a tiny grin. It was worn-out and strained, but *far* better than nothing.

"I'd tell you to quit it, but I know it's not that easy," Henry said.

"I appreciate that," Oliver murmured, then sat straighter. "I'll get him. One of these days, I'll get him."

"Yes, you will," Henry said, and when he spoke again, his tone had softened in a way that made Ellie suspect he was looking at Helen. "You both will."

There was a short pause that Helen finally broke. Her voice sounded thick, as if she were trying not to cry. "How soon do you think you'll make it to Homer?"

Ellie reached for her phone. "By my map ..." She squinted as she did the math. "Four days. Maybe three."

"Please don't do it in three," Helen said. "You'd be in no state to help us close the gate by the time you got here."

"It depends on if more of them find us," Oliver said. "If we can stop to sleep, we will, and we'll do it in four, maybe five. If not ... the quicker we get to Seldovia, the better."

Silence.

"How *is* Seldovia?" Oliver finally asked.

"Declining, like the rest of Alaska," Henry said. "But hanging in there as best we can."

Oliver nodded. Then, seeming to share Ellie's thought that there was no point in asking for more details on the little town, he went on. "And you, Henry? How're you feeling?"

"Stable," Henry grunted.

Ellie looked out the window, suddenly feeling like an intruder despite what Helen had said earlier.

"I'll take it," Oliver said.

"You and me both," Henry said.

After a tense silence, they said their goodbyes. Ellie leaned back against the leather seat, stretching her arms out in front of her, trying to work some of the blood back into her legs before they, presumably—*hopefully*—got out of the truck. "Well, that was an interesting conversation."

"Yeah." Oliver stared forward, his expression contemplative and still very much on the glum side.

"At least we know they're still okay," Ellie offered.

Oliver just nodded, his expression unchanged. "That's something."

Ellie looked at him for a moment longer, then turned back to her window, suppressing a sigh. She knew he would talk if she pressed him, but it was also clear he needed a minute. Instead, she gazed out at the farmland, at the little houses and the big, round bales of hay lining the sides of the road.

It was intensely frustrating to not be able to touch Oliver. This was a moment when words couldn't help, but maybe a touch to his hand or shoulder could. And she so badly wanted to comfort him, to comfort *herself*. But she couldn't watch him endure that pain again.

"How about we stop and get lunch?" Oliver's voice, quiet and mild once more, interrupted her thoughts, and her heart quickened a little at its sound. "We haven't eaten since breakfast. And I don't know about you, but those two protein bars from Sam's stash aren't going to last me until dinner."

He met Ellie's eyes, and then to her delight, his lips quirked up in a smile. It was small, but it still warmed her like the sun on a summer morning.

"Food pretty much always helps," she agreed, sitting up and reaching for her water bottle. She drank, then handed the open bottle to Oliver and lifted her phone, squinting at the little map on the screen. "You, Oliver, are amazing. Thank you for letting me sleep for so long."

"You needed it." That smile inched back across his lips, this time tinged with mischief. "Plus, you're cute when you snore."

"I—what? I don't snore!"

"Just a little. Every once in a while." He glanced at her and his smirk widened. "You're cute when you blush, too."

"Stop it," Ellie said, but couldn't help a grin from rising to her own lips.

"I struggle to stop doing anything that makes you smile like that."

Ellie's heart melted into a little golden puddle. "If you keep saying those kinds of things, you might never get rid of me."

"I could live with that."

This time, the silence that settled between them was much more comfortable, and as they entered the city limits, Ellie just let it be. It felt good to be able to enjoy a quiet moment like this with someone. It was almost its own kind of intimacy.

That said, Oliver had spent the last thirty minutes—no, the last few days, *weeks*—helping everyone but himself. Ellie felt a pang of guilt, resolving not to let her own issues overshadow his in the future. His turn was long overdue.

If he wanted it, that was.

"Before we get out," she finally said, "will you update me on Wormwood?"

The sharp lines of his jaw tensed again. "There's not much to update. I've been fighting him on and off all morning. Just more of the usual."

"Why didn't you wake me up?" She hesitated as a potentially devastating thought struck her. "Do I ... help? Or ...?"

"You help," Oliver said quickly. "You definitely help. But ..." He gave a small shake of his head. "He attacks at any time over anything, without warning. A jibe here, a taunt there ... It's a mental game. When I'm talking with you, it's just different things. But you take the sting out of a lot of it just because you're *you*."

Ellie sighed, settling back in her seat. "That's a relief. Still, I wish I could do more."

"I'd let you drive if you want. Once we get over the border."

Ellie grinned. "I could drive right after lunch if you wanted."

"Done. And *I'll* take a nap." Oliver smiled, then hit the brakes, nodding to a McDonald's sign on the side of the road. "Speaking of food, want to stop?"

Ellie wrinkled her nose. "Not there."

Oliver blinked at her. "You don't like McDonald's?"

"Nope."

"Seriously?"

"Yeah. There are way better places to go!"

"I guess ..."

"We can go," Ellie said. "Really. If you love it—"

Oliver shook his head, his expression turning troubled. "It's not my favorite. It's fine, but really it's ... well, it's *cheap*."

Ellie stared at him. She hadn't even considered that.

"We can go somewhere else as long as it's fast," Oliver said. "I just—"

"Oliver." Ellie's heart clenched as he met her eyes, his own full of what looked like shame. "I can pay for all our food."

He looked back at the road, frowning, his eyes tracking the McDonald's sign until it slid past Ellie's window and out of sight.

"It's okay," he said. "I can get my own. I don't want to ..." He sighed. "You should pick a place. One that's fast, though. I don't think we have time to sit down somewhere."

"Oliver," Ellie sighed.

"Pick a place." His tone was mild, but his eyes were still pained.

It took Ellie moments to find a nearby sandwich shop, and almost as little time for them to pull into its parking lot.

"I want to buy, Oliver," Ellie said, as they walked toward the door. "Let me."

"Ellie, it'll be fine. Really. I've saved plenty."

"Let me rephrase," Ellie said, lowering her voice as he opened the door for her. "I'm *going* to pay for our food on this trip. All of it. And you can get whatever you want. Money isn't an issue."

Oliver was silent as they joined the line, the low buzz of human conversation masking their own. "It just feels wrong. I feel like I'm your dead-beat boyfriend who's just mooching off you."

Ellie shook her head. "Not even a little. I happen to have a lot of resources in the financial department. And you need to *save* your money. It's simple logic, Oliver. Please let me do this for you."

Oliver sighed and ran a hand through his hair, his eyes darting around the room. Ellie found herself doing that, too. Peering into all the corners, behind the counter, making sure all the faces in the line were human.

Not that that was always reliable.

Ellie put her hands on her hips and faced Oliver squarely. "I don't know what Wormwood's saying to you right now, but listen to me, not him."

Oliver blinked; his mouth opened, then closed as Ellie went on.

"We're doing what has to be done. It's logical. No one would judge you for it." She softened her gaze and her tone. "One of these days, you can take me on a real date with nice food and all the romantic stuff and I'll let you pay then. Fair?"

Oliver broke their gaze, staring up at the menu with a frown on his face. Then he shook his head. "Deal." Then, very quietly, "Thank you, Ellie."

She smiled. "It's the least I can do."

Chapter Ten

They ate their sandwiches in the car. Oliver insisted on driving again—just until the nearest gas station—so Ellie could eat in peace. She'd only protested a little, and her warm, grateful smile had made him all the more happy to override it.

Between Wormwood, the Lady, his lack of financial resources, and the thousands of miles that still stood between them and the gate, Oliver was starting to feel like driving was the only thing he could do that made any difference.

"Was Wormwood pestering you in the sandwich shop?" Ellie asked around a mouthful of roast beef. "Did I guess right?"

"Yep."

"Is he still?"

Oliver shook his head. "He's gone quiet for now. What I don't understand is—" He cut off on instinct, then almost laughed at the ridiculousness of it. Wormwood was in his head. If he'd already thought the thought, it didn't matter whether he said it out loud. The demon would know.

"What?" Ellie asked.

He forced his eyes forward, looking down the road at the gas station in the near distance. "I don't know why he holds off on the headache. Why he specifically reserves it for when we touch."

"I've wondered that, too," Ellie admitted, then shoved the last bite of her sandwich into her mouth as they turned into the Conoco. "It'd be much more debilitating for both of us if he just incapacitated you. I think it confirms our earlier guess."

"That they must have limits on their power? There doesn't seem to be any other explanation."

"Yeah." Ellie stretched, her body arching in a way that made it difficult for Oliver to keep his eyes on the road. Instead, he made himself focus on turning into the gas station. And when Wormwood's gravelly laugh grated through his mind, he made himself ignore that, too.

He pulled up next to a pump and unbuckled his seatbelt. "I assume you're not letting me pay?"

"That's correct," Ellie said, hopping out and flashing her sweetest smile at him. "And don't even think about feeling bad."

I wonder how long it'll take before she realizes you have nothing to offer.

Oliver slammed the door then shoved his hands in his pockets, trying to arrange his face into a mostly clear expression.

I'm shocked she hasn't already, actually.

"I'll do my best," Oliver said as he stepped around the front of the truck.

Ellie pulled her card out of the reader, then reached for the pump. "I'm holding you to that."

Better not let her know how hard you're failing when it comes to getting rid of me, Ollie.

He fought to keep his expression neutral, glad she wasn't looking closely at him. "I'll run to the bathroom, then we can switch if you'd like."

"Sounds good. Let me know if there are any snacks or drinks that you want."

This time, Oliver overrode Wormwood before he could even begin, pacing backward so he still faced Ellie. "Oh, I'll find lots of snacks." He caught her eye and forced a grin. "Hangry Ellie—while still beautiful, smart, and brave—is *not* as much fun as Fed Ellie."

She smiled sweetly. "You know me so well."

"I'll meet you back here in five minutes."

"Got it."

Oliver let his eyes linger on her for a few seconds longer than was necessary. She wasn't looking at him anymore, but her lips still curved in a little smile and her waist-length chocolate hair rippled in the breeze—a silky, bronze curtain covering the ever-dulling bruises on her throat.

You're only making it harder for yourself. Not that I'm complaining.

Suppressing a snarl, Oliver turned. At least Wormwood couldn't kill them, and he couldn't seem to touch Ellie at all. He had already survived a month of this. What was another week?

Oliver reached for the door, his muscles relaxing at the warmth of the sun on his back. It felt more powerful down here than it was in Alaska, as if it were only too happy to give heat and light to a land that wasn't so bipolar. He let his hand rest on the hot metal handle and allowed himself a second—a single long blink's worth of time—to enjoy it. During the first disorienting days of Wormwood's mental invasion, he'd discovered that little things like that somehow made a difference. They grounded him.

It'll be okay, he told himself. They could make it. They'd already made it nearly to the Canadian border, they'd probably left the Lady far behind them, they had at least some guesses how to kill any others they might encounter—

Oliver snapped his eyes open as a thought hit him with so much force that it nearly bowled him over. Then he groaned, burying his face in his palm. And inside his head, Wormwood laughed and laughed.

I was wondering how long it'd take you to figure it out. You're so stupid, Ollie.

"I'm such an idiot," Oliver whispered. He didn't have a passport. He wasn't going to make it into Canada.

***

Ellie leaned against the door of the truck, half-listening for the telltale pitch change of the rushing gasoline that would signal that Sam's truck was finally full. It took much longer than her little Impala, and when time was of the essence ...

She looked down at her phone and found herself clicking through to the picture Sam had sent that morning, almost as if her hands were on autopilot. Despite the warm sun, the hair rose on the back of her neck as the image appeared on her screen. There was nothing on earth that could convince her that the most ragged of the four petroglyphs wasn't the Lady. And the other cloaked figure, the one with green shells for eyes ... could that be Silverskin? What were the other two, then? One just looked like a normal sick figure with what Ellie presumed was a headdress—maybe a chief of some sort—and the other was a hulking monstrosity that barely looked—

"Ellie Forth."

Ellie's head shot up, every nerve in her body racing into overdrive at the sound of the unfamiliar voice. No one out here except Oliver should know her name. Especially not the random guy stepping around the pump holder holding the most massive pair of pliers she'd ever seen.

For an instant, Ellie stared at him. Then, she ran.

"Ellie." His voice was shockingly calm given that he was about to kill her.

Well, try *and kill me,* said the small, recklessly brave part of her that she still didn't quite know what to do with. She wrenched open the passenger's side door, her heart beating into her throat, and fumbled for the knife she'd bought earlier that morning. Her hand closed on its hilt and she looked up.

The man was gone.

"Ellie, please—"

She whirled, ripping the knife from its sheath and slashing the naked blade in a vicious arc. It hit nothing; the thing was standing about five feet away with both hands raised in the air, the picture of innocence. One she didn't believe for a second, not with that ... that *torture device* he was holding.

Ellie scrambled away from the truck. Her eyes darted toward the convenience store and her heart sank. With the way the demon was positioned, there was no way for her to slide past him without putting herself within reach of a blow from his tool-weapon. She looked frantically back to the stranger just in time to see a completely unexpected emotion enter his eyes.

Panic.

He lowered his hands. Slowly. As if she were a trapped dog he was trying to rescue from a gutter, and Ellie hesitated. That *face* ... there was something familiar about him.

"If I were a demon, you'd be dead by now," he said. His voice was quiet and intense, but also ... oddly reassuring. Or, maybe it would be under other circumstances.

Like right after a massive structure fire, for instance.

Ellie's jaw dropped; she barely registered the clunk of the gas pump shutting off. "You're the EMT. The incompetent one."

"Incompetent? Oh, come on—"

"You didn't even check Oliver's vitals! You—this isn't important." Ellie tightened her grip on the knife. "Who are you and what do you want with us?"

For a moment, Ellie thought the man was going to smile. But he didn't, and when he spoke, there was no trace of humor in his voice. "I'm a friend who has a vested interest in keeping both you and Oliver alive."

"Why—?"

"And I'm already starting to run out of time, so be quiet and listen or you'll both die."

The newborn part of Ellie, the reckless part, couldn't just let that fly. She narrowed her eyes. "Why not wait and tell us both, then?"

"Oliver is compromised until he can get rid of Wormwood. Plus, *you'll* listen." The man jerked his head toward the convenience store. "There's no guarantee he would."

Anger rose in Ellie, sharp and raw. "You have no idea the battle he's fighting—"

The man overrode her like she hadn't even spoken. "Oliver doesn't have a passport, and even if he did, you'd still be killed at the border."

"*What?* You're lying. You can't *possibly* know—"

"Ellie! Stop interrupting!" The man put a hand to his forehead, which, now that Ellie was paying attention, was paling visibly. "You can't go to the check station. Death is waiting for you there. Instead, there's an exit a mile before Sweet Grass—that's the name of the border town—called Dell Ranch Road. Take it, turn west, keep going for a couple miles until you come to an intersection."

"Wait ..." Ellie whipped her phone out of her pocket and opened her notepad app, her fingers skittering across the keys, misspelling almost every direction. *As long as I can remember what they are, it'll be fine.*

She paused. *You sure trusted him quickly.*

"Ready?"

The man's voice was hoarse, weaker-sounding than before. Ellie looked up and her eyes widened. He was *fuzzing* around the edges, the circles under his eyes darkening like bruises on fruit. The pliers dangled from fingers that were now limp and weak-looking. Pity pricked at Ellie; for a moment, she couldn't believe she'd ever found him threatening.

"Go," she said. "Tell me."

"Take your first right—north. It'll be a few miles. Then drive straight through. You'll cross a cattle guard, then the road will turn into a two-track that runs through a hayfield."

Ellie's suspicion ballooned again. "That sounds like trespassing."

"The farmer and his help are gone for the day, and the nearest cameras will be disabled."

Ellie didn't even bother to ask how.

"Once you get to the fence, cut it with these." With effort, he tossed the pliers to Ellie. Her stomach lurched as the heavy, cold metal landed in her hands; she nearly dropped her phone trying to catch them, and did drop her knife. The tool looked brand new, its angled edges sharp and wicked.

Cut the border fence? She shook her head. *We'll end up running from both the demons and Canadian law enforcement.*

"There's a dirt road right over the border. Go east until you reach the highway, then go north as fast as you can, as far as you can." His eyes closed. "If you can make it to Edmonton you'll be safe for the night. Or as safe as you can be, anyway. I still suggest you take turns sleeping and watching. I ... dunno what else is starting to crop up out there, so be ... be prepared."

The man staggered back a step, and Ellie realized she could see the outline of the gas pump through his body. "You *cannot* tell Oliver until ten minutes before your exit. Less if you can manage it."

Ellie trembled. "Or what?"

"Death will find you," the man gasped.

"Wait!"

But the man was gone. He'd disappeared in front of her eyes, gone like he'd never existed.

"What the ever-loving *hell*?!" Ellie seethed. She whirled in place, scanning the fuel station, the litter-covered median, and the highway for people, figures, anything that might be coming for them. But there was nothing. The gas station was empty except for her.

Oliver's compromised. He can't know ...

Ellie turned and threw the pliers into the back seat, then dragged the bow case they'd bought that morning—with the bow in it—over them, hiding them from view. *And WHY aren't you going to just tell Oliver? What* exactly *is making you trust that ... ghost or whatever he was?* Crossing her arms, she stared at the bow case for a second, every line of her body tight and thrumming with the tension of a war with herself that she felt like she was somehow *losing*.

She growled and stomped to where her knife lay, glinting against the dull concrete, and snatched it. "You want me to just *trust* you? Just like that?" she muttered at the spot where the stranger had vanished. "I don't know who you are, or *what* you are, and you think I'm going to—"

"Ellie?"

She whirled, clamping her mouth shut. Oliver stood a few steps away, his head cocked to the side, confusion in every line of his beautiful, familiar face. The apparition's words thundered through Ellie's head. *He can't know.*

"Are you okay?" Oliver paled as he looked down and saw her knife. "Why do you have that? Were you attacked?"

He took a step forward, reaching for her, and dammit if she didn't just want to throw herself into his arms and cry and howl until she felt better, then kiss his perfect, sensuous lips until she felt *great.*

"*No* I'm not okay!" Ellie dodged his arm and stomped around the truck to the driver's side, sheathing the knife as she went, and slammed the pump back into its holder. "I'll fill you in as we go."

When Ellie turned, Oliver was gaping. "Do you need to ..." He gave a helpless little shrug-gesture toward the convenience store, "I don't know, go to the bathroom or anything?"

But Ellie was already in the driver's seat. "I went at the sandwich place."

It was nearly a mile before Oliver broke the silence, but his fidgeting told her everything she needed to know about his state of mind. That, and the fact that he was perched on the rich leather seat like it was a cactus.

"Do you want to tell me what happened?" he asked.

Yes. Yes, yes, yes. She shook her head. "I ... need a minute to process it."

"Were you attacked?" Oliver shifted to look at her, but Ellie kept her eyes fixed on the road. She knew what she'd see if she looked over there. He'd have that pin-you-down look that made her feel both exposed and like she was lying on a beach, basking under a tropical sun. The combination of care and disquiet in those cobalt eyes would have her spilling everything in ten seconds or less; she just knew it.

The hard, dull asphalt, on the other hand, would keep her secret. At least, until she decided whether to trust the gas station ghost or not.

"No," she finally said. "I wasn't attacked." It was true. The man hadn't made a move to harm her. And based on her limited experience, that probably meant he'd been telling the truth—that he *wasn't* a demon. They didn't seem to plan; just feed and destroy.

But if he wasn't a demon, then what was the other option? An angel?

Ellie gave a bemused little shake of her head. *That's not how I imagined them being.* And if the man had been an angel, ghost, visitor from the other side, whatever ... why hadn't it been her mom or Lily? Why hadn't someone she loved come to help?

The thought made her throat tighten, and the racing yellow lines on the asphalt blurred in front of her.

A quiet rustling brought her back. Out of the corner of her eye, Ellie saw Oliver lean forward in his seat and rub a hand across his face. Resisting the temptation to look at him, she fixed her eyes on a big red barn near the side of the road, staring at it until they whizzed past. Was his agitation all for her, or was it because he'd realized he couldn't make it into Canada? She couldn't broach the subject, not without revealing the escape plan.

The one that she was *still* on the fence about trusting.

Unless ... If Oliver *did* have a passport, that would disprove the whole thing. Ellie had just opened her mouth to ask when he spoke again.

"As long as you're not hurt, I'm all right with waiting until you're ready to talk about whatever happened. But I have a problem, too, and I'm afraid it can't wait."

Ellie's heart started to pound. He didn't have one. The ghost was right. And if that were true, then she should assume there was an ambush waiting for them at the border and act accordingly. Including not letting Oliver know the plan until the right moment.

Half-consciously, Ellie started tapping out a violin etude she'd memorized months ago on the steering wheel. *First, keep up appearances.*

"What's your problem?" she asked.

"I don't have a passport."

"I ... that's really bad."

"Yes." He twisted in his seat, peering into the back, and Ellie fought the temptation to glance at the bow case to make sure it still covered the pliers. "We have a tarp, right?"

"Sam always keeps one in here, in his survival kit." *And we've got waterproofed matches and a hatchet, too.* If they were charging straight toward a fight for their lives and she was the only one who knew it was coming, then she'd better start taking stock of their assets.

Oliver plunked back down in his seat. "If I hide under that tarp in the back and you say I'm a load of wood you're delivering, what are the odds we can get across?"

"Probably zero. And if they realize we're trying to smuggle you over, they'll likely detain us." Ellie's stomach clenched. If something was waiting to kill them, like the apparition said, there was absolutely *no way* they could escape it once they were in custody.

Oliver pulled out his phone and started typing something, then shook his head and let it fall into his lap. "No service. I can't look anything up. Do you know anything about the border itself? Is there somewhere we could get across … illegally if we have to?"

Ellie didn't dare look at him. "I don't know. I *wish* I knew, but I didn't even think about this being a problem."

Oliver pressed a hand to his eyes. "I'm so sorry, Ellie. I can't believe I didn't get a passport, didn't even figure it *out* until now—"

"There was no reason for you to get a passport, Oliver. We never could have guessed we wouldn't be able to fly, especially since that's how you got here in the first place." *Darien guessed,* she realized, but didn't voice the thought. "How long do we have until we get to the border?"

Oliver glanced at her phone, at the map she'd downloaded for the times they wouldn't have cell service. "Forty-five minutes."

This is going to kill me. Ellie stepped on the gas, watching the speedometer inch upward until it hovered right on the line between her sanity and becoming a highway patrol target.

"We could turn around and get to a different airport," Oliver said. "Billings, maybe."

"I …" Ellie squeezed the steering wheel. *Talk. Distract him.* "I'm scared to death to fly, Oliver. We didn't even *know* about Silverskin until he burned the Luxembourg House to the ground, remember? What if something else is out there and it finds us while we're waiting in an airport security line?"

"They don't like to hunt in the open, though—"

"But what if one just … burns down the airport?" She shivered, trying to shut out the memory of the burned kitchen workers, of their crispy, shiny-red skin. Their screams.

"That would be awful," Oliver said.

"And how fast is the Lady? For all we know, she's already made it to Billings and Wormwood will tell her the second we turn around."

For a moment, Oliver was silent. Then, he rested his elbow on the windowsill, cupping his chin in his palm, his face set in hard, icy lines. "Points made. Flying is still out."

The pressure in Ellie's chest intensified, and she stroked her thumb across the ridged laces on the steering wheel. *Shut it out. Stay grounded. All you have to do is make it a few more minutes and then you can tell him everything.*

Ellie gritted her teeth as she realized she'd only strengthened the ghost's case. For better or for worse, following his directions was their only option now. She could only hope she'd made the right decision.

"Do we ... do we just keep going, then?" Ellie asked.

Oliver shook his head slowly, then glanced at her. "Do you have any other ideas?"

"I have no idea what to do. My only thought is to ... is to see if there's a way to get through if you only have a driver's license. If there are any special provisions for that or anything."

The silence that filled the truck was thick, heavy, *suffocating. Though*, thought Ellie, *maybe that last one was only reserved for liars.*

"I see one problem with that," Oliver said.

"What?"

"The demons seem to be able to communicate with each other. We know there are others out there, but not how many or where they are. And Wormwood's known this whole time that we'd get delayed at the border." Oliver folded his arms over his chest, staring at the road with a look of quiet, desperate rage. "If I were him, and knew we'd be sitting ducks at the Canadian border, I'd tell every demon within a hundred miles to come and get us."

Ellie's hands started to tremble. He was figuring it out too quickly. She pressed on the gas, watching the speedometer approach one hundred. If the ghost could take down a surveillance camera, maybe he could take down a radar as well.

"How long?" she burst out.

Oliver looked at her, his mouth slashing down in a suspicious frown.

"How long until we get to the border now?"

"Twenty minutes." He leaned over, peering at the dashboard. "How hard are you speeding?"

"As hard as I dare."

"... Do you have a clever plan you're not telling me about?"

Ellie flexed her hands on the steering wheel, the fingers on her left side launching into a passage from her last recital piece. *I have a crazy, half-baked escape route given to me by a parking lot ghost.*

"My only plan is to get there and see if your driver's license works," she said.

Oliver shook his head. "I really think we should turn around. I wasn't sure if we should keep going in Shelby, but then something happened. That you clearly don't want to talk to me about, even though we promised ..."

Guilt seared through Ellie as Oliver looked out his window, letting out a long sigh through his nose. "Look, I might not be as smart as you and your family, but I'm doing the best I can to get us out of this. And I'm at least smart enough to realize when you're not telling me something."

"Oliver." Ellie swallowed her anger; it burned in her stomach like molten lead. "Don't ever say you're not smart again. Ever. It's another one of Wormwood's lies."

She finally looked him in the eyes, letting the hurricane in her chest bleed onto her face. He held her gaze, and everything she felt was mirrored there: fear, desperation, rage, and what might have been love. If they weren't going to make it, she might as well admit it, if only to herself. In the face of imminent death, suddenly the challenges of *living* seemed so much simpler.

Oliver turned forward, his voice quiet. "You're veering."

Ellie jerked the steering wheel, nearly overcorrecting before settling the truck back into a smooth, straight line. "How long?"

"Fifteen minutes."

"Tell me why you don't swear."

Oliver's head whipped around. "What?"

"Just ... talk to me for a few more minutes. Please."

He stared at her, and she glanced at him before turning back to the road. Then, he leaned back again, slowly, his posture so tense the seat might as well have been a torture rack. "I do swear, just not often. My mom didn't like it, and my friend I lived with before the gang ... his family had a no swearing rule."

"That sounds very zealous of them."

"It was. They were very churchy. I thought they were zealous about a lot of things." To Ellie's surprise, Oliver let out a little chuckle. "Then again, Helen and Henry go to church every Sunday and they can both out-cuss most sailors."

Ellie snorted. "Well, we all need an outlet."

"I guess so." Oliver's smile faded. "I'm not sure why that's the thing I focused on in jail. Everything was so out of control, and I felt so terrible about ... aiding drug and human trafficking ..."

He swallowed and looked back out the window. "Maybe it was ridiculous, but I needed to prove to myself that I could control ... *something*. Make and hit a goal of some type. That's probably also why I became such a reader."

Ellie nodded. "That makes sense. Also, you didn't knowingly aid either of those things. The blame rests on the shoulders of the people who made those calls, who *knew* what they were doing." She glanced at him. "You didn't know."

For a long time after she'd looked back at the road, Ellie felt Oliver's eyes on her. "No, I didn't," he finally said.

Ellie just nodded, her heart leaping into her throat as they crested a hill and a big road sign glided into view, flashing neon green in the sun. It was too far to make out the words, but ... "How far now?"

"Ten minutes."

"Yes! Oliver, we made it." She hit the brakes, then the blinker, relief raising a lump in her throat as she read the sign: **Dell Ranch Road**. Oliver's eyes widened as they coasted onto the exit ramp, taking in the empty farmland around them and the dusty dirt road in front of them.

"Does this mean I finally get to know the plan you've cooked up?" he asked.

"Yes." Ellie flinched as the truck skidded on loose gravel as they approached the intersection. "As I'm telling you, though, reach back and get the pliers underneath the bow case."

"The *pliers* ...?" Oliver wriggled out of his seatbelt, then reached into the back seat as Ellie accelerated onto the dirt road.

"While you're at it, can you get the bow out, too?" Ellie asked.

"Yeah. *What* ...?" A second later, Oliver landed back in his seat, holding up the pliers. "These are wire cutters, Ellie."

"Ah. That makes more sense."

"Serious wire cutters." He examined them for a second longer, then set the tool points-down in a cupholder and reached back for the bow case, clearly being careful not to brush against her. "So, Ellie, tell me how you got ahold of a pair of incredibly heavy-duty wire cutters in the *three minutes* I was in the bathroom, because I don't remember buying them on our supply run earlier. And then, I'd love to know what you're planning on doing with them."

Ellie sighed, then launched into the strange, short story of the last hour of her life. With each word, it seemed like Oliver's frown deepened.

"I know it's insane, but it's true," she finished.

"He just walked up to you and told you to trust him?"

"Yep."

"And then told you to trespass, cut a fence, trust that the surveillance cameras were down, illegally cross an international border, then handed you these?" He held up the cutters.

"That about sums it up."

"And then you tried to knife him?"

"Yep. Not that it did anything. He stayed out of reach."

Oliver grunted, and when she glanced at him, his face was approving. "Still, nice job. What did he look like?"

Ellie shrugged. "Pretty generic. About your height, dark hair, dark eyes. Generally European-looking. He looked about our age." She frowned. "Not unattractive. If I'd have seen him on campus, I would have thought he was just another student."

"Hmm."

"At first, I thought he was the Lady posing as you. But she'd gotten a good look at you, and he looked different enough ... it just didn't sit right. Then I realized he was the incompetent EMT." Despite herself, Ellie's lips pulled up into a thin smile. "He didn't like it when I called him out on that."

Oliver let out a soft breath that might have been a laugh. "I'll bet not." He stretched his arms out in front of him, leaning over the bow in his lap, then rolled his lean shoulders.

Ellie focused on the sagebrush that snaggled the side of the road, furring across the prairie and up the yellowish sides of the buttes in the near distance. The less she thought about wrapping her arms around Oliver, about how it felt to snuggle into his strong, solid chest, the better. For now, at least.

"How far did you say it was to our turn?" he asked.

"A few miles. He wasn't very clear on that." Ellie chewed her lip. "Like I said, it seemed like he was on a hard timeline, so he was trying to cram as much information in as possible."

"But you don't think he was a demon."

"He didn't act like one. I really think if he were, he would have just killed me." She frowned. *Cameras ...* "Then again, maybe he didn't want to kill me because he didn't want it to be caught on the security cameras."

"Maybe. Maybe this is all an elaborate ruse to lure us away from safety and *into* an ambush."

"But when have they ever planned like this?" Ellie shook her head. "I don't know, Oliver. I'm still not convinced I've made the right call, so if you think we should turn around, I'll listen. They've just ..."

"No, you're right. This isn't how they usually behave." Oliver scratched his chin. "And the fact remains that I don't have a passport, and flying is out of the question."

He twisted in his seat, reaching for something. "Want to try the wooden arrows first?"

"We might as well. I'm really hoping we don't need them, though."

"Me, too." There was a rasp of wood on wood, then Oliver faced forward again, clutching a handful of arrows. "Where's the lighter fluid?"

"On the floor behind you."

"Okay." Oliver paused, seeming to consider his words. "I think you made a good call, Ellie."

"Really?"

"Really. I don't want to think about what they have waiting at the border, not when they've had so much time to prepare." Oliver's chest rose and fell as he took in one long, slow breath. "So the only thing I think we can do is be prepared."

"And hope we haven't been duped." Ellie squeezed the steering wheel again, trying to ignore the way her blood felt like it had turned into a river of sparks, pulsing and crackling under her skin.

"Do we have toilet paper somewhere?" Oliver asked.

"Yeah, but ... can it wait until we get across the border?"

Oliver stared at her, then started to laugh. "No, not for that. I want to see if I can make some fire arrows. Just in case wood isn't the answer."

"Oh! Yes, it's in the center console. Great thought, Oliver." *The kind of thought I might have had if I didn't have to fend off a stupid anxiety attack.* "Let's not put the lighter fluid on them until right before we get out, though, or I think I might be sick."

"Wise." Oliver started unrolling the white paper. It trailed across his lap, looking uncomfortably like the pale version of one of the Lady's cloak tassels. Ellie's anxiety seethed down her throat and settled, boiling, in the pit of her stomach; she might be sick even without the stink of lighter fluid. She willed her shoulders to relax, then her core.

"Just breathe," Oliver said. His voice was quiet, soothing, a night breeze on a summer weekend.

"I'm okay. I can handle it. I've been doing it for years."

Oliver shot her a tense smile. "I know you can."

Ellie returned his smile, but it disappeared as she caught sight of a road ahead, branching north. "I think I found our turn."

Oliver just gave a nod. Dread bloomed and flared in Ellie's stomach as she hit the brakes, letting the truck coast the final hundred yards or so. Not for the first time, she wondered if her renewed anxiety attacks were the result of a demon, if maybe she had one that had latched onto her like Wormwood had to Oliver. But it felt so familiar, so much like what she'd experienced in the past. So ... normal.

She sniffed. That wasn't a comforting thought, either.

Gravel crunched under the truck's tires as it turned, then rolled to a stop. The road narrowed in front of them, squeezing itself over a cattle guard before withering into two tire-sized lines. They stretched onward, brown against a field of golden grass.

Ellie pushed down the squeezing feeling in her chest, then released the brake.

The truck trundled forward, grating over the metal bars, then settled into a slow crawl as Ellie guided it down the barely-road. Oliver's head turned back and forth, his keen eyes darting across the field. What seemed like miles of golden hay rippled in all directions, caught in a lazy slow dance with the summer breeze, but other than that, there was nothing to be seen.

Still, Ellie didn't feel right. Quite the opposite: she felt stripped, naked, exposed out there on the prairie, with no trees or cover of any kind and the mountains too far away to be anything but blue smudges on the horizon.

"For what it's worth, Ellie, I think you're handling this incredibly well."

"Same to you," she said, the words coming out more tersely than she'd intended. She swallowed. "Sorry, I'm not ... mad, just ..."

"Scared."

Ellie nodded and stole a look at Oliver. His jaw was set, his eyes icy, grim as the reaper himself. A deadly but reluctant fighter, waiting for—and dreading—what might be coming.

"I am, too," he said softly. "Wormwood's been very ... active in the last few minutes. I can't tell if that's a good thing or a bad thing."

Ellie's heart jerked. "Do you think we should turn around?" Now that they were here, she realized she didn't want to retreat. It had been hard enough picking a course of action the first time. The thought of going back, trying to figure out something else ... that would be *awful*.

"No." Oliver's voice was still soft, but had gained a razor-edge. "Because you're panicking."

Ellie flinched. He might as well have punched her.

"Oh!" Oliver smacked his forehead. "No, Ellie, not you. I'm so sorry. I was talking to him, in my head, and I must've said the last part out loud."

Ellie nearly ground her teeth. "That's not much better."

A fence seemed to rise up out of the hayfield, stretching in front of them as far as she could see in either direction. It was barbed-wire, with metal strands stretched tightly across wooden posts set far enough apart to drive a truck through. And as the first fence came into view, so did a second one, only a few yards behind it.

It was much taller—taller than the truck—and its metal posts gleamed dully in the afternoon sun. The wires stretching between them were almost as thick as the grass snakes that sometimes climbed onto the Shack's front porch to sun themselves. Everything about it screamed *do not cross*.

She felt more than heard Oliver's deep breath. "Did your friend at the rest stop say anything about the border fence being electric?"

"No, he didn't," Ellie said. "That seems like such a needlessly convoluted way to kill us, though."

"True." Oliver shook his head slowly. "Well, if it is, we can only hope our friend found a way to turn the current off."

The fences seemed to march toward them of their own accord. Though Ellie was driving, was technically in charge of where they went and what they did, she couldn't remember ever feeling so out-of-control.

"If I cut, will you cover me?" Oliver asked.

His voice was unbelievably calm. Ellie didn't trust herself to speak; she just nodded.

"Unless you want to switch?"

"No." Ellie swallowed. "You're stronger. I'm sure you'll be faster."

"That's what I was thinking. Plus, I trust your aim."

Caught between the warmth of his belief in her and the cruel knife of self-doubt lodged in her chest, Ellie hit the brakes. The truck bumped to a stop in front of the barbed wire. Beside her, Oliver scanned the area around them, and when he spoke again, his voice was a tense whisper. "I don't see anything."

"I don't, either."

The truck's engine idled quietly under their feet as their eyes met. Oliver's burned with fierce determination, and as she watched, the intensity in them flared. "Let's go."

Then, he was out of the truck and halfway to the fence.

Ellie scrambled after him, snatching the bow and quiver full of paper-wrapped arrows. Leaving the truck door open, she pulled the arrows out and poured a little lighter fluid on the wadded up toilet paper at their tips. A metallic *thnick* met her ears; she looked up to see Oliver move to the second wire, the first one dangling limply above it. She shoved all but one of the now-stinking arrows back into the quiver, nocked it, then jogged to where Oliver crouched just in time to see the second strand of wire go slack.

"One more," he grunted, clamping the final wire between the jaws of the cutter. With one quick press of his hands, the whole fence sagged. Carefully, he grabbed one of the clear sections between the jagged barbs and started to drag the broken fence to the side, out of the way. "Help me with—"

But Ellie had already set down the bow. "On it." She grabbed the other loose strands—Oliver had cut the fence clean in half between two poles—and hauled them out of the truck's path.

"There," Oliver said as he let the broken fence crash to the ground. Ellie tried not to feel too guilty as she looked down at the twisted mess of wire and wood at their feet.

"Let's go, Ellie," he said. She turned to see that he'd picked up the bow and was looking at her with his head cocked, his eyes sympathetic. "The farmer will be okay."

Ellie turned away. "I know."

"Your life is worth a lot more than some minor property destruction." Oliver gestured with the bow toward what looked like the roof of a barn peeking above the golden field in the distance. "And if the owner knew what was really going on here, he'd agree."

"I'm sure he would. I'm just…" She frowned. "And *your* life. Don't leave yourself out."

For a second, Oliver just looked at her. Then he smiled, sudden and delighted. "I really didn't mean to. I was just … thinking of you. Anyway…" He cleared his throat, then offered her the bow. "What if I drive, and you get in the back of the truck. Then I can work on that behemoth—" he nodded at the border fence "—and you can keep watch."

"Works for me," Ellie said. She took the weapon and hoisted herself into the bed of the pickup. "This gives me a lot more visibility ..."

Movement caught her eye. Shading her eyes with her free hand, she squinted across the field of swaying gold at ... at ...

What is that?

She snapped her free hand downward. "Hand me those binoculars. Under the seat."

Oliver disappeared and reappeared seconds later, holding them out. Ellie snatched them and pressed them to her eyes, trying to pinpoint that figure she'd seen—

There.

Her mouth went dry, her hands starting to shake. She nearly dropped the binoculars as she fell into a crouch. "Go, Oliver. Go now!"

The blood drained from his face but he didn't question her, just rushed for the truck. She wanted to kiss him for that alone—if she ever got the chance. Because she'd just seen what looked like the Grim Reaper, scythe and all.

And it was headed straight for them.

Chapter Eleven

Oliver didn't know what Ellie had seen, but judging by the terror on her face, he didn't want to.

He threw himself into the truck, slammed the door behind him, and hit the gas. The border fence was only about ten yards from the farmer's but the prairie was bumpier than it looked. His teeth rattled as a the truck hit a hidden pothole, jolting it so hard that, behind him, the arrows clattered in their box like dried bones.

Oliver glanced in the rearview mirror and breathed a sigh of relief. Ellie crouched on her knees in the truck bed, one hand gripping the side wall and the other clutching the bow. She was impressively well-balanced, her limber form swaying and adjusting to the truck's movements as if she'd grown up racing across the countryside in the back of a pickup.

Which, she probably has. He spared half a second to marvel at her, then slammed on the brakes as Wormwood's laughter scraped through his brain.

You can't make it. You're not going to save her.

Oliver snatched the wire cutters and scrambled out of the truck, clutching them in a vise grip. *We killed Silverskin and made it this far. I wouldn't count us out.*

Oh, but you don't know what's coming for you, Ollie.

He'd start at the bottom, while they still had some distance between themselves and whatever was coming after them—

You'd kill yourselves if you knew what was coming.

Fear dragged chilled fingers down the back of Oliver's neck. He shoved it into the same mental box he'd shoved Wormwood's voice, figuring they could keep each other company.

Actually, knowing you, you'd kill Ellie to spare her and then die horribly, and I'd probably get enough entertainment out of it to last me a century.

Oliver clamped the cutters down on the first strand, gritting his teeth. This fence made the barbed wire look like fishing line.

Besides. Silverskin was only one. He doesn't matter in the grand scheme of things.

Sweat broke out on Oliver's brow, cooling immediately in the incessant prairie breeze. Where was this thing and how fast was it coming? How much time did he have?

Not when there are millions of us.

All the blood drained from Oliver's face, his hope threatening to go with it. *What?*

A gloating laugh was Wormwood's only response.

Oliver's eyes flicked up to Ellie. She stood silhouetted against the sky, the sun glinting off her dark hair but dulling when it hit the night-black bow. Her eyes were fixed on some point in the distance, her face pale as a skull.

Hurry up, Ollie. Death is coming.

Snarling, Oliver leaned into the cutters, throwing his whole body into the task, and the first cable exploded apart.

"Yes!" He reached for the next one.

"Oliver?"

"One down!"

"It's getting closer!" Ellie's voice was high, petrified-sounding, and Oliver briefly wondered if she'd be able to shoot if the time came.

The second cable snapped and Oliver repositioned himself so he had better leverage. Despite his best efforts, terror ghosted around his mental fortifications like smoke. If worst came to worst, he wasn't honestly sure Ellie could cut the fence, either. She was strong, but he had several inches and probably sixty or seventy pounds on her, and it was taking everything *he* had—

Oh look, there it is. I knew you still doubted her. Did you *know? Well, I guess now you do.*

Oliver bore down with the cutters, ignoring the pain starting to build in his palms. "Shut *up*. Shut up, shut up, shut up—"

The third cable hissed apart and he was already scrambling to his feet, positioning the cutters for the fourth—

There's no way Ellie could do this. She's not strong enough, and you might not be, either.

"Shut up," Oliver muttered again. Though this time, he wasn't sure if it was Wormwood he was talking to, or himself.

The fourth cable struck him in the stomach as it shivered away from itself, leaving raw, stinging pain in its wake. Oliver ignored it and moved to the fifth. It was the last one he could do while standing on the ground; he'd have to get in the back of the truck to reach the others.

Halfway there. He flexed one burning palm. *Halfway there.*

Ellie stifled a sound, probably a scream, and sympathy seared through Oliver. His fear was strong enough to nearly hijack him, and *he* didn't have clinical anxiety. She did. And she was still standing, still staring down whatever creature was coming for them, armed with only a bow and a few flimsy wooden arrows.

Oliver jerked back as the fifth cable snapped; it missed his eye by inches.

"Three more!" He vaulted into the truck. "Just ..."

Movement to the east caught his eye, and Oliver's jaw dropped as he finally saw it. A horse and rider. They were still several yards away but were closing the distance with nightmarish speed.

"CUT THE FENCE!" Ellie screamed.

Oliver forgot about his burning hands, throwing all his strength into the sixth cable. It coiled as it snapped, like an angry silver snake. The seventh followed. He seized the eighth in the clipper's jaws.

"Last one," he gasped. But even the adrenaline couldn't stop the pain now; it felt like he was shoving the clipper's handles *into* the flesh of his palms.

"Hurry! It's almost here!"

She's dead. You're dead.

Oliver gave a desperate pull. With a slithering, metallic hiss, the cable burst apart.

"Got it, El—!"

Oliver felt her shift behind him, heard the rush of air from her lungs, and knew she'd drawn the bow. He whirled, his eyes falling on the ax, and he rushed for it—

RUN.

The voice was so different from Wormwood's that it nearly bowled Oliver over. It was the same one, the one that had saved him from the Gatekeeper, from the fire. Oliver threw himself over the side of the truck, stumbling on the packed brown earth. "Come on, Ellie!"

The thunder of hoofbeats roared in his ears, and he looked up to see a pale figure on a moon-white horse, like Death itself had ridden straight out of the Bible and onto the golden Montana grassland.

"I have a good shot! I think I can hit him!"

"We don't have time—"

"Then GET IN so you can drive if I miss!"

Cursing, Oliver flung himself into the truck. The twang-click of the bowstring reached his ears; he jerked his eyes to the rearview mirror just in time to see Ellie's knees hit the truck bed.

"DRIVE!" she screamed.

Oliver threw the truck into reverse, twisting around to guide them backward. He only needed a few feet, just enough to make the turn without getting tangled in the wires. Ellie was only partially visible through the window but she was scrambling for something ... another arrow. She nocked it, drew, then aimed again—

Oliver let out a ferocious laugh, his heart full of fear, admiration, and more than a little pride. *Maybe I doubt her aim, Wormwood, but never her courage.*

It doesn't matter. Nothing you do matters now.

"You'd better hope so, for your sake," Oliver snarled, and hit the gas.

The truck pitched forward, and through the open window, he heard Ellie cry out. His eyes snapped to the rearview mirror just in time to see her send the second arrow flying toward the demon. She hadn't managed to light this one or the first one, but the fact that she had enough self-possession to do what she *was* doing was incredible.

But it wasn't enough. The horse kept coming. How the animal was moving so quickly, Oliver had no idea. Up close it was a sickly white color, so bony he could see every rib. It looked like it shouldn't even be able to get up, let alone charge across the prairie with speed that bordered on supernatural, *while* carrying a full-grown man on its back. A man who matched the animal: bone-white, thin-faced, red-lipped, wearing white rags that wrapped around his skinny, birdlike form. The blade of a scythe rose over his shoulder, wicked, black, and glinting.

The creature met Oliver's eyes and smiled. Then, he reached behind him, his hand closing on the shaft of the weapon, and turned those mad pink eyes on Ellie.

***

Ellie knew screaming wouldn't do anything, but she needed the release, so she did it anyway. The reaper was right beside the truck, his scythe held in one hand as he drew it back to strike. She scrambled for another arrow, knowing it would be useless—she'd missed her other two shots and the lighter fluid was in the truck—but she couldn't freeze. Not again, not if she could stop this thing from killing Oliver, even if she was only a distraction so he could get away.

The fear was insane; her ears rang, her vision tunneled, and she wondered if she would die from the terror alone. Ellie didn't know how she nocked the arrow, only that she was drawing the bow as the reaper-demon raised his huge scythe—

The truck lurched right just as she fired. Ellie was flung forward, barely catching herself before she smacked her face into the side of the truck. Her left forearm seared like it was pressed to a hot stove; the bowstring must have clipped the sensitive flesh there, and she had no idea where the arrow had gone.

The road. We have to be close. She desperately hoped it was well-maintained, not just another two-track. The arrows weren't working; she wasn't good enough. Speed might be the only thing that could save them.

Gritting her teeth, Ellie forced herself to her knees as the truck bounced and swayed underneath her, its powerful engine roaring as Oliver put on another burst of speed. Her heart leaped with frantic hope as she saw it, just ahead. The road cut a wide, tan swath through the sagelands, and they were almost on top of it; it was within *yards*.

The truck bulled through a fierce snarl of sagebrush, throwing Ellie forward again and filling her nose with its pungent spice. Then they were through, fishtailing onto the hard-packed dirt, and Ellie let out a sob of relief as she looked up—

Her whole world narrowed, swallowed up in a pair of pale-pink eyes, a rictus grin, and an upraised scythe.

Ellie threw herself backward, and the sound of the scythe hitting the truck drowned out her scream. It was terrible, the screech of metal on metal like a thousand untuned violins playing a dissonant, hellish symphony. The truck ground almost to a complete stop and Ellie slammed into the back of the cab. Something hard hit her in the face—the bow. She groped for it, willing her head to clear as her hand closed on the cool, hard metal.

Underneath her, the truck seethed. Its tires spun in the dirt, gaining inches, then feet, dragging the Reaper behind them. Ellie looked up just long enough to see he wasn't smiling anymore before heaving herself onto her knees, searching frantically for an arrow. There had to be one close by, but her vision wasn't working right and every part of her body was shaking. But if the Reaper's scythe was dug into the tailgate, then he was probably in his physical form. She could hurt him, distract him, *something*—

The roar of the engine changed pitch, climbing even higher. The metal screamed again, bending and warping under the pressure. Oliver yelled her name. The rest of his words drowned in the cacophony, but it was enough to make Ellie realize ...

Oh, hell.

She looped her arm through the bow then threw herself at the side of the truck, slinging an arm over it, clinging to it with everything she had. With a final, tortured screech, the tailgate gave way.

The truck shot forward.

Ellie let out a cry as the force nearly flung her out onto the prairie. Half-listening to Sam brag about his truck's acceleration was one thing; experiencing it—especially like *this*—was another. She didn't even hear the tailgate hit the ground; for the first few seconds she just held on, the tears on her cheeks whipped away by the wind.

A bitter scream split the air, supernaturally loud and furious enough to freeze her bones. Ellie raised her head. The Reaper had glided over the twisted remains of the tailgate and was still coming for them, but he was falling behind. She would have dissolved into tears of relief right then and there if the demon hadn't raised the scythe above his head and hurled it straight for her face.

***

Oliver was thrown back in his seat when the tailgate finally gave. He'd tried to warn Ellie, but if he'd known Sam's truck was capable of that kind of acceleration, he wouldn't have floored it. Wrestling the fishtailing vehicle under control, he looked frantically between the road and the rearview mirror. Ellie was still there, safe—or as safe as she could be—and they were leaving the horseman behind. Relief made him so weak he thought his heart might crack.

"I'm so sorry, Ellie," he rasped. She couldn't hear him, but he repeated it again, then again, then ...

The horseman raised his scythe, its beast putting on one last unearthly burst of speed. His white arm blurred and then the scythe was winging through the air like a fan blade, directly at Ellie.

Oliver screamed her name and jerked the steering wheel.

Ellie dove for safety.

The scythe hit in an explosion of sparks and screeching metal.

Sam's truck bucked and skittered across the road and Oliver's instincts took over. He wrestled it back into a straight course, every second feeling like a year. He had spent years driving on frozen Alaskan roads. This wasn't all that different.

Except that he might have just lost his best friend.

Shaking, he raised his eyes to the mirror again, afraid of what he'd see. She wasn't gone, *couldn't* be gone. He'd tried to angle them so the scythe's trajectory should have taken it to the other side ...

He gasped, horror nearly locking his every muscle. It had. One of the sides had been completely sheared off, the metal still glowing a sullen, cherry red. And Ellie was nowhere to be seen.

"Ellie!" he cried. He should *never* have left her back there, he should've made her come with him—

Her head popped up, still attached to her shoulders, her eyes wild and frightened.

Oliver let out a choked sound; his chest hurt so bad that he was half-afraid his heart might fail. But Ellie was alive, the horseman was falling behind, and without his scythe—

Oliver's eyes shifted to the horseman. He stood in the middle of the road like a sentinel straight from Hell, falling farther and farther behind. As Oliver watched, the scythe re-formed in his hand, but it didn't matter. They were too far away. As long as they put some distance between themselves and the demon, they would make it.

Ellie peered through the back windshield with huge eyes, her hair wild, her face pale. Her mouth formed one word: GO. Then she hooked her arm over the remaining side and braced one foot against the wheel well.

Oliver hit the gas, not as frantically as last time, but enough that he watched Ellie as much as the road to make sure he wasn't accelerating too fast. But she was rock-solid, curled into a ball and locked into place. She didn't shift, didn't so much as budge until the highway appeared in front of him. Only when he'd finally pulled to the side of the road did she stir, pushing herself backward, trembling so hard he could see it from where he sat.

Oliver piled out of the truck, sparing one glance behind him to make sure the horseman hadn't caught up, before sprinting to where Ellie wobbled on the slashed-off edge of the truck bed. Somehow, she was still holding the bow.

He caught her just as her feet hit the ground, crushing her against him. Instantly, the headache sliced him from temple to temple, but he didn't care. She was *alive*.

"Oliver." Her voice was raw from screaming, weak from terror, and she shook like she had hypothermia.

"I'm so sorry, Ellie, I should've made you come with me …"

She let out a little whimper that sounded like the words "my choice."

Oliver just bent, slid an arm under her legs, and picked her up. The bow clattered to the dirt but he ignored it; he'd come back for it in a minute. Ellie tried to push against his chest but he just tightened his arms around her, stumbling through the haze of pain to the passenger's side of the truck.

"Wormwood … your headache," she mumbled.

Oliver fumbled the door open. "I don't give a damn." He nestled her in the seat but kept his arms around her, burying his face in her neck. "I don't care. I thought you'd died."

Ellie's chest convulsed and then she was sobbing, her arms encircling him with a strength he was amazed she still possessed. He held her as the dam burst, as she gasped and cried, and the last of his own terror left wet lines down his cheeks.

"Maybe that's not the job for me," she hiccuped.

"It's not the job for *anyone*." He kissed the side of her mouth. She turned her face a fraction, her lips brushing over Oliver's, and he—

A scream split his mind, shrill, irate, and maybe even afraid. Wormwood. Pain drove through the top of his skull, radiating down into his shoulders as if an invisible hand had gripped his spine and dug its nails into it. His eyes flew open and, instead of seeing Ellie's face, he saw a wall of black and white spots.

Oliver stumbled backward, clutching his temple, a harsh noise issuing from between his clenched teeth. He stood there for a minute, catching his breath as the pain subsided and his vision returned to normal.

"Oliver—"

"You're worth it." Oliver let his hands fall from his face, blinking in sunlight that was suddenly too bright, and looked back down the road. He didn't want her to see how badly it still hurt, not if there was a chance she'd blame herself for it.

"Is he coming?" Ellie's voice sounded like she was trying to hold it steady, and maybe it would have fooled someone else, but not him.

"I don't see him, but it doesn't matter. We need to go." Oliver gave her one last, long look. She had a cut on the bridge of her nose, and the skin around one of her eyes was already starting to bruise. Sickened, he turned, scooped up the bow, then staggered to the driver's side and got in, tossing it behind him.

"I lost the rest of the arrows," Ellie said, tugging her door shut.

"We have more in the box. Plus, we have a full tank of gas, and food and water. All we have to do now is run."

Ellie let out one long sigh and closed her eyes. Her hair had come half-loose from its ponytail and drooped down her shoulders, neck, and face as if it were as exhausted as she was.

"Oh, Ellie." Oliver pointed the truck up the on-ramp, his stomach finally unclenching as they sped onto the nearly-deserted Canadian highway. "You did so well."

"I thought I might be able to hurt him. Slow him down." She buried her face in her hands. "I was so stupid."

"How many times did you shoot?"

"Four."

"Four shots," he repeated, "from the back of a moving truck that was being attacked by one of the Four Horsemen of the Apocalypse." He glanced at her, seeing her eyes come open, a frown crossing her face. "Maybe it wasn't the smartest, but if *that's* not courage, I don't know what is."

Slowly, Ellie pushed herself upright, her face still scrunched in a frown. Oliver wished for the hundredth time that he could pull her into his arms and lay back on something soft, stroke that long, silky hair until she—or he, or *both* of them—fell asleep in the warm comfort of each other's arms. If he'd known that last night had been their last opportunity for who *knew* how long, he would have done exactly what she'd suggested and stayed right there.

That's shockingly nonsexual, Ollie. What's the matter? 'Fraid you won't be able to make her—?

"Please talk to me, Ellie." He swallowed down the rage, the *hatred* that reared in the pit of his stomach. They'd escaped. Again. He should've known Wormwood was going to take cheap shots; he had no other option.

"I'm worried about you," Oliver added.

Ellie gave a helpless lift of her shoulders. The fear had hollowed out her eyes; they were dull, haunted shades in her pale face. A drop of blood tracked a crimson trail from her nose to her lip. Oliver fished for the toilet paper, handing her a few squares.

"Thanks." She took them and pressed them to her nose. "I don't know how to process what just happened." Her eyes fell closed. "I'm so tired. And Sam's truck …" Two big tears slid down her cheeks.

"I think he'll just be happy we're alive."

Ellie nodded. "He will. He just … he loves this thing."

"So do I," Oliver said fervently. "It just saved our lives."

For a moment, they lapsed into an exhausted silence.

"Edmonton is where we need to get to, right?" Oliver asked a few miles later.

Ellie nodded.

"How far is it?"

She reached for her phone and squinted at the screen. "Six hours." The words fell from her lips like a death sentence, then Oliver heard her sigh. "I can take a turn driving."

"After what you just went through?" Oliver shook his head. "You relax for a minute."

"You need to rest, too."

"I'm good for a while still, especially if I can turn on the radio or listen to one of your podcasts." He tried to smile. "That one about music history is *especially* riveting."

Ellie raised an eyebrow.

"No, really! I want to know what that guy Kolshinsky was going to do—"

"Stravinsky."

"Stravinsky, yeah. He sounded like a rebel."

One corner of her mouth twitched. "Oliver, I'm so glad you're here with me."

Oliver's first instinct was to come up with a quip, something that would get her to laugh. Or even smile; a real Ellie smile right now would give him everything he needed to keep going and then some. But all he could think about was the sight of the sheared-off truck wall in the rearview mirror, the awful realization that he didn't know where she was.

The image of her mangled body lying on the prairie, her blood stark red on the tawny grass.

He looked over at her, the sudden depth and sharpness of his feelings threatening to overwhelm him. There were no words. So he cleared his throat, stared at the road, and settled for, "I feel the same way." He swallowed and steadied his voice. "Rest, Ellie."

For a few minutes there was silence, and Oliver just drove, feeling his body calm as the last dregs of adrenaline drained from his system. He flexed his bruised palms, one after another, then chanced a look over at Ellie. To his surprise, she was gazing at him with her head cocked.

He cleared his throat again. "So ... it seems like something *might* be bothering you, since you aren't asleep."

She snorted. "Astute."

"My specialty." Oliver waggled his eyebrows at her, raising a small smile to her lips again. A smile as beautiful as a sunrise, and which faded just as quickly.

"Your hands are hurt," she said.

Oliver shrugged. "It's nothing a little ibuprofen won't fix."

Ellie dragged a hand over her eyes, then turned and reached into the back, unzipping her suitcase. "What did you mean when you said the demon was a ... like, a horseman?"

Oliver blinked. "He was a tall, albino-looking guy riding a white horse that looked like it was about to drop dead of starvation."

Ellie plopped down in the seat again, seeming steadier. Even if the frown on her face matched the confusion he felt.

"Isn't that what you saw?" he asked.

"No. It's not."

"Oh." Oliver scrubbed a hand over his eyes, then winced as it throbbed. "So ... what did you see?"

"The Grim Reaper."

Oliver's eyebrows shot up. "What?"

She nodded. "Just like you'd imagine him. No horse, just a massive, cloaked man with a *huge* scythe."

"How did he keep up? Was he ... running?"

"No. He sort of glided, a little like the Lady but more smoothly. But he wasn't a skeleton," she added. "I thought he was at first, but he turned out to be ... well, just like you described from what I could see. An albino. He had pink eyes and everything. He was just wearing a black cloak and hood."

Oliver stared down the road. They'd seen the same demon completely differently. What did *that* mean? "Maybe it's one of his unique abilities, or whatever."

"Maybe." Ellie fiddled with the ibuprofen container until the lid popped open. "One or two?"

Oliver shifted and his ripped shirt brushed the cut on his stomach, sending a fresh, stinging wave of pain through his body. "Two." *One for my hands, and one for that cut.*

Ellie stuck an uncapped water bottle into the cupholder next to him, then shook two rust-red pills onto her palm. Oliver gasped. The flesh of her left forearm was scraped and raw, and a massive bruise blossomed from the inside of her elbow nearly to her wrist.

"Ellie." He bit back the guilt again, nodding at her arm. "Bowstring?"

She nodded, then hovered her hand above his so she could drop them into his palm without touching him. "It's all good." Another taut smile. "It's nothing a little ibuprofen won't fix."

"How's your neck?" he asked as she popped two pills of her own.

"Better by the hour." She looked ruefully down at her arm. "It's definitely lost its spot as the thing that hurts the most."

Oliver shook his head. "Between all our injuries, we might make one functional person." Gingerly, he probed the scratch on his stomach with one aching hand. As painful as the cut was, it seemed to have stopped bleeding on its own. He breathed a sigh of relief.

"Oliver, is that blood?" Ellie leaned over the center console, gaping down at the hole in his shirt.

"One of the big cables got me when I cut it. It's just a scratch."

"A *big* scratch." She looked up at him, uncertainty in her gray eyes, her face even paler than it had been a few seconds ago. "Can you tell if it's still bleeding?"

"I don't think it is."

She sighed and settled back in her seat. "That's a relief. I'd do my best, but I'm definitely not cut out to be a nurse."

"It's fine. It really is. Why don't we put half an hour between us and the horseman? Then we can switch and I'll put some antiseptic on it."

"That sounds good." Ellie leaned back again. "The more distance, the better. I can't imagine the reaper ... horseman, whatever ... was the only one waiting for us at the border. Though he was certainly capable of doing the job on his own."

"That he was." Oliver hesitated as Wormwood's words came back to him. *Millions.* He opened his mouth to say something, but the thoughts died unspoken on his lips as he caught sight of Ellie. She was slumped back against the seat again, her eyes closed, face still ashen. Her expression suggested she was in pain, but he didn't know if it was the physical kind or the kind that went deeper. The kind that came from horror and helplessness, from realizing that, as hard as you'd fought, the only reason you were still alive was sheer dumb luck.

"Ellie," he murmured, "sleep."

"But you—"

"I'm okay." Oliver swallowed. *I'm not sure if I'll ever sleep again.* "You can spell me in half an hour."

She looked at him through half-open eyes, then reached down to lean the seat back. "Half an hour. Then you'd better pull over."

"Start that podcast about Stablevsky for me, would you?"

Ellie let out a weak chuckle. "Stravinsky. You're getting there." She tapped her phone, then set it in the center console and lay back as a voice came over the speaker. "Music history never fails to put me to sleep."

"And it never fails to keep me awake."

Above her closed eyes, Ellie's brows lifted. "Oh yeah?"

"All two times I've ever thought about it."

Her quiet laugh warmed him, comforted him.

"I'll stop talking now," he said softly. "Sleep."

"Mmm-hmmm."

And she did. It couldn't have been more than five minutes before her body relaxed, her breathing deepening.

Oliver only half-listened to the podcaster drone about the long-dead musician. He'd requested it with pure intentions; he *wanted* to learn more about her world and the things she was passionate about. But as he drove, his mind started to wander. He kept stealing glances at Ellie, at her long lashes, her trim figure, her pink lips, slightly parted in sleep. Maybe it was infatuation, but everything about her was stunning to him.

He sighed and leaned his head back against the headrest. It didn't feel like infatuation, though. At least not *only* infatuation. There was a depth to it, an energy, like the slow, rolling power of the ocean, that he'd never experienced before. Unintentionally, Ellie had entwined herself into the very fabric of his life, and he wanted, he *needed* her.

He ... loved her?

Big words.

Oliver shook his head. Dean had told his mother he'd loved her, too, and in the end, he'd run off and left them. That couldn't have been love; it couldn't *ever* have been love. Love stayed. Love tried.

Your idealism is disgusting, Ollie. People are just animals who throw words instead of crap. You know that.

Oliver bit down on his retort and settled back in his seat, ignoring the weird twitching that had started up again in his fingers.

Who's to say you won't be just like your daddy?

I say.

It's in your blood.

Oliver reached over and turned the volume up, trying to drown out Wormwood's poison. When he put his hand back on the wheel, it spasmed, sending a shivery little ache up into his forearm. He let out a long, silent breath. He'd said thirty minutes. What he'd meant was "as long as Ellie slept."

So he drove on.

Part II: The Hunt

Chapter Twelve

"So, anything else we should be looking for besides fire weapons?"

Sam's voice was low in Darien's ear as they walked hand-in-hand down the palm-lined path. A warm breeze tugged at the fronds above them, brushing against her skin with gentle wisps that smelled like salt. She was still a little in awe of the cultural program they'd enjoyed after lunch, but was glad for the chance to walk off all that pulled pork and pineapple.

Plus, she wanted answers. And she wanted them fast.

"Folklore," she said. "Local ghost stories. Anything that sounds like it could be connected."

Sam's fingers twitched in hers, and she gave his hand a sympathetic squeeze. She knew he'd had enough of ghost stories to last a lifetime, and couldn't blame him, but all he said was, "That makes sense."

They strolled the last few paces to the door of the huge museum and Sam tugged it open. Darien stepped through, her skin prickling as the temperature dropped by a few degrees. Still, it wasn't uncomfortable. In the summer, Coloradans seemed to feel the need to run their air conditioners until the insides of buildings felt like ski slopes. Darien was often *grateful* to step out into dry, ninety-degree heat after shopping or eating out. Here, though, the climate was so naturally comfortable there was barely a need for temperature control. And she was loving it.

Behind her, the door swung shut, and Sam took her hand. "All right, let's go look for clues."

"You got it, Sherlock."

Sam grinned. "Nah. Of the two of us, *you're* definitely Sherlock."

"Fine. Let's go, Watson." Darien looped her arm through her husband's and started forward.

The place was huge and they took their time, carefully scanning every display, plaque, and infographic they came across. With each fascinating but unhelpful exhibit they passed, Darien started to wonder ... had she just been seeing things when she'd picked up that brochure? Had her mind been so eager to make a connection that it had forged one where it didn't really exist? In her text, Ellie hadn't seemed to think so. But here in the light of day, surrounded by tourists, Darien couldn't help but wonder.

That wouldn't be surprising, Darien reflected as she examined a wall of bowls and baskets. A second thought followed hard on its heels. *Maybe we should quit looking and just enjoy our honeymoon.*

But Darien sighed. She couldn't bring herself to do that, and she knew Sam couldn't, either. Even if this was just a gigantic, tropical, wild goose chase—complementary mocktails included—they needed to feel like they were helping somehow.

Darien released Sam's hand and wandered over to a different section. A collection of ancient musical instruments caught her eye: drums, long pieces of wood with a single string stretched down their middle, and ... she squinted. *Nose flutes?*

She smiled, thinking of Ellie. Not only would she *want* to try and play one of those, she'd probably be instantly good at it.

"Oh look, a hula skirt made from human hair," Sam remarked. "That's fun."

Darien wrinkled her nose. "Not for the person the hair belonged to."

"Valid." Sam took her hand again, scanning the huge room. He nodded to a display on the other side. "There's the weapons. Want to go take a look?"

"Yes. Let's take our time getting over there though, so we don't miss anything."

"Sounds good."

Sam's free hand fell to his left pocket—the one where he always kept his phone. The movement seemed so casual, so automatic, that Darien wondered if he even realized he'd done it. Darien fought the urge to check her own messages; Ellie and Oliver were probably somewhere in rural Montana, out of reach of cell service. They'd send updates when they could. Still ... worry wormed through Darien's stomach, small and irritating, like a parasite she couldn't get rid of.

She tried her best to ignore it as they fell into a slow walk, letting her eyes wander over the other displays. They were nearly to the weapons wall when she saw it: a dimly-lit alcove studded with strange-looking pictures. The sign above it read "Hawaiian Legends and Folklore."

Darien stopped, her skin prickling. "Wait, Sam." She took a step forward, her hand tightening in his. "That might tell us something."

"Like how to avoid all of them?" Sam half-joked, but he'd gone tense. Darien saw it in the set of his jaw, felt it in the stiff lines of his hand.

"We have to know what they are first." Darien shot him a smile as they stopped in front of the display. He returned it. Sort of. Suppressing a sigh, Darien started scanning the pictures, the titles ... anything that looked or sounded like what Ellie and Oliver had described.

"Menehune," Sam murmured. "Small, industrious people who live in the forest." He shook his head. "They don't seem terrifying enough."

Darien's eyes fell on another picture and her eyebrows went up; it was easily one of the most stunning she'd seen that day. An ageless woman stared back at her, bathed in sullen lava-light, her fiery hair flowing down her back and curling into smoke at its ends. Her face was intense, serious, and her traditional-looking dress wrapped around generous curves. She was harsh. Beautiful. A mother, a creator, and a destroyer all rolled into one.

Damn, Darien thought. *That's a woman who's got her life figured out.*

"Pele ..." She cocked her head, reading. "Goddess of fire, volcanoes, creator of the Hawaiian islands ..." She went quiet for a moment, studying the picture, then shook her head. "Fire aside, I don't think she has anything to do with the demons. I can't imagine anything associated with them would be so revered."

"Agreed," Sam said. "But ... I don't know, Darien." He folded his arms over his chest and eyed the picture of the goddess in front of them. "The connections are stacking up. Their weapons were made mostly out of wood, and they worshipped a fire goddess. Though that makes sense just because ..."

"Of the active volcanoes?" Darien supplied. "And the fact that they didn't have metal to work with until colonists arrived?"

"Yeah ..." Sam pinched the bridge of his nose. "I want answers so bad that I'm probably just seeing what I want to see."

"I know the feeling." Darien laid a hand on his arm. "Any connection could be important. Just because we haven't found anything definitive doesn't mean we won't."

Another picture caught her eye; she sidestepped over to it and a chill ran down her spine. An army of what looked like specters glared sightlessly down at her, muscled and fierce-eyed and unnaturally pale, all armed with spears, daggers, and clubs. If Pele's picture had been the most beautiful she'd seen today, this was easily the most unnerving.

"I keep thinking ..." Sam stopped dead, staring down at the picture. Then he let out a low whistle and wrapped his arms around Darien from behind, resting his chin on her head. "I would *not* want to play football against those guys."

"*I* wouldn't want you to play football against those guys. Based on what the plaque says, they'd kill you."

"Huaka'i Po," Sam said. "Night Marchers. They look a little demonic. Do you think ...?" He paused, presumably reading. "Oh, no, not if they're the spirits of important chiefs and they *protect* the islands."

"Yeah. Their legend seems too positive to fit what we're looking for, despite the kill-you-on-sight part. " Darien snuggled back into Sam's arms, blinking at the picture and wishing she could unsee it. Vengeful Hawaiian spirits who patrolled old battlefields and could kill with a glance? And all their victims heard beforehand were drumbeats and chanting.

"Still," she said, "now that I know about these guys, I vote we don't go out much after dark."

Sam gave her a squeeze. "Fine with me. There are other things I'd rather be doing after dark anyway."

She chuckled, then made to move away. Sam released her immediately, stepping around her to gaze up at another infographic, and his eyebrows went up. "Oh good, now there are dragons, too."

"Dragons?" Darien backtracked to where her husband stood. "Hawaiian dragons?"

"Maybe? They're called Mo'o. Looks like they protect the water on the islands. They start as harmless geckos until you make them angry, and then they turn into dragons and eat you."

"So be careful around water, got it." She studied the picture. The animal looked like a giant Komodo Dragon. "Of all the ones on this list, they might be the coolest."

Sam folded his arms, staring at the display. "They're cool until they're real." He blinked, then looked down at her. "Sorry. Uh, I think the Mo'o have the same problem as the

Night Marchers: overall, their legend is way too positive." His voice lowered, taking on a dangerous edge. "Our demons don't seem to protect, only destroy."

"I agree." Darien reached for Sam's hand again. "Let's go look at weapons, shall we?"

A shadow of Sam's easy grin returned; he draped his arm around her. "I'm in."

They sauntered over to the weapons wall, leaving some room between them and a middle-aged couple who were examining a case of clubs embedded with shark teeth. Darien tried not to think about what those would do when they connected with human flesh.

"Well, we have spears, clubs, slings, daggers, and lots of creative uses of shark teeth," Sam said, then glanced around. "Where's that fire dance, though? Do you know what I'm talking about?"

"I think so," Darien said. "I've never been here and don't know much about Hawaiian culture, but I've definitely heard about the fire dance. I'm surprised we didn't see it during the lunch program, actually." She looked around. There had to be a staff member or tour guide around here somewhere—

There. Darien locked eyes with a tall, stocky man with a deep tan and raven-black hair, wearing the museum's uniform. She tugged Sam's arm. "Why don't we go ask an expert?"

"Might as well."

The man grinned as they started his way, his eyes crinkling at the corners along well-worn smile lines. "You two look like you have a question."

"We do," Darien said brightly, then peered at his name tag. "Kaleo ... did I pronounce your name right?"

"Kah-ley-o, yes. What can I help you with?"

"Can you tell us if ancient Hawaiians used fire weapons?" Darien asked.

"Not that I'm aware of." Kaleo gestured around the room. "And I'm aware of most of it."

"Huh." Sam rubbed a hand along his cheek. "So ... there *is* a fire dance, though, right? I remember coming to Hawaii as a kid and going to a luau, and seeing these guys doing amazing things with burning knives and spears."

"Yes, there is a fire knife dance, you're remembering correctly. It's just a Samoan tradition, not a Hawaiian one."

"Ah," Sam said. "Gotcha."

"It's a beautiful tradition. In fact, they'll be performing it tonight during our luau, if you plan on attending that."

"Unfortunately, no," Darien said. "It sold out before we could get tickets."

Kaleo shook his head. "Ah, well, you'll have to come back, then."

Darien grinned up at Sam. "I'm pretty sure we will."

"Oh, most definitely," Sam said. "Kaleo, thanks so much for the help, we appreciate it. Darien, should we keep wandering?"

She squeezed his arm. "I'm all for it."

***

Several hours and a relaxing beach dinner later, Darien and Sam fell through the door of their decadent hotel room, laughing and teasing each other. Sam closed the door behind them and Darien didn't bother to turn on a light. *The moonlight and nightlight will do just fine.*

"Well, I wouldn't say we found answers," Sam said, "but it was still a good day."

"I agree." Darien groaned, rubbing her stomach. "That shrimp was amazing. I ate way too much of it. And that *sunset* ... just wow."

Sam came toward her, his eyes turning soft and playful and heated. "The question is, can we make it even better?"

Darien let a slow smirk curl her lips. "I think you know the answer to that."

Sam smiled right before he kissed her, a tiny and smitten upturn of his lips that made it all the sweeter when they met hers. A sigh escaped Darien; her husband responded by pressing closer, his hands tightening around her waist. Dazed, Darien broke away and reached for the hem of his shirt. "I don't think you're going to need this."

"Nope!" Sam pulled it over his head with enthusiasm and tossed it, and Darien had three seconds to enjoy the eye candy before he pulled her into his arms again. This time his kiss was deep and passionate; he lifted her off her feet, and she threw her arms around his neck, pouring every fierce ounce of her love for him into the kiss. There was nothing in the world but the familiar press of his body, his lips, and the thunder of his heart underneath her palm as it started to race.

Sam lowered her until her bare toes touched the soft carpet, then started to kiss his way down the side of her neck, nibbling at her shoulder. She let her hands wander up into his feather-soft hair as his fingers caught the hem of her shirt—

Pain erupted in Darien's ankle; it felt like something had sliced it with a knife. She cried out and Sam jerked back.

"Dar, I'm so sorry, did I hurt you?" He let his hands drop, and for maybe the first time ever, he looked like he didn't know what to do with them. His strong figure blurred in front of Darien as her eyes filled with tears.

"I'm so sorry," Sam repeated, and suddenly his warm hands were on her shoulders, steadying now instead of sultry. "I was trying to be careful with you and the baby but you said earlier you still want passion—"

"I'm fine, the baby's fine, you just ..." Darien closed her eyes as her foot twinged; a tear slid down one of her cheeks. "You *have* to watch your feet!"

Absolute bewilderment crossed Sam's face; he straightened. "What?"

"Look!" Darien pointed to her ankle. Even in the dark there was a visible wound, and though it didn't look as big as it felt, it *stung*. "You stepped on me again."

"No." Sam's frown deepened. "I can very confidently say that I did *not* step on your foot, not this time."

Darien stared at him, at the wounded look in his eyes and the way his bare chest still rose and fell unevenly, and the ugly little suspicion she'd managed to keep at bay for the last day finally reared its head.

"If *you* didn't ..." she whispered.

Fear flickered across Sam's strong features. "Oh, *hell* no."

"Sam ..." Every hair on the back of Darien's neck stood at attention. "What if they're here?"

Sam went predator-still. The shaft of moonlight falling through the window illuminated his eyes as they changed from molten silver to razor-edged steel. His head turned, first one way, then another. Darien scanned the room behind him, cursing how quickly the darkness had changed from accomplice to antagonist. Something warm trickled down the inside of her ankle, trailing over the arch of her foot.

Over by the bed, something rustled.

"Turn on the light!" she shrieked, but Sam was already most of the way across the room, his arm flashing white in the gloom as he hit the switch. Light flooded the suite, gleaming off polished wooden surfaces and elegant marble, brushing bright fingers across the cozy, white bed ... and throwing the grotesque shape beside it into sharp relief. It huddled on the carpet, all snarled black fur, clawed hands, and savage yellow eyes.

Darien screamed at the same time Sam yelled. He grabbed her arm and yanked her backward, toward the door. The creature growled, its lips pulling back to reveal a pair of sharp, gleaming incisors. Then, it scurried under the bed and was silent.

For a moment, Darien and Sam just stood there with their arms around each other, shaking.

"What did that look like to you?" Darien finally whispered.

Sam's eyes didn't move from where the creature had disappeared under the bed. "An aye-aye."

The breath went out of Darien's lungs in a rush.

"I assume they're not native to Hawaii," Sam murmured.

Darien shook her head, trying to steady her breathing. "Madagascar. And they're endangered, so the odds of one just wandering around *anywhere* are basically zero."

They stared at the spot where the creature had disappeared for a moment longer. Then Sam released her and took a tentative step forward.

"Sam—"

"I'm not going any closer, I just want to see ..." He crouched, squinting at the space under the bed. "Can you hand me my phone?"

Darien grabbed both their phones and handed Sam his. He turned on the flashlight, then pointed it under the bed. Darien knelt beside him. The beam was fairly diffused; it was hard to tell for sure, but it looked like ...

She turned on her own light and the second beam removed any doubt. The creature was gone, the space under the bed empty.

Sam looked at her. "There's no way it could've escaped without us seeing it."

Darien squeezed her phone, her fast heartbeat stinging in her ankle. Sam looked down at it, at the blood trickling into the arch of her foot and the small crimson stains on the carpet that showed exactly where she'd stepped. He took her hands, and she let him pull her upright, then lift her gently into his arms. "Let's get that cleaned up."

"I could've walked," she said, snuggling into his broad chest as he carried her toward the bathroom.

He kissed her on the forehead. "But it's easier to cuddle like this. Even if it's only for a second."

Carefully, Sam set Darien down on the edge of the jetted tub. She reached for the tap and closed her eyes as the cool water rushed over her ankle, splattering pink across the tub's white floor. It didn't take long for the crust and clotting to melt away, revealing a four-inch-long scratch that was deepest in the middle. Darien examined it, then breathed a sigh of relief.

"Do you think it needs stitches?" Sam asked. He kept glancing between her and the door, as if afraid the demon was going to come skittering through it at any moment.

"Probably not. It's pretty shallow. A couple of big Band-Aids should cover it, and I bet the hotel desk has those." She rubbed her eyes. "I'm not sure how much salt water I'll be wading in after this, though."

Sam cast a worried glance at her ankle, then let out a silent sigh. "I'm trying to decide what to do. Do we transfer rooms? Move hotels? Go home?" He rubbed his face absently, his eyebrows pulling into a thin line. "Any thoughts?"

"If we transfer rooms, it'll either follow us or terrorize the next tourists who are unfortunate enough to sleep here. Unless we want to call it and fly back to Colorado, and take our chances with whatever's there, I don't think there's any getting away from it."

"I think you're probably right. And I'm not sure going back to Colorado is the right answer, either."

Darien fiddled with the hem of her shirt. "What if ..."

Sam looked at her, his eyes questioning.

"What if we try and study it?" she asked.

Sam's eyebrows flew upward. "*Study* it? I was thinking *kill* it."

"If we have to, yes, but ..." Darien shifted, ignoring the pain in her foot. It had quit bleeding; as long as she took it easy for the night—or tried to—it would be fine. "Sam, it showed up as an aye-aye. *Exactly* what we were joking about this morning."

Disgust flickered across Sam's features. "How long do you think it's been here, watching us?"

She shuddered. "I don't think I want to know. But ... it's just too crazy to be a coincidence."

"So what, you think we ... *manifested* a demon?"

Darien shrugged. "I think we better find out. We wanted answers, right? Well, maybe here they are."

Sam was quiet for a moment, staring down at her ankle. Then, he met her eyes. "Well, if we're not safe here, we're not safe anywhere. And if we can influence them in some way then that's a game-changer, so we might as well experiment."

"Let's do it."

Sam stood, offering her a hand. "Let me check and make sure that monster isn't hiding under our bed, and then you can at least sit somewhere soft while we call the front desk. Then ..." He turned to look at her, his eyes dark with fear, frustration, and determination.

Darien returned his stare, anger burning into her very bones. "Then we've got plans to make."

Chapter Thirteen

I t was 9:30 when Ellie and Oliver shuffled into their hotel room. Ellie collapsed onto the closest bed and Oliver sank onto the other, a relieved look on his face.

"I'm glad we didn't try to keep going," he murmured.

"After sixteen hours on the road that included almost losing a fight with the Grim Reaper?" Ellie's eyes fell closed. "I couldn't have. I was at the end of my rope."

"I know you were. I wish you'd woken me up sooner."

Two quiet thuds drifted to Ellie's ears, then a soft rustling and a sigh, as if Oliver had kicked his shoes off and lain back on his bed, too. It was amazing how attuned she felt to him, even though he was halfway across the room and untouchable.

She rolled onto her back and winced. Her ribs, her face, her neck, her arm where the bowstring had bruised it—was there anything that didn't ache? She sighed, then stretched, working some of the last, lingering car-stiffness out of her body. Folding her arms over her stomach, she peeled her eyes open.

Oliver lay on his back, watching her, his eyes soft in that way that made her feel not just desired, but *cherished*. Ellie's throat constricted as emotion washed over her, sharp and wistful and all-consuming. Two tears leaked out of the corners of her eyes, dripping down her cheek and nose. They could have been for any reason—her pain, Oliver's pain, the horror they'd narrowly escaped at the border ... but maybe ...

Maybe it was because this moment felt peaceful, and that feeling was all but a stranger now.

Ellie wiped her eyes, drew in a deep breath, and pushed herself up. "Can you keep watch while I take a quick shower?"

"Yeah." Oliver sat up slowly, rubbing his eyes.

"Thanks." Ellie rose and rummaged in her suitcase. Clutching a bundle of clean clothes and other necessities, she stepped into the bathroom, then turned on the shower, trying not to imagine a demon sailing through the wall while she was stark naked and covered in soap.

Ten minutes later she padded out onto the thin carpet, dressed in a tank top and shorts with her hair up in a towel. Goosebumps rose on her skin as the cool, dry air washed over her, and she shivered.

Oliver rose from one of the comfy-looking chair by the window. "Feel better?"

"Much better." Ellie pulled the towel off her head and shuddered as her hair spilled across her shoulders in a wet, freezing tangle. "I always underestimate how chilly the world feels after getting out of the shower. Let me find my jacket and I'll switch you places."

Oliver bent and grabbed something out of his suitcase. "My sweatshirt's right here. Catch."

His gray-white hoodie sailed across the room like a limp, floppy ghost. Ellie caught it and pulled it gratefully over her head. The hoodie's fleece lining was soft against the skin of her shoulders, and it smelled like him.

Oliver scooped up his own pile of clean clothes and started toward her, grinning. "You look good in it."

"You might never get it back."

He laughed, short, low and genuine, his eyes crinkling at the corners. "That's fine."

"I'm holding you to that." Ellie stepped aside to let him pass, then took his seat by the window and pulled up a book on her phone. She probably wouldn't read much of it, but maybe having it close could help her stay more alert. "Enjoy your shower, Oliver."

"I will."

The door closed behind him. Ellie skimmed a few sentences, then looked out the window. The last bleed of the sun's color sat low on the horizon, fading every second she watched, leeched away by time and the ceaseless turn of the earth. Below her, the tiny town sprawled in a heap of streetlights and window lights, its edges swallowed up by the darkening Canadian wilderness.

Ellie pulled her legs up and wrapped her arms around them, resting her chin on her knees. The Northern Rockies were out there somewhere, brooding in the darkness. Throughout most of the day's drive they'd marched in a rigid line in the distance, lording over the flatlands like cold, arrogantly beautiful sentinels. Exploring them, especially—her skin tingled—exploring them with Oliver, would be incredible.

But now is not *the time.*

In that moment, she realized something. The fears she'd struggled with before the demons' escape—of getting outside her comfort zone, taking a risk, falling for some-one—they had all become muted. In fact, they almost seemed trivial. She felt like she'd aged ten years since her father's death. Maybe with all the shock, all the helplessness and heartache and rage, had come courage.

Or maybe she'd just graduated to larger fears.

Ellie buried her face in Oliver's sweatshirt, breathing in his sweet, masculine scent and imagining she was in his arms. After a second, she forced her eyes open and scanned the quiet street for anything strange-looking, but kept her nose and mouth tucked into the soft fabric. At least he was here with her. And at least they'd be safe tonight.

She frowned. *According to the parking lot ghost, that is.* But he'd known a lot of important things: that Oliver hadn't had a passport, how to get over the border, that the cameras were down—

A memory hit Ellie and she cocked her head, watching the meandering headlights of a passing car. *Death will find you.*

"Death," she whispered. The demon at the border had appeared to her as the Grim Reaper, and to Oliver as a gaunt, apocalyptic horseman. Had he somehow embodied what they each thought death looked like? The flesh on Ellie's back started to crawl. What kind of terrible power did *that* demon have, that he could read their darkest, most subconscious thoughts that quickly and then make himself *embody* them? Wormwood could hear every thought, read every emotion, and he was awful enough. But, presumably, he couldn't kill them, or they'd be dead already. The Reaper, on the other hand ...

We'd better beat him to the gate, or it'll be a bloodbath.

A quiet click floated through the air as the bathroom door opened. Oliver stepped out, wearing a black T-shirt and the same lounging pants he'd worn when they'd played games at the Calls' house all those eons ago. "That shower was wonderful. I almost didn't leave."

Wearily, Ellie uncurled herself and faced him, cross-legged. "Hey, I just thought of something."

"What's that?" He tossed his clothes into his suitcase and flopped down in the chair opposite her.

Quickly, Ellie told him about the parking lot ghost's odd wording, and her growing suspicion that it meant more than he had been able to express. "So when the ghost said 'death,' what if he meant capital-D Death? Not just 'you're going to die if you try to cross the border' but 'Death himself is coming for you'?"

Oliver sat back. "Now *there's* an interesting thought. It's possible, I guess."

"Why a horseman for you?"

"Bible story." He shrugged. "My mom dragged me to church a few times. I never felt like I understood what the preacher said, but I do remember a story about the Four Horsemen of the Apocalypse. Death—capital-D Death—was one of them. He rode a pale horse, which was exactly what I saw today."

"Huh." Ellie yawned, drooping. "And the Grim Reaper is obviously a cultural thing for me. He's pretty much everywhere, especially around Halloween." She scrubbed her hand over her eyes, grateful she didn't have to worry about smudging makeup. When she forced them open, Oliver was looking at her with deep sympathy.

"Let's finish this discussion tomorrow," he said. "You need to sleep."

Ellie cast a longing glance at the bed. "Are you sure? You didn't sleep as much as you needed to in the car—"

"Not all resting is sleeping." He smiled. "I got plenty of it talking to you and listening to stories about Stravinsky."

Ellie blinked. "You learned his name." A slow grin crossed her face as her heart warmed. "That brings me a ridiculous amount of happiness, Oliver."

"Good. Go to bed."

"Okay." Ellie stood; her head swam and her body still throbbed, but the sweet, melty feeling in her heart helped almost as much as the painkiller she'd taken right before her shower. She'd tottered halfway across the room before she realized she was still wearing Oliver's sweatshirt. Wrapping her arms around herself, she half-turned. "Do you want your hoodie back?"

"I'm not cold." His voice was so gentle, his outline an inky-black shadow against the navy sky. "If you want it, take it."

Ellie smiled. "Thanks, Oliver." She shuffled to the bed and lay down, nestling into the creamy sheets and soft, downy comforter, breathing in Oliver's comforting scent. "Wake me up in four hours. Promise."

"I promise."

"Don't try to be a martyr."

"I won't."

"You have problems with that."

"I know."

"I'm ..." She faded, her eyes fluttering closed. "I'm so glad ... you're ..." *here with me.*

The pain finally faded, and the world went dark.

***

Oliver gazed at the bed on the other side of the room where Ellie lay, sleeping silently in his sweatshirt. He was relieved she hadn't fought harder to take the first watch; she desperately needed the rest.

And he didn't know if his will would've held up. Not when he knew he was in for four more hours of mental torture.

That's right, lover boy. It's just you and me now.

A few weeks ago Oliver would've come up with a frustrated retort, made it as scathing as possible. Tonight, he just raised his phone and read a few more paragraphs of *White Fang.*

What's the matter, Ollie? Wolf got your tongue?

Oliver didn't reply.

Oh, you're no fun.

Oliver stood, slid his phone into his pocket, and stepped to the window, gazing out at the lights below. The night was clear and the stars winked overhead. Valleyview was a good size—big enough to have far more resources than Seldovia did, but not so big that its light blotted out the sky. It didn't afford the same view of the stars as Helen and Henry's house, or the Shack, but it was far better than a city the size of Denver, or even Anchorage.

Trying to distract yourself isn't going to work. You know I can outlast you.

Oliver folded his arms. *How many of you are there?*

Millions.

Oliver's mouth fell open; Wormwood had answered so quickly! And on the heels of his shock came fear, crawling through his veins as that single, ruinous word sunk in. He took a deep, silent breath, making himself relax. Wormwood was a liar; there was no way there could be that many demons—

Because the world would've ended by now? Is that what you're thinking?

Yes. And Ellie and I wouldn't be halfway across Alberta. So you must all be incompetent, then. Oliver let a tiny, humorless chuckle escape his lips. *That's comforting.*

We're far from incompetent. Wormwood sounded like he was bristling, as if, for once, Oliver had gotten to him.

Oliver smirked, his eyes tracking a rabbit as it crossed the hotel sidewalk. *Not from what I've seen.*

You're one to talk. Face it, Ollie: the only reason you're still alive is sheer dumb luck and because you hide behind people who are way better than you.

Oliver clenched his teeth, but he couldn't stop their faces from flashing through his mind. His mother, Ellie, Helen, Henry, Bill, Robert—

They're fighting so hard. And all you've done this whole time is fail them. You couldn't die for them, you left Helen and Henry behind to suffer, you hid behind your girl today and let her take the fall—literally.

Cold sweat prickled on Oliver's forehead. He put his hands to his temples, as if it would help, as if he had any control at all over the monster in his head.

You know it's true.

"I know you're a liar," Oliver whispered.

When we've all awakened, you'll know I wasn't lying. Well, you'll be dead, but your ghost will know.

Awakened? Oliver managed a derisive snort. *That explains a lot, if a bunch of you are sleeping on the job.*

Quip all you want, Ollie. It won't change its inevitability. This world is horrific on its own; it didn't even need *our help. There's so much food out there ... it won't be long.*

Oliver lowered his hands, crossing his arms over his chest again. *If you kill us all, then what will you eat?*

For a moment, his mind went totally, blissfully silent. Then ...

How many cattle ranches have you driven by in the last two days? Wormwood let out a grating cackle. *And you* still *didn't put it together on your own.*

Oliver felt like he might throw up. He sank down in the chair Ellie had sat in, clutching its arm so hard his knuckles went death-white in the light of the streetlamp. He had nothing to say. Nothing at all. Not when dying had just become the fate of the lucky.

You know nothing is going to come through the window, right?

I don't know that.

Why would we do that when we can just float through a wall and you'd never see us coming?

Oliver closed his eyes. Wormwood had a point. He sighed, rubbing his hand through his hair. *As long as we're just chatting, tell me. Why don't you headache me all the time?*

There are different kinds of suffering. I try to maximize all of them.

Oliver's eyes opened; they felt puffy. *I barely ever touch Ellie now. We've got a good system down—*

Except when she gets hurt, which is going to be a lot, since you're incompetent.

Oliver flexed the hand he'd nearly broken against the Calls' cabin wall the first time he'd tried to punch Wormwood, and took a deep, controlled breath. *At least you have your limits.*

What gives you that idea?

Your wording. It implies prioritization. People—beings—who have unlimited resources don't need to do that. Oliver smiled, thin-lipped and razor-edged. *You're still making mistakes, Wormwood.*

This time, the silence stretched. A minute ticked by, then another, and another. Oliver let himself gaze over at Ellie's dark shape for a few seconds, then lifted his phone again. A sentence, a glance out the window. A short paragraph, a scan of the room.

And nothing from Wormwood.

Oliver wasn't foolish enough to think the demon had actually gone; he had too many dark, lonely nights of experience. Foreboding started to build in the back of his mind, layered with anxiety, with shame, with a cocktail of unpleasant thoughts and emotions. Smoke and fire and imminent, horrific death. The gang and that girl's scared brown eyes, the way she'd looked at him like he was a monster. Memories of his mother's wan, pinched face, of watching his friends' fathers pick them up from school with a deep longing that he didn't think he'd ever be able to put into words.

Could he ever, *ever* be good enough for the people in his life?

Oliver ran a hand through his still-damp hair. In—he squinted at the glowing clock on the bedside table—three hours and forty-five minutes, he could sleep. He could escape. He could make it that long; he'd done it before, and that was without Ellie in the room, quietly snoring through her swollen sinuses, comforting him just by virtue of her presence.

Oliver settled back in his chair, going still except for his silent breathing and the constant darting of his eyes.

***

"Ellie."

Even in sleep, Ellie still felt Oliver's low voice like a caress. But this time, it wasn't entirely welcome.

"Ellie. Ellie, wake up."

The aches were the next thing to break through the silent, wonderful blackness of her deep sleep. Her neck, her side where she'd hit the cab of the truck, her face and nose where the bow had smacked into it, and ...

A tiny moan escaped her lips. The inside of her left arm burned like it had been lit on fire.

"I'm so sorry to wake you up, El."

Ellie cracked her eyes open. Oliver knelt by the bed, propped against it on one carefully-placed elbow. The moon had risen while she slept; its faint, silvery light haloed his head but made it impossible to see his face. His voice, though ... now that she was more or less conscious, she realized that his voice sounded utterly spent.

"S'okay." She pushed herself upright, pulling tendrils of now-dry hair out of her face. "Scoot so I don't accidentally touch you."

Oliver stood. "How do you feel?"

Like I almost got beat to death by ... Death? Ellie rose, exhaling her impulse to wince, hoping the moonlight wasn't so bright that he could see the pain on her face. If he could, he'd probably do something noble and stupid like try and stay up all night so she could go back to bed. "A little better. My arm's the worst but it's all superficial."

"Good." Oliver slumped onto the other bed. "I'm glad."

"How're you?"

Oliver let out a stifled groan. "Been better. Nothing some sleep won't fix, though."

"How's your stomach?"

"Fine. Healing." He stretched out on the bed with an audible sigh.

Ellie's heart twinged. She stuffed her hands in the pocket of Oliver's hoodie and picked her way to the chairs by the window. "Your hands? Your lungs? *Your* neck bruises?"

"My lungs are fine. My bruises are almost gone. My hands hurt, but I can live with it."

"Do you need Tylenol?"

"No." His words were starting to slur. "Won't be awake that long."

"Are you sure?" Ellie half-stood. "I can get you one—"

"It's just like … the first week on the fishing boat. My hands hurt then … too …"

Ellie hovered between sitting and standing for far too long before she realized he wasn't going to finish that sentence. She blinked at his prone form; he had one hand on his chest and the other by his side, half-outstretched toward her. His eyes were closed, but even in sleep his face looked drawn. Hugging herself, Ellie buried her face in his sweatshirt again, and an idea struck her.

She stood, padded across the room to her bed, and tugged off the soft, downy comforter, still warm from her body heat. Crossing the aisle, she draped it carefully across Oliver. He didn't move, but she thought he looked more peaceful, more comfortable that way.

And all without touching him or waking him up, she thought with no small amount of pride, settling back in the chair. *It's the little victories.*

Ellie pulled up her eBook, then started the routine: read, then scan, then read, then scan again. Overall, it was an effective system; though it didn't totally drive away the drowsiness, it kept it at bay.

For the first two hours, at least.

Sometime around 4:30, Ellie stood and started pacing. Oliver hadn't moved since falling asleep and she was grateful she could hear his deep, soft breathing. It put her at ease. She did some stretches, skimmed an email about the symphony rehearsal schedule, scrolled aimlessly through some of her friends' social media posts … and sighed as her eyes returned to the window every time.

Would she still relate to any of them when she got back? She'd never be able to tell her friends; never be able to talk about this with anyone except Darien, Sam, the Calls, and the beautiful, broken man sleeping behind her.

That's it. That's the answer. Your family is now the people who know what's really going on and will love you through it. Don't let any of them go.

Five-thirty came and went. Quietly, Ellie rummaged through the closet, casting glances out the window every few seconds until she found a spare blanket. Relieved that Canada followed the same noble tradition as American hotels of shoving one in a room *somewhere*, she curled up in the chair and draped it over her legs.

Only an hour to go.

A few deer crossed the road, but nothing else moved. Lights started flickering on in the houses and restaurants below. The horizon was lightening, just barely. Ellie leaned her cheek against the chair's roughish upholstery and started to let herself relax. It wouldn't be long now and she'd wake Oliver, then they'd get back on the road and she could take a nice, long car nap ... she'd definitely earned it ...

***

Get up.

Oliver was lying on Helen and Henry's oversized, comfortable couch. A fire burned low in the hearth, cheerfully crackle-popping its way into ash, and in his arms, sleeping peacefully, lay Ellie.

For a second, he was stunned. There was no headache, no leering giggle in the back of his mind, no shame.

He was *free.*

Oliver tightened his arms around Ellie, pulling her flush against his chest. She let out a sleepy little sigh and tucked her head under his chin but didn't wake up, and Oliver, baffled but overjoyed, was content to just savor this moment. She smelled delicious, like the Mexican vanilla Helen used in her cookies, and her hair spilled across the bare skin of his chest in lustrous brown waves—

The bare skin of his chest?

Oliver's eyes widened, and he moved—not enough to wake Ellie but enough to tell him that he was, indeed, wearing pants. He raised his head just slightly, taking in her dimly lit form. She was dressed in her warm, flannel pajamas.

Flummoxed, he let his head fall back against the soft pillows. He'd *never* wander around without a shirt, not even in his aunt and uncle's house—it still made him feel too vulnerable. The only way it would have come off was if she'd taken it off. And he was pretty sure he would have remembered that.

"Get up, Oliver."

Oliver jerked his head up so quickly his throat started to hurt. Henry was standing by the door, stock-still.

"How long've you been there?" Oliver's voice was hoarse, his body leaden, as if he hadn't moved or talked to anyone in hours. They were clothed enough—and in the middle of the *living room*—that Oliver didn't think anything beyond mild canoodling had happened, but he still felt embarrassed.

Henry didn't move, but his voice got louder. "GET. UP."

Oliver frowned. It wasn't Henry's voice; it was the other one. The one that told him to run from the horseman, the one who helped him at the gate, and in the fire, and …

He gasped as he remembered. The man behind him on the airplane, when he'd first flown to Denver. The incompetent EMT.

They all had the same voice.

GET UP RIGHT NOW!

Oliver bolted upright, cursing as he found himself tangled in a massive white comforter that smelled like Ellie—she must have pulled it over him while he was asleep. The sun beamed through the open window, lighting the room like it was midday. A patch of light half-draped itself over the chairs, illuminating the limp figure curled up in the leftmost one, huddled under a thin blanket.

MOVE! SHE'S ALMOST HERE!

"Ellie!" Oliver scrambled out of bed. The figure in the chair jerked and a rush of pure relief went through him; she was okay. He pivoted, rushing to grab their things from the bathroom. "Ellie, wake up!" He grabbed things off the counter and threw them in bags just as Ellie's curse hit his ears.

"I'm so sorry, Oliver, I didn't mean to—"

Oliver darted out of the bathroom, glanced at the clock, and nearly stumbled. It was almost 11 a.m.

"Put your stuff in your suitcase," he said, "and keep your eyes up while you do it because something's coming."

Ellie's face was bright red, her eyes full of tears, but she sprang into action anyway, stuffing yesterday's clothes into the case, pulling on her socks, lacing up her tennis shoes— "You think it's the Lady?"

"I don't know. I just know we have to go."

Ellie's face went from red to sheet-pale so fast that Oliver was afraid she might faint. "That would be horrifyingly fast."

"We did give her over thirteen hours to work with."

Ellie closed her eyes. "I'm so sorry, I can't *believe* I—"

"It's done now. Let's just get out alive." He tugged his suitcase after him. "Come on. We can get dressed after we put some distance between us and here."

"Yep. Let's—"

A ribbon of black flashed at the corner of Oliver's vision. He didn't stop to think, just dove at Ellie, flattening her to the floor as a searing burst of heat and light cracked overhead. Ellie gasped underneath him but he didn't have time to feel guilt—or the headache. He just flipped, coming to his feet as pressure started to constrict his throat—

He stumbled, heaving. It was worse this time; the Lady was going straight for the kill. Through watery eyes, Oliver made himself look up. The demon was hovering between them and the door, the ends of her rotting cloak twitching like dying fish. A low crackling sound reached his ears a second before the stench of smoke curled into his nostrils.

Oliver panicked.

His vision fogged, spiraled; he stumbled to one knee. He couldn't *breathe. The smoke was all around him, choking him, ripping his lungs open from the inside out. He was back in the Luxembourg House and Silverskin was going to flay him alive and then do the same to Ellie—*

Something struck living flesh with a horrible crunch. The sound penetrated Oliver's mental maelstrom like a lighthouse beam, and the pressure on his throat released. He gasped, his head clearing—it was the Lady, not Silverskin, and they were in a hotel, not the Luxembourg House. The smoke ...

The smoke was real, though, as was the growing, nightmare roar of a structure fire.

Something heavy thunked against Oliver's foot; he kicked out at it, sending it skittering away before realizing it was the alarm clock. An instant later Ellie stepped up next to him, clutching one of the long, wicked hunting knives they'd bought in Montana. For a split second, Oliver stared at her, putting it all together. She'd hurled the clock at the Lady, buying him enough time to breathe again, to get himself under control.

"Nice—" he started.

But the Lady twisted back around, her gaunt hands falling from her face, which was still contorted in pain. She snarled at them, tendrils of bluish-white energy starting to arc between her skeletal fingers.

Ellie shrieked, grabbed his hand, and pulled, taking them both to the threadbare green carpet between the beds. He threw his body over hers as the heat and blinding light arced over them again. Ellie cried out, and Oliver had a sudden, awful vision of the knife blade driving deep into her body, of her scarlet blood covering the carpet, splattering the white bedding—

The lightning cut off. Oliver looked up, coughing as the smoke thickened. Flames were devouring the bed he'd slept in the night before, licking at the walls. A jolt of adrenaline shot through him; it wasn't just *their* lives at stake anymore.

"Now's our chance," Ellie breathed. She pressed the hilt of the knife into Oliver's hand and he nearly went weak with relief when he saw that it was gleaming and unstained.

"Get her." Ellie's eyes burned up into his. "I'll get the other knife."

Oliver grinned down at her. "Or you could just throw a lamp."

Then, he leaped to his feet and dove for the Lady. The demon's death-black eyes went wide with shock; she obviously thought her last bolt had killed them.

"Nope," Oliver snarled, and plunged the knife into her side.

The Lady screamed, a high, keening wail that Oliver knew would bring security down on them in minutes. He twisted the hilt, driving it deeper, cutting upward until he hit something that felt like bone. It stopped the knife dead but Oliver jerked it sideways, tearing the blade out of her back instead. The demon bowed in agony.

"Can't handle a little pain?" Oliver growled, then struck again. The blade hurtled through empty air.

Oliver stumbled, then shook himself, realizing the way was clear. "Ellie, the door!"

She was already at his side, coughing from the smoke but with a snarl on her face, clutching one of the tarnished bedside lamps in her hand. Oliver grabbed her hand, ignoring the shiver of pain in his head, and they bolted for the door, the Lady still screaming and writhing behind them. They flung themselves out into the hallway just as the fire alarm went off.

"About damn time," Ellie gasped. An instant later the sprinklers whirred to life, showering them with freezing water.

"You have the keys?" Oliver coughed, throwing the door to the stairwell open.

"Yeah," Ellie panted as she rushed past him and down the stairs. "Lost the other knife, though. You have your wallet?"

"Yep."

"Okay."

They sprinted across the parking lot and dove into the truck. Despite the abuse it had taken yesterday and how beat-up it looked, it still started with a roar that Oliver could have sworn was defiant. Ellie threw it in reverse and Oliver looked up at the window that had been theirs. Flames wreathed it, writhing and devouring, but maybe ... maybe with the sprinklers, they could still be brought under control. There was no sign of the Lady.

They peeled out of the parking lot and headed north, both panting like they'd run much farther than they actually had. Oliver's heart didn't start to calm down until they'd left the hotel and the distant wail of sirens far behind.

Neither did his Wormwood headache.

"So ..." Ellie said once they were far enough from Valleyview that the whole town was visible in the rearview mirror. "That went better than yesterday. Aside from me ..." Her cheeks colored. "... sleeping in."

Oliver shook his head, remembering his own exhaustion after throwing himself head-first into the life of a commercial fisherman. This was more than comparable. And she wasn't used to it at all. "I understand. It still wasn't great, but believe me, I get it. And actually ..." He let a small smile curve his lips. "Not only did we survive, but we hurt the Lady pretty badly. That's something to celebrate, if you ask me."

"What'd you do to her? All I saw was lots of flailing."

"I stabbed her. If she were human, she'd be dead, but ..."

"But she's not." Ellie's eyes darkened. "Still, I bet she won't be coming after us for a while. Which is good, because unless we want to drive thirty more hours and fight who knows how many more demons in our pajamas, we need to buy clothes."

Rage.

It was all Wormwood felt; it consumed his mind. But it was the tight, perfect control of it, not its scorching intensity, that scared him the most. Death had learned how to weaponize it, use it as fuel.

"She's not incompetent," Wormwood said.

"She has one last chance," Death replied.

Wormwood watched a little town whiz by out the truck's window and couldn't help the longing he felt. All those people ... and they weren't fighting nearly as hard as Ollie. They'd be so deliciously easy. If there was one thing humans were prone to, it was pride, and therefore, shame. It was everywhere ... everywhere ... he could feel it ...

"She will heal quickly," Death said. "We share that advantage with the humans. She is already pursuing them."

"That's good." Wormwood hesitated, then decided to voice the little thought that had been nagging at his mind for the last few hours. "I feel ... like I'm not meant to be this bound to you."

For a moment there was silence, and Wormwood felt something from Death. Displeasure? Uneasiness?

"I can bind anyone I wish," Death finally said. "Other than your privileged position as spy, you are no different."

A particularly decadent individual called to him somewhere in the near distance, but disappeared just as quickly.

"You have a job, Wormwood." Death's voice had turned silky, predatory.

"I know."

In an instant, Death's voice—and his rage—vanished. Wormwood was alone again.

Chapter Fourteen

Sam jerked his leg up and scrambled backward across the creamy white couch, shuddering. There was a flash of gray-black fur, a weird, chittering hiss, and then silence. The goosebumps didn't stop, though. They just slithered across Sam's skin like water from an icy shower.

Except ... less pleasant.

"Are you okay? Did he hurt you?"

Sam wrenched his eyes up to where Darien sat cross-legged on the bed, fully clothed, staring at the space between the couch and the floor where Ankle Tickler had just disappeared. Earlier that morning, they'd come up with a plan to lure the demon out on *their* terms. A few minutes ago, Sam had moved to the couch—the only other place in their room with a gap big and dark enough to hide the creature—and took up his post there. Then, they'd both lowered their bare feet to the ground and waited.

Luckily—or maybe horrifyingly, Sam hadn't made up his mind yet—the demon had taken the bait almost immediately, latching onto his ankle with greedy little fingers that felt like cold nails pressed against his flesh. Over the last few days, he'd tried to sympathize with Darien as she'd grappled with her skittishness. But after feeling *that*, he wasn't sure how she hadn't torn this place apart.

"I'm good." Sam rolled his ankle, which—other than that lingering cold-nails sensation—was completely fine. "No cut, not even a bruise."

"Sam ..." Darien's eyes flicked to his, excitement taking the place of the fear. "I think our manifesting idea is working. I think we can have some degree of control over them."

"I hope so, Dar. I didn't give him a lot of time to work with, but—"

"True, but as we learned last night, he doesn't need much time to leave a mark. *And* he looks healthier this morning."

Sam's eyebrows went up. "I mean, I know you love animals but he isn't *actually* an aye-aye. It doesn't matter how healthy he is—"

"No, listen. Remember when we were first joking about a demon that just ran around grabbing ankles?"

"Yes." Sam beat back the heavy sigh threatening to escape. He remembered—especially the *joking* part.

"You said something about it looking like a sick, creepy version of an aye-aye. Well, when I was up watching TV last night so I didn't fall asleep, I actively imagined him as a healthy, normal aye-aye. And now ... well, I wouldn't say he's healthy or normal, but he looks more like a creature from our world with really bad mange than an alien monster."

She squinted at the dark space underneath Sam.

"Can you see it?" he asked.

"Not unless he can camouflage himself." Darien's eyes widened and she fixed him with a stare. "Which he *can't do*. Quick: actively imagine him *not* being able to camouflage himself."

"Oh, I'm imagining. We don't want to be dealing with that."

"Okay. So he must have gone through the wall, like the Dark Lady did in Ellie's room. There's no other way out."

"How did he touch me if he isn't solid?"

Darien shrugged. "I don't know. Magic?"

Sam gave a weird, strangled chuckle. He didn't know why; it was mostly a vain attempt to bridge the part of him that said *it is what it is* with the part that still screamed *none of this makes sense*.

"Let's run one more experiment," Darien said. "You take a second and imagine him as a healthy aye-aye."

"I don't really know what—hang on." Sam pulled his phone out of his pants pocket. "All of human knowledge at my fingertips and I'm using it to look at pictures of one of the weirdest animals on the planet."

Darien snorted. "And yet somehow, the picture's now relevant on what might be a world-saving level."

Still studying the picture, Sam allowed himself a grin. "Life's weird." He looked up. "Ready?"

"Yep." She uncrossed her legs and scooted toward the edge of the bed.

"Wait—" Sam started.

"Listen, I don't think he's going to hurt us anymore. I think we've ... tamed him? Gentled him? And even if he does ..." Darien wiggled the toes on her injured ankle. Or rather, her *formerly* injured ankle. The cut's shallow edges had sealed without leaving a mark, and only a crusty scab remained over its deeper middle. "It'll heal."

Sam couldn't help but shake his head in wonder. She was right; at the rate the cut was healing, it would be gone by lunchtime. It was nothing short of supernatural—just like Ellie's bruises had been after the Lady's attack in Portlock. He'd passed that off as simple good luck: the injury must have been much less severe than they'd first thought. Now he just tried not to think about it so the guilt didn't eat at him as much.

"Plus, if he runs out from under the couch, we'll know he was hiding under there the whole time," Darien said. "If not, we can assume he walks through walls and just went around."

"Or became invisible." Sam frowned. "But if he could become invisible, why would he *ever* show himself to us? I'd think that would be a liability. And the unseen monster is always scarier than the seen."

"That's what I'm thinking." Darien dangled one foot over the edge, looking apprehensive but determined. "Are you ready?"

I'll never be ready to watch you put yourself at risk. But Sam just said, "Yep."

Darien lowered her foot to the floor, her bare toes curling on the clean, thick rug. "He's healthy, remember? He's a healthy, normal aye-aye."

"Yep." Sam glanced at the picture on his phone again, willing the demon to look like the creature he saw there. And, more importantly, willing it not to be violent. If it hurt his wife again, he'd rip it limb from limb—starting with its healthy, normal-looking aye-aye ankles.

"The waiting is the worst part," Darien murmured. "I wish he'd just get it over with."

"Maybe he decided bacon's better than human terror and went downstairs to have breakfast."

Darien laughed. "Well, if he doesn't get out here soon, I'm going to give up and go shove *my* face full of bacon—"

A flash of dark fur.

Sam yelled at the same time Darien shrieked. He was off the couch and two steps across the room before he knew what he was doing, but stopped dead as Darien threw up a hand.

"Wait!"

To Sam's shock, she lowered her other foot to the floor. "He didn't hurt me, and we need another look."

"You're *sure* he didn't hurt you?"

"Yes. Now please go sit down, or your giant football physique will scare him off."

"I doubt that," Sam grumbled, walking backward. He wasn't going to take his eyes off Darien for even a second. "I know firsthand how tempting your legs are."

She shot him a grin.

And then they waited some more.

"Maybe he's given up," Sam finally said.

Darien's eyebrows contracted. "How afraid of him are you now?"

"Honestly? Still some, but not as much as I was before."

"Me neither. I'm wondering ... now that our dread is gone and he's out in the open, do you think it's harder for him to get enough to ... eat? Or however that works?"

Sam shrugged. "That'd make sense. It would contribute to their desire for secrecy." He cocked her head, studying Darien as she stared down at her feet, her hands folded in her lap. The gentle rub of her right thumb over the ring on her left hand was the only sign of her nerves.

"There may be no one on earth better suited to tame a demon than you, you know that?" he asked softly.

Darien glanced up, surprise in her eyes. "Why's that?"

"Because you can have compassion for something as ugly as an aye-aye, for starters."

She grinned. "They're not that ugly."

"*And* you're amazingly brave. Do you know how many people would do what you're doing right now?"

"You did."

"That's true, but—"

"The house my family lived in when I was really young had a mouse problem," she said. "It was a good, solid house and we loved it, but every winter they'd get in and get everywhere. We'd see them scampering around in the day, hear them all night long ..." She grimaced. "They'd run over our feet sometimes. So, I'm a little desensitized."

"That's nasty. We'd get them, too, but never that bad."

To his surprise, Darien smiled. "Ana and Sophie and I would try to save them. We made a live trap out of a bucket and some peanut butter, and—"

She gasped, and Sam looked down in time to see clawed fingers wrap around her foot. He leaped up, but Darien shook her head. "He's not hurting me."

"He's scaring you."

"Fear won't kill me."

Sam perched on the edge of the couch, coiled like he was waiting for the snap. Another skeletal little hand wound its way around Darien's other foot, and she shuddered visibly.

"What about the baby?"

"The baby's fine, Sam. This isn't …" She let out a strangled little half-laugh. "This isn't that much scarier than an organic chem test."

"I …" *disagree?* But he didn't dare say it; he didn't know *what* to do other than not break Darien's concentration. They needed this information. Ellie and Oliver, Helen and Henry … if they could find *anything* the Alaskans could use to their advantage, they had to do it.

Sam only wished it'd been him Ankle Tickler had chosen to torment instead of his pregnant wife.

He leaned to one side, flattening himself against the couch so he could peer around Darien's ankles at the creature hiding behind them. It had curled up behind her legs like a hiding cat, doing its best not to be observed.

"Can you see him?" Darien whispered.

"Not well." Still … Sam squinted. He could just make out the curve of what might have been its rump. Though the fur was still black, it looked thicker, and a few little white hairs poked up, catching the daylight streaming through the balcony's glass door.

"I think he looks more normal, Dar."

She let out a shaky breath. "Okay, maybe try coming closer. Slowly, though."

"I'll be careful." Sam slipped off the couch onto his hands and knees, craning his neck. The demon didn't move.

Sam crawled left but the demon shifted, too, putting Darien's feet between him and it. Inwardly, Sam cursed. There was no clear line of sight, though he did have a perfect view of the long, spidery fingers still wrapped around his wife's ankles.

"You just know how to torture all of us, don't you," he muttered.

The fingers shifted, and Darien let out a string of Spanish curse words.

Sam's stomach clenched. "Hang in there, babe."

He inched forward, then some more, pulling his phone out of his pocket as he went. The demon still huddled behind Darien. Sam stopped and turned on his flashlight, then started forward again. "I'm going to keep coming, and he'll probably run. I'll try and get a good look at him before he goes through a wall—"

A strange little face popped out from behind Darien's feet and fixed Sam with an orange-eyed stare. He froze; he couldn't help it. Those eyes were so much more feral, so much *hungrier* than the animals' in the pictures had been. Then, he flipped his phone up, shining the flashlight straight into its eyes.

The thing hissed, revealing two buck teeth, a long tongue, and pink, healthy gums. Then it darted under the bed and through the wall.

Sam only felt the slightest discomfort that *that* was the thing that surprised him least. *I'm getting better at this.* He stood, then sat heavily next to Darien and pulled her into his arms. Despite her apparent composure, she was trembling, and didn't protest at all when he pulled her into his lap.

"That went shockingly well," she said.

"It did. I thought I'd end up trying to kill it. And probably failing. But here we all are, alive and unhurt." He looked down into her eyes. "He didn't hurt you, right?"

"No. He just ... tickled my ankles. Which was really, really weird and unpleasant."

"I'm sure." Sam hugged her tighter. "You're amazing. I'll buy you all the food and we can do anything you want today."

Darien chuckled. "Deal. Let's eat bacon and go see a lava cave."

"You got it."

"But before we go, let's recap."

Sam hid a smile. *Always the scientist.*

"We've learned we can affect how they look and act based on how we imagine them. Which is *huge*."

"It is huge. And based on the fact that Ankle Tickler is here crashing our honeymoon, I think it's safe to assume the demons are everywhere. Likely worldwide."

"Though why they aren't destroying everyone and everything is beyond me," Darien said. "You'd think there'd be more chaos."

Sam frowned. "What were you watching last night?"

"*Titanic.*"

"That explains it. I turned on the local news during my watch and things are getting ... weird. Crime spikes, three murders in one night, that kind of thing. Then I got curious and checked one of the national channels, and ..." He shook his head. "I'll spare you the details. I'm sure you'll hear about them later, but ..."

"That bad?"

Sam thought about the people whose faces he'd seen flash across the screen, the causes of their deaths, the sheer, overwhelming statistics—and that was only what he'd had the stomach to watch. He swallowed and forced a wry smile. "I wouldn't want to ruin your honeymoon or anything."

Darien snorted. "My honeymoon's fine. All I need is you." Her stomach gave a massive grumble. "And bacon."

"Let's go get you some, then." Sam let her go. Her feet touched the floor and she moved to the center of the room, away from anything that could conceal Ankle Tickler.

"Want to call Ellie and Oliver over breakfast?" she asked as she slipped on her sandals.

"Yes." Sam slipped on his sandals. "Has she texted you at all today?"

"No."

"Me neither." Sam swallowed his nerves and opened the door for Darien. "After you, my beautiful wife."

She smiled, brushing against Sam as she stepped into the hallway, the heady scent of her fruity shampoo stirring such wonderful memories. Part of him wanted to just take her back to Denver, leave this place and the demon behind. But he knew what was waiting for him there. And he didn't want to see how it had evolved in the two days they'd been gone, not even if there *was* a way to change it.

Sam looked back, casting his eyes around the sunlit room, but nothing stirred.

The other option, said a small voice in his heart, *is to go to Alaska.*

He scowled, pulled the door shut, and turned to follow Darien.

***

A late, decadent, bacon-filled breakfast later, Sam and Darien strolled out to their rental car. Sam couldn't help but check the space between the car and the asphalt for a pair of mad orange eyes before getting in, but there were none.

Of course it would only bother us in our hotel room, Sam thought morosely as he slid into the rich leather seat. *And don't think of its eyes as mad, either. They're ... friendly ... adorable ... demon eyes.*

He sighed. Now that he was aware of them, it seemed like his brain made assumptions and connections about the demon a mile a minute. Keeping his thoughts deliberate was a feat by itself.

"Ready?" Darien asked.

Sam shook himself. "Yeah. Just trying to keep our pet demon visualized correctly in my brain so he doesn't try and rip our feet off while we sleep or something."

"I know the feeling. My entire brain feels like a rabbit hole." She rubbed her eyes. "I thought it was just pregnancy."

"Nope," Sam said as he pulled out of the parking garage and onto the street. "You're not alone."

"It's making me wonder ..." Darien leaned back and cracked the window open, letting the warm, humid air spill into the sedan. Sam waited as she gathered her thoughts. "It makes me wonder how effective this thought-control thing might actually be."

Sam hit the gas and the car whirred onto one of the local highways. "I've wondered that, too. Especially since it seems like everyone who sees the demon has to be in agreement to make any major changes."

Darien nodded. "I don't think we have a prayer of changing one like the Dark Lady, not when she's *literally* legendary."

Sam tightened his grip on the steering wheel, frustration bitter in the back of his throat. Had this whole morning just been an exercise in futility?

"Why don't we call Ellie and Oliver," he sighed.

"On it." Darien whipped out her phone and dialed, then put it on speaker.

Ellie picked up on the third ring. "Hey. Give me a second, we've got to finish checking out."

Darien frowned. "Checking out? Isn't it, like, one o'clock there?"

Oliver's voice crackled over the speaker, interrupted by a weird, tinny beeping, but Sam couldn't make out what he said. He exchanged a bewildered glance with Darien as Ellie made a muffled reply.

" ... here, take my card." Her voice became clearer. "We're in a Walmart. Not a hotel. Sorry, Oliver's going to finish checking out while I fill you in."

"We've got some stories for you, too," Sam said. "Very important ones."

"Did you have a nice chat with Hawaiian Bigfoot on a beach or something?"

"No, but Darien got her foot cut open by a demon."

Silence.

"*What?*" Ellie finally asked. Then, muffled again, "Darien got hurt. By a *demon.*"

Oliver's response was indistinct, but his shocked tone was not. Ellie mumbled something back. Or maybe she was trying to talk to *them*; Sam couldn't tell, especially after a new sound echoed over the receiver: the brittle clatter of a shopping cart bouncing over asphalt.

He fought the temptation to close his eyes in frustration. "We're having a hard time hearing you, El—"

"Sorry, we're on the run from the Lady. Like, *seriously* on the run. Our first priority is getting stuff loaded and then once we're in the car we can talk."

"Want to call us back?" Darien asked.

"No, I'll bet we can do this in two minutes or less. Hang on, I'm chucking you in the passenger's seat."

There was a muffled thump, then quiet, punctuated occasionally by more far-away thumps and the sound of Ellie and Oliver's voices. Seconds later, they heard a door slam, then Ellie's voice came over the line again. "We're good. I'm putting you on speaker. I assume we're talking to both of you?"

"Yep," Darien said. "Who wants to go first?"

"You guys go first," Sam broke in. "I feel like we have the good news, so we should save it for last." *And I have to know what's going on with you before I have a heart attack.*

Oliver snorted. "The best news we have to offer is that we're alive."

"And we now have clothes. And toiletries," Ellie muttered.

"*What?*" Sam asked. "Did you lose your suitcases or something?"

"Yes. This morning," Ellie said. "The Lady attacked us and we barely got out with our lives, let alone our stuff."

"But," Oliver said, "we've learned some interesting things about the demons. Things you need to know now that they're everywhere."

Sam set his jaw. "Tell us everything."

What followed was one of the most harrowing stories Sam had ever heard. With each word, his tension ratcheted higher. Darien finally slipped a hand over his, tracing her fingers up his arm. She looked frightened.

"So let me get this straight," Sam said. "The Lady's attacked you twice and can shoot lightning now, and nearly burned down a hotel."

"Yep," Ellie said.

"She can also shake off a stab wound that would kill a person, so killing them still isn't simple."

"Yep."

"And Oliver has a guardian angel who will only talk to Ellie, and he still can't get rid of Wormwood."

"Yep."

"Not for lack of trying," Oliver muttered.

"And Wormwood's somehow contacting other demons and setting them on you," Sam went on. "Like the one who attacked you while you were chopping up the Canadian border fence, who seemed to conform to your *individual* ideas about how death is personified."

"Yep."

Sam exchanged a significant glance with Darien.

"I think you're going to find our news really interesting," she said.

"But first," Sam said, "and I'm sorry to be so pedantic, but I want to make *sure* we're on the same page. You've also noticed that the demons can switch between solid and ... and ghost-y?"

"Incorporeal?" Darien suggested.

"Yes," said Oliver.

"Okay," Sam said. "And they can only be hurt when they're solid ..."

"Which means you pretty much have to wait until they're actively attacking you," Ellie said.

Sam let out a long, slow breath, caught between pride at her courage and terrified rage that she was in the situation in the first place. Darien started rubbing his shoulder again. "And Oliver's in Canada illegally, so you can't get hurt or pulled over."

"Yep. And we ... I'm so sorry, Sam, but your truck is ..."

"It's wrecked," Oliver said.

Sam shook his head. "I don't care about the truck. I just want you two to stay alive."

Ellie let out a humorless laugh. "We're doing our best."

There was a moment of silence, broken by Oliver. "How about that good news?"

"Well, it's good and bad," Darien said, then told them everything they'd learned in the last twenty-four hours. Sam added in an occasional comment, but mostly he just listened, glancing at the ocean every once in a while.

"So clearly the demons are everywhere, because I'd imagine Hawaii would be one of the *last* places to be invaded," Darien finished. "But here's the good news: we can influence them. At least, Sam and I were able to have some control over what Ankle Tickler looked and acted like. Which is *really* interesting when put in the context of the Horseman-Reaper attack at the border."

There was silence in the sedan, broken only by the smooth hum of its engine and the whir of the air conditioner.

"That's huge," Ellie finally said. "That so perfectly explains what we saw."

"They only have as much power as you give them," Oliver murmured. "That has to be what the Nantinaq meant."

"So, if we imagine the Lady as a puppy or something—" Ellie started, but Darien cut her off.

"I don't think the effect is as straightforward as 'Lady to labarador,' unfortunately. Sam and I could change Ankle Tickler, but we both had to have the same vision. On my own, I could only change him partially. He still retained some of the characteristics Sam imagined him with. I think the Lady would be almost impossible to change, given that so many people know about her."

"That's also made us pretty sure we're the only people Ankle Tickler has interacted with," Sam added. "And ... well, there's been no indication that we can fundamentally change his *nature*, either. He still feeds on what seems to be frustration. Maybe annoyance."

"And fear, the good old stand-by," Ellie said.

"Yes," Sam acknowledged. "Though a nature change is today's experiment, courtesy of Darien, our resident optimist."

Darien smiled and shrugged, accepting his words for the compliments they were. "It's worth a try. This is your exit."

Sam pulled off the highway and into a palm-lined parking lot, positioning the sedan in the shadiest spot he could find. When he looked over at Darien, she was staring down at the picture-perfect beach. Sam wondered if she was actually taking in any of it.

She shook her head. "We'd better let you go. But please let us know what's going on with you if you can. I know things are crazy, but ..."

"We're really worried about you," Sam said. "Especially now that we know how close the Lady is, and how fast she can move."

"I'm sorry, Sam," Ellie said. "We'll be better at updating you."

They said their goodbyes. Oliver's seemed stiff, and he'd talked less than usual during the conversation, but Sam reminded himself that the man had a demon in his head. A demon who, in all likelihood, had been actively tormenting him the entire time they'd been talking. It was amazing how much easier it was to forgive a person once he knew the subtext underlining their actions.

Plus ...

Sam grimaced. Based on his own track record, he wasn't in a place to judge.

Chapter Fifteen

S am and Darien were quiet during the walk down to the beach, which, aside from a few surfers and two bikini-clad women reading books, was empty. Sam adjusted his backpack, then kicked at the fine, ivory sand, thinking of Ellie. She'd definitely still stretch out on a beach and read a book; nothing would probably ever change that. But after Portlock, would she go inside a lava cave? Was that adventurous spark in her, the one that had just barely started to come back to life, gone for good now?

Sam reached over and took Darien's hand, then made himself focus on the lapping of the waves, the infinite blue of the ocean, and the black, jagged cliffs that rose above it all.

"This is gorgeous," Darien said. "I'm surprised it's so empty. I would have expected tourists to be all over this place."

Sam glanced down at the ocean again, where waves upon unending waves broke over the shoreline. Darien's steps slowed and finally stopped. He watched as her lips parted, her brown eyes sweeping across the gorgeous beach in front of them, the light of the sun flecking her already beautiful irises with gold.

"Did you know they also call this 'Eternity Beach'?" she asked.

"I did *not* know that." He leaned against the rough bark of a palm tree, breathing in Hawaii's sea-brine scent, and tried to let himself relax. "How romantic."

Darien winked at him. "If there's no one in the cave, we'll have to kiss. For the honeymoon's sake, you know."

"Oh, yes." Sam fell into step beside her. "I'm still determined to romance you, even if our hotel room options are pretty much out now."

"I think you're doing beautifully," Darien said.

They came around a bend in the cliffs and slowed, taking in the sand, the cliffs ... and the mouth of the cave. Sam sized it up; it was a smudge of pure black against the lumpy, rusty-charcoal rock around it. A sign posted outside its entrance read: **Fragile ecosystem. Please do not touch the walls or petroglyphs.**

"It's not as big as I thought it would be," Darien said.

"Me neither." Sam forced a smile; if he forced it, he might feel it. "According to your brochure, though, it's more amazing inside than it looks on the outside. And if we're lucky, it might have answers."

"I can't wait to find out."

Sam turned his attention back to the cave. It gaped at them, a sandy, rock-strewn pathway snaking into its dark throat. He eyed it, fidgeting with the straps of his backpack again. Right now, its ceiling was high enough to fit his six-foot-four frame, but before too long he'd have to crouch, which would make it difficult to defend or run. From what they'd researched, though, the tunnel didn't go too far before becoming impassable. Maybe a half mile or so. And it was well traveled.

Plus—he shrugged the backpack higher on his shoulders—they'd brought flashlights, water, paracord, and lots of snacks.

"Are you still okay to go in?" Darien asked.

Sam forced away thoughts of the other cave that had been involved in his life recently. He hadn't actually been inside it, and it looked nothing like this. "Thousands of people have probably been in there. I'm sure it's safe." And before he could lose his nerve, Sam took her hand again and stepped into the tunnel.

Immediately, the air around him cooled. He'd been right—he could straighten to his full height but only barely, and in parts he'd have to be careful not to hit the top of his head on the rough ceiling.

"This is nice," Darien said mildly. "I'm loving the shade."

"Me, too." Sam unzipped the pack and pulled out two flashlights, then handed one to Darien. They picked their way over the uneven floor until the light from the entrance faded to a dim gray, then Sam turned on his flashlight. The beam easily illuminated another ten yards, which looked similar to the ground they'd already covered. Except with more ... litter. And a surprising amount of graffiti.

Darien made a disgusted little sound through her nose as she nudged an empty chip bag with her toe. "I don't understand why people can't clean up after themselves."

"It's gross," Sam agreed. He followed the beam of Darien's flashlight as it slid over the walls. The first thing it illuminated was an initialed heart with an arrow through it—definitely not a petroglyph. But the next picture was of an intricately detailed flower, then what looked like a bunch of Hawaiian tribal symbols.

"Look at those," Darien murmured. "I wonder how old they are."

She stepped forward, and Sam followed her as the darkness deepened around them, his light sliding over unmarked rock until ... "Darien."

He stared at a line of what looked like tribal-style spears that stretched along several feet of wall, stepping closer. "I think these are the ones in the brochure. Come look."

Echoing footsteps sounded behind him, then Darien appeared out of the darkness, first as a ball of light, then as a ghostly silhouette. She peered at the little drawings, her arm brushing against his. Even though she seemed calm, he could feel the goosebumps on her skin.

Sam put his arm around her, tucking her in close to his body, then turned back to the cave wall. "I really think that looks like fire."

"I think it does, too." She pulled out her phone. "Let me send a picture to Ellie."

Sam held his flashlight up so it illuminated the petroglyph for her camera. "We've got to be getting close to the picture of the maybe-demons, right?"

"I'd think so." Darien hit a few more buttons, the phone's illumination lining the curves and angles of her face in blue-white light. Then she put it back in her pocket and clicked her flashlight on. "I'm *really* intrigued by all this. It just ... feels different from other places I've visited. Do you get that feeling?"

Sam considered that, placing his feet carefully to avoid all the little rocks and bumps on the cave's moist floor. "Maybe. But that could just be because lava tubes are so unique."

"Maybe." She didn't sound convinced.

The air cooled even more as they walked. Water dripped somewhere ahead of them, but even that sound seemed tentative, muffled, as if it were trying to fall as softly as possible. This underground world was silent in a way that even the mountains weren't, as if the earth itself had secrets it didn't want to share.

They passed a few more petroglyphs, pausing to examine each one, but none were what they were looking for. Sam started to worry, wondering if they'd missed it, or if it was in a farther section of the cave where they didn't dare go, until Darien froze, her body tensing against his side.

"There it is," she whispered.

Now it was Sam's turn to have goosebumps. They broke out across his arms and shoulders as he followed the beam of Darien's flashlight with his own, and he drew in an involuntary breath. Five humanoid figures stared out at him from the wall, massive and intricate in a way the brochure photo could never adequately convey. It wasn't that they were more detailed than any of the petroglyphs around them, but they had a sort of *life* in them that none of the other ones did. It was almost as if they were staring back at him.

Especially the one with the green shells for eyes.

There it is, indeed, he thought.

"Which ones do you think they are?" Darien asked. Her voice was hushed, as if the petroglyphs were listening, and Sam found himself imitating her quiet without realizing it.

"I think we definitely have the Lady and Silverskin."

"Agreed," Darien said. Her flashlight beam slid across the wall and stopped on the central figure, which looked like an elongated skeleton and was easily the creepiest thing Sam had ever seen. "I don't know *what* that is."

Sam fought down the irrational fear the petroglyph brought on and took a step closer. "It almost looks like the xenomorph. You know? But without the tail. And with a more ... human-skull head."

"I don't really watch sci-fi," Darien said.

"Well, neither do I, but *Alien*'s a classic." Sam forced an uneasy chuckle that fizzled and died faster than the snowball he'd thrown in their wood stove when he was eight. "Anyway ..."

They moved on to the next two: the chief and a strangely lumpy figure that looked like it might have been made out of rock. Sam released Darien and moved forward until he was a mere foot away from the wall. Up close, he could see that the chief's eyes were made out of shells, too, only they were pink instead of green.

"Hang on, keep your light there," Darien said. "Let me take a picture of these three so we can get Ellie and Oliver's opinions on them."

Sam took a step back, holding his flashlight up again. "You got it."

Once Darien had sent the text, they eyed the wall for a little longer, the silence thickening between them. Sam marveled. He knew the petroglyphs couldn't hurt him, weren't magical, didn't have any power of their own. But he couldn't deny this place seemed outright oppressive all the sudden.

"Ready to go?" he finally asked.

"Yeah." Darien stepped around him and shone her flashlight down the passage. "I was thinking of going until the rockfall that ends the easy part of the cave, but after seeing this … Wait, what?"

Sam pointed his light in the same direction and his eyes widened. The brochure had shown a picture of the cave's end—or at least, the end of its walkable section. It had been just a pile of black, volcanic rocks, settled there after a cave-in who knew how many years ago.

But that wasn't what he was looking at now. It was as if the wall had just … come *down*. Rocks had tumbled loose, some rolling all the way to where he stood, maybe fifteen yards away. Beyond it, the tunnel seemed to continue.

"Well," said Darien. "I didn't expect that."

"And that sums up our honeymoon in five words."

Darien just looked at him, her eyebrows raised so high he thought they might disappear into her hair. Sam's expression froze on his face. But then, to his relief, his wife burst out laughing. And then *kept* laughing.

"That shouldn't be this funny," she finally gasped, holding a hand to her face.

"Enjoy it," Sam chuckled. "It's the stress leaving your body."

"Or maybe it's the pregnancy." She wiped at her eyes. "Or both."

"Probably both."

Still hand-in-hand, they moved forward, stepping around bits of rock that had rolled away from the wall and up to a sign that looked like it had been posted recently. Darien held her flashlight up, and together they read:

RECENT SEISMIC ACTIVITY HAS OPENED PREVIOUSLY IMPASSABLE PARTS OF THE HALONA LAVA TUBE. USE CAUTION IF CONTINUING, AND DO NOT DISTURB THE PETROGLYPHS.

"Huh," Darien said. "Want to keep going?"

Should we? Sam wondered. But … they'd come this far and been fine. Plus, they *had* found some interesting connections, and maybe there were more ahead. He shrugged. "If you're up for it. We have all day and plenty of snacks. If conditions get iffy, we can just turn around."

Sam held his flashlight up again. It was clear the second part of the cave was less traveled; it was rockier, its stone edges weren't as rounded, and there was no litter. But … He squinted in the dim light. There were footprints in the sand. Several sets of footprints, both in and back out again. Something inside his chest eased. "Realistically, if it wasn't safe, they probably would've shut the whole cave down."

"That's what I would think." Darien looked up at him with those huge brown eyes. "So ...?"

Sam couldn't help but grin. "Let's do it."

"Yes!" Darien tugged him after her, but it didn't take long before the passage narrowed and he had to let go. Soon they were dodging rocks and snaking their way around boulders.

"We're lucky we did this now," Darien said as she squeezed through a particularly narrow part of the passage and disappeared around a corner. "In three more months I'll be too—"

There was a scrape of rock on rock, a short scream, then silence.

"Darien!" Adrenaline flooded Sam's body; he shoved his way through the passage, pointing the flashlight beam ahead of him. Even in early pregnancy, Darien was smaller than him, and it took precious seconds to work his way through. "Darien!"

He ripped himself free and found himself in a wider cavern decorated on all sides with ancient, silvery petroglyphs, but they weren't what arrested his attention. A jagged hole sprawled the length of the floor, and Darien's flashlight lay beside it, still on. Sam's heart nearly stopped. The crevasse's lip was inches from his foot; one more step and he'd have fallen in. Icy air blasted from its depths, carrying the faint cry of a devastatingly familiar voice.

"Sam!"

"Darien!" Sam fell to his hands and knees, scrambling to the edge. He couldn't see the bottom but she was alive, and that meant it couldn't be too far away. "I'm here!"

"Where ... you? ... can't see you ..."

"You can't see the top?"

"No! ... so ..." Her words dissolved into what sounded like coughs.

"Hang on!" Sam wriggled out of his backpack and fumbled with the zippers, then rummaged until his hand closed on the paracord. It was four hundred feet long—longer than a football field—and his wife's voice sounded close. It should be more than enough.

Sam knotted the rope's end around a huge black rock, wondering even as he did it if he should just call 911. But what if Darien was bleeding and needed help *now*? He could call from the bottom if he had to; he just had to *see* her, touch her, make sure she was all right.

Sam wrapped the rope around his hands and leaned on it. When it took his weight, he hurried over to the side of the pit. "I'm coming, Darien!"

Her voice echoed back to him but it was indistinct, weak-sounding. His heart jolted. If she had hit her head, or was bleeding … if the worst had happened …

"Hang on!" Sam grasped the rope and lowered himself onto his belly, then wriggled backward until he was dangling from the lip of the chasm with one hand, clutching the rope in the other. He took a deep, jagged breath.

Then, he let go.

His feet struck earth mere inches later. He yelled in shock, scrambling for purchase, but the incline was steep and rocky and he was sliding, desperately clinging to the rope so he didn't lose it in the pitch darkness. Something hit the dirt next to him and rolled away. His flashlight.

"Darien!" Sam yelled. "My flashlight—"

The world went pitch black.

Thousands of miles to the north of Death, a primal roar shattered the rich atmosphere. He looked up from the elk on which he was feeding, the animal's huge, terrified eye starting to glaze.

"Wait," he crooned at it, stroking a finger along the soft hide on its face. "Wait."

Then he sat back and closed his pink eyes, letting his fingers sink into the brown prairie dirt, running them up a thin, woody stalk of grass. The wind caressed his face, his hair.

I want this world, he thought. Then, he pushed down the thought, the need, and reached out to one he rarely had reason to interact with: the Gatekeeper.

The feelings hit Death with such power that they nearly knocked him over: violation, invasion, darkness, suffocation.

"Interesting," he said. "Keep me apprised."

The Gatekeeper didn't speak; in fact, Death had never heard him speak. Instead, the ancient one sent another impression: of hunger, of power, and of purpose. Then, he closed the connection, and Death was left alone.

"Hmm," he said, then returned to his meal. It was by no means paltry, but it also did not carry the same satisfaction as a human. Animals were different. Animals saw him as he really was. And that, as a whole, made for a less … entertaining experience.

"Still," he said, putting his hands on the elk's face again. The animal let out a coughing little wheeze, quivering with terror. Any second now, its heart would give out. "Your life is worth experiencing. Do not think otherwise."

Chapter Sixteen

When Sam careened out of the darkness and landed next to Darien in a heap, her heart sank clear down into the bottom of her stomach and settled near the baby's. Shivering, she groped toward his still form, squinting in the near total darkness. "S-Sam?"

He groaned, pushed himself upright, then pressed a hand to his eyes. "I ... I can't see. I didn't think I hit my head, but—"

"No, it's just that dark." Darien pressed against him, soaking in his warmth, and sucked in a deep, slow breath. Her mind was starting to fog; she felt like she'd been slowly suffocating ever since falling into the crevasse. Sam's arms came around her and he pulled her tightly to him. She let her eyes fall closed. He was so warm, *so* warm. She would have cried if she'd had the energy. Or the oxygen.

"Are you hurt?"

"I tweaked my ankle." *As if it needs more abuse.* "But—"

"You didn't fall hard? You ... you think you and the baby are both okay?"

"I th-think so." Darien forced the words through her chattering teeth. "I caught myself early enough, it was ... m-more of a controlled slide."

Sam let out a long, shuddering sigh. "It doesn't make sense that it's this cold." He looked up to where a murky glow—presumably from Darien's dropped flashlight—filtered through the top of the crevasse. "You didn't happen to catch my flashlight, did you?"

"N-no. And I'm sure you saw, m-mine's up there."

"I did. I left it on. We should be able to see it." Sam put a hand to his head. "Hang on ... mine was still on, too. When I came down here. It should still be ... be shining." He shook himself. "I feel woozy."

"Me, too. There's s-something …" This time when Darien shuddered, it was from fear as much as cold. "There's something wrong. Wrong with this place."

"Then let's get out. There's a rope; I brought a rope. It should be close."

Darien closed her eyes in relief. "A rope. Sam, I *l-love* you."

"I think I held onto it until I landed." Sam pulled away, still clutching her hand, and started sweeping his other hand across the cave's floor. "It should be right here."

Darien gritted her teeth. *Come on. Get up and help.* Feeling like she was swimming through half-frozen molasses, Darien forced herself to her knees, then ran her free arm across the gritty floor.

"Carbon monoxide," Sam muttered.

"I was wondering about that, t-too." Darien rested her forehead on her outstretched arm and sucked in another breath. "Doesn't explain the cold. Or …" *The flashlights.* She frowned. They were brand new and heavy-duty, built to withstand activities like spelunking, rock climbing, and backcountry camping. If the slide into the crevasse hadn't broken Darien's extra-vulnerable body, there was no way it should have killed Sam's flashlight. And hers was *up* there; they could *see* it. Sort of.

A shiver passed down Sam's arm; the cold was finally getting to him, too. "We'll … we'll get out. The rope is here somewhere—"

Darien's hand knocked against something cold, smooth, and hard. She seized it, her heart leaping. "A flashlight! I found your flashlight." She fumbled with it but her fingers were so numb they were nearly unresponsive. A jolt of panic went through her. *Frostbite.*

"Oh, thank—"

"No," Darien moaned. "It's not working."

"What?"

"M-my hands are freezing. Here, you try."

Sam took the flashlight and clicked it. Nothing happened. He cursed. "*How?* These are supposed to be able to work at the top of Everest—"

Darien's sandaled foot brushed against something thin and fibrous. A bolt of adrenaline shot through her; she shoved herself upright and snatched for it, willing her insensate fingers to work. "Sam, I have the rope!"

"Oh good." Sam tugged on her hand. She crawled to sit next to him and passed him the rope. "It's still attached up there. We c-can get out. Can you climb?"

Darien pushed her hair out of her face, then forced her legs underneath her. "It's climb or d-die, isn't it?"

"Let me help." Sam lurched to his feet, took Darien's hand, and pulled her upright. His breathing was shallow, his strength clearly waning, and he was shivering as hard as she was now. Still, he put his frigid hand on her waist, guided her in front of him, then pressed the rope back into her palm. Darien clutched at it, trying not to throw up as the black cavern tilted and spun around her. By her estimate, she'd been in here for three or four minutes longer than Sam.

And in this place, it seemed like that might make all the difference.

Darien forced herself forward, two fat tears leaving delicate films of ice on her cheeks. "I'm afraid f-for the baby."

"Let's just get out. It'll ... it'll be okay."

Darien stumbled as the incline sharpened, scrabbling for purchase on the loose lava rock. Normally she would have cried out, but all she could manage was a weak gasp.

"I've got you." Sam's voice was hoarse with fear as he stepped up behind her, pressing his body against hers and looping his arm around her waist. "H-hold onto the rope with both hands and just b-baby-step it."

"I can ... do it ..." Darien took another step, pulling herself hand-over-hand up the incline. Her fingers were shooting spikes of pain down into her wrists and Sam's body was shaking uncontrollably. But hers ... she was starting to feel warmer. The shivering was ... was *stopping*.

Heat rises, she thought stupidly. *It's warmer up here.* But that didn't make sense. The only other option was ... *stage two hypothermia.*

And without knowing she'd started, Darien was laughing. The sound reverberated through the cave, swooping over their heads like the caw of a raven about to feast.

"Why are you laughing?" Sam wheezed.

"I'm going to freeze to death in Hawaii. That's the stupidest way to die."

"So, d-don't do it." Sam took a giant step, shoving her forward and upward. "You're too smmmart to die stupidly."

Darien sniffed. "You're right. This death is beneath me." She threw her hand out and caught the rope again, pulling herself forward with all her fading strength. A foot, then two, then three. Darien allowed herself a tiny, tired sound of joy at her progress. Then, she leaned over the rope and threw up.

Sam's hand moved to her back, drawing small, soothing circles. "When you're d-done, we'll d-do another st-tep."

Darien gasped in air, heaving like she was running. "Go," she managed to choke out. And Sam did. In one mighty surge, he shoved her upward and—

Her head ... broke the ... *surface*?

Darien blinked; her flashlight blazed through the crevasse's opening, almost blinding her after the total darkness of its bottom. She sucked in a giant breath, then another, her head clearing, strength trickling back into her arms and legs.

"Sam!" she called, then heaved herself upward, climbing faster now. He said something but it was muted, as if he somehow *wasn't* right behind her, and fear seized her by the gut until—

Suddenly he was there, his cry of shock loud in her ear. "What the *hell*?"

"I don't know!" Darien gasped, forcing herself forward and upward. Her top half was blanketed in warm, humid air that smelled like mildew and salt and life, but her legs were still cocooned in the cold, in the dark, in that other ... *place*. Stronger now but shivering again, Darien forced her tingling hands higher on the rope, grateful beyond words that she wasn't further along in her pregnancy.

If ... Her stomach nearly convulsed again. *If there's still a pregnancy.*

Darien raised her head. The lip of the crevasse was right there, and her heart leaped. There was hope; hope for all three of them. There had to be.

"We're almost there, Sam." Fingers throbbing, Darien reached for the edge but came up short by more than a foot. She let her hand fall, biting down on a cry as warm blood rushed into it, pulsing, *burning* from the inside. There was no way she could hang on, not as weakened as she still was and with fingers that felt frostbitten.

"I can make it. Just hold onto the rope." Sam stepped around her, sized up the cliff through still-bleary eyes, then leaped. His hands caught the edge, then, grunting with the effort, he dragged himself up and over. An instant later, his haggard face appeared above Darien. "That was way harder than it should've been."

"Can you pull me up?" Darien didn't even try to keep the fear out of her voice. She felt better than she had at the bottom of the pit, sure, but it didn't take much to accomplish that. Worse, her legs from the calves down were still encased in that icy, toxic ... *place*, and numbness was creeping up them, replacing the needles of seconds before.

"Of course I can." Sam knelt and offered her a hand, looking affronted enough that some of Darien's worry eased. She grabbed on, fighting a bizarre urge to smile as he muttered, "Four years of college football practices have done *something* for me. Ready?"

Darien tightened her grip on his wrist and felt him do the same. "Yes."

"Go." Sam grunted and pulled. Darien clung to him, pressing her numb feet against the wall, and climbed. She threw her arms over the lip, Sam released her, and then he was kneeling in front of her, grabbing both her arms, practically carrying her the rest of the way. She collapsed on top of him and buried her face in his chest, and that's when the tears came.

"We made it," Sam said, rubbing her back. "We're alive."

"I'm ... Hang on, I have to f-fall apart for a minute—"

Sam shook his head weakly. "Crying means you're breathing. Cry all you want."

His arms came around her, one still-cold hand tangling into her hair and pressing her head down against his chest. Darien let the sound of his heartbeat, of his slowly calming breathing, soothe her. For a long moment they lay there in the warmth and quiet and dim, harsh light, grateful to be alive.

"What was that place?" Darien finally whispered.

"I have no idea," Sam said. "I've never experienced anything like that."

"Me neither." Darien pushed herself up. "Are you hurt at all?"

"I don't think so. My head still aches from whatever was in the air down there, but ..." Sam sat, rubbing his eyes. He still looked drawn, and pale as the moon.

"What about you?" He went up on his knees and took her hands, his worried eyes boring into hers. "Are you okay? Any ... any bleeding?"

"Not that I can feel, but ..." Darien's lower lip started to tremble; she bit it to keep from breaking down again. "I don't know. And I don't know what was in the air down there but I'm *so* afraid it hurt the baby. Sam, I'm ... I'm *so* scared." She choked on a sob.

Sam pulled her to him again, rocking her gently. "We should get you to a hospital."

"Yes," Darien sniffed. She stood shakily, gritting her teeth as her toes started to tingle and burn.

Sam stood, then shrugged on the backpack and put his arm around her waist. "Let's get out of—"

A single, clarion tone vibrated through the air.

Sam fell silent, his eyebrows contracting as he looked at Darien, then back toward the cave's entrance.

"Did that sound like a horn to you?" Darien asked.

"Yeah. That's good though, right? People mean help."

"We need to warn them about the crevasse—" Darien cut off as the unseen horn blasted again, closer and more strident, unlike anything she'd ever heard. On and on it went, and when it stopped ...

Drumbeats.

Sam took an uncertain step backward. "Is this ... are they doing a religious ceremony?"

The memory that had haunted the dusty corners of Darien's mind since the cultural museum burst to the forefront: of a murderous army of hulking ghosts, pale and black-eyed, blowing conch shells, beating drums, chanting ...

And killing everyone in their path.

Darien tugged on Sam's arm. "We have to get down."

"What?"

"On the floor. Right now. Get down and don't look up."

Darien dropped to the cold, rough stone and hid her face in her hands. To her relief, Sam hit the ground next to her. "It's probably real people doing something ceremonial," he muttered, but he was shaking.

"It could also be the Night Marchers."

"Even if they do exist, they only march *at night*."

"How can you still not believe in—?"

"Look, I know supernatural stuff is real now, but for hell's sake, they can't *all* exist."

"Well, with how this day's gone, I'm not taking any chances," Darien hissed. "Now put your face down."

Sam didn't protest, which was good because a new sound had joined the first: the low rhythmic murmur of human voices. Terror jolted through Darien as the chanting and the drums and the stomping of feet grew closer, louder, until it filled every cell in her body. And the smell ... Darien gagged. It was like the smell that hung around the necropsy room in the vet lab.

Darien squeezed her eyes shut, her breath coming fast and shallow. *Don't throw up, don't look up, don't throw up, don't look up—*

A trembling arm draped around Darien and she jumped before realizing it was Sam. A moment later, she felt the press of his body against her back; he was shielding her.

"I'm convinced now," he whispered hoarsely.

"Just don't look up. Whatever you do, don't—"

Flickering orange light flooded the room, so bright Darien thought it might sear her eyes even through her closed lids. Her stifled cry was lost in the thunder of the drums, the earth-shaking footfalls of the army, the stench that oozed into her nose.

Tears filled her eyes. *This wasn't how it was supposed to end.* She turned her face into Sam's and waited for the blow to fall.

Chapter Seventeen

"N A'U!"

The voice was so commanding that if Darien had known what the word meant, she would have obeyed instantly. As it was, she just lay there, shaking and gasping as the cavern fell into a dead, stifling silence that stretched the seconds into weeks.

Finally, the voice spoke again, quieter but with no less authority. "Look upon us."

Neither of them moved. Then, slowly, Sam raised his head. He gasped, his body going ramrod stiff. Darien jerked her head up and her mouth fell open.

In front of her stood the most terrifying, beautiful group of people she had ever seen. She couldn't tell how many there were—the procession stretched back into the original lava tube—but six had arranged themselves in a semicircle in front of the others, staring down at Sam and Darien with expressions as hard as the cave's walls. Three were men, three were women.

All looked lethal.

Darien locked eyes with the marcher who stood at the front, and her gaze fell almost immediately; she couldn't look at that exquisite, flinty face anymore. But where else was there to look? Aside from a crested helmet, a short cape draped around his powerful shoulders, and a loincloth, he was naked—and if anything, that made him all the more frightening. There was no hiding his killing strength, the fluid, predatory grace in his arms and legs, the easy familiarity with which he held his spear and torch.

Her eyes slid to the female marchers, hoping to find compassion in those dark eyes, but they were as grim as the men's. They were tall and no less fit, carrying their spears and what looked like slings with an easy familiarity. They wore functional-looking skirts and wraps around their chests—clothing that was clearly designed to *not* get in their way.

The final couple—the ones on the far left—were different. The man's headdress was the largest in the room, and both wore robes that fell almost to the floor. Or ... Darien blinked. They would, if the marchers' feet weren't hovering several inches above the ground.

"You may look in our eyes," said the marcher in the middle, who was closest to them. His wasn't the voice that had first called out, but it was still persuasive enough that Darien found herself looking straight into his face again.

"We will not harm you," he said. He was the tallest of the six, as tall as Sam but looked older, as if he might be in his mid-thirties.

If he were ... alive, Darien thought.

"You are lucky," said the woman beside him. Her face was stern and cool, her glossy black hair tied back in a plait that fell to her waist. "We would have destroyed most intruders by now."

Darien gaped, then stole a glance at Sam. He looked as shocked as she felt. In fact, the only other time she'd seen an equivalent expression on his face was when the Dark Lady had shown up in Ellie's bedroom.

The woman-marcher's eyes narrowed; she shifted her spear to her other hand and the movement drew Darien's eyes. The spear itself was as long as she was tall, straight and slender and darker at the tip, as if it had been dyed or soaked in water.

Or ... thought Darien, *soaked in pitch.* Their group text was about to get very interesting. If they got out of here, that was.

Sam eased away from Darien, coming up onto his knees. "Aloha. Thank you for ... for sparing our lives."

Darien's heart skipped a beat; she pushed herself upright to kneel next to her husband and reached for his hand. If something was going to happen to him, it might as well happen to both of them.

"Thank you," she echoed.

For a moment, the marchers stared at them, their expressions unreadable. Then, the middle marcher inclined his head, something like approval flickering in his torchlit eyes. "Aloha. We are members of the *Huaka'i Po*, the guardians of these islands. I am Ikaika." He gestured to the statuesque woman on his right. "This is Kailani, my *wahine*."

Kailani inclined her head a fraction of an inch. Darien returned the gesture.

The marchers on the right took a step forward and Sam's arm twitched toward Darien as if to shield her. The warriors stopped, and the corners of the man's mouth twitched upward. He looked younger than the other two, as if he were in his twenties, and had by far the friendliest expression of the bunch.

Darien gulped. *Not that that's saying much.*

"I am Kekoa." He turned, sweeping his arm toward the woman standing next to him. "And this is—"

She batted his arm away. "I can speak for myself, *ipo.*"

Kekoa's smile broadened. "That you can."

The spectral woman shot Kekoa a fierce grin, then turned her heart-shaped face toward them. "I am Alaula." She offered a gracious nod, looking between Sam and Darien with mischievous eyes, eyes that were almost playful.

If only she wasn't a terrifying, powerful, potentially bloodthirsty apparition, Darien thought. *We could be friends.*

"And this," Ikaika said, gesturing toward the final two marchers, "is our *ali'i,* Kukahi, and his *wahine,* Malia. As Kukahi has said, you may look upon them."

Darien did. Kukahi was shorter than Ikaika by a few inches, but he and Malia had an unmistakable air of power and nobility. Both their eyes were implacable.

Darien looked away. "Why ..." Her eyes flicked to Kailani's; she swallowed her fear and held the warrior's hard stare. "Why haven't you killed us? Why are you here?"

Ikaika gestured toward the petroglyphs on the wall. "Because you need to be able to fight the *kaimoni.* The demons, as you call them"

Sam looked at Darien. "So, they *did* escape before. Here."

Darien looked at the crevasse, her stomach clenching as a terrifying thought occurred to her. "So that's ..."

"Their world that you fell into, yes," said Ikaika. His voice was almost gentle.

Darien's heart sped up, thunking painfully in her chest. Beside her, Sam sat back, his face full of stunned disbelief. "It's a gate. Like the one in Alaska."

"Are there more gates?" Darien asked. "Gates in other places?"

"Few, and of those, even fewer are crossable," said Ikaika. "But for our purposes only one matters: this one. We have come to help you, but though we are powerful, our time is limited. You must listen."

Darien closed her mouth and exchanged another bemused glance at Sam. Who were they to argue? She looked back at Ikaika and nodded, and the marcher began to speak.

"Our people fought the *kaimoni* hundreds of years ago and prevailed, but not without terrible destruction and loss of life. When I was young, perhaps your age, an earthquake opened a new passageway in this cave. This passageway." He gestured around them. "It had been a safe place, one where children often played. Much like you today, we did not know things had changed until it was too late."

Ikaika glanced at Kekoa and Darien thought she saw compassion soften his face. "A child was drawn in, and her death unleashed the *kaimoni* upon us."

"My sister," Kekoa murmured, and now the sorrow on his face was unmistakable. "She was deceived and paid for it with her life." His eyes flicked up to theirs, hardening. "When we felt the balance of the earth shift, we knew it had happened again. Someone had been tricked, and was trapped, and the gate was open. The *kaimoni* had returned."

"How can we beat them?" Sam asked. "How did you?"

"We burned everything," Ikaika said.

Darien couldn't stop herself from flinching. "You burned ...?"

"Because fire's what kills them, isn't it?" Sam said. "You went full scorched-earth."

"We tried to protect the children and the elderly," said Kailani. "But, as is the way of our people, most of us chose to fight. To defend our *'ohana* and our lands. We would rather die free than live as slaves."

"And many of us did die that night," Alaula said. "Kekoa, myself, our *ali'i* ..." She gave a respectful nod to Kukahi and Malia. "Nearly everyone you see here, and more that you don't."

Ikaika nodded. "We set fire to the forest and brush all across this area in an attempt to deter the *kaimoni*, to force them either away from us or into the open. You see, they can turn from flesh and blood to shadow in the blink of an eye—"

"We know that," Sam said.

Ikaika raised his eyebrows, and Sam gulped. "Sorry. We've been studying a demon during our time here. And my sister and her ... uh, boyfriend ... they're trying to get back to the gate in Alaska to try and close it, and they're being hunted by a demon called the Dark Lady. We've compared notes, and ..." He frowned. "We've actually figured out quite a bit."

Ikaika nodded. "Very well done. Tell us what you already know about the *kaimoni*. That might save us time."

"They turn corporeal when interacting with the physical world. When they're attacking, for example," Sam said. "But they seem to spend most of their time in their ... *shadow* state. I assume for protection. Fire being their weakness was on our shortlist, and thanks to you, now we know for sure."

"The fire has to get *inside* their bodies to kill them," Kailani said. "It is very important that you remember that."

"Hence the flaming spears," Sam said.

Kailani and several of the other warriors nodded.

"They also seem to want to hunt alone," Darien said. "More like cats do than dogs. And we were able to drive off the Lady when she attacked Sam's sister, so we assume they don't like to be outnumbered."

Ikaika nodded. "Very good. Anything else?"

"We can influence them through our perceptions," Darien added. "The one we're studying, we've been calling him Ankle Tickler. Sam and I were able to change his appearance by envisioning him differently than he already was."

The cave went silent; even the shiftings of the army stopped. Ikaika peered at them. "That, we did not know. I am impressed, and that does not happen often."

"We don't know how much of a difference that little tidbit is going to make, but ..." Darien shrugged. "The more we know, the better."

"I agree. You have learned much on your own, and I have faith that you can turn the tide. Now let us finish our discussion, for we have much to tell you."

Darien nodded and settled cross-legged on the floor next to Sam. Then, they sat, listening like schoolchildren to the most bizarre, frightening storytime ever invented.

"Malia and Kailani led the largest part of our force to the other side of the island, hoping that their fear, grief, and rage would draw the majority of the *kaimoni* there to feed. A second, smaller force, including Kukahi, Kekoa, and myself, stayed on this side with one goal: close the gate. Then, our warriors scorched the island's interior, putting a wall of flame between our two armies.

"In the end, over half our island was destroyed, but the tactic worked—at least, it worked well enough. The *kaimoni* were confused, disoriented. Their desperation made them more dangerous, but it bought us enough time. Still, we fought with a desperation this land had never known before that night, and we would have been utterly defeated were it not for Kekoa."

Ikaika looked over at the young warrior, who nodded, then took up the story.

"I was one of the warriors who made it into the cave itself," Kekoa said. "We did not know what to expect; no one who had gone in to find my sister had come out again. There were *kaimoni* along the way, and they took some of us, but five made it to the end, including myself."

Kekoa paused and took a deep breath. "Waiting for us was a creature the likes of which I have never seen before or since. He was *their* guardian, and the fear he inspired in us ..."

A shudder passed through Kekoa's frame, but he composed himself. "My fellow warriors were my brothers-in-arms. One—" Kekoa glanced back at the assembled army, like he was looking at someone Darien couldn't see "—was my brother by blood. We had fought together, won and lost together. We knew how to manage fear, both in ourselves and in each other. So, we lit our spears, and we engaged.

"I do not have clear memories of what happened. Fear made us slow. We were all hurt, but one of us must have injured the Gatekeeper in return. He went mad with fury. He ..." Kekoa closed his eyes. "You do not need to know the details of what he did. It is enough to say that I saw an opening and took it, running into this very room, where I saw a hole in the floor spitting air too cold to belong in any part of this world but the highest mountains."

A small, frigid smile curved the warrior's lips. "And this is where their ability to inspire fear destroyed them in the end. After what I had just fought, seen, *experienced* ... after watching my brothers cut down ... Dying was more merciful than living with that fear.

"And so, I threw myself in. It was quick and painless." He grimaced. "Though it was very cold. When I overcame the shock of it all, I saw my sister and a far-off glow, like a sunrise." His voice went quiet, almost reverent. "It drew me toward it. It was beautiful."

Darien stared at him with her mouth open. *Did I just hear testimony that heaven exists?*

Sam's grip tightened, driving the thought from her mind for the moment, and when Darien looked at him, his eyes glistened in the flickering torchlight.

"How did you get her out?" he asked.

Kekoa looked at Sam for a long moment, his expression sympathetic. "Is someone you know trapped?"

Sam managed one small nod, then looked down, a tear spilling out onto his cheek. "My father."

Darien felt like her chest might collapse looking at him, but her empathy turned to horror at his next words.

"Is there *any* way to get to him?" Sam asked hoarsely. "Is there any way I could just end this right—"

"Sam, no—"

In an instant, Sam had her by the shoulders, his fingers tight on her skin. "Darien, the Gatekeeper's not here."

"You're not thinking clearly—"

"If there's a chance ..." He pressed his forehead to hers. "I would take it. To save you, and our baby, and Ellie. Dad, your family, *everyone* I love."

Ikaika's voice cut in. "There is no way, Sam. Your father is on the other side of their world, and you would die within minutes. There is a reason the Gatekeeper only needs to guard the gate where his victim lies."

Sam just nodded, and Darien didn't know whether she wanted to hug him or slap him. "We're going to have a discussion about this later," she whispered.

"That's ... fine." Sam released her and looked up at Kekoa again. "So, what did you do when you got there?"

"Leilani's spirit was ... frozen. Immobile. I took her hand, said her name, and told her to come with me."

Sam looked up. "And did she?"

"Yes. I do not know which did it: my presence, the sound of her name, or my ..." Kekoa hesitated, "touch, though that is a different experience as a spirit. But it worked. She was deeply shaken, but she managed to arise and walk with me toward the place of light. Every step we took rejuvenated her, restored her, until we were there, passing through."

Another tear spilled onto Sam's cheek, and this time he didn't bother to wipe it away. "Was your sister ... okay? In the end, was she all right?"

"She has moved on peacefully. Her ordeal was terrible, but she is happy now, and your father will be, too." Kekoa took a step forward, holding Sam's eyes. "The human soul is resilient. And suffering—all suffering—*will* come to an end. Do not let the storms and horrors of this world make you forget that."

Sam swallowed and wiped at his eyes, and Darian remembered what he'd said that morning, the way his face had fallen when he'd talked about what he'd seen on the news.

She slung an arm around her husband's waist and gave him a comforting squeeze, then looked up at Kekoa. "And after that, the demons just ... went back?"

Kekoa shrugged his huge shoulders. "Yes. I was not truly in either our world or theirs, but I saw ... *shades* of them, screaming and howling as they were pulled back into their void."

"The fighting stopped almost instantly," Ikaika said. "Which was a blessing, because there was much to do."

For a moment, the cave was quiet.

"How did you know *we* were involved?" Darien asked. "How did you know it was us you needed to talk to?"

Ikaika glanced at Kukahi; for a moment, he looked uncomfortable.

"We communicate with ... others. Other ... Guardians and spirits. And I will say no more about it."

"Okay," Sam stammered. "Can I ask, though ... we planned this trip eight months ago, long before the gate was open. What if we'd decided to go to Spain, or Iceland, or—?"

"You would have been found," Ikaika said. "It does not matter where you had traveled. One of the other Guardians would have found you, and you would be having this conversation with them instead of us."

"So, you *are* like the Nantinaq," Darien murmured. "You don't just watch over the people here, but also ..." she couldn't help but glance at the gaping tear in the floor, "... guard the rifts between our world and the demons' world."

"Not just between this world and the demons' world, but between this world and *all* the worlds."

Sam's jaw dropped. "Are you saying ... are you saying there are *more* worlds out there?"

Ikaika nodded.

"Are they all full of demons?"

"No," Ikaika said. "There are many worlds that border this one. More than you can imagine—more than even we have seen. And within those worlds, there are many creatures that could be called demons."

"But there is also great beauty," Alaula added, "and wonder."

At those words, it seemed to Darien like every flinty face in the room softened.

"Yes," Ikaika said, and smiled. "Do not let this revelation make you afraid. The earth itself has defenses against other worlds. Immunity, if you will. It is rare for rifts to open, and only as the result of some kind of …" Ikaika cocked his head as if in thought, "some sort of … injury to it."

Darien put a hand to her head. *Defenses, immunity, injury…* "You're making the earth itself sound almost like a living organism."

"It is," Kailani said, and to Darien's shock, the regal woman actually rolled her eyes. "I will *never* understand why it is so difficult for some cultures to accept that."

Ikaika just shrugged.

Darien stole a glance at the pair that hadn't spoken yet: Kukahi and Malia. Both stood like statues, their grave faces framed by gray-streaked hair, their skin lit by a healthy glow in the writhing light of the torches. For a moment, Darien wondered how these ghosts managed to look healthier and stronger than most of the living people she knew.

Then, Kailani stepped forward, cutting off Darien's thoughts as completely as if she'd used her spear to do it. "Yes, the earth is a living thing, with a soul. As are other worlds. But they want to stay separate from each other."

Ikaika nodded. "But like a human body, the earth is imperfect. It endures injuries, has vulnerabilities, and they open up rifts."

"Yes," said Kailani. "Most of these rifts create conditions that are inhospitable: volcanic eruptions, deep-ocean vents and trenches … most forms of life that attempt to come through are destroyed."

Alaula broke in. "And even if a rift opens in a hospitable place, such as this," she waved one elegant hand around the cavern, "conditions here may poison beings from other worlds. As you two just experienced."

Darien sat back, her mind reeling. This was more than she'd *ever* bargained for.

After a moment, Sam spoke, his voice still a little hoarse. "You're dimming."

Darien blinked and looked more closely. He was right; the marchers didn't glow like they had at first, but their luster had dimmed so slowly that she hadn't noticed until her husband pointed it out.

"Our power is nearly spent," Ikaika said.

"Wait …" Darien glanced between Ikaika and the royal couple, Kukahi and Malia, who still hadn't spoken. They'd simply stood and watched with those dark, impassive eyes. "May I ask one more question?"

Ikaika inclined his head. "Be quick."

Darien crooked a thumb at the crevasse. "Will there be any ... lasting side effects from falling in there?"

For a moment, nobody moved. Then a whisper shivered through the crowd and Malia stepped forward. The cave went silent, all eyes turning to her as she walked the air between them on featherlight feet.

"*Ali'i,*" Ikaika said as she passed. She gave him a nod, but kept walking, finally stopping in front of Darien and Sam.

"Stand." Her voice was deep, feminine, and richly accented.

Darien obeyed, feeling Sam scramble upright next to her, and looked up into Malia's face, trying not to tremble too hard. For a moment, the chieftainess just studied her with discerning brown eyes, her expression both appraising and matronly.

"Neither you, nor any member of your family—" Malia's eyes flicked to Darien's stomach, then she fixed Darien with a significant look "—will have lasting physical damage."

A sigh of relief exploded out of Darien. "That's—"

Malia held up a hand. "*However* ... traveling between worlds changes a person. As my *'ohana* have told you, very few manage to do so and live to tell about it. Those that do are usually the ones who travel between the earth and the realm of spirits, and then return to the earth, to their physical bodies."

"Are you meaning ... near-death experiences?" Sam asked.

Malia inclined her head a fraction. "Yes. Since that is the natural path of the human soul, their consequences are fewer and less intense than yours will likely be."

The blood drained from Darien's face; she couldn't stop the hand that flew to her stomach. "What about the baby?"

"She will be affected," said another voice. One with authority—the one, Darien realized, that had shouted when the marchers first came into the cave. Kukahi was coming to join them, the silence of his footsteps drowned out by his warriors murmuring a single word: "*Ali'i.*"

"I suspect that all three of you will be more sensitive to things unseen, and to the demons of *that* world in particular." Kukahi gestured to the pit. "I do not know what form that sensitivity will take, but you might find it a useful weapon as you seek to purge them from our earth."

The chieftain stopped in front of Sam, who swallowed but didn't flinch. "We did not have the weaponry available to you now when we fought these *kaimoni.*" He stared unblinking into Sam's eyes, seeming to size him up, then nodded to Darien. "Nor did we have whatever advantage the two of you might provide."

Kukahi stepped back to stand beside Malia, and Darien felt Sam relax fractionally. He still stood so straight he might have been a soldier at attention, but the fear seemed to have left him.

The marchers' outlines were starting to blur around the edges, their faces many shades paler than their original golden, hale glow. As if he'd read Darien's mind, Kukahi spoke again. "We are out of time and have told you everything we can. Like the Nantinaq and others, our existence is known but not widely believed, and we ask you to keep it that way."

Mutely, Darien and Sam nodded.

"Make use of the tools and courage you have, and above all, rely on your *'ohana*. Your love for each other will be what saves you."

"Wait," Sam said, a note of desperation that Darien had never heard before entering his voice.

Kukahi raised his eyebrows.

"Will you help us fight?" Sam asked. "In Alaska, at the open gate?"

Kukahi shook his head. "As spirits, we are bound to certain places and people. We will not be able to help you once you leave Hawaii. These islands and our people are our charge, and we guard them above all else."

A lump rose in Darien's throat. She looked around at the assembled warriors: the six who had spoken and the army that stood at their backs, and couldn't help but think of her own mother and father, of Ana and Sophie, of her grandparents in Mexico and her friends in Colorado. Of Ellie, Robert, and Oliver. Resolve stiffened her spine; she grasped Sam's hand and raised her chin. "Thank you."

Kukahi nodded. "May you go in safety and, in the end, find peace. *A hui hou*, Sam and Darien. Until we meet again."

Then the Marchers were gone, fading as silently as early-morning mist after sunrise, and Darien and Sam were alone. For a long moment they were still. Then, Sam tugged gently on Darien's arm.

She fell into step beside him, then squeezed through the narrow passage into the larger cave. The warm air wrapped around her like a sea-scented blanket and she sighed; she hadn't realized how cold she'd still felt, sitting on the ground next to the frigid crevasse.

For a while they walked quietly toward the cave's mouth, hand-in-hand, not looking at any of the petroglyphs. There was no need; they had what they'd come for.

Sam finally broke the silence, his voice quiet and reflective in a way Darien had rarely heard before. "I know the Night Marchers said there would be no lasting physical damage, but I'd still feel better if we went to an urgent care at least. Is that all right with you?"

"Yes." Darien glanced up at Sam's face. He looked tired and subdued. *A lot like I feel, in fact.* She sighed and let her head fall briefly onto his shoulder as they walked. "I won't push you, Sam, but at some point we need to talk about …" She swallowed.

Sam squeezed her shoulder. "I'm sorry. I …" He let out a heavy sigh. "I felt like if there was a way to end it, I needed to."

"I understand, Sam, but …" Darien bit her lip. "You *can't* leave. Don't you *dare* leave me a widow and carrying your child at twenty-three."

Sam's face looked suddenly older. "Not if I can help it. But …" He shook his head. "Someone has to die, Darien."

"Maybe we can find another way."

Sam smiled; it looked forced, but it was still there, and that was something. "If anyone can, it's you. Any thoughts off the top of your head?"

"Oh, I've got thoughts. Many, many thoughts. I just need to organize them first."

"It's good to hear you say that. Means you can't have been too damaged."

Darien snorted. "My fingers say otherwise." She gave them a good wiggle, wincing as they throbbed, but from what little she could make out by the flashlight's illumination, they didn't look black or blistered. She glanced down; neither did her toes. "I think they're just being dramatic, though."

Sam's smile disappeared. He leaned over and kissed her on the forehead, his voice suddenly husky. "I love you."

Darien found herself blinking away tears. "I love you, too."

"I have no idea what the next few days or weeks will hold for us. Or the world. But you're my foundation. You and our new little person. Whatever happens, nothing will change that."

Darien waited for him to say more, but he didn't. They came around a long, sweeping curve in the tunnel and blinked as its entrance came into view, bright as light reflecting off a diamond. She threw up her hand to shield her eyes and made out two figures coming toward them.

Sam must have seen them, too, because he stopped. "Hello!"

"Hello!" The answering voice was male and lightly accented. "Did you guys go all the way to the back?"

Darien and Sam looked at each other, then Sam shrugged. "Yeah."

They started forward again, and Darien squinted as the people drew closer. Both were men, and both wore some sort of uniform, though the backlight was too intense for Darien to make out details.

"Into the newly opened section?" the man asked, stopping in front of them. He looked Hawaiian—dark-haired and tan-skinned, with a solid build—and had the same look on his face that Darien had seen on park rangers in Colorado when tourists weren't behaving.

"Yes," Sam said.

"And we suggest you seal that part off," Darien said without preamble. "There's a crevasse that's opened in the floor. We ..." She glanced at Sam. "We nearly fell in."

The big ranger nodded. "We got a report of that about an hour ago. We were just coming to check it out."

"It wasn't here yesterday," said the other ranger. He was shorter, with Asian features, and looked small sandwiched between the Hawaiian and Sam. His shrug, however, was as confident as they came. "Things like that happen. This island may not be actively volcanic anymore, but seismic activity is still common, and these lava tubes can be labyrinths. Sometimes all it takes is a little jolt to open up a new passageway."

"Well, it's dangerous back there," Sam said, and Darien could tell he was trying hard to keep his voice neutral. "The crevasse is just around a blind corner, so be careful."

Something rumbled behind them, echoing down the tunnel. All four of them froze. Sam yanked Darien against him, a shudder passing through his body, and they listened as the noise went on and on. Then, as suddenly as it had started, it stopped.

"Rockslide," the big Hawaiian said, then glanced at his coworker. "That what that sounded like to you?"

"Yeah." The second ranger shook his head, his face bemused, then turned back to Sam and Darien. "Well, you two get out of here. After what we just saw, there's good odds we close the cave to tourists for the time being."

Darien glanced back down the tunnel, and Sam did the same, his eyes narrowing.

"I think," he said softly, "that is a *very* good call."

Chapter Eighteen

Ellie was *not* thrilled to learn it was possible to be too tired to sleep.

"I used to be able to nap anywhere, you know," she grumbled as her seat dragged itself upright, and her with it.

Oliver hit the pause button on the dash. "You can keep trying. I've got your podcast. Prokofiev's even more fascinating than Stravinsky."

Ellie shot him a look. "You're pulling my leg."

Oliver assumed his teasing face, the one that looked profoundly serious except for the way his eyes twinkled. "I would if I could."

Ellie giggled, then glanced at the clock in an attempt to distract herself before she blushed too hard. It didn't work; she could feel a flush creeping into her cheeks anyway.

"Three twenty-five," she said, ignoring Oliver's smirk. "My body is so confused. My sleep schedule's all off, my meal schedule is broken … and speaking of which …"

Ellie leaned behind her and grabbed their bag of snacks, then plunked it down in her lap. "Want anything?"

"Nah."

"Are you sure? You've hardly eaten today."

"I'm not hungry."

Ellie peered more closely at Oliver. Even with their watches, they had both gotten over eight hours of sleep last night thanks to her little mishap. She was still tired—with the situation they were in, she figured that was to be expected—but Oliver didn't look like he'd rested at all. His face was pale, and the skin under his eyes was a dull purple, the same color as the bruises around his neck.

He glanced over, caught her staring, and smiled. "I take it you like routine?"

You're deflecting. Ellie turned back to the bag. "I do. I like life to be predictable enough that I can feel comfortable being unpredictable sometimes. You know what I mean?" She pulled out a bag of white cheddar popcorn and popped it open.

Oliver shrugged. "Maybe?"

"It's all about feeling like I can be spontaneous."

"In a way that's *completely* controlled."

"Exactly." Ellie held out the bag. "Want some?" When he didn't reply right away, she shook it gently. "No's not actually an option here."

A smile ghosted onto Oliver's face. "Sure." Careful not to brush her fingers, he reached in and grabbed a handful, then popped it in his mouth. "This is good."

"Better than Pop Tarts?"

Oliver's grin blossomed; he looked like he actually felt it now. "Nothing's better than Pop Tarts."

"Not even Helen's cooking?"

"That's a different kind of good."

"The wholesome kind?"

"Exactly. There's 'good and good for you' and then there's 'so good you don't care that it's bad for you.'"

Ellie laughed. "That's true."

They lapsed into another comfortable silence, and Ellie turned her attention out the window. The scenery looked much the same as it had half an hour ago when she'd first closed her eyes: little hills, copses of tall pine trees, and rippling golden hayfields. Outside Oliver's window, thickly forested mountains still brooded in the distance. They were closer now.

Ellie crunched more popcorn, fixing her eyes on the road ahead of them, its asphalt grayed by years of sun and storms. According to her map, the Alaska Highway—which, at some point, had become its official name—would soon take a hard turn to the west and start winding its way through those behemoths. Towns of any size would become less frequent. Cell service would be rare to nonexistent.

With what she now knew about how the world worked, it might not be an exaggeration to say they had better chances of running into Sasquatch than getting help out there.

She ate another bite, then offered more to Oliver without really registering what she was doing. How fast would the Lady come after them? How injured had she been? They couldn't keep up this breakneck pace forever; they had to stop to eat, use the bathroom, sleep ...

"Thanks," Oliver said as he took another handful.

"Yep." Ellie snuck another glance at him, then returned her gaze to the road. Though it seemed like he was getting better at fighting Wormwood, Oliver still hadn't gotten rid of the demon. Which meant that any time they stopped, they ran the risk of another, unknown demon finding them.

Ellie shuddered, pushing away memories of the Reaper. They were about to enter the harshest, most remote stretch of their route. Anything could be lurking out there in that pristine wilderness.

And then what? She let out a deep, silent sigh. *We better figure out how to kill these things.*

Ellie's eyes flicked back to Oliver. When he thought she wasn't looking—like right now—his face became as broody as the mountains in the distance. She fought the familiar urge to reach out and touch him. Instead, she deliberately relaxed her shoulders, looked forward, and made her voice sound casual. "How are things on the Wormwood front?"

Oliver thought for a minute. "I'm making progress. It's just ... too slow."

"Is there anything I can do to help?"

"Other than just being here and being you?" Oliver shot her a tight smile. "I don't think so. It's not your fight."

Ellie turned in her seat, facing him squarely. "If it's your fight, it's my fight. That's how relationships work. So, if you plan on sticking around, you'd better get used to it."

Oliver stared at her long enough for the truck to veer a little. "This shouldn't be as difficult as it is," he muttered as he turned forward, correcting their course. "Just ... know I'm working on it."

"Good." Ellie settled back in her seat again. "So—and the answer doesn't have to be yes—but *is* there anything you want to talk about? Any problems you want to try and solve? World problems, personal problems, general demon problems ... I'm here for it."

Oliver nodded, then thought for a moment. "Wormwood's bothering me less about the gang."

Ellie's eyebrows went up. "That's got to be a good sign."

"I think it is. The biggest issue now is that he's finding other things."

"Like what?"

"Anything he can. My hopes for the future, the fact that my dad left when I was a baby, our relationship ..." Oliver gave a tired shake of his head, his voice turning hollow. "I didn't realize he had so much to work with."

Ellie frowned. "Is there something wrong with our relationship?"

"No! Sorry, I don't want you to think that." He met her eyes just long enough for her to see the sincerity in them. "Crazy circumstances aside, this is the best relationship I've ever been in."

"Well ..." Ellie shrugged. "Me, too." She leaned back, crossing her ankle over her knee. "So, what is it that's bothering you? It better not be that you're not good enough for me or whatever."

Oliver looked sheepish.

"Is that it?"

"Pretty much, yeah."

"Why?"

"Other than the fact that I'm a poor kid from the wrong side of the tracks, and you're a well-bred, upper-class woman of means and talent? That's a pretty obvious ..." Oliver's jaw tightened. "Sorry. Wormwood's here. He has been ever since we woke up this morning, and here I am saying the exact same things he is."

Ellie let out a long, unsteady breath, and looked out the window. When she was sure her voice was steady, she spoke again. "It's hard for me to tell when you're fighting him. You hide it so well."

"Oh, good."

Ellie whirled. "It's *not* good! How am I supposed to help you if I never even know when you're struggling?"

For a moment, they were silent, Oliver's face pensive. Then, slowly, he nodded—maybe to himself. "Vulnerability doesn't come easily to me."

"Apparently, neither does self-compassion," Ellie muttered.

Oliver's eyes flashed. "Ellie, I'm working on it, okay?"

She blinked as a wave of guilt hit her, and looked out her window again. They had come to a wide, burbling river that glittered in the sunlight, studded with islands that stood out like emeralds on a silver chain. The tone of the truck's wheels hollowed as the highway turned into a bridge, arcing across the ambling water. It wasn't until they reached the other side and coasted into the outskirts of a small town called Taylor that Oliver spoke.

"I didn't mean to snap at you. I'm sorry."

"No, I'm sorry. I pushed you too hard."

"It's okay. I know it's because you care, and you're stressed because we're about to have even fewer resources than we already do." Oliver's grip tightened on the steering wheel and he let out a low growl of frustration. "I *have* to get rid of him. I keep thinking I'm close. He seems more and more desperate. But he always comes back. I don't know what else to do."

For a moment, he was quiet, and Ellie didn't think he would say any more. But then ...

"I never, ever want to let him come between me and the people I care about. You, Helen, Henry, the crew—that's been my number one goal going clear back to Seldovia."

Ellie shook her head. "I know how it feels. I only spent three days fighting him and I was ready to give up and die by the end." She sighed. "Anyway, I think you're right, and you're actually on the verge of beating him. That's why he's throwing so much at you. Maybe these are his parting shots."

"We can hope. It just better be soon." To Ellie's surprise, Oliver smiled, though the expression still looked tired. "He does call me 'boring' a lot now."

"That's ... good?"

"It is. After the last few years of my life, I don't mind boring."

Ellie's phone buzzed. Then buzzed again. And again.

"You're popular," Oliver said as she pulled it out, then offered her a tentative smile. When Ellie returned it, he relaxed visibly.

"It looks like this is the second-to-last town before—" Ellie froze as her phone unlocked and she saw her many, *many* notifications. "Oh my gosh."

"What?"

"I must have only just gotten service, and I've missed five calls from Sam and three from Darien, and ... hang on, they've texted."

Ellie tapped the screen, bringing up Sam's all-caps text.

FIRE KILLS THE DEMONS

She gasped. "Oliver! It's fire! Fire's what kills them!"

"What? Yes!"

"We were on the right track the whole time! What if we ..." Ellie clutched the phone, her eyes roving around the part of town that she could see, looking for somewhere to pull off.

"There's a Walmart," Oliver said. "Let's pull in there and sort it out."

Ellie sized it up. It wasn't big but it was busy, and presumably had security cameras everywhere. "Yes. We need to hear this story. Then we can keep running."

Oliver pulled into the parking lot, then guided the truck to the gas pumps. "Might as well fill up while we're here." He threw the truck into park. "I'll get gas if you hold the phone."

"Deal," Ellie said, "if you take my card."

She held it out to him and, to her surprise, he took it without batting an eye. "No shame."

Ellie grinned, a wave of happiness swelling within her. "No shame."

Oliver got out and Ellie dialed, then opened her door so he could hear. Sam's phone rang three times before he picked up, and when he did, Ellie blurted, "Tell us everything."

"Get everything flammable you can. Lighter fluid, a can of gasoline if you can get it, plus there's hand sanitizer and a can of Sterno in our survival kit, and I think we also have bug spray—"

"How did you figure it out?" Ellie interrupted. "Did you kill Ankle Tickler?"

"No. No, we ... agh, how do I explain this, Darien? We accidentally fell into the demons' world, dragged ourselves back out again, and then were ambushed by an army of Hawaiian ghost warriors who fought the demons hundreds of years ago and wanted to give us some pointers."

"*What*?" Ellie met Oliver's eyes, relieved to see he was just as confused as she was.

He took a step closer to the phone. "We can't stay long, and we'll probably lose service as soon as we leave town, so give us the five-minute summary."

Sam managed it in three and was done before the gas pump clicked off. "And that's the Cliffnotes version."

"There was more, but we can fill you in later when we have time to catch up," Darien said.

"Yeah," Sam said. "The point is, now if the Lady shows up and starts throwing lightning, you can shoot back. Just make sure you get the fire inside her body somehow. Stab her."

"You don't have to tell me twice." Ellie sat back, stunned. "And you're *sure* you two are okay?"

"Well, the people at the Urgent Care seemed to think so. Other than some scrapes, bruises, and a little frostnip, of course."

"Frostnip." Oliver chuckled as he set the pump back in its holder, then took a step forward and leaned against the truck's door. "Only you two would manage to get frostnip in Hawaii."

"Hey, it'll make a great bedtime story one day," Sam said.

"I am *not* telling our baby that story at bedtime. Or any other time," Darien said. "And if you do, then *you* can stay up all night with her when she has nightmares."

Oliver grinned but caught Ellie's eye and mouthed "we should go."

Ellie nodded, stretched her legs one more time, then forced herself back into the truck, unable to stifle a soft groan.

"You okay, El?" Sam asked.

"Yeah, I'm just shoving my body back in the truck, and it's mad about it."

Beside her, Oliver's door clunked shut, the keys jangling as he put them in the ignition. "Human beings weren't meant to spend this long driving." The engine turned over, and he guided them out of the parking lot.

"How're you doing, Oliver?" Sam asked. "How's Wormy?"

"Funny you should ask. Ellie and I were just talking about that. As usual, he's a manipulative, lying, cruel bag of scum, but I'm making progress. I've decided not to listen to anything he says."

Sam grunted. "I'm surprised you didn't decide that earlier, knowing you."

"I did. Clear back in Alaska." Oliver sighed; for the first time, frustration snuck into his tone. "It turns out that's one of those things that takes *practice*, which takes *time*, which we *don't have*."

For a moment, the truck was quiet.

"Do you want to know what I think?" Darien asked.

"What do you think?" Ellie asked.

"I think this seems a lot like ... well, like depression. I've never had to go through that, but the people I've talked to who have all say it's one of the hardest things they've ever faced."

"It's definitely one of the hardest things *I've* ever faced," Oliver said softly.

"Plus, yours is supernaturally-caused, which no one in living memory has ever dealt with before—"

"And based on the Lady's lightning-shooting, it could evolve and kill you at any moment," Ellie added.

"Yes," Darien said. "So, there's an extra layer of complication on top of all that."

Sam's voice came over the line, serious and sincere. "Listen, I've had a demon in my head, too. It was only for a couple days, but ..." He was quiet for a second, and Ellie could just imagine him shaking his head. "I don't know how you've lasted this long, Oliver. For what it's worth, I really do have deep respect for you, and am glad you're with Ellie. In every sense of the word. It doesn't matter what your past looked like."

A slow smile spread across Oliver's face and he straightened in his seat, as if their collective words had lifted a weight off his shoulders. "Thank you."

"You're welcome," Sam said, his tone businesslike again. "And I'll never say anything that sappy to you again, so I hope you took good notes."

Oliver snorted. "I never was a good note-taker, but the important things still stuck."

"Oh, so you'll remember basically everything I've ever said, then," Sam said. "That's goo ... ecause I ... always ..."

"We're losing you!" Ellie said. "And you're not always right, Darien is!"

The phone blipped just long enough for laughter to echo over the speakers before the call died, swallowed up by the wilderness. Ellie smiled, her heart lighter than it had been in days. Judging by the look on Oliver's face, his was, too.

"We know how to kill them now," he said. "We actually *know!*"

"And we were on the right track to begin with! I don't know about you, but that makes me feel better."

"That does feel good."

Ellie looked sideways at him. "Do you feel good?"

He cocked his head, his lips turning up in a little smile. "Yeah. I do actually. And that's astounding given what Wormwood's saying to me *literally* right now."

Ellie leaned as close to him as she dared. "Did you hear that? He's not buying it, you creep, so get out of his head and find someone else to bug!"

Oliver started to laugh, then winced and put a hand to his head. The floating, happy feeling in Ellie's heart deflated.

"I'm sorry—"

"It's okay. What you said is true, and he knows it, or he wouldn't have headached me." He let his hand fall to his lap. "Maybe we should switch drivers soon, though. Just in case."

Ellie nodded. "And for the record, I'm proud of you for opening up. I feel like that's a universal human struggle, and you're kicking it to the curb in a way that also seems really balanced and healthy, so ... yeah."

"Thanks, Ellie. I'm starting to realize ... " He was quiet for a moment. "I've struggled with this for a long time without knowing it. But now that I know ... well, I'm done letting it taint all the good things happening in my life."

"Wise words."

They lapsed into silence, and Ellie's thoughts turned to the Lady, their new knowledge, and the half-formed ideas that had flitted through her brain earlier as she'd tried to nap. She glanced over at Oliver; his expression was thoughtful, almost calculating.

"You look like you might be thinking along the same lines as I am," Ellie said.

Oliver's eyebrows rose. "What lines are those?"

"That we ..." Ellie hesitated. Oliver seemed closer to vanquishing Wormwood than he ever had before, but still hadn't managed it. Anything she said would reach the Dark Lady's shriveled, moldering ears. But if Oliver was already thinking it—and if she knew him at all, he was—then Wormwood was already tipped off, anyway.

Besides, what choice did they have but to risk it?

"That we ambush the Lady," she said. *And I'll just have to think of a backup plan. One Wormwood doesn't know about.*

Oliver nodded. "Yes, and I think we should do it tonight. We're rested, she's injured, and we haven't put as much distance between us as usual, so it shouldn't take her long to catch up."

Fear shivered through Ellie, but she wrapped her arms around herself and lifted her chin. "Let's do it."

"Okay, then. Would you mind pulling out your phone for the map?"

"Already on it. And all our supplies are in here somewhere, right? We were smart enough to leave them in the truck before we got to the hotel last night?"

"All except your knife, which we replaced."

"Go us," Ellie muttered as she pulled up her map. Then, she looked up at Oliver, bared her teeth in a foxlike grin, and said, "Let's kill ourselves a demon."

Chapter Nineteen

Oliver eyed the little cabin as Ellie pulled into the dirt driveway and threw the pickup in park. Silently, they sized it up, the truck rumbling underneath them. The structure was like many of the cabins he'd seen in Alaska: log walls stained a dark mud-brown, its single story capped with a green metal roof. A few fingers of aspen and pine had snuck within a stone's throw of the building, but otherwise, the area was clear of everything but grass and sage for at least a hundred yards in every direction.

It was gorgeous. Peaceful.

"What do you think?" Ellie asked.

That I wish we were here under very different circumstances. But Oliver shoved the thought aside; now wasn't the time. The back porch with the stunning view was so they didn't get ambushed, the cozy wood stove and gas cooking range were for emergencies only, and the bedroom wouldn't be used at all.

"I think it's defensible," he said.

"Great. That was my goal."

"I'm just impressed you were able to find this place during the fifteen minutes we had in Fort St. John."

A wry smile lifted Ellie's lips. "I get really motivated by cute vacation cabins. It's hard to beat both solitude *and* hot running water."

Oliver snorted. "Being able to wash my hands with warm water was definitely my biggest worry about tonight."

"Not using yourself as demon bait?"

"Nah. I'd almost forgotten about that part." Oliver unbuckled his seatbelt and opened the door. "All right, let's try not to burn this place down."

You'll all burn. You can't win this fight.

Oliver slammed the door, swallowed his anger, and opened the back, his eyes scanning the packed bench seat. They'd learned their lesson from last time; they'd take only what they needed to make tonight's plan work. Showers, fresh clothes, a good night's sleep—it would all have to wait until the Lady was dead.

Silently, Oliver thanked Bill for driving him so hard. This wasn't going to be all that different from a really, *really* long day of fishing.

Keep telling yourself that, Ollie.

Across from him, Ellie started shoving things into a bag. Oliver caught the glint of the sun off a can of Sterno before dropping his eyes. If he knew Ellie at all, she had a backup plan.

And he didn't want to know it.

Instead, he pulled the bow case out and started fishing in the truck for the quiver. "Let's go over the plan again while we unload and get stuff set up."

"Sure."

You know the Lady has more firepower than everything in your pathetic little arsenal put together. And that's only in her first shot.

Oliver grabbed the quiver of arrows, Sam's hatchet, and the can of bear spray, then nudged the door shut with his toe. He trudged to the front of the truck, still keeping his back to Ellie. "We make a fire in the firepit out back, then send you off to a secret spot that only you know about."

Ellie's voice sounded muffled; she must still be digging for stuff. "And when the Lady comes for you—because historically, you've been the bigger threat, so we're assuming she'll target you first—I'll shoot her with a flaming arrow." She stepped up beside him, all messy hair and resolute eyes, the bag slung over her shoulder.

I can't wait for you to watch her die.

"Did you get enough Sterno?" Oliver asked.

"Three of our four cans. That's enough to last the night and then some, right?"

"It should be." A thought occurred to Oliver. "I might take the fourth. Use it to coat the hatchet as another backup."

"Good idea."

They stumped toward the cabin, following the thin dirt trail that led to the porch. Oliver breathed in the scent of pine and sage and, just for a second, let himself enjoy it.

Careful. It's that kind of thinking that'll kill you. Enjoyment, pleasure ... they're all just different words for weakness. They just mean more things can be taken away from you. More pain. More anguish. Just kidding, enjoy all you like. It's better for me—

Oliver willed himself not to reply as the demon went on. Instead, he said, "I was also thinking I'd keep a supply of sharpened sticks in the fire, just in case."

"In case I miss?"

You jerk. Should've thought before you said that one.

But Ellie just nodded. "I think that's a good idea. A miss is a distinct possibility. I'm trying to be confident, but I'm not going to lie. She's ... daunting." Ellie bit her lip, then reached for the screen door. Its squeaky hinges nearly swallowed up her last words, but Oliver heard them anyway. "I'm afraid of losing you."

He grabbed the screen and held it open for her. "Hey. Neither of us is going to die tonight."

You're dead wrong.

"And even if I'm wrong," Oliver added, "hope is the one thing they can't take from us. If we die hoping, we die victorious."

Ellie turned to face him. The lazy evening sun lit her nearly flawless skin; she practically glowed. Oliver became aware of every beat of his heart; she had no *idea* what she did to him, even tired, stressed, scared, bruised, and slightly smelly.

"Listen," she said, "let's make a deal. Either we both go, or we don't go at all. And given that we'll be far enough away from each other that a lightning strike won't kill us both, we'll just have to settle for option two."

"I'd prefer option two. I've got a lot to live for."

Ellie searched his eyes, and he let everything he felt for her show on his face. Her eyes started to glisten; she blinked, turned on her heel, and marched inside.

You just can't say anything right, can you, lover boy?

Let's not jump to any conclusions, Oliver thought as he stepped inside. The cabin wasn't huge, but the nearly floor-to-ceiling windows overlooking the back deck and the wide-open meadow beyond made it feel plenty spacious. A couch and ottoman took up most of the living room, facing—Oliver blinked—a dull-black wood stove and a neatly stacked pile of split logs. *That could be helpful.*

Yeah. In burning down the cabin.

"How long would you say we have before sunset?" Ellie asked.

Oliver turned. She stood in the pool of light that spilled through the windows, twisting her hair into a bun at the nape of her neck, a hair tie between her teeth. He stepped forward, laid the bow case and quiver on the sturdy wooden dining table, then joined her. "An hour, probably."

"So, plenty of time."

"Yeah." He nodded at the fire pit a few yards from the back porch. "And that's as perfect a setup as we could ask for."

Ellie took the hair tie out of her mouth and wound it into her hair. "I'll make sure—" She cut off. Oliver didn't ask what she had been about to say.

"So, you'll hang out there ..." Ellie nodded at the firepit, "with your knife, the bear spray, the hatchet, and your discount flaming swords."

Oliver grinned. "Well, they worked so well last time, I might as well try them again."

A flicker of self-doubt crossed Ellie's face; she shook her head. "No. I'll get her. I'm en-visioning myself succeeding. Isn't that what they tell you to do about stressful situations?"

Oliver's smile softened. *That's my girl.*

Enjoy her while you've got her. Or ... a snide chuckle. *Enjoy her as much as you can anyway. Even if you do manage to beat us, one day she'll wake up and see you for who you really are, and then it'll be goodbye, Ellie.*

Oliver folded his arms. He didn't believe that anymore—at least, he didn't *think* he did. Still, the spot was sore enough that Wormwood's words were irritating. "I might light a fire in the wood stove as an extra precaution. Do you want to go find a spot while I do that?"

"Sounds good. Then we should go through the closets and see if there's anything else we can use."

Oliver nodded. "In a place like this, we might find some real treasures."

"As long as none of them are dead mice." Ellie moved to the table and slung the quiver across her shoulders. Inside, a dozen arrows rattled lightly, their movement constrained by the cotton balls Oliver had soaked in hand sanitizer and stuffed onto their field tips as they'd driven. She ignored them, unzipped the case, and lifted out the bow.

Ellie turned the bow over, examining it, and Oliver joined her. A long, gray scratch ran the length of its bottom limb, but the weapon's injury paled in comparison to the bruise it had left on Ellie's forearm. Oliver had always loved the way the golden-hour sun bathed the whole world in vibrant color, seemingly as a parting gift. But the way it brought out every mottle of that bruise ... it tugged at his heart like a black hole.

"It looks like it survived yesterday," Ellie said, then looked up into Oliver's face. Her stance was as firm as ever, but those gray eyes were nervous. "I think I'm out of excuses."

It took everything Oliver had to step back and let her pass. "Scream if you need me."

"I'll always need you." She turned and slipped toward the door. "But yes, I'll scream if I get in trouble."

Then she was gone, the screen banging shut behind her.

Oliver stared at the empty front porch for a second, then sighed and moved toward the wood stove. By the woodpile sat a basket full of old newspapers for kindling. He reached for them, then froze.

Propped against the woodpile was a heavy iron poker.

His heart skittered as memories accosted him, vivid and awful and reeking of burned flesh. Jag holding the poker, searing the blood rose into his skin inch by painful inch.

You put your back to your enemy, Ollie. Gave *it to him.* Wormwood chuckled. *What did you expect? It's your own damn fault you weren't smart enough to see them for what they were beforehand.*

Oliver made himself grab a handful of newspaper, then threw it into the belly of the stove. "I was a boy who didn't understand what family was, or what life could be like."

You did, though. Your mother sold herself so you could have that kind of life. You'd seen it in Kyler's family, and you walked away. You knew even back then that you weren't good enough for it.

Oliver grabbed a log, running his thumb along the rough, splintery grain. Even unshaped and destined for the fire, the pinewood was beautiful; it reminded him of the staircase to Helen and Henry's loft.

To his room, which they'd given him because they loved him.

Oliver tented the wood over the crumpled-up newspaper, leaving enough space for air to circulate and feed the flames. "I made my choices, and I'll own them—good and bad. I will not be a victim, not to my time in the gang, not to loss, grief, or abandonment, and *especially* not to you, Wormwood."

And yet, here I still am. The demon's voice turned silky with what sounded like barely disguised glee. *Holding your attention.*

Oliver paused. Something about the way the demon had said it ...

Ellie!

Oliver leaped to his feet. He crossed the room in two strides, shoved the door open, and had just set foot on the porch when realization hit him like a thrashing halibut. He looked down, closed his eyes, and listened.

A squirrel chattered, a few birds chirped, the trees murmured in a light breeze.

And that was it.

Oliver took a deep breath, then let it out. *Get it together.* Yes, she was out there alone, but she was armed, and she wasn't the type to not call for help when she needed it. Plus, whatever spot she'd end up choosing had to be within bowshot range, which meant she hadn't gone more than thirty yards, maximum. *Trust her.*

Oliver turned and stepped back into the cabin.

"That was a good bluff." He settled in front of the stove and pulled a lighter out of his pocket. "You nearly got me."

She's dying out there, and you're sitting here doing NOTHING! NOTHING AT ALL!

Oliver ignored the twist in his gut and held the flame to the newspaper. "You're overdoing it. You're not going to trick me into giving away her hiding place."

The fire caught, licking greedily up the edges of the newspaper to gnaw on the spears of kindling he'd laid out above it. In the seconds before he could close the door, a little woodsmoke drifted out, wreathing Oliver in its sweetish scent.

Another memory bowled into him, *of searing-hot flames and glowing green eyes. The absolute knowledge that he was alone, trapped, abandoned inside the building that was about to become his pyre. The smoke was burning his eyes, his nose, his throat, his lungs, it was everywhere, but it wouldn't kill him fast enough; he was going to burn alive—*

Oliver didn't remember jerking away from the stove, but he must have, because he was lying on his back, looking up at the log ceiling. His breath came in short gasps; his heart was racing so fast his chest hurt.

And Wormwood was laughing.

Fury simmered in Oliver's stomach. He pushed himself upright, took two steps, reached down, and grabbed the poker.

The laughter stopped.

Breathing deeply, Oliver leaned down and closed the stove's door on the dancing flames. Then, he examined the tool. The iron was unsullied by rust, heavy and stout in his hand. He gave it an experimental swing and didn't fight the vicious smile twisting his lips. "I think I'll take this with me tonight."

Oliver stood and headed to the kitchen to see what resources the cabin owner had left for them.

And Wormwood was silent.

***

A few minutes later, Ellie slipped back into the cabin, bow in one hand, his sweatshirt tied around her waist. Oliver's relief was immediate and intense; it was all he could do not to smash her against him in a bear hug.

"Find a good spot?" he asked.

"Yes, I did." She propped the bow against the side of the ottoman, looking satisfied, then turned to him. "How's the stove?"

"Good. Burning. And I started looking through the kitchen and hall closet." Oliver wasn't totally aware of the steps he'd taken toward her, but now he found himself stopping only a few inches away. He could see every fleck of blued steel in those gray eyes, every lash and freckle, the way her blush pinked her cheeks. She was vibrant and beautiful and so very *alive*.

Ellie took a deep breath, her chest rising and falling, looking like she was having similar thoughts about him. "Did you find anything useful?"

"Oh boy, did I." He turned away. "Come look."

Ellie followed him down the short hallway, stepping back as he swung the closet door open. Her eyes widened. "That's a huge first-aid kit."

"It's got everything. Bandages, disinfectant, bug bite stuff, burn cream, medical tape …"

Ellie glanced at him. "You went through it already?"

"I was worried about you. I had to do *something*."

Ellie's arm twitched toward him as if she wanted to put it around his waist. Instead, she smiled. "That's really sweet."

He returned her smile, then watched her as she took in the rest of the closet's contents. "More hand sanitizer, that could be helpful … ugh, I *wish* we had time to just sit and play Yahtzee ... I like all these books, though. Dutch oven cooking, camping guides, a field medicine manual ... very practical."

Her eyebrows rose when she saw the two bottom shelves, which had been packed so full of toilet paper that Oliver doubted even a mouse could squeeze between the rolls.

A grin split Oliver's face. "That's a pretty magnificent hoard of toilet paper."

She giggled. "It's weirdly reassuring."

"Come on, there's more." Oliver stepped back and closed the door, then led Ellie to the bathroom. "He's got extra quilts in the bedroom closet—plus towels and sheets—and a couple of MREs in the pantry."

"Dang, this guy was *prepared*."

"But what I really wanted to show you was this." Oliver tugged on the mirror; it swung forward, revealing a row of little orange bottles.

Ellie blinked. "Those look like prescriptions."

"Yep. Painkillers, muscle relaxants, and a couple others I don't recognize."

Ellie looked at him, that shocked expression still on her face.

"There's a bottle of penicillin in the freezer, too," Oliver added.

"You're kidding."

"Nope." He leaned his hip against the vanity, facing Ellie.

She gestured at the mirror. "Why risk keeping all that? And why rent the cabin out *with the drugs still in it*?"

"I think it makes perfect sense. Think about it. We're a hundred miles away from the nearest hospital. The closest grocery store might be fifty-plus miles away. And we have no cell service. If someone got stranded here in a blizzard, or if an accident happened, you'd want to be prepared."

"Okay, the meals, the toilet paper, the blankets, that I all get," Ellie said. "But leaving your prescriptions in the cabin you plan on renting?"

Oliver nodded toward the mirror. "Would you have looked in there?"

"It doesn't *look* like it has a secret storage compartment, so probably not."

"There you go." He shrugged. "Living ultra-rural changes the way you see things. We *have* to rely on ourselves, to be prepared. You'd be shocked at the number of people in Alaska whose cabins look just like this. They store food, supplies, extra blankets ... and yes, many of them hang onto their prescriptions."

Ellie shook her head, bemused. "I'd never even thought of that. And I thought *I* grew up rural."

Oliver smiled. "Rural's relative. Compared to the rest of Denver, you probably did. Compared to Seldovia?"

"Fair enough." She stepped out into the hallway, and Oliver followed. "Are there any other secrets you want to show me?"

"Nope. That's all."

"Okay." She cast a glance toward the freezer and shook her head again. "While I'm really hoping we don't need it, I have to admit it's comforting the medical stuff is all here."

Oliver folded his arms, trying not to imagine the kind of injuries they might be facing tonight. Ellie's bumps and bruises were bad enough already.

"Me, too," he said softly.

For a moment, they both stood, letting the sun sink lower on the horizon and the breeze caper through the sage. But it was too much of a luxury to stay, and they both knew it.

"Well, I'd better be off to the discount flaming sword store before I lose control and do something like kiss you," Oliver said. He grabbed the hatchet off the table and reached for the back door.

Ellie's footsteps sounded behind him; it sounded like she was heading for the bathroom. "Don't tempt me, Oliver. I'll take a pit stop, then meet you out there."

"Sounds good. Don't do drugs."

Her laughter followed Oliver as he stepped into the cooling air, his shoes making hollow thunks on the wooden deck. He scanned the skies, the meadow, the spaces between the trees.

Nothing stirred.

Warily, he descended the stairs and started hunting for sticks sturdy enough to stab a demon with. A few minutes later, Ellie joined him. She'd grabbed the bow again and was wearing his sweatshirt now.

"Here's a good one," she said, holding out a stick so thick it could have doubled as a club. She smiled when he took it from her. "Darling."

"Thanks." He grinned. "Babe."

Ellie let out a rueful chuckle. "We really need to work on our domestic bliss."

"Well, we got off to a rocky start," Oliver drawled, "but I still think we can make it work."

She laughed, and a little spark of joy flared in Oliver's heart.

"So, what else do we need to do?" she asked.

"Well ..." He eyed the massive stack of wood not twenty feet away; it was bigger than it had looked from the cabin. "I've got plenty of wood and discount swords now. I think all that's left to do is sharpen a few of them. Is there anything you need before I sit down and start doing that?"

Her face went carefully blank. "Nope. In fact, I can help you, if you want."

"I do want that."

"Excellent. Let's get started."

The sun hung low on the horizon by the time they'd finished sharpening the sticks, flaking bits of bark and wood off with their knives until the tips gleamed in the evening light, pale and—hopefully—deadly. Now, they sat, silent and not quite touching, watching the sun fire the bases of the clouds into pink and orange ribbons that feathered across the sky like an aurora.

"Someday I want to show you the Northern Lights," Oliver said.

"I would like that. I've always wanted to see them." Ellie sighed and burrowed down into his hoodie. "It's probably about time. Do you want this back?"

"I'm good. I've got a fire. You keep it."

"Well, I have canned fire." She stood and stretched. "Something tells me it's not going to be this cozy, though."

"Probably not. Think of how good it'll feel to have the Lady dead, though."

"I do think about that. A lot." Ellie looked toward the horizon and the fading colors there. Her expression dimmed. "I just hope Wormwood hasn't found any other demons to attack us, and that we'll only be dealing with the Lady."

"Me, too." It was a thought they'd debated on the drive, but decided this part of the world was so remote that most demons had probably bypassed it on their way to greener pastures.

Still, Oliver thought, *if there are millions of them like Wormwood said ...*

But he shook his head; that was probably just another one of the demon's lies.

"I'd better go while there's still some light," Ellie said.

"And you're sure you'll be all right?"

Ellie shrugged. "As sure as I can be. And as all right as you are."

Oliver swallowed, then nodded. "I'll go inside for a minute while you get to your spot. Then I guess it's game on."

"I guess so." She offered a brave smile. "Scream if you need me."

"I'll always need you."

Ellie let out the smallest laugh, then her face grew serious. "Oliver ..." She blinked once, her expression troubled, then said, "I'll see you on the other side."

"Back at you." He climbed the steps.

Back at you? Mentally, he cursed himself. *What if that's the last thing you ever say to her?*

He started to turn.

"Go inside, Oliver!"

Not worth it. She probably doesn't love you back, anyway.

"Shut it," he whispered, but stepped inside the cabin.

Chapter Twenty

The light was a washed-out shade of gray, the details of her surroundings fading quickly by the time Ellie got to her spot: a copse of young, bushy pine trees with limbs that snarled around each other so tightly she doubted even a deer could wiggle through. Earlier, she'd nearly walked right by this place; a strange trick of the land made the copse look smaller, bushier, and altogether less useful for her purposes than it really was. Luckily, a backward glance on her way to an ostensibly better stand of trees made her pause ... then stop dead.

What had looked like a useless, stunted thicket was actually a trap-setter's paradise. The trees carved a half-moon into the meadow, enfolding a section of grass and a few errant sagebrush in their embrace. And in almost the very center stood the grand prize: a small, dead tree, maybe three feet taller than she was, its rust-colored needles a torch waiting to happen.

It was perfect. And because of how it looked from the cabin, Oliver would never guess she would choose it.

Ellie dropped everything and went right to work.

Her plan was simple. Which, she reflected, was good. Less could go wrong that way. While driving, she and Oliver had built the entire scheme—loudly and unambiguously—around the assumption that the Lady would attack Oliver first. He was the stronger fighter, the bigger threat, and—Ellie suppressed a shudder—the demon really seemed to want to torture Ellie into madness before killing her, which Oliver would never allow if he were alive. From the outside, that plan of attack seemed the most likely, the most *logical*, even.

But if *Ellie* were in the Lady's shoes, if Wormwood had been feeding *her* every scrap of intelligence he could gather ... she would do exactly the opposite. Which meant she'd needed a *serious* backup plan, and one that Oliver couldn't know about.

Ellie put her hands on her hips and surveyed her setup. The first thing she'd done was scrape a makeshift firepit out of the dirt, placing it at the apex of the little meadow, between the spread arms of the half-moon. The trees should protect her from a lightning strike on three sides but the fourth was wide open, and her biggest vulnerability. Luckily—between the full moon and the open space between Ellie's copse and the forest proper—she should see the Lady coming if she stayed alert. Since she would already be watching over Oliver, bow in hand, Sterno burning, ready to light her arrow and shoot anything that attacked him ...

It should be easy to pivot and shoot the Lady if she appears behind me, right? The demon was a large target, and would be closer, and Ellie had not one, but *two* bonfires ready to distract her if she threatened to shoot lightning—

A bolt of nerves shot through Ellie; she looked more closely at her woodpile. Was it ... had a log been moved?

She took a few steps toward it, squinting, but it was just the way the shadows lay as the last motes of sunlight slipped away. Relieved, Ellie withdrew, wrinkling her nose. The logs still smelled like hand sanitizer; she'd upended almost everything in Sam's sixteen-ounce bottle over them before jogging back to the cabin. She may not have had as much experience with starting insta-bonfires as her brother but figured that much alcohol should do the job.

Ellie turned and cast a cursory glance over the dead pine—her second backup plan. No breeze stirred the trees, which meant the fishing line she'd dunked in hand sanitizer and strung into its death-red branches hadn't budged. It was a morbid string of Christmas lights, waiting for a spark to set it alight.

That's a great way to start a forest fire.

Ellie let out a frustrated sigh. Yes, it was less than ideal, but if it came down to either incinerating a remote woodland or leaving the Lady alive?

She wasn't sure what she hated more: the fact that *that* was her choice, or that the answer was obvious.

Twitchy, nervous, cursing the demons for invading her world, Ellie turned away from the fire pit and followed the fishing line toward the back of the copse, where she'd tied its translucent end around a stump to keep from losing it in the dark. She double checked the string's proximity to her sitting spot; it needed to be close enough for her to light it quickly, but not so close that the line—and then the tree—would go up in flames if she accidentally bumped her Sterno can. Satisfied, Ellie leaned the bow against a nearby trunk, crouched, and peered through the small, pine-framed opening she'd made earlier.

Needles scraped her arms, sharp even through Oliver's hoodie, but they weren't nearly as irritating as the thorns of doubt that prickled at her insides. She hadn't ever been great at estimating distance, but she'd guess she was between thirty and forty yards away from the firepit, where Oliver would soon take his place.

As bait.

Ellie stared at the cabin's back door for what felt like a very long time—long enough that the anxiety dozing in the pit of her stomach started to unroll and sniff the air for food.

He should be out here by now. She took a deep, controlled breath, willing her hands not to tremble. Could the Lady have caught up to them that quickly? Could she *already* be in the cabin—?

Oliver slipped out the back door, down the porch steps, and to the fireside with his characteristic wolflike grace. Ellie breathed a sigh of relief and let herself study him for a moment. *I should have told him how I feel.*

Her reasons had been good; she hadn't wanted to take his mind off the task ahead of them. But now, watching him stand there alone ...

Ellie tightened her grip on the bow. Those thoughts were secondary; first, the Lady had to die. And if everything went according to plan—*either* plan—Ellie would be the one to kill her. A shiver of something, maybe rage, maybe disgust, washed through her as realization hit.

She *wanted* to kill the Lady.

Ellie sat back, the corners of her mouth tugging downward. She'd never wanted to kill anything in her life. *But freak monsters from another dimension? Those change people.*

For a moment, Ellie was silent and still as she tried to reconcile the girl she had been with the new woman wearing her skin. Then, she just shook her head and opened the bag she'd stashed earlier on her scouting trip.

Four cans rolled around its bottom: three Sternos and a barely-used can of bug spray. She held up the latter. It was too dark to make out its list of ingredients, but she remembered that it had been near the top of Sam's list of flammable things he had in his truck, so she'd grabbed it. Her brother would know, too; Ellie distinctly remembered their mother dragging him inside the house with singed eyebrows and a shocked expression, yelling at him for turning the bug spray into a blow torch. The memory was almost enough to make Ellie smile.

She set the can down within easy reach, then pulled out a Sterno tin and her lighter. Heat flared from its top, then settled into a steady, low-profile flame. Ellie nocked an arrow. Then, careful not to swing its cotton-balled tip anywhere near the Sterno, she settled down by her peephole to keep watch. Below her, Oliver sat on the log bench, his elbows on his knees, staring into the flames.

And they waited.

The minutes stretched. The air grew steadily colder. Ellie pulled the hood of Oliver's sweatshirt over her head and huddled down, wishing she'd brought her heavier jacket. Then, she shook her head. Warmth meant comfort, comfort meant sleep, and sleep meant calamity.

She'd already learned that the hard way.

Ellie was just starting to relax a little when Oliver sat bolt upright. She mirrored him instantly, wrapping her fingers around the bowstring and coming up onto her knees to draw, her heart pounding in her throat. An attack this early would be a surprise; it had taken the Lady far longer to catch up to them in Valleyview. Still ... they hadn't put nearly as much distance between themselves and the demon this time, and even though she was injured, who knew what she was capable of?

Ellie stared at Oliver. He was stock-still, his posture tense, his eyes fixed on some point beyond the fire. But he hadn't reached for his burning sticks, or hatchet, or fireplace poker, or even his knife.

Instead, his lips were moving.

Understanding hit Ellie, and she drooped back into a sitting position. *If only I could shoot Wormwood for you.*

A few minutes later, Oliver got up, stretched, slouched to the woodpile, and returned with an armload of logs. Then he drew his knife out of its sheath, picked up a long stick, and began to whittle its end into a sharp point.

Ellie snuck a quick glance at her phone, keeping the screen behind a little hillock so its light didn't catch Oliver's attention and give away her hiding place. She winced. It wasn't even ten o'clock.

They'd only been doing this for an hour.

Letting out a silent sigh, she wiggled a little to get the blood back into her legs. *Some things don't change after all. You're still a lousy huntress.* She forced herself to be still, and to wait.

The night deepened, the moon rose, and the quiet kingdom it ruled began to stir to life. At some point a small woodland creature skittered up a tree some yards away, scaring Ellie so badly she doubted she'd calm down for a week.

It's good for you, she told her thundering heart. *It'll keep you alert.*

Midnight snuck by. Ellie switched the now-guttering Sterno for a fresh can. Oliver had burned through all his original stick-swords and more besides. Every so often he would murmur something out loud. Ellie never made out the words, but oddly, he seemed to be getting calmer by the minute. Hope surged within her. Whatever battle he was fighting with Wormwood must have been going well.

Near one o'clock, an owl hooted and was answered by another, a ways down the meadow. They talked back and forth for a while, then the one at the bottom of the meadow took flight, its black silhouette ghosting across the star-spattered sky.

Two o'clock came and went, then three.

Ellie's nerves intensified.

Below her, Oliver stood and paced to the woodpile for the sixth or seventh time. This time he lingered, turning in a slow circle, scanning his surroundings. When he finally returned to his seat, he dumped the wood and picked up his hatchet and poker, examining them.

Ellie lit her last can of Sterno. It was nearly four. The sun would rise around 5:45.

It shouldn't be long now.

Oliver sat with his hatchet in one hand and the poker in the other. Every line of his body was rigid, coiled, the angular planes of his face like flint. It seemed like even the skittering night creatures had gone quiet, as if everything in the meadow was tense, readying itself.

Suppressing a groan, Ellie fought the urge to stretch. Her muscles ached from sitting and the strain of being constantly at the ready; her neck hurt from craning it back and forth between Oliver and the space behind her. But she couldn't relax, not when both his life and hers depended on staying—

Behind her, something crackled.

Ellie whirled, staring frantically across the meadow to where the Lady hovered, blue static licking up her arms—

Ellie threw herself sideways, and not a moment too soon. Blinding light seared across her vision, so close that heat sizzled on her skin. The strike's impact knocked her onto her back, a thunderous *boom* resounding in her ears. For a second, she lay there, gaping at the clear, starry sky, unable to move, barely able to breathe, every cell in her body tingling like a fallen-asleep limb.

Some part of her registered a second light out of the corner of her eye, orange and steady and ... growing now, flowering, *exploding* upward as it feasted on the dead tree in the center of the clearing.

It worked. Not in the way she'd intended, but maybe it was enough to buy her some time—and Oliver time to get to her. He wasn't far distance-wise, but he'd have to run to the top of the copse, without knowing there *was* a top, *in the dark.*

Still reeling, Ellie shoved herself up, blinking hard to clear her vision. The light illuminated the clearing with an eerie, flickering glow, including the Lady, who looked as stunned as Ellie felt. Her jet eyes were wide as she stared at the burning tree, her face slack with shock and what might have been fear. Even across the clearing Ellie could see the jagged tear Oliver's knife had put in her dress, but the pallid skin underneath was whole and undamaged.

Not for long. Ellie snatched the bow, grateful the arrow was somehow still nocked and the cotton ball attached. Slinging the quiver over her shoulder, she half-snuck, half-staggered to where she'd left her Sterno can.

Some part of Ellie hoped the tin had survived, that the little flame that had kept her company all night would still be there, but no. It was gone, obliterated, and the alcohol on the fishing line had burned off. She dug in her pocket for her emergency lighter but it, too, was gone; lost when she'd been blown backward by the first lightning strike.

Pressure started to wrap around her throat; the Lady had recovered. Frantic, Ellie abandoned the fire idea and scrambled to her feet. Even if shooting the demon with a regular arrow wouldn't be fatal, it would throw her off long enough for Ellie to breathe, and then—

SMACK!

Oliver's hatchet buried itself in the Lady's shoulder. The demon let out an eldritch scream and the pressure on Ellie's throat vanished. Heaving for breath, she lurched toward the burning tree and held the arrow out. It ignited. She nocked it again with trembling fingers, then edged backward only to see the Lady's cloak tassels whip out of sight.

Apparently, Ellie wasn't the only one who had decided to use the burning tree for protection.

"Ellie!"

"Oliver!" She went weak and nearly dropped the burning arrow. "You—thanks for the hatchet—"

"No time!" He held up the poker; the light of the fire glittered off the flammable gel on its tip. "Let's flank her—"

A howl of pain and rage echoed through the clearing. Ellie whirled in time to see the Lady burst out from behind the fire, rip the hatchet out of her shoulder, and fling it. On instinct Ellie threw her arm up, using the bow as a shield. The hatchet hit its metal frame with a deep *clang*, knocking it back into Ellie's face and sending her staggering. Pain burned across her face and neck, the skin stinging like it had been whipped.

Half-dazed and trembling, Ellie regained her balance, but the Lady was closing in on them, her face contorted in an inhuman snarl.

Oliver stepped in front of her. One of his hands flew to his throat, and his chest heaved, but he still held the metal high in challenge.

"Plan ... A ..." he choked out.

You distract, I shoot. Ellie fumbled for the bowstring. Her fingers clamped on an end of it—

An end of it?

The bottom dropped out of Ellie's stomach. It was broken, cut clean in half, useless.

"The bow's broken!" she gasped.

Panic flared in Oliver's eyes. The Lady rushed forward in a sudden burst of speed, so fast that Ellie barely had time to react. She dropped the bow and brought her nearly useless arrow up, but Oliver was faster, and his weapon much stronger. He swung the poker in a desperate arc and connected, burying its gelled tip in the curdling flesh of the Lady's stomach.

The demon let out the same weird, wailing shriek she'd given in the hotel and Oliver gasped.

"YES!" Ellie snatched another arrow out of the quiver and charged toward the tree. The flames were starting to die down, but there was still more than enough to catch the alcohol-soaked cotton ball. It flared, and Ellie sprinted back toward where Oliver wrestled with the Lady.

The demon had clamped both skeletal hands around the poker as if she *wanted* to keep it there. Oliver twisted it and she thrashed, but still wouldn't let go. Instead, she pulled the metal deeper into her own stomach, a wide, horrible smile stretching her mouth, and Ellie realized what was about to happen a second before it did.

"OLIVER!" she screamed, but it was too late. Another blinding flash cracked across the clearing. Oliver's hands and arms seized, his body arching, face contorting in agony.

The light went out, and Oliver fell.

He hit the ground and lay utterly, completely still, his eyes glassy and unseeing.

The Lady let out a long, satisfied hiss, then turned to face Ellie. She looked worse for the wear; hunching as if in pain, her hair and cloak limp, her face even more craggy and pitted than usual. But her eyes glittered as malevolently as ever, and now there was triumph in them.

Pressure encircled Ellie's throat, squeezing her consciousness away, supernatural terror striking her with the force of a moving car. She let out a strangled whimper and fell to her knees.

The Lady's face changed, relaxed. She drifted closer, lazily now, as if content to take her time. Her grip on Ellie's throat loosened just slightly. Just enough to prolong her life. Just enough for the demon to enjoy more of Ellie's fear.

Just enough for Ellie's mind to clear some. Enough for a crazy, desperate idea to form in the small part of her mind that was still sane.

"I'm almost sad to see you go," the Lady rasped.

Ellie wanted so badly to say something. Instead, she let herself choke on the words, hoping she could hold the anxiety back long enough to execute this last, desperate plan, begging the universe to please let the tiny flame on the tip of her arrow be enough.

"No, I'm not letting you speak," the Lady tutted. "You'll never speak again. You just let me *enjoy* you."

Ellie's mind was fogging; she clutched at the only coherent thought she still had. *The fear isn't who I am.*

She shook and whimpered and let herself fall forward, scrabbling on the ground but keeping the arrow—and its embers—out of the dirt. The Lady drifted closer.

It's not me.

Closer. Ellie let her eyes stray to Oliver, who lay on the ground, unmoving, and her tears came in earnest. *I'm more than my grief, and I'm more than my fear.*

Feet away, the Lady stopped. Pressure still constricted Ellie's throat; every breath was labored, her act wasn't totally an act. She could only hope it had been enough.

It was now or never.

Ellie lunged, throwing all her strength behind her swing. The arrow wouldn't break the Lady's skin, but she wasn't aiming for that. Instead, she was aiming for the little bit of gel, shimmering in the firelight, that had scraped off the still-embedded poker and onto the tattered folds of the demon's dress. The Lady's eyes widened, but it was too late; the tip of the arrow touched the gel.

It ignited.

Flame erupted in a great gout, engulfing the demon. Ellie cried out and fell back; the heat was so intense she thought the skin of her face might blister. She flung an arm over her head and dragged herself away, toward Oliver's body. Coughing as the pressure on her throat released for the last time, Ellie threw herself over him and looked up at the writhing fireball that had been the Lady.

The demon burned with a brightness and heat that put Ellie's beacon-tree to shame. For a few seconds, she hung there like a second sun. And then, as quickly as the flames appeared, they guttered, a black substance leaking out of her eyes, her ears, every split in her skin. As Ellie watched, it flared, dripping like a fiery waterfall to puddle on the earth. The Lady fell, and what was left of her body shattered on impact, bursting into an unrecognizable heap of glowing coals.

Ellie collapsed over Oliver's body, dazed and shaking. The meadow was as still and silent now as …

As Oliver.

Whose chest wasn't moving.

Any triumph Ellie felt was snuffed out. "Oliver?"

Nothing. He lay spread-eagled on his back, his eyes wide open, beautiful and dead as sapphires.

With trembling fingers, she felt under his jaw for a pulse. His skin was still warm, but his face had gone pale as death.

"*No!*" Ellie scrambled up and put her hands on the center of his chest. "*I won't lose you, too!*"

It had been years since she'd learned how to do chest compressions and she wasn't sure she'd *ever* done them right, but she'd be damned if she just sat here and let Oliver slip away.

"I. Need. You." She punctuated every word with a compression. Beneath her hands, his ribs bowed in his lifeless chest. Anguish swept over her; she was hurting him, *breaking* his body but she couldn't—wouldn't—stop, and then the dam burst. All the insanity she felt came pouring out and she was sobbing and screaming in the red light of the dying fires.

"If you don't get up, I don't think I will, either. So COME!" She slammed the heels of her hands into his chest. "BACK!"

Nothing. She was alone in the dark again. And this time, she didn't have the strength to get up and leave. She could only stay right here, bent over Oliver, trying to bring him back, until the end found her.

"She's dead," Wormwood said. "And ... and so's Oliver."

A sense of freedom spread through him, so intoxicating it made him dizzy. He barely registered Death's shock, his words, his ...

"... and watch," Death was saying. "We must make sure the girl dies, too. You must wait by her until—"

"I have to feed!" Wormwood roared. He drew back, away from the scene. "Oliver hasn't been fully satisfying for days!"

Death snarled, and Wormwood flinched even as resentment welled within him.

"How soon can you be back to them?"

"Soon. Everyone's ashamed of something. All I have to do is find any human that isn't her."

"Go," Death spat. "Then get back to her and report to me."

Chapter Twenty-One

Oliver sat up.

He blinked a few times, trying to clear his vision. When that didn't work, he rubbed a hand over his eyes. But that was weird, too; his hand didn't feel right on his skin. The sensation was more like the *impression* of a touch than an actual touch.

Oliver clutched his temples, trying to remember. He'd jabbed the poker into the Lady's belly, trying to gut her like a salmon. A flash of light, a surge of agony that had locked every muscle in his body, then ... he'd sat up. He didn't remember falling, or blacking out, but he must have.

Self-disgust rose in his throat, bitter as bile. The poker was *metal,* and with electricity involved ... *That was idiotic.*

Groaning, Oliver opened his eyes again. His eyesight was dim, blurry, the night so black that Ellie's tree must have burned out some time ago. Dread fuzzed the edges of his thoughts; something was seriously wrong. If that much time had passed and he was still lying here, then Ellie was either unconscious somewhere nearby, or she was ...

Oliver stumbled to his feet, casting around for a slender, still form lying on the ground. But it was so dark, *everything* was so dark—

Except ...

He stopped. The tree *was* still there, and still burning. It was just ... muted. Hazy. As if what he'd first thought was vision damage was actually a real, physical barrier between him and the flames. And ...

Movement caught Oliver's attention, and his heart seized. Ellie *was* there, right in front of him, his strange, warped vision making her seem ghostlike in his gray hoodie. It was hard to make out details, but she clutched what looked like an arrow in her hand, its end alight.

He went weak with relief. She'd done it. All they had to do now was light the gel he'd smeared all over the poker—

Slowly, *too* slowly, Ellie's hand went to her neck.

"Ellie—" A sickening realization hit Oliver as she started to fold in on herself. The fact that she couldn't seem to see him, her torpid movements, the barrier between them ...

He reached for her, needing to touch her, feel her, feel *pain* if that was what it took, because that was preferable to feeling nothing. To being ...

Oliver couldn't let himself think it. He just stretched out an arm—

"Oliver?"

He froze. That voice.

It was *the* voice.

"Oliver." Where it had once boomed with power, compelled him to action, now it was ... quiet.

No, not just quiet. Unsteady. *Stunned.*

Oliver turned. A man stood a few feet behind him, the same man who'd checked his burns after the wedding. His head was cocked to the side, his mouth open, shock plastered all over his face. He looked solid, real, normal. Behind him, the Lady floated with her hand raised, a blurry, slow-swirling black shape against an even blacker night. Those pitiless eyes stared right though Oliver to where Ellie hunched, gasping in slow motion.

Horror crashed over Oliver. "I ... I'm dead. *God*—" He choked on the word, name, prayer, *whatever* it was; he guessed he'd soon find out. "I'm dead." Another thought hit him, even more terrible than the first. "And this is Hell, isn't it."

The being stood stock-still, that profoundly disturbed look still on his face. Then he shook his head. "For some, yes. But I don't think you—"

Oliver panicked. He pivoted, trying to orient himself, but there was no moon, no stars in this place. Just distorted visions of people he loved and creatures he hated, and he could do nothing about either.

He whirled back to Ellie. "No, I have to go back. I can't leave her." His voice broke. Even through the barrier, he could see her struggling to breathe, see the pain on her beautiful features, the desolation.

He glanced back. Behind the ... the *angel* that had helped them, the Lady came on. Oliver took a shaky breath. He probably didn't need to do that anymore, but the familiarity of it gave him comfort. And he needed that, needed a clear head. The angel obviously had some level of power. Maybe there was still a chance.

Oliver faced him. "You're the angel."

"I wouldn't call myself that."

"You've been helping us, though. You were there at the gate, in the fire, before the border crossing, you were even on my plane to Denver."

"Yes."

Hope rose in Oliver's hollowed-out, empty, impression-chest. "Can you send me back?"

The angel shook his head. "That's not within my power. But Oliver," he added when Oliver pressed a hand to his face, threatening to buckle, "don't count yourself out. The shock stopped your heart, so clinically, you're dead. But there might be a way—"

Oliver bolted upright. "How? I'll do anything—"

"How much do you believe in her?" The angel nodded toward where Ellie quailed, arrow in hand.

Memories blurred through Oliver's mind; Ellie standing on the lawn of the Luxembourg house, her pink dress rumpled from where Grandpa Forth had stopped her from running into a burning building after him. The terror that Ellie had faced at the gate, the Nantinaq's clear respect for her. The arrows she'd shot at the Horseman, those dazzling gray eyes boring into his as they sat on her porch swing, full of peace, hope, clarity. How they'd looked right before he'd kissed her ...

He took a step toward her, close enough to see the terror on her face and the fierce little spark in those eyes. The way she could reconcile those two things amazed him.

Oliver glanced at the angel. "She's one of the smartest, most capable people I've ever met. There's no one I'd rather trust with my life."

"Good. You've noticed the wounds the demons cause heal quickly. If Ellie can give you a chance—rescue breathing, CPR—you might pull through. Wounds aside, your body is strong and healthy. It wants to live, and you obviously want to return to it." The angel crossed his arms, turning his eyes on Ellie. They were difficult to read, but Oliver thought there might really be hope in them. "All we can do now is wait. And trust."

The Lady started to glide through the angel, pieces and parts of her blending with him in a way that was disorienting, *disturbing*. Her tattered cloak drifted around him as if caught in a slow-motion squall. When the angel caught sight of her, he grimaced, sidestepped, and turned his attention back to Ellie.

Oliver studied him. Ellie's description had been accurate; he was about Oliver's height and build. But his outfit was ... surprising. He wore jeans and a gray tee shirt—the kind of simple, comfortable clothes that would've looked at home in Oliver's own closet. And his face, with those high cheekbones and wavy dark-brown hair ... It was so familiar—almost piercingly so—that Oliver couldn't help trying to place it.

Of course it's familiar. I saw him when he checked my burns. But no, it was more than that. He racked his addled brains, trying to remember, but decided to just give up. "Who are you?"

The angel blinked, then his face went blank. "Someone who cares about you." Again, he nodded at Ellie. "And the people *you* care about."

Inwardly, Oliver sighed. *Not helpful.* Though ... blue jeans aside, the being *was* an angel. Or at least, he seemed to be. And they probably had full license to be as cryptic as they liked.

Still, Oliver watched him for another second, head tilted. He was getting more and more convinced that his first impression had been right: that the angel was *profoundly* agitated. He had the same look on his face that Oliver associated with people who suddenly found themselves in over their heads and had no idea what to do about it.

Though that could be because I just died.

Oliver began to pace back and forth, circling Ellie like she was the earth and he the moon. Everything—both their fates—hinged on what she was about to do. The least he could do was be there for her, even if she couldn't see him. And—he trembled—especially if she didn't win. If she ended up ...

No, he thought. *You can do it, Ellie. Don't let the next time we see each other be here.*

The Lady floated closer with each unbearably slow second, away from Oliver's body, lying prone on the ground.

Another dull pang of shock hit him at the sight.

He glanced at Ellie and the Lady, his gaze more calculating this time. Based on their positions, it hadn't taken him long to wake up in this ... place. Still, some part of him worried about brain and organ damage. Even if Ellie did save him, it wouldn't do any good if he woke up a shell of his former self.

"How long have I been dead?" he asked.

Still watching Ellie with a deep frown, the angel shook his head. "I don't know for sure."

Oliver raised his eyebrows. For a being that was supposed to be all-knowing, that didn't sit right. Suspicion stirred in him, and with it, dismay. "All right."

Oliver started to pace again. He was separated from his body. How did he still have this much need to *move*?

"Time matters less here," the angel said. "Spirits don't experience it the same way physical bodies do. By my best guess, you've probably only been dead about twenty seconds, maybe less."

Oliver stopped. "*Twenty seconds*? This is unendurable." He started to pace again. "How have you not gone insane?"

"I have my ways. I get to see the triumphs of … the people under my care, and you'd be surprised how therapeutic that is. Plus, I talk to other spirits, and other beings in your world who are more sensitive to, well, *presences* like mine."

More dots connected in Oliver's mind. "Like the Nantinaq. He told me he talks to angels. I'd almost forgotten."

The angel chuckled. "*We* haven't talked much, but yes. Though his communication is dicey. He isn't from our world, either, so he just has to piece things together as best he can. Which is why," he said, turning to Oliver, "you have the misconceptions you do about me. 'Angel' isn't the right word. 'Spirit' or 'ghost' is more accurate. And better reflects my abilities."

"They … don't seem as earth-shattering as I'd hoped," Oliver admitted.

"That's fine," the angel said absently.

Oliver looked sideways at him. There was no question he was fighting some kind of internal battle; Oliver had been there too many times to not recognize the signs on another man's face.

That weird, familiar face.

He shook himself, returning his gaze to the sluggish scene in front of him. "How long can I be dead before my body's permanently damaged?"

The ghost shrugged one shoulder. "Five minutes, give or take. Even then, I wouldn't count you out, though. If there's one thing I know about you, you're a fighter." A tiny smile lifted one corner of the man's lips. It looked awkward, like he wasn't sure it was supposed to be there. "Just like your mother."

"Like my mother ..."

The revelation hit.

Memories of old photographs he'd seen, all those long years ago, before his mother had finally put them away. Maybe thrown them away. Maybe burned them in a barrel with every other memento of *him*, the man who had abandoned his wife and baby son and left them to fend for themselves.

Of course his face looked familiar. Oliver saw its features in the mirror every day.

"Dean," he snarled.

Dean's face closed off, all except his eyes. They gave him away totally, gave away all the sadness, the guilt, the regret he must feel. The regret he'd *better* feel. "Oliver, I'm so—"

"*Don't* say you're sorry! Don't you *dare* tell me you're sorry."

"Oliver—"

"I hope you've suffered," Oliver growled. All those years of watching his mother deteriorate, of his own feelings of unworthiness and shame and devastation—took over. The agony spilled from his mouth like the poison he knew it was, but he couldn't stop. He advanced on Dean, stalking right through the Lady as he did, his body—his *spirit*—shaking with rage.

"I hope the last twenty-two years have been hell for you. I hope you watched every. Single. *Second* of what we had to go through. Of what Mom had to go through. You ... you ..." Oliver drew in a ragged breath. He would *not* shed tears in front of this man. Even if he could, Dean wasn't worthy.

"I did watch," Dean said quietly.

"She had to sell herself to feed me! She had to go without food, without medicine, without any comfort, or rest, for *years*, because you were too much of a coward to stand by the woman *you said you loved!*"

"I know, Oliver." His voice was still so maddeningly, infuriatingly, QUIET!

"And then you couldn't even stick around to help raise the baby you made!" Oliver thumped his chest so hard that if he'd still had a body, his fist would have left bruises. "ME! Did you ever even hold me? Or did you run away the second Mom got home from the hospital?" His voice broke. "Was I really such a bad kid that I drove you to not only abandon us, but to *overdose on heroin*?"

Dean was silent, his eyes full of something Oliver couldn't read. Sickened, Oliver looked away, back at Ellie.

Just in time to see her collapse.

He was to her before her knees hit the ground, reaching out on instinct, but his hands passed right through her body. Hot rage burned through him; rage at the man behind him and at his own helplessness. He breathed again, willing the rote motion to calm him enough to not just … *hurl* himself at Dean. "Was it on purpose?"

"My death? No." A beat of silence. "But when I woke up here, well … I wasn't devastated."

Oliver half-turned, not bothering to hide his fury. It was so sharp and bitter in his throat that he could barely speak. "You … you bastard, Dean. You—"

"I woke up the morning after I left knowing I'd made the biggest mistake of my life. I couldn't look in the mirror. I hated myself." Dean gestured around. "I ended up here less than a month after I ran. And the *first* thing I did was look for you and Autumn. "

"I don't *care*—"

Dean held up a hand and damn it if Oliver didn't fall silent.

"Listen, Oliver. You're right about me being a bastard. Literally. I didn't know who my father was. I never knew. And, as you know, that leaves a hole. I was always reckless, emotional, prone to acting—and speaking—without thinking. I got involved in drugs, but harder than yours, and from a much younger age. I was hooked hard."

"Don't try and justify yourself."

"I'm not. I'm hoping some context will help you realize my actions weren't your fault."

Oliver glared at him, but Dean ignored the hint.

"When I met your mother … well, Autumn was brilliant and beautiful. She made me feel more deeply than any other woman I'd ever met."

Dean paused again, and despite his rage, Oliver was struck by how calm he was. Where Oliver's insides felt as scorched as the remnants of the Luxembourg House, the dead man was practically *clinical*. There was no hint of either self-justification or self-derision in his tone or demeanor; Dean was simply stating facts.

"I got clean for a while. It was easily the best time of my life. Within a year, I'd asked Autumn to marry me, and she said yes."

"One of the only bad decisions she ever made," Oliver muttered.

"Well, *you're* here, so it wasn't all bad."

Oliver looked away. "I'm not sure getting me here was worth all that pain."

Dean's eyebrows lifted. "Oh, you are. There isn't a soul out there that isn't worth the pain. And given some of the souls out there, that's saying something." He fixed Oliver with a flat stare. "Quit putting yourself below everyone else. It's both demonstrably false and a waste of energy. And you're going to need all the energy you have."

Ellie's knees finally hit the ground, and Oliver crouched in front of her. She still hadn't let go of the arrow, but in her current state, would she be able to use it?

"Listen," he said, "I know I'll be going right back to a fight if this works. But if I can get back to her, I'll thank God—or whoever's in charge of this ... this *mess*—for every second, no matter how bad." He shot a venomous look at Dean. "It can't be worse than being stuck here with you."

Dean ignored his last jibe. "There's no denying you're in for a fight. But Oliver, what comes after the fight?"

Oliver watched Ellie's mouth open wide in a silent scream, and helplessness sent another surge of fury through him. "Are you seriously trying to teach me something right now? *Dad*?"

Dean barely reacted. "Eventually, this will end. And when it does, I bet you'll have some very good times. I want you to have energy to enjoy them, Oliver. To thrive. Please, don't waste it on hating yourself when there's nothing—*absolutely nothing*—to hate."

The words struck Oliver to his core, fanning the maelstrom there. It felt so good to be comforted by his father. And so pathetic.

He'd never been more confused.

"Any other ... *confessions* you want to make?" Oliver spat.

"You know how the story ends," Dean said softly, then sighed. Oliver looked up at him, but he was watching Ellie, and there was pain—deep and tearing—on his face. For a moment, they were both silent, watching her fold in a slow-motion bow. The Lady drifted to a stop, a look of lazy triumph on her face.

"I don't know how much that helped, Oliver," Dean said. "And I am *truly* sorry. You just ..." For the first time, his voice betrayed him. He swallowed and went on. "Don't ever—*ever*—take the responsibility for my immaturity, my bad decisions, on yourself. What I did was not your fault."

Still kneeling in front of Ellie, Oliver bowed his head. If they'd have been on the same plane of existence, their foreheads would have touched.

"You punched a hole in my soul, Dean," he finally whispered. "It's been festering for almost twenty-two years. And you think one lousy pep talk is going to make me forgive you?"

"I'm not asking you to forgive me." Dean's voice was soft but resolute. "I don't expect you to. All I want—all I've wanted for years—is for you to let this burden go so you can *live*."

"Well, I'd like that, too." Oliver was aiming for sarcasm, but he choked on the words as he realized how truly, desperately, he wanted to be free of the shame. It was a black, bottomless shaft that bored all the way through him, that influenced every part of who he was, and it felt all the uglier now that Dean had bared it.

"Shame lies, Oliver, and you're too smart to listen to it. I'm proud of the work you've done, and I *know* you're strong enough to finish the job." Dean took a step closer, and out of the corner of his eye, Oliver saw him lift a hand, as if he wanted to rest it on Oliver's back. Oliver tensed; he couldn't help it.

Dean let his hand fall without changing his expression. "You're a good man already. Overcome this, and you'll be great."

Oliver didn't know what to say. For a moment he was grateful he didn't have a heart, because it would have cracked in half right then and there. Through the haze in his eyes, he focused on Ellie. He could see the terror in every perfect line of her body, the *hurt*. Slowly, Oliver placed a hand over hers. Neither of them could feel it, but if there was the slightest chance his belief in her, his *love* for her, could help …

"Come on, you amazing, brilliant woman," he murmured, hopefully too low for Dean to hear. "You're more than your fear. You've beat it before, and you can beat it … again …"

Ellie raised her eyes, looking in the direction of his body, and the defiant spark in her eyes flared.

Understanding hit Oliver. "She's baiting the Lady with her fear! She's got it completely under control!" He reached up, tracing the outline of her face with a finger. "Well done, you."

Something floated by Oliver's vision; it took him a moment to realize it was one of the Lady's cloak tassels. She must be hovering right behind him.

"Come on, Ellie," Dean said, and Oliver had to admit … there was no way the concern in the dead man's voice was an act. "You're more than your grief."

"You stole that from me."

"It was wise."

A horrible thought occurred to Oliver, and his face twisted in disgust. "Do I ever have any privacy, or do you stalk me all the time?"

"No. I value privacy and dignity. There are moments, conversations, that are only yours, and I respect them."

"Well, that's—"

Ellie made her move. Oliver snapped his mouth shut, his nerves leaping as she stabbed the tip of the arrow toward the Lady's gut ... and the flammable gel there. She moved slowly enough that Oliver had time to lurch to his feet and scramble out of the way. For a second, he and Dean were both silent, tense, but her trajectory looked good, and ...

"YES!" Oliver yelled as the ember caught. Flame burst upward, searing across the Lady's torso with explosive force. "You beat her!"

The raging red light caught Ellie's face, illuminating her terrified expression. Oliver's gut clenched in sympathy; he knew firsthand how hot the creatures burned. True, that supernaturally-hot feeling might have been because *everything* had been on fire at the time, but judging from Ellie's reaction, he didn't think so.

Oliver looked up to see Dean watching him, a hint of a smile on his face. Then, the dead man folded his arms and looked back at Ellie, who had hit the ground and was starting to roll away. "She's amazing. A great woman."

"I know. And I'm going to treat her that way."

"I have no doubt you will, son. You're a better man than I ever was in life."

Oliver jerked his eyes to Dean, caught somewhere between rage that Dean would dare call him "son" and ... how wonderful his compliment had felt. Suddenly, he found himself blinking back those odd tear-impressions again. Folding his arms over his chest, he swallowed and turned back to Ellie. She'd come up onto her hands and knees and was crawling toward his body. Nerves pricked him. It would have to be soon.

Oliver's gaze flicked to the Lady, suspended in the air. The flames were *eating* her, devouring her dress and the rotted flesh beneath, pouring out of her eyes, her ears, her stretched, screaming mouth. They seemed almost gleeful. More like Oliver had thought he would feel when she finally died.

He did feel something. Triumph maybe. Certainly relief. But it was all muted, buried beneath rage, confusion, and fear that somehow he wouldn't be able to make it back. That he'd be stuck here with the man behind him.

Oliver glanced sideways at Dean, who was watching Ellie with open pride and relief. It was such a fatherly expression that it made Oliver pause. How many times *had* Dean looked at him like that, from beyond death itself? A small, desperately painful part of his heart—a part he'd rarely allowed himself to *look* at, let alone feel—twinged.

"Why didn't you warn us this time?" he asked.

"That the Lady was about to attack, you mean?"

Oliver nodded.

"I yelled and screamed at both of you for a good fifteen minutes before she got here. I just ..." For the first time, frustration colored Dean's tone. "I couldn't make you hear me this time."

"Why not?"

"I don't know. I ..." Dean ran a hand through his hair. "I'm not supposed to be here, Oliver."

"What do you mean?"

"I mean that I belong in the spirit world, not this ... in-between place."

"So, there's a spirit world?"

Dean looked over at him, his expression guarded. "Yes."

"Where the souls of the dead live?"

"Yes."

"And this—" Oliver gestured at the odd shroud that blurred details and slowed time "—this isn't it."

"No. I don't exactly know what this place is, other than some sort of in-between. I came here briefly when I died. Saw myself—my body—in that room, watched them carry it away. Then, I was ..." Dean frowned. "I don't know how to describe it. I was *pulled* into the spirit world."

Questions whirled in Oliver's head. He glanced at the Lady, who was now so charred that none of her features were left, and quickly looked away. Just because he didn't feel any pity for the demon didn't mean he enjoyed watching her burn alive.

"And you can see ..." Oliver waved his arm at the scene in front of them "... *this* world, the world of the living ... from the spirit world?"

"Yes."

Something far more painful than a heartbeat started thumping in Oliver's chest. "Is Mom there?"

"Yes."

"Is she ..." Oliver's voice was suddenly unsteady. "Is she okay? Is she happy?"

Dean smiled. "Yes, she's happy."

The dead man's expression was so paternal. Oliver's eight-year-old self would have glowed if Dean had looked at him like that. His twenty-two-year-old self just wanted to punch the look right off his face. But he shook off the rage; there were other questions he wanted answered. And this next one ...

He steeled himself. "Why didn't she ...?"

Dean waited for a moment as Oliver struggled to finish the sentence. Then, in a soft voice, he said, "Why isn't she here, too?"

Blinking, looking anywhere but at Dean, Oliver nodded.

"She tried, Oliver. I don't know why I made it through and she didn't, but ..." Dean cocked his head, considering. "When one barrier opens, strange things often happen to the others. Usually, they get weaker."

"That ... makes sense?" Oliver said, thinking back to Darien's immune system analogy.

"But it only lasted for a few minutes at most, and the shift was subtle. I'd been trying to help you from the other side ever since my death, so I was *right there*, ready to take advantage of it. That few seconds might've made all the difference."

Dean paused. "It also seems like living a life full of mistakes and regret makes it harder to move on. All that stuff about ghosts and 'unfinished business' has to come from somewhere. Your mother, well, she doesn't carry the guilt I do. Intent, how *invested* a person is ... it matters."

The words cut Oliver to the bone. Did that mean ... had some part of his mother not wanted to come back?

Dean went on, seeming oblivious to Oliver's sudden agony. "Autumn did the right thing from the beginning. I, on the other hand, have a lot to make up for." He shrugged. "Maybe it's the universe's way of ..." His voice changed, concern coloring it as Oliver started to shake. "Oliver?"

Oliver took a deep breath; it was so strange, the way his ... ghost? ... responded to intense emotion the same way his body would have. It was like it hadn't quite separated itself. For a moment, he let himself be distracted by the sight of the Lady's remains hitting the ground, her charred body shattering into embers. They glittered through the black barrier, a scattered handful of angry stars. A profound sense of relief swept through him. *If nothing else, at least Ellie's free of her now.*

Oliver turned his attention back to Dean, folding his arms to try and hide his trembling. "Did she see it all?"

"Everything."

Shame. It was a tidal wave, as strong as the ones in Seldovia, sucking him out to sea with unrelenting force. He couldn't speak, couldn't look at Dean, or Ellie. It was all he could do not to fall to his knees.

"And," Dean said, "she's proud of you. Not just that, she's amazed by you."

Tear-impressions started to slide down Oliver's cheeks with abandon. He let them.

"We both are."

Oliver hid his face in his hands as the sobs broke free. They shuddered over, around, *through* him, hollowing and purging and ... cleansing?

"You don't fully understand the magnitude of what you've overcome, Oliver. But you need to try." Dean was silent for a minute, but when he spoke again, his voice was closer. Oliver looked up to see the dead man only an arm's length away. "*Please*, son. Forgive yourself. Let yourself be happy."

For a moment, Oliver held Dean's gaze, those eyes full of nothing but compassion and love. Then, breathing heavily, Oliver looked back at Ellie before Dean's gaze broke him again.

Am I breaking, a small part of him wondered, *or is this how it feels to be put back together?*

Ellie turned to look at where the Lady's embers lay, then, slowly, she pushed herself up. Her hand slid to Oliver's neck, as if she were checking for a pulse. Oliver's spirit-hand drifted to the spot where hers rested against his skin; he could almost feel its softness, its warmth.

"Come on, Ellie," Dean said. Then, he took a step closer, raising his voice. "CPR!"

Oliver reeled forward. He'd just taken a shaky breath to join Dean's encouragement when Ellie surged, coming up onto her knees.

"She's going to do it!" A wide smile split Dean's face as Ellie's hands came together in the center of Oliver's chest. "She didn't even need us!" He whirled to Oliver. "You're badly injured, but since most of the injuries are demon-caused, they'll heal very quickly. There's a—"

"Why do demon-caused injuries heal more quickly?" Oliver interrupted. "Is that—?"

"The same reason it was so hard for me to get those wire cutters and knock out that camera. We don't belong in this world, so we aren't as … permanent. Because of that, my energy goes quickly and takes a long time to build up again. But on the flip side, it's easier for the body to heal from demon-caused injuries, apparently." Dean shook his head. "I don't fully understand how it works, but I'm grateful it does. Now—"

A jolt of energy hit Oliver square in the chest. He staggered, his gaze swinging to where Ellie crouched over his body. She rose in slow motion, then started to come down again. Oliver barely had time to brace himself before he was jolted again, and with it came pain. He gasped.

"The fact that it hurts can only be a good sign, right?" he gritted out.

"Yes. Oliver, listen—" Dean glanced to where Ellie was winding up again, crying openly now. This time the surge of emotion that went through Oliver had nothing to do with CPR. *I'm coming, Ellie.*

"You're going to hurt so bad you might wish you were dead again," Dean said, "but don't give in to the pain. It'll pass. Use the stuff in the closet. Clean your burns, bandage them tightly—"

Ellie hit Oliver again; he doubled over.

"Oliver!" Dean's voice was sharp, commanding again. "Focus, then you can go! There are virtually no demons nearby. Get cleaned up, then both of you sleep. You should be safe for about eight hours—"

Pain splattered across Oliver's chest as Ellie hit him again and he groaned, falling to his knees. She was moving faster, and the world was whirling around him, he was *suffocating*—

"Goodbye, son."

The world flipped upside down and Oliver tumbled, disoriented and in agony and completely out of oxygen. Everything narrowed, overpowered by a single, desperate urge.

To *breathe*.

Chapter Twenty-Two

Ellie sobbed, fighting waves of agony and revulsion every time Oliver's ribs bent under her hands. She remembered that CPR, when properly done, could break them, but no amount of classroom instruction could have prepared her for what that really meant, what it *felt* like. She begged, pleaded, whimpered his name with every compression, barely aware she was saying it. Time bent around her; she couldn't have been doing this for more than three minutes, but it felt like days. Already it was sapping what little physical strength she had left.

Focus. Stayin' alive. One hundred beats per minute. The notes—the beat—swooped like bats over the hell that was her terror. She snatched at them, clung to them. *Stayin' alive, stayin' alive ...* Her arms started to tremble. *Stayin' alive.* One more compression. *Stayin'*—

Oliver's body jerked.

Ellie jumped. Recovering, she leaned over and pressed two fingers to his neck. For one long second, there was nothing.

Then the bare whisper of a pulse shivered at her fingertips.

Panic bubbled up in Ellie's stomach but she forced herself to think, to pare the situation down to its core. *Rescue breathing.*

Ellie didn't remember the right technique, but Oliver's pulse wouldn't last long if he didn't get any oxygen. She had to try. Awkwardly, she tilted his head back and chin up, his pulse flitting weakly at her fingertips like a trapped butterfly. She took a deep breath and leaned down—

Oliver gasped.

Ellie shrieked, clapping her hands to her mouth. The sound was ghastly, more like a death rattle than the breath of life. Panic threatened again; once he was breathing, how did she keep him that way? Especially since his lungs sounded *full of fluid?!*

Oliver arched, his head turning slowly toward the smoldering tree, the last dance of its flames reflecting in his glassy eyes. For what seemed like hours he stayed there, every muscle strained, as if his body were trying to decide if the oxygen was enough to coax it back to life.

Ellie seized his hand. "Don't give up!"

The breath whistled out of him in a rush. He heaved in another, as labored and wet-sounding as the first, and held it again.

"Oliver ..." Ellie's voice cracked. His skin was waxy, his eyes wide and staring. Wherever he was, it still wasn't here.

He exhaled, then sucked in another lungful of air, and maybe ...

Hope hit Ellie. Yes, that breath seemed to have come easier. Shaking nearly as hard as Oliver, she placed a hand over his heart. It thundered with a vengeance, as if trying to make up for the minutes it had lost. "Oliver, I know what's in here. I know what you're capable of, and I know you can beat this. Come back to me!"

Oliver's eyes closed. His hard-fought breath released as a tortured groan, his face contorting with pain. Ellie gripped his hand, hoping, praying, willing him to pull through.

His eyes slit open, and finally—*finally*—they focused. "Ellie."

A lump rose in Ellie's throat; she squeezed his trembling hand. "You made it back."

Oliver's eyes fell closed again, his face twisting, and he let out a long, pained cry. It went through Ellie like a knife. She bolted upright, her hands hovering over him, but she didn't dare put them anywhere.

"Where does it hurt?" she asked.

"Everywhere! My insides are—"

He cried out again but cut off as a coughing fit seized him. They sounded wet and awful, like he was dying of pneumonia, and racked his entire body. Ellie forced herself to breathe, to not give in to the panic clawing at the edges of her mind. She'd been an idiot for thinking he was out of the woods; he'd taken an electric current straight to the chest! And with no hospital within a hundred miles, and no cell service for who knew how far ...

She was all he had.

Ellie put a hand on his spasming chest. "Can we roll you onto your side?"

Oliver was hacking so hard he couldn't speak, but he pushed, trying to roll toward her. Ellie grabbed his shoulder and waist and pulled. He came to rest on his side, still coughing. Ellie kept a hand on his shoulder until the coughing receded. It wasn't much, but it was the only comfort she could offer.

He groaned again, his breath hissing through his teeth. "I don't like ... how often we ... end up here."

"Let's never do it again."

"I'll ... try."

Oliver gasped again, his eyes squeezing shut. His jaw clenched and he trembled. Through tear-filled eyes, Ellie looked up at the cabin. Maybe she could run in and grab some of that painkiller, then—

His hand twitched around hers, tightening. "Help me ... inside."

"We should get you to the truck, so we can get to a hospital."

"No." He groaned, clutching his stomach. "No hospitals."

"Oliver, *look* at yourself. Even with a closet full of medical stuff, I can't—"

His cry of pain shattered Ellie's sentence, so desperate and agonized it was all she could do to keep from screaming herself. She scrambled to her feet, babbling, "Let me get some painkiller, let me—"

"Wait! I can ... can feel it ... healing. Give me ... time."

He screamed again, and Ellie knew she would never get the sound out of her head for as long as she lived.

"Stay," he gasped when it was over. "Wait."

Crying, Ellie bowed over him, clutching his hands. "For how long?" *How much of this could he endure?*

She would never know the answer to the first question, but the answer to the second was: enough. Gradually, Oliver relaxed, his full-body tremors subsiding until they were more like shivers, as if he were cold.

"I think ..." He clenched his teeth as another spasm racked his body. "I think I can make it ... inside."

Ellie glanced up. If they could make it to the cabin, they could also make it to the truck. Who knew if Wormwood was still around? And what *else* lurked in the shadows of the trees? If there was anyone—or anything—within a few miles, Oliver's screams would have given them away.

"I still think we need to get in the truck and get away from here." *And closer to a hospital, just in case.* If it were a choice between legal troubles and losing Oliver again, she'd take the former.

"No." To Ellie's shock, Oliver pushed himself onto trembling arms, panting. "We're safe for a few hours."

Ellie frowned. "How do you know?"

"I—" Another tortured groan escaped Oliver, but he managed to get his knees underneath him. Slowly, he raised his head, and for the first time, Ellie got a really good look at his face. His eyes were clouded with pain and exhaustion, and ... some deep, lingering shock, something *haunting*.

Ellie shook her head. *He just had a near-death experience. What do you expect?*

"Help me ... up," he panted. "I'll tell you ... on the way. But be careful, I ... I think I'm burned."

Memories of the wedding—of the crisped skin of the kitchen workers—filled Ellie's mind and her stomach swooped. She stood anyway, offering Oliver her hands. "Let's get you inside and we can deal with it there."

Oliver grasped her hands, then let out one long moan and slumped forward, his head resting against her stomach. Staggering, she looped her hands under his arms and leaned into him, a jolt going through her before she realized he was still breathing.

After about ten seconds, Oliver mumbled, "Sorry. I'm ... I'm back now."

"Quit apologizing. I'm just glad you're alive."

A breath whooshed out of Oliver; it almost sounded like it could have been a laugh. "Me too. You ... ready?""

Ellie braced herself. "Yes."

Oliver forced one foot underneath him so he was on one knee. "One, two ..."

"Three," Ellie puffed. She hauled back with everything she had and Oliver staggered upright, gasping and shaking. The little color that had come back into his face drained from it. He swayed, and Ellie seized him around the waist. "Don't collapse on me now. Here ..."

She ducked under Oliver's arm, draping it around her shoulders. His head flopped against hers but he managed to keep his feet, and together they shuffled to the cabin's back door. Shoving it open, Ellie made for the couch and eased Oliver down onto it. He collapsed, his eyes rolling back in his head, and Ellie's heart shot into her throat. "Oliver!"

She fumbled for the closest lamp, flooding the room in artificial light that seemed too bright and rich after the glowering, skulking bonfire. It threw Oliver—and the fact that he was, indeed, unconscious again—into sharp relief. She scrambled to him, putting two trembling fingers to his exposed neck, and nearly cried when she felt the strong, steady beat of his pulse against her fingertips. He was still breathing, too, easy and noiseless.

Unsure what to do, Ellie bent over him, rubbing his shoulder. It was so quiet she could hear her own heartbeat.

This is when I should be cleaning his burns. She gulped. *While he's passed out.* But what if something had gone wrong internally? What if the healing ability just hadn't been enough? What if he'd slipped into a coma?

For a wild moment, she was tempted to haul him to the truck and take off for the nearest hospital, consequences be damned. But before she could get up, Oliver let out a weak cough, then spoke.

"... wasn't kidding ..." he mumbled.

Ellie stared. "Oliver? Are you ... are you with me?"

"I'm with you." He coughed again, and his eyes slit open. They were glazed with pain but lucid. "'M glad we made it to the couch."

"Me, too. And after seeing that, I *really* think the best idea is to get you to a hospital."

"No, Ellie."

"Oliver, your body is wrecked, and I'm not qualified to do this. Please—"

"I'm healing." With a groan, he pushed against the couch, trying to sit up. "We need to ... to bandage my burns, then rest. My body will take care ... of itself if we can just ..."

Ellie steadied him as he rose. His eyes squeezed shut, his face contorted in pain, and he let out another long cry. Every muscle in his body was tensed in agony. Tears coursed down Ellie's cheeks but she made herself look him in the eye. "Give me one good reason to stay."

"Dean," Oliver whispered.

Ellie blinked. "Dean?"

"I talked to D ..." He let out a snort that was clearly derisive. "The *angel*. He was ... was Dean the whole time."

"Like, your *father*?"

"Yeah."

That explains the haunted look in his eyes, Ellie thought.

"He said ... he said to get cleaned up and then sleep," Oliver said. "We have eight hours. Besides ... as you said, we have hospital stuff."

"I did say that, didn't I," Ellie muttered. "You're *sure* you trust him?"

For a moment, Oliver didn't say anything. Then ...

"Yes. And you ... trusted him ... first."

Can't argue with that. Ellie stood and jogged for the closet. "Okay, then. Let me find that field medicine book and let's do this."

She threw the door open, snatched the book, and flipped to its table of contents. Relief washed over her. "It's got an entire chapter on treating burns."

"Oh, good," Oliver said. His breathing was still shallow, but that seemed to be because of pain now, not because it was nearly impossible for him to do it. Given the circumstances, Ellie would take it.

She skimmed the most important points in the chapter, trying to ignore the way the blunt, clinical descriptions made her stomach churn. Then, she grabbed the first-aid kit, hurried to the bathroom, and threw open the mirror cabinet. With a shaking hand, she reached for the bottle labeled **Oxycodone, 15 mg**, then rushed back to the couch, where she unsnapped the kit and laid all the supplies out on its soft upholstery. She spared a second to be thankful the section on burns was smack in the middle of the manual; she could lay it down on the couch and it would stay open to the right pages on its own.

"It says to keep the victim warm," she explained. *Which makes sense.* She knew what it felt like to have goosebumps erupt underneath a sunburn, and was sure Oliver's burns were far, far worse. All the same, it was impossible to know whether she was doing the right things in the right order. All she could do was trust the manual and hope its information wasn't wrong or outdated.

She swallowed her fear and moved to the wood stove. "You started a fire in here, right?"

"Yeah, but I haven't ... tended it ..." Oliver clenched his teeth and dropped his head to his hands.

"It's fine, don't worry about it." Ellie swung the door open and her heart leaped. Embers still glowed in the stove's belly. She stuffed a few handfuls of newspaper and some logs in there, then, when they ignited, she swung the door shut.

Plus, that's a resource if we're attacked again. She'd trusted the parking lot ghost and the EMT, but now that she knew he was the man who'd abandoned Oliver as a baby ...

Well, precautions were never unwarranted.

Ellie hurried back and plunked down next to him, flipping open the manual again. "There. Getting you warm should help with the shivering, which should help with the pain."

"Thank you. It ... hurts."

Ellie could have smacked herself. *I should have given him the painkiller already!* She grabbed it, fumbling with the lid. "Here. Painkiller. I'm ... I'm sorry I didn't do that first thing—I was going to, but there was so much—"

Oliver groaned, his voice raw with barely suppressed agony. "S'okay. You're stressed."

Ellie shot to her feet again. "Let me get you water so you can take one of these." She rummaged in the kitchen cabinets, trying to ignore Oliver's half-stifled groans. "Does it help to talk?"

"When I ... can."

Ellie snatched a glass and filled it, then hurried back and squinted at the label. *One pill every 4-6 hours ...* But how much was 15 milligrams? Too much? Not enough? And *how did she know if oxycodone was what was actually in there?*

Oliver doubled over, a harsh scream issuing from between his teeth.

"God help us," Ellie said. It was the closest she'd ever come to praying in her life.

Might as well, she thought helplessly. There were no more options. Hoping she wasn't about to kill Oliver, Ellie held out the pill with trembling hands. "Here."

He stared at it through bleary eyes. "What is it?"

"Oxycodone."

Oliver dropped his head. "No."

Ellie stared at him. *You've got to be kidding me.*

"Oliver, please. You'll probably only need one pill at the rate you're healing, *maybe* two—"

"Then let me ... heal ... on my own."

"*Why?* You just *died,* came back, and now we have to ..." She closed her eyes, shutting out images from the wedding, of blistered, crisping skin and faces stretched in agony. "We have to clean your burns. That's going to hurt. There's *no reason* not to be kind to yourself."

Oliver let out a pained little noise, resting his forehead in one hand.

"Damn, it, *just take the pill!*"

"No."

"Why?!"

"I don't ... trust myself."

Ellie cocked her head as a strange thought occurred to her. "Have you ... never taken prescription painkillers before?"

"No."

"Wisdom teeth? Tonsils? Appendix?"

"Still have 'em all."

"Not even after you ... broke your ribs?"

Another shake of his head.

Ellie threw up his hands. "Well, Mister Perfect, welcome to the real world. This is how the rest of us get by, and we mostly come out fine—"

"Ellie, Dean died of an opioid overdose."

Ellie snapped her mouth shut; he'd told her that ages ago, when they'd walked together after her father's death. Still ... she swallowed her embarrassment, reached for his hand, and placed the little pill in his palm. Then she put two fingers under his chin, tilting his face up until she could see his tormented eyes. "I'm sorry. That was insensitive. But Oliver, you're not him. And *I* trust you."

Oliver's eyes fell to the pill in his palm, and it seemed to Ellie like something changed in his gaze. Slowly, he raised his hand and popped it in his mouth.

Tension went out of Ellie in a rush. "Thank you," she said, handing him the water.

"It's thrown me off ... seeing him."

"I can't even imagine what that was like."

For a second, there was silence except for Oliver's ragged breathing. A log popped in the wood stove.

"I was thinking," Ellie said softly, "well, we have a few minutes before the painkiller kicks in, and we probably want to wait to clean your burns until then."

Oliver grunted in agreement.

"If you wanted to talk about what happened after ... the Lady ..." She put up a hand as Oliver raised his head. "Don't feel like you need to, but if it helps ..."

He stared at a point on the wall for a moment, then let out a sigh. "I think it might."

Ellie listened as, haltingly, he told her what had happened after his heart stopped. Of the barrier that had been between them, how strange it felt to lose his body, of the weird time warp he'd found himself in. But mostly, she listened to him talk about Dean and their conversation in heart-wrenching detail. His voice changed as time passed, growing smoother as the pain lessened, evening into that quiet, rich timbre that was so achingly familiar.

He didn't stop shaking, however, until he was done. Ellie looked up in time to see a single tear trickle down his cheek, lined in golden lamplight. She reached up and wiped it away.

Oliver's eyes fell closed. Slowly, he reached up and brushed his fingertips along the back of her hand. It was the first deliberate touch they'd shared in days, and Ellie felt it in the depths of her soul.

Anxiety tugged at her. "Am I ... is Wormwood still hurting you?"

"I can't tell. I don't ... feel right." A deep frown tugged at the corners of Oliver's lips. "I don't like it. I never wanted to be high again."

"I don't like heavy painkillers either, but I think you're about to be really grateful for them." *I already am.* Ellie shoved back another wave of her seemingly ever-present fear and skimmed the manual again. She wanted to do this as efficiently as possible, for both their sakes. "Are you ready for me to clean these up?"

"Yes."

"Okay." She glanced over at the kitchen, where a pair of scissors stuck out of a knife block on the counter. "Will you be devastated if I cut off your shirt?"

"It's already ruined."

"Perfect. That's going to make things a lot easier." Ellie grabbed the scissors, then returned to Oliver and sized up the situation. If she cut one long line down the back of his shirt, she could doctor whatever she found there, then ease it off from the front. That way, he wouldn't have to move much to get out of it. With those long sleeves of his, that was probably their best option.

Ellie gulped. *No matter what you see, just don't pass out.* She sank down on her knees beside him and started snipping the dark fabric at the nape of his neck. *This is* not *how I imagined taking your shirt off.*

"You imagined taking my shirt off?"

Heat rose in Ellie's cheeks as she realized the thought had escaped through her mouth. She spluttered something but stopped as Oliver's shoulders convulsed in a short, painful laugh.

"You're blushing, aren't you," he said.

"Nope."

"Don't lie. I can feel the heat from here."

A smile broke across Ellie's face as she worked. "Quit it," she said, letting a hint of laughter seep into her voice.

"No. Your laugh is so pretty. I love it."

An ache pierced Ellie. *He's high as a kite.* A fact she became grateful for seconds later, when she tried to lift a section of fabric and found it stuck to his skin. Nausea rose in her throat but she set her jaw anyway. "Oliver, I'm going to have to pull on your shirt a little, and it might hurt."

"Be fast."

Ellie pinched the fabric and jerked. Something *crackled,* scrunching under her fingers like tissue paper, and Oliver cried out. Ellie's nausea reared again, so strong that she doubled over this time. She was going to throw up, pass out, she couldn't handle what was under there—

Yes. You can. Now get up and do what you have to.

Ellie shuddered out a breath, then did just that.

"You okay?" she asked Oliver. His head was bowed, his elbows resting on his knees again, his breath coming in shallow gasps.

"Better than dead."

"... Okay. I'm a little more than halfway through. Hang in there."

Trying not to imagine what exactly her scissors were cutting, Ellie continued. Once past the ... blockage ... the going got much easier, until she snipped through the last bit of cloth holding the shirt together. Carefully, she parted the ruined fabric, revealing a mess of angry red burns. And in the center of his back—where her scissors had hit that nasty patch of resistance—was a charred, gray spot the color of burned wood right before it crumbles to ash. A faint, acrid smell wafted through the air.

Ellie held down a gag through sheer force of will. "I'm going to push it off your shoulders now."

"Fine." His voice was a whisper, full of some emotion Ellie was too tired to read.

Shirt off, antibiotic cream, bandages, bed. Four steps.

She could do four steps.

Ellie eased the shirt off his shoulders but paused as her fingers slid across a rough, raised patch at the top of his left shoulder blade. Oliver flinched, and Ellie realized she'd just touched his brand.

"Sorry," she said. "I—"

"Just keep going. It's okay for you to see it."

Fear pricked Ellie, but she made herself push the fabric away and down the upper part of his arms, revealing the hale skin of his strong shoulders, muscled by years of hard work. Even in this situation, her heart gave a wobble.

It didn't last, though, because now there was nothing to hide his burns. They radiated from that chalky, central mass in an amorphous blob, fading from a deep, purplish red to the livid cherry of a sunburn at their edges. So many emotions coursed through Ellie at the sight that she just decided to shut them behind a wall and deal with them later. Instead, her eyes flicked up to his left shoulder, and the raised scar there.

Her eyes filled with tears.

The brand was larger than she expected, almost the size of her hand. Someone had burned a perfect circle into his flesh, and within the circle was a rose, not quite in bloom. It was rough, jagged, and the thought of how much it must have hurt made Ellie's already angry stomach churn again.

"I can't believe someone could do this to another person," she whispered, almost to herself.

Oliver turned his head slightly. "It's okay now, Ellie. I'm not ashamed of it anymore." He relaxed, his head bowing. "That's ... *so* freeing."

Careful not to brush against his burns, Ellie leaned down and kissed Oliver's shoulder, right in the center of the rose. "You never needed to be."

A visible shiver went through him; he sighed. Ellie blinked and a tear fell onto his skin, trickling down the curve of his back, toward his burns. Quickly, she wiped it away—salt would feel horrendous on those wounds—then straightened, forcing her tired mind to focus.

"Are you doing okay, Ellie?"

"I'm fine." She reached for the bacitracin. "I'm glad we're safe for a while, though. After this, we'll both have earned a nap."

"Yeah." His voice went low, his words slurring. "Naps are ... *awesome.*"

Ellie blinked at him, then shook her head and popped the tube open. "I'm going to put bacitracin on your burns now, so—"

Oliver giggled.

Giggled.

"Baaasss ... uhtraysin. That word's funny."

High. As. A. Kite. Ellie hoped to anything and everything holy that she hadn't accidentally overdosed him. Or misdrugged him entirely. One pill should've been safe ... right?

If not, she resolved, *I'll bait Dean's ghost in and find a way to murder it for encouraging us to stay here.*

"That kiss felt good," Oliver murmured.

Ellie's throat constricted; she wondered how much of this he would remember in the morning, and how much of it—especially the triumph over his shame—he actually meant. She squeezed some of the goopy paste onto her hands, then took a deep breath. "Think of it while I put the antibiotic on. Even with the painkiller, it might still hurt."

"Okay."

Ellie pressed gentle fingers to his back and started to smear the paste across the burns—the least awful-looking ones first. Oliver tensed, his breath hissing through clenched teeth again. Fumbling, Ellie squeezed more paste onto her hand, then steeled herself and pressed it to the central, gray section.

Layers of charred skin flaked away, sticking to her fingers like papery layers of Helen's biscuits.

Oliver arched and cried out. Ellie gagged, and the world started to swirl. She flopped backward, her cheek hitting the couch's soft upholstery, and took deep, desperate breaths ...

" ... Sally ..."

What?

"... would've been funny ..."

Feeling returned to Ellie's limbs, and she became acutely aware of the goop on the tips of her fingers. She didn't let herself think about what else was on there.

Sucking in a breath, she made herself sit up. "What?"

"I said why didn't your parents name you Sally? Sally Forth? Would've been funny."

Ellie almost smiled. "Are you making a joke to try and cheer me up?"

"Yeah. Can't kiss you, so ..." He tried to shrug, then winced. "Ow."

"Hold still and let me ... let me finish this." Taking another deep breath, Ellie made herself look at his injury. She sagged in relief. "I actually ... I think I got it. Let me move to the front."

"Goody. Then I can look at you."

Oliver raised his head as Ellie moved in front of him, his gaze traveling slowly from her battered tennis shoes to her face. He gave a lopsided smile as she sat, his eyes tracking hers with enough focus that some of her tension eased. That *had* to be a good thing.

"You're so pretty," he said. "You look good in myyy sweatshirt."

Ellie's heart warmed, her smile breaking through. "You're killing me, Oliver."

"No. No." He shook his head, his eyes going solemn. They were so blue and deep, like a summer thunderstorm on the edge of the horizon. "I'll save you. I'll do ... *whatever* ... it takes."

Ellie reached out and touched his cheek with her goop-free hand, her feelings suddenly so tender she could hardly speak.

"Let's finish this and get you in bed," she finally managed.

"And you."

"And me." Ellie dropped her hand and steeled herself again. The burns on his back had been bad enough; who knew what they were in for now? She reached for his shirt, still bunched at his shoulders. "Let's get this off."

"Ooo-kaay."

The ruined fabric didn't stick this time, but as it slid down his arms, Ellie paused. Then, her mouth fell open. Delicate red lines webbed across his skin, crisscrossing over and around each other like little forks of lightning. Or ... like blood vessels.

Ellie gulped. *Those can't be good.*

"Uh ..." She glanced at Oliver's face. He was staring down at his arms with the kind of look Ellie had seen on young Sam's face when he'd found an extra interesting bug.

"Cool," he said.

"*Cool?*"

"They're so fancy."

"Oh my hell—"

"Look. They're doing stuff."

Ellie frowned. He was right; the outermost lines were fading before her eyes, disappearing back into his skin like they'd never been there. Despite her fear and exhaustion, a little bit of wonder snuck into her voice. "And they don't hurt, you say?"

"Nope." He chuckled. "Wow. Look at them *go!*"

Well, if they're going to fix themselves … Ellie rubbed her eyes, then finished tugging Oliver's shirt off, revealing a chest and stomach every bit as sculpted as his back. To her relief, the damage wasn't as bad as she'd thought it might be. He was burned across his pectorals and down to his mid-abdomen, the skin there livid and hot, but she couldn't see any hint of the hideous grayish patches that marred his back. A scabbed-over cut about four inches long gaped just below the burn line, his only relic of their fight at the border.

Ellie briefly wondered why the burns were worse on his back than his chest—where he'd actually been *hit*—but didn't have the energy to dwell on it. She wadded his shirt into a ball and chucked it, then looked back to find Oliver watching her.

His eyes were so openly adoring that Ellie almost forgot how to breathe.

"You're incredible. I …" He winced and clenched his teeth. "Ow."

Ellie reached for the bacitracin. "Here, sit up. You can get sappy on me after we deal with this."

Oliver sat as straight as he could, and she managed to cover his burns quickly and with minimal wooziness. Then, following the manual's instructions, she wrapped non-stick bandages around his torso. Once finished, she sat back and studied her handiwork. It would do for tonight, but she *definitely* wasn't cut out for nursing school.

"Is that comfortable?" she asked.

"Yeeep." He looked at her, grave now. "When we get out of here, we should find sommme … Starbursts."

"Okay." She stood. "Bedtime. Let me help you up."

Ellie held out her hand and Oliver took it, leaning heavily on her until he got his feet underneath him.

"That was easier than last time," he grunted. He didn't look like it—his eyes were half closed and he slumped against Ellie enough to make her stagger, but when they started forward, he did seem steadier. Which was good, because now that the pressure was off, Ellie was crashing hard.

Together, they stumbled into the bedroom. Ellie released Oliver, pulled back the covers on the queen-sized bed, then helped him lower himself onto it. "Let me get you water. You'll probably need lots."

When she returned with the biggest glass she could find, Oliver was lying on his side with his eyes closed, his breathing quiet and even. She hesitated. Should she pull the covers up around him? She'd wrapped his burns well enough that the sheets shouldn't irritate them, and the field guide *had* said to keep the victim warm ...

Ellie reached for the blankets and was just pulling them up around Oliver's waist when he stirred. He grabbed her hand, his eyes fluttering open. "Stay with me."

Emotion flooded over Ellie, turning every beat of her heart into a throb. She glanced at the closet; she'd been planning on curling up on the couch underneath one of the many quilts stashed in it. But the lure of a real mattress, with real sheets, and with *Oliver* next to her ...

She shouldn't. What if she rolled into him and tore at his burns while they slept? What if sleeping next to him was too *distracting* for him? He was in no state to do anything about it, but he needed sleep above all else. And so did she.

"Oliver ... I ..."

"Please," he whispered.

"... Okay."

Ellie pulled his sweatshirt over her head and tossed it onto the foot of the bed, leaving her in her tee shirt and hiking pants. *Lucky for me, they're comfortable,* she thought as she swung her legs into bed. She hoped Oliver's were, too, though he was so exhausted he probably didn't care.

Carefully, she lay down and pulled the blanket over them both. Oliver let out a soft sound, then his arm draped around her waist. He tugged her closer, closer, until her back just brushed the soft bandages around his chest. A sigh escaped Ellie as his warmth seeped into her. For the first time in days, she felt safe.

Oliver nuzzled her hair, then his lips brushed the nape of her neck in a soft kiss. "I love you."

Ellie melted. Sleep was forcing her eyes shut, and judging by the way Oliver slumped against her, he was already gone. With how drugged he was, he probably wouldn't re-member what he'd said in the morning, but Ellie still let the words wrap around her, as warm and strong as his arms and bringing a depth of joy she'd never known.

"I love you, too," she whispered, and was gone.

Chapter Twenty-Three

Sam took a disproportionate amount of solace from the fact that he could at least take his traumatized wife out to a nice dinner. And it was a *nice* dinner. Brazilian-steakhouse style, with an open buffet, fruit so fresh he wouldn't have been surprised if they'd picked it that morning, and the most sumptuous, high-end cuts of meat money could buy. He was relieved when Darien tucked in with abandon. She and their baby needed it.

Sam had been hungry, too. Until he'd seen the shadow.

It was a flicker at the edge of his vision; nothing more. If he hadn't been on edge from the events of the day, he probably wouldn't have noticed it. But he was. So, he did. And when he'd turned, there had been nothing there.

Sam wrote it off as exhaustion and cut into his honey-glazed ham, smiling at something dryly observant that Darien said, relieved that she seemed more or less normal. He had just finished the ham and was taking a sip from his glass of wine—the only one he'd allowed himself on this whole trip so far—when another shape rose on the edge of his vision and hovered there. Within an eyeblink, it was gone.

Sam set his wine glass down.

"Sam?"

"Yeah?"

"Are you okay?"

"Uh …" Sam picked up his fork and started twirling it. "I think I'm more tired than I realized. Don't get me wrong, I'm glad we decided to keep our reservation anyway, but man …"

"Me, too." Darien wrinkled her nose. "My emotions feel weird."

"Well, we've had an insane day, *and* you're pregnant. I think it's amazing you're only feeling weird and not … worse."

"That's true, but ... I don't know. They're ... I don't know how to describe them." She eyed a tray of bacon-wrapped beef filets that a waiter was offering to some diners across the aisle. "At least it hasn't affected my appetite much."

"That's good." Sam glanced toward where he'd seen the last shadow. It had seemed ... human shaped. Maybe that wine was stronger than he'd first thought.

Maybe you're just losing your mind. Seeing demons where there are none.

"Maybe we should've just gone back to the hotel," he said absently.

"Our room isn't exactly restful anymore, though." Darien lowered her voice. "Not since we've implemented our demon-taming program."

"Yeah. Being *this* deliberate with my thoughts is a lot more work than I thought it would be."

Darien nodded, then flagged down the waiter and watched with open anticipation as he piled their plates with steak. Sam's lips quirked up as he watched her.

Darien smiled. "*This* looks—"

Movement.

Sam's eyes flicked to the next table over as a humanoid shape materialized behind a petite, middle-aged woman. It was tall—taller than any of the wait staff—and seemed to warp the light around it as it bent over her, reaching toward her head.

Sam pushed his chair back with a rasp of metal on tile, ready to get up, to run to her aid. But as quickly as it had come, the thing was gone.

"Sam?"

He turned. Darien was staring at him with her mouth half-open, steak forgotten. "What's happening?"

Sam leaned over the table and she mirrored him, her face deeply concerned.

"Did you see the demon?"

Her eyes widened. "No. There's one here? Over there?"

"Yeah. He was there for a second, then disappeared."

"Wait ..." Darien put a hand over his and glanced around. "That doesn't make sense, though. This place is packed. Someone else should have seen it, too, and no one's ..."

"Panicking?" Sam supplied.

"Acting like they did, yeah. Plus, they shouldn't *want* to hunt in a crowd. They—"

A shape oozed across the floor behind Darien, following a waiter. Sam swore and rocked backward, nearly pitching over before he righted himself. A man at the next table over turned to look at him, frowning.

"Sorry," Sam said, then frowned and looked down. He'd put his elbow in the center of his plate, knocking steak and a half-eaten ring of pineapple into his lap.

"Sam?" Darien's eyes were huge and intense. "You're freaking me out!"

"There was another one. Following that waiter. It looked ... different, though. I think it was a different one."

"Do we need to leave?"

Do we need to ...? Sam shook himself. "Have you eaten enough?"

"Have *you*?" She pointed her fork at the plate he'd filled minutes earlier at the salad bar—the one out of range of his flying elbows. "You've barely touched any of that."

Sam looked down at his lap and sighed. The filet was juicy and pink in the center, exactly how he liked it. And on his salad plate, three strawberries as big as his nose glistened next to rings of pineapple, scoops of parmesan-covered vegetables, and a heaping spoonful of fluffy, richly seasoned quinoa.

He looked up at Darien again. "I'm fine, I ..."

Another shadow rose behind her. Sam stiffened as it came closer, closer, and bent over her, warping the dim restaurant light into a sickly amber halo.

Her eyes went wide with terror. "Is there one behind me?"

Sam swallowed and nodded. "It doesn't look like either of the other ones. It's something new."

Darien twisted to look behind her, straight at the creature. It didn't move, and judging by her lack of panic, she couldn't even see it.

"What do I do?" she asked.

Sam took her hand. "If pattern holds, it should—"

But it was already fading, gone as if it had never been there.

Sam sagged with relief. "It's left. I might need a box."

"Let's flag down a waiter."

Minutes later they walked out the door, carrying their leftovers. No other shapes had materialized but Sam could swear he'd seen more shadows, flitting just on the edges of his vision.

"Can you see any more?" Darien asked as they crossed the parking lot.

"Not at the moment. Do you think they're demons? They don't look like the Lady or Ankle Tickler—they don't really have shapes. But I can't think of what else they would be."

Unless they're part of some other *urban legend I don't know about.* Sam tried not to shudder visibly as the implications of that thought hit him. What if this was how he'd see the world for the rest of his life?

Darien shrugged. "That makes the most sense, but ... I don't know. There are so many accounts of things people see out of the corners of their eyes ..."

"They *feel* like demons," Sam said firmly.

"Well, the Night Marchers said we'd probably be more sensitive to the demons and their world, so I vote we assume that's what's going on." Darien rubbed her forehead. "Maybe you can now see demons that other people don't."

"Lucky me." Sam opened Darien's door. They didn't usually do that but tonight was—should have been—special, and some part of him wanted to cling to that. Darien sat heavily and pinched the bridge of her nose. Sam's heart unraveled a little more as he looked at her. "Are you all right, Dar?"

"I don't know. We're probably safer in there with all those people, but I feel better out here. I'm ... weirdly relieved."

"Well, let's get back to our room," Sam said as he slid into the driver's seat. "If nothing else, we can make sure we both get enough sleep tonight."

"Maybe we'll have tamed Ankle Tickler enough to trust him."

"Maybe." *And maybe Santa Claus will show up with my mom, dad, and Lily in the back of his sled and tell me this has all been one big fever dream and that everything's fine.*

Sam drove out onto the street and cracked the window, the warm, tropical air wisping across his skin, through his hair. For a minute, neither of them spoke.

"How're your feelings now?" Sam asked.

"Better-ish?"

Sam waited, but Darien didn't speak again. When he glanced at her, she was staring out her window at the last light of the sunset. Nature had always brought her solace; Sam swore she could find beauty even in scrubby, sage-covered wastelands. He, on the other hand, would have driven right past the sun's last revelry and not even looked at it if not for her. Not when he was seeing demons left, right, and center—demons that didn't look like the ones he'd encountered before, and that no one else could see.

"How do you do it?" he asked softly.

Darien looked at him. "Do what?"

Rolling up his window, Sam gathered his thoughts as he merged onto the highway that would take them back to the Four Seasons. "How is this not rocking your whole world?"

"The Night Marchers? The demons? The shadows you're seeing?"

"Yeah." Sam stole another glance at Darien. Her dark eyes were thoughtful, her skin lit by the dimming sun with a fiery, rosy glow.

"Give me a minute to think about that one," she said.

"That's fine."

With that, she was quiet, and Sam let her be. He just drove through the Hawaiian dusk, past cheerfully lit neighborhoods and dark snarls of forest. Were the Night Marchers out there somewhere? Protecting those they loved?

Movement flitted in the rearview mirror, and Sam looked back. A gray shape was following them; it warped the wine-red light of the sunset into the deep scarlet of new blood. Adrenaline shot through Sam until he realized it was falling behind; they were outdistancing it. After what couldn't have been more than five seconds, it faded away.

Sam swallowed and fixed his eyes on the road. If this was going to become a regular thing, he needed to get his reactions under control so he didn't drive Darien insane.

Or *seem* insane to, well, everyone else.

Even though I feel insane.

And with that, the top blew off his internal volcano.

"What's *real*, Darien? More importantly, what *isn't* real?" He gripped the steering wheel. "I was just starting to come to grips with alternate dimensions. Like, yeah, that's something straight out of science fiction, but it theoretically could happen. These ... demons ... they aren't actually *demons*. They're living creatures from another world, like aliens. I can live with aliens—even if they don't make sense, they can still *make sense*. As a concept, at least."

Darien reached over and put a hand on his shoulder, but didn't interrupt. Sam was grateful; it felt so good to finally voice his turmoil that he didn't want to stop.

"But we just talked with the ghosts of ancient Hawaiian warriors! They had names, families ... idiosyncrasies! They were *people*!" His voice shook. "I was doing okay until *souls* got involved. Now I don't know what to do, or think."

"How did you reconcile the fact that your dad's spirit is what's holding the gate open?" Darien asked.

Sam briefly closed his eyes. Darien had a gift for asking direct questions in a way that didn't make him feel ridiculous or judged, and this one was no different. He thought for a moment. "I guess I assumed it was his ... energy? That somehow they'd harnessed the physical energy from his ... body as he'd ... died?"

"That would take incredible technology, and we've seen no evidence of that."

"Unless it was something their biology could do. Unless ... gah, but it doesn't matter! What matters, what's getting me, is ... Darien, the *empirical evidence* that souls exist not only looked me in the eye earlier, but implied they might've *speared* us if the situation had been different."

"Yes."

"I should've asked them more questions. I should've—"

"What, like, 'where do we go after we die?'"

"Yeah!"

"They wouldn't have told you."

"Why the hell not?"

"Because those are the types of conclusions you have to come to on your own."

Sam nearly threw up his hands. "I *did* come to the conclusions! I went to counseling, to family therapy, I talked to teachers and good friends, and my grandparents, and what I came away with was the comfort that Mom and Lily never had to suffer again."

Sam's voice broke. "They lived amazing lives. Were they too short? Yes. But they laughed so much, and they did so many wonderful things. Dad, too. Even though they're gone, their impact won't die for ... for decades, maybe longer. Lily's memorial bench at her elementary school—it's going to last for as long as the school is there. Many, *many* people loved them, will remember them. I'd found peace in that. I'd come to terms with it.

"And it made me value *life*, Darien." Sam scraped his teeth across his lip, as if he could get it to quit trembling through sheer intimidation. When that didn't work, he barreled on. "It's so fragile, and short. If this is all we got, we have to *live* it. I think that's the attitude that's gotten me through school, that got me onto the team, that gave me the courage to ask you to marry me."

He attempted a smile. It failed.

"But now that there's more ... what do I do? I don't *know* if I want to live forever. What will I *become* if I live forever? That seems like a good way to go insane."

"If it's any comfort," Darien said gently, "many religions think we'll be more or less happy after we die. Sure, there are some hellfire-and-damnation sects out there, but that's not the view I subscribe to."

"How did you pick?" Sam asked.

"Which one to go to?"

"Yeah. There are so many out there. And it seems like they don't agree on *anything*." He rubbed his face. "And none of them say anything about Night Marchers or ... or interdimensional *misery* vampires."

Darien let out a wry laugh. "That's true." She considered for a moment. "It's evolving. I'm always looking for the truth. There's a ... feeling, sometimes, that I get at church—at my current one, at least—that I've never found anywhere else. That's why I keep going, even if I am sporadic."

"What if you die and find out you were wrong?"

"Then I'll hope the fact that I tried to stick to my morals, that I was kind and compassionate and worked hard and loved the people—and animals—around me will be enough."

Sam looked over at her. "That level of uncertainty terrifies me."

"That's the nature of life. It comforts me that Oliver and Ellie seem to have a guardian angel of some kind, though. I like to believe that's how it really is. That our loved ones are still out there watching over us." Darien squeezed his shoulder, then traced her fingers across the back of his neck. "But nothing is certain."

"Why should whatever's on the other side be any different?" Sam murmured, almost to himself.

"I actually think getting to the other side will clear a lot of things up."

Admiration and exasperation swelled within him. "I have no idea how you reconcile it all. I admire it, I do. I don't think you're crazy or silly."

"I don't think you are, either," Darien said. "I respect the work you've done to get to the philosophy you've arrived at. I hope you don't think I'm trying to preach to you or anything. We've both got a lot to figure out here."

"You're just handling it so well. I'm ... envious, honestly."

"Less well than you might think," Darien murmured.

They didn't speak again until Sam pulled the sedan into the hotel's parking lot and turned off the engine. He twirled the key absently between his fingers.

"I think what I need to figure out first," he said, "is where to draw the line."

"What do you mean?"

Sam scratched behind his ear. He felt calmer now, but only a little. "I mean, I thought I knew how lightning worked. But what if I'm wrong, and it actually *has* been Zeus this whole time? Or Thor? Or whoever."

Darien took his hand. "Sam, rule number one of a faith crisis is to never throw what you already know out the window. If all you know right now is how lightning works, you cling to that."

"It's not Zeus?"

"I highly doubt it. I mean, Zeus might exist. If Bigfoot can, why not? But if he does, he's probably some interdimensional ... *something* ... with the ability to create lightning."

"But that doesn't make him the source of all lightning," Sam said.

Darien nodded. "The world we live in is the same one as it was five days ago. The *only* difference is that we know a little more about it now."

"I guess that's true."

They sat in silence for another moment, watching the last dregs of gray sunlight leach away.

"Shall we go check on our pet?" Darien asked.

"Might as well." Sam got out, opened Darien's door, then took her hand. "I'm hoping that by the end of the night, we'll have convinced him to go from grabbing ankles to giving foot massages—"

Another shadow. This one hovered lazily to the side of the door, revolving in the pool of light that spilled from the entrance like it was a luxury swimming pool. Sam stopped.

Darien's hand tightened within his. "Another one?"

He nodded. "Right by the door. We're going to have to walk past it to get in."

"Have you ever seen one hurt somebody?"

"No, but my sample size isn't very big."

"True." Darien's eyes darted around the area, everywhere but at the thing itself. She looked hesitant, afraid.

"Wait ..." Sam peered at the thing; its movements weren't changing but it seemed to be growing more transparent. "It's fading."

Sam watched the apparition until it disappeared. "It's gone. I didn't see it move away, but ... Do we risk it?"

Darien squared her shoulders. "Well, to borrow a point from our earlier conversation, we've probably walked right by a lot of these things without knowing it. Even if they are demons, they've been here for over a month at this point and we're not dead yet."

"That's true." Sam tried to swallow his trepidation. "All right, let's go."

They walked by the place where the shadow had hovered with no problem whatsoever. It could have been any other patch of balmy, humid air for all the difference it made.

"Well, that's comforting at least," Sam muttered as they stepped into the huge lobby. Hundreds of little lights reflected off the impeccably polished floor, warm and inviting, beckoning him toward rest. Sleep. Peace.

What a cruel illusion.

They were almost across the lobby before Sam spotted it, looming behind the smiling hotel clerk like it had stepped out of a nightmare. A demon. Solid, actualized, humanoid. He stopped dead.

It was as tall as Sam, with a heavily muscled chest and arms, but that was where its similarity to him—or *any* human—ended. Its unnaturally long neck shriveled as it ascended, forming into a grotesque, doglike head. It leaned over the clerk, its deformed jowls nearly touching her shoulder. And she smiled, helping the customers in front of her like nothing in the world was wrong.

"Another one?" Darien muttered.

"It's behind the clerk. It looks totally different, like a man with a dog's head." *But, like, a* mummified *dog's head.* "You can't see it?"

"No."

Sam gulped, trying to bring his voice down to its normal range. "It's ... it's not just a shadow. It's very ... realized." *And very horrifying.*

Darien seized his arm. "Quick, look away."

"Why?"

"I think we can safely assume you can see demons now, even the ones that are invisible to everyone else. That gives us an advantage. Let's not give it away."

Sam tore his eyes away from the monster, shaking.

"Also, if you're the only one who's seen that one, we don't want you accidentally changing him into something even more terrifying. Come on." Darien tugged him after her, and he followed meekly to the elevator. "There's nothing we can do to help her, and everything we have to gain from keeping this under wraps."

A few mercifully demon-free minutes later, they stepped into their room and let the heavy door close behind them with a *click*. Sam sank down on the soft couch, still shaking. "I don't like this superpower."

"I'll bet not," Darien muttered, plopping her purse on the end table. She settled down next to him.

"Where's your mystical ability?"

"I don't know," she said softly. "Yours took a minute to show up. Obviously mine needs a little longer." She didn't sound excited.

"Thank your lucky stars," Sam said.

"I am." Darien frowned at the wall for a second, then shook herself and peered under the bed. Sam followed her gaze. Orange eyes glinted back, reflecting the light of the full moon as it rose over the gleaming ocean.

"Can you see Ankle Tickler?" Sam whispered.

"Yes."

Sam let out a sigh of relief. The eyes blinked and tilted, as if the creature were trying to decide what to make of them. Then, defying convention, it crept out from underneath the bed.

Sam's shoulders tensed. Next to him, Darien leaned forward, lips parted, eyes wide. The creature stopped and sat, curling its thick, furry tail around its front paws like a cat. Then, it just stared some more.

"Are you hungry?" Darien asked. Slowly, she lowered her feet to the ground, and Sam's heart leaped into his throat. He wished she wouldn't do that, but the creature did seem to have a clear preference. In solidarity, he planted his feet on the floor next to hers.

The creature cocked its head the other way, opening its mouth as if scenting the air. Then, it uncurled itself and padded forward with a lithe, predatory gait.

"It doesn't move like an aye-aye," Darien said.

"No?"

She shook her head. "They're more awkward. But this ... this is interesting ... behavior ..." She stopped talking as Ankle Tickler reached her. The demon twined around her ankles like a cat, then settled on her bare feet, stroking her ankles with those impossibly long fingers.

"Are you not afraid of us anymore?" she asked.

It didn't respond; just sat there staring out the window, almost as if it were admiring the view.

Curious, Sam tapped his foot lightly against the ground. Ankle Tickler twisted its neck up to look at him, those luminescent eyes feral, guarded, but also ... innocent? *Is that the right descriptor?*

"Great, so you're the family cat, now," he grumbled.

"He's a little cold. Cats are generally warmer." Darien leaned forward more, resting her elbows on her thighs and meeting the creature's eyes. It stared up at her. "What are you feeding on? Because I'm not really afraid of you anymore."

"Probably me," Sam said.

The demon cocked its head at him.

"Let me clarify," Sam said. "I'm afraid of many things. The shadows, the afterlife, the ... thing downstairs ... but I'm not scared of *you*. I'll still tear you limb from limb if I have to. Punt you like a football."

The demon blinked, then yawned.

That's just insulting, Sam thought. "Anyway, now that we've cleared that up ..." He turned to Darien. "I think ... please don't be too frustrated with me about this, but I think we should consider going to Alaska."

"I was going to suggest the same thing," Darien said.

"Really?"

"Yes. Especially after tonight. They're in for a fight, and they're going to need all the help they can get. With you being able to see things others can't, you could save lives."

Sam's heart sank even as determination rose within him. He nodded at Ankle Tickler. "What are we going to do with him?"

Darien bit her lip and looked down at the demon, who was still rubbing its too-long fingers lightly across her ankles. "I don't know. After this, I almost hate to leave him here." She paused. "I guess we could take him with us."

Sam's heart squeezed. "Dar ... yes, we could take him with us, if he wanted to go. But our primary objective still has to be to close the gate. In the end, he'll have to go back to his world."

"I know. I won't get attached."

"Okay." Sam started to rub her back. "Your compassion is beautiful. It's one of the things I love most about you. Don't ever, ever think it's a problem. I just don't want you to get hurt by this thing."

Ankle Tickler stretched, then uncurled himself and ambled under the couch. The hair on the back of Sam's neck threatened to rise; no matter how friendly the thing had become, no matter how much they seemed to be able to influence it, he couldn't bring himself to trust it.

Darien sat for a moment longer, then straightened. "Let's find some plane tickets, then get a good night's sleep."

They shared a glance and Sam knew they were thinking the same thing: it might be their last decent night for a while.

Death trembled as he extended his consciousness to the limits of his ability. Two more had Awakened within the last several hours but it was the one in Hawaii that he kept going back to. The one that felt more primitive, more raw. The one that had yet to speak back to him.

He fell to his knees. He would need to feast *after this. He needed his strength, especially since Wormwood—*

Wormwood. *How long had it been?*

Death tore his thoughts away from Hawaii and searched closer, honing in on his hateful little mentee. There was no denying the resentment there, the mutual loathing. Soon, he might have to do something about it.

"Wormwood," he snarled. The other demon was sated, heady, deliriously happy; all reason had deserted him.

"What?" came the surly response.

"Get back to Ellie. NOW!"

Chapter Twenty-Four

The first thing Ellie became aware of was cool air on her back. She stirred, blinking, trying to coalesce her memory's foggy haze into something solid and understandable. The fire, the fight, the Lady blazing white-hot against a backdrop of stars. Oliver's dead, staring eyes, his awful burns, helping him ease his wrecked body onto the bed ...

His lips, soft on the nape of her neck. His words.

Something rustled behind her.

A bone-deep ache shivered its way into the pit of Ellie's stomach. She pushed herself up and turned. Oliver was sitting with his back to her, silhouetted against the morning light that blushed around the edges of the curtains. The water glass she'd put on his bedside table the night before was gone; she assumed he was holding it.

"Oliver?"

He half-turned. "Hey, Ellie." His voice was tired-sounding, but steady.

She scooted toward him. "How are you feeling?"

"Better than I was."

Grimacing, Oliver leaned over and set the glass on the table. Ellie surveyed him. His bandages still seemed reasonably tight and clearly he was in good enough shape to get himself water. But what state were his burns in? Especially after he'd held her in his sleep for the last few hours?

Mentally, she kicked herself. *I shouldn't have let him.*

Awkwardly, Oliver shifted so he was facing her and shot her a pained smile. "Look, I can move."

Ellie hesitated. She had no idea what time it was, or how long it would take the drugs to wear off, but ... "Are you still, um, loopy?"

The smile slid off his face. "I don't think so. It's hard to tell you're high when you're ...
high. But I don't feel like my head's going to float away, and I'm not sick anymore, so ..."
He gave a painful-looking shrug.

"Do you need more medicine?" Ellie scooted forward, then leaned around him and
examined the dressings on his back. They looked ... as good as could be expected? She bit
back a surge of frustration at her own lack of knowledge. Demons aside, they needed to
get somewhere with cell service so they could video call Darien and have *her* take a look.

"Not right now."

Ellie raised an eyebrow.

Oliver smiled slightly. "I really do feel better, and I really will take more medicine if I
need it."

"Okay." Ellie sank back onto her knees in front of him. His eyes tracked her movements
perfectly; they were clear and steady, and ... and so soft. For a moment, Ellie just stared
into them. *Did you mean what you said last night?*

She tore her eyes away from his, reached for his hand, then hesitated. "Tell me if this
hurts."

Oliver swallowed, and she knew he wasn't thinking about pain caused by his injuries,
either. "I will."

Ellie took his hand, and when Oliver didn't flinch, she examined his arm. The skin was
clean, healthy; no evidence remained of the branching red lines that had crisscrossed it
only hours before.

She took his other hand, turned his arm over. "The lines are gone."

"Uh ..."

"That's incredible." Ellie looked up at him. "I don't know how much you remember
... but ..."

The look in Oliver's eyes—the tenderness, and yearning, and ferocity there—stole her
ability to breathe. She felt transfixed, captivated in a way she never had before. It was a
dreamy sort of madness, an ache as intense and deep as hunger. It was as if her *soul* needed
his.

It was terrifying.

"Do you remember the last thing you said to me before you fell asleep?" she asked.

Oliver's steady gaze didn't waver. "That I love you."

Ellie's voice dropped to a whisper. "Did you mean it?"

"Yes, I meant it. Both then, and now. I love you, Ellie." For the first time, uncertainty seemed to cross his face, but as quickly as it had come, it was gone. "If it's too soon for you, I understand. But—"

Ellie put a finger to his lips. "I love you, too, Oliver." His eyes widened and she smiled, letting her hand fall. "I told you last night, too, but you'd already fallen asleep—"

And then his mouth was on hers.

Ellie gasped at the sweet, searing shock of it. His lips were cool from the water, but they were the only thing about the kiss that was. It was hungry, lingering, and fierce, as if he were dying of thirst and she was an oasis. He wrapped an arm around her waist, his other hand splaying into her hair, cupping the back of her head. Ellie eased her hands across his bare shoulders, brushing the rose scar with the tips of her fingers. The muscles underneath were hard as iron, but his skin was velvet-soft, and his bandages—

His *bandages.*

Ellie broke this kiss. "Don't hurt yourself—" She started but Oliver kissed her again, seemingly heedless of his injuries. He paused just long enough to say, "I'm fine," before pulling her in again, tighter, tighter, and one of them overbalanced and they were both falling ...

Ellie hit the bed with a gasp, Oliver's arm still under her back, arching her against his bandaged chest. He let out a soft grunt of what might have been pain, but then his lips were on hers again, heated and insistent, his hand still cradling her head. They both smelled like smoke and sweat but Ellie didn't care because he was alive, and he was hers. His tongue brushed her lower lip, light as a butterfly's wingbeat. Ellie sighed, letting him deepen the kiss, losing herself in it.

Oliver shifted, taking some of his weight on his elbow. A pang of loss went through Ellie as he pulled back, his eyes closed, his head still bowed toward hers. But he was hurt, too hurt to be doing *this*—

He kissed the side of her mouth.

"Oliver ..."

His lips traced a slow, burning path across her cheek, along her jawline. He stopped, sighing, his breath warm on her neck, raising goosebumps that tingled through every cell in her body. "Yes?"

Don't hurt yourself.

Don't stop.

"Yes, Ellie?" His words were barely a whisper, his lips brushing against her skin with each one. Ellie's hands tightened on his shoulders; they *needed* to stop, to fix him, to move. But finally—*finally*—they were in each other's arms, and who knew when they'd have this chance again? So she twined her fingers into his silky black hair and she pulled his head down, down, until his lips touched her neck.

Ellie's breathing hitched, and Oliver's grew unsteady, too. His arm tightened around her waist, his lips lingering over her pulse before moving on, trailing featherlight kisses down her neck to her collarbone. She turned her face into his hair and weaved her fingers through it, and there was a reason they should stop but she couldn't remember it; she could barely remember her own name. Not with the way he was holding her, as if she were the most precious thing on earth. Not with the way his lips were circling the hollow of her throat; not when her heart was aching with the fiercest, most powerful joy she'd ever known.

Slowly, almost lazily, Oliver kissed his way back up her neck, pressing the last one to the sensitive skin behind her ear. "Eleanor," he breathed.

Ellie couldn't manage anything more than a whimper.

Oliver laughed softly, then kissed her lips again, gentler now. Another kiss, slow and serene, and a third, each more tender than the last. He dropped his head, his breathing shallow and uneven against her neck. Then, with a little groan, he collapsed on his side next to her.

Alarm punched holes through the butterflies in Ellie's stomach; she came up on her elbow. "Are ... are you okay?"

"I'm great." His eyes flickered open. "It's just a little pain."

Ellie stroked a thumb across his stubbled cheek. "Just a *little* pain?"

Oliver snorted. "After last night, I have a new perspective." Something changed in his expression, the humor fading from it. "Ellie, I'm sorry if that was ... too much. I didn't mean to get carried away."

That beautiful ache settled in Ellie's heart again; she leaned down and kissed him, soft and lingering and gentle. He reached up and laid his hand on her cheek, then slid it into her hair, easing her down next to him.

Ellie nuzzled his face, relishing his sigh. "Nothing I've experienced has ever felt like this before. Not in high school, college, Italy ..." Ellie angled her head, letting her lips brush his with every word. "It means *so much more*."

His lips curved upward against hers. "Nice to know I can do a better job even when I can't finish the job."

Ellie giggled, a strange combination of heat and nerves shrouding her like a blanket. Someday, they'd cross that bridge. Someday …

But not today. Today, they really needed to get on the road.

Apparently, Oliver was thinking the same thing, because he let out a heavy sigh. "We should go."

"Yeah. And your bandages need to be changed—"

"Well, *this* is compromising."

Ellie's eyes shot open to find Oliver's already wide and glinting with carefully controlled rage. Revulsion coursed through her; she bolted upright, peering in the direction of that raspy, snide voice, and let out a shocked cry.

She'd only seen Wormwood once—in the chapel right before the wedding—and her memory failed to fully capture the utter *weirdness* of him. Those too-large eyes set in a too-round head, that thin nose and slightly pointed ears … he looked like a devil straight out of an old storybook used to frighten children into obedience.

The demon's mouth stretched wide in an expression of glee. "I love the looks on your faces. I love stripping you down to your naked, ugly emotions in front of each other." The demon licked his lips. "There's no *end* to how much torment I can inflict that way."

Ellie felt Oliver move. She glanced back. He'd sat up and was scooting to the side of the bed.

"Oliver," she whispered, but he shook his head.

"He's always got to play the hero, Ellie," Wormwood said as Ellie scrambled to her knees. "It's the only thing he can do to convince himself he's worth anything."

Ellie felt like she'd been stabbed. She put a hand on Oliver's shoulder; it was painfully tense, but his eyes were determined and … *calm*?

"And he's right, Ellie," Wormwood added. "I've been in his mind for a long time. I know him better than anyone—even his own mother." The demon chuckled. "And definitely better than his father. Pretty face aside, he's not all he's cracked up to be."

Ellie whipped around, incandescent rage flooding her veins. "You have no right—you never had *any* right—"

Oliver's hand slid over hers. Then, gently but firmly, he pushed it off his shoulder and stood. His face twisted in pain.

"Don't believe him," Ellie said.

"I don't."

"Yes, you do," Wormwood scoffed. "You started all this, remember? Everything you've felt in the last month is all you. *I'm* just an opportunist."

Oliver stepped forward, rounding the corner of the bed. Wormwood watched his slow progress, amusement coloring his angular, wicked features.

"To hell with this." Ellie snatched the lighter off the bedside table and turned to face the demon, ready to murder him, *obliterate* him. "I killed the Lady, and I can kill you, too."

Wormwood smirked. "I'm not stupid enough to turn physical, you idiot. Besides, if you did burn me, I'd take the whole cabin down. And I don't think Oliver could get out in time; he's too weak and slow."

Ellie glanced at Oliver. He was rounding the bed's other corner now, still with that implacable look in his eyes. Despite what Wormwood said, she snuck closer to the demon. When it came to getting out of the cabin, she had faith in both herself and Oliver. If there was an opportunity to kill Wormwood, she was taking it.

"What did she think when she saw that little souvenir on your shoulder, Ollie? Was she more scared of it or your roasted back?"

"I'm not afraid of him," Ellie snarled. "Or you."

"Well, I know neither of those are true. Don't forget, I was in *your* head, too." Wormwood shot her a look that was far too knowing for comfort, then turned back to Oliver. "I think this is the worst state I've ever seen you in. And that includes the time back in Seldovia when you were considering bashing your head in just to try and get rid of me."

A sob rose in Ellie's throat; she tried to choke it back but didn't quite succeed.

Wormwood's grin widened. "I mean, what do you expect? Your daddy clearly had issues, and your mama, too. What makes you think you can live a happy life when they probably gave you all their problems?" The demon's voice lowered. "What makes you think you have a *right* to live a happy life when your mother suffered so much just to keep your worthless carcass alive? Especially after you turned right around and *caused* so much suffering."

Oliver's eyes flashed.

"Some way to thank her," Wormwood growled.

Feet from the demon, Oliver stopped. Ellie tensed, ready to take a swipe at the creature, but Oliver met her eyes and shook his head.

Wormwood let out a sardonic laugh. "Not hiding behind your girlfriend this time, Ollie? That's so *unlike* you."

Oliver still didn't say anything. Instead, he cocked his head, examining the demon with an expression that was suddenly calculating.

Wormwood's smile slid off his face. "What's the matter? Don't know what to do now that no one's taking the fall for you?"

A slow grin spread across Oliver's face, and Ellie's eyes widened. It was razor-thin and hard as iron, as far from his usual kind, lopsided smile as she could imagine. This was the grin of a wolf.

"You can't get inside my head."

The room went dead silent. Ellie could swear Wormwood paled.

"I *can* get inside your head," the demon snarled. "I can—"

Oliver tapped his temple. "Then why aren't you here? Why are you standing out there?"

Wormwood growled.

Oliver's eyes flashed again, and suddenly his grin was gone. "Come on. Hop on in. Make me hate myself again."

For several long seconds, man and demon stared at each other, the soft morning light wrapping around them both. It gilded Oliver's face and shoulders; he looked like a tattered, indomitable angel.

"Liar," he whispered.

Wormwood's face twisted. He let out a roar of rage, a scream that went on and on and on.

"You finished?" Oliver said softly. Wormwood started to snarl something but Oliver cut him off, still in that quiet, deadly tone. "There is *nothing* you can say to me now that I'll believe, and you know it. You're powerless, Wormwood."

"I can still fly after you!" the demon screamed. "I'll tell—"

"No, you won't." Oliver turned to Ellie and offered her his hand. She took it, climbing off the bed to stand straight-backed beside him. Then, pouring every ounce of her defiance into the look she leveled at Wormwood, she slipped her arm around Oliver's shoulders, feeling his go around her waist.

"I'm not ashamed of what I did," Oliver said, "because the boy who made those decisions isn't who I am now. But I'm grateful for him, because if I hadn't done that, been through that, I wouldn't be here." His eyes narrowed. "Overcoming you. Protecting my family and the woman I love."

"You don't have a family," Wormwood scoffed.

Oliver let out a humorless chuckle. "After a month of living inside my head—our heads—you still don't understand human beings." His arm tightened around Ellie's waist. "Goodbye, Wormwood."

The demon stormed after them. "You're still not free. There are millions of us. You can't break the Gatekeeper, and Death is coming for you."

"We've beaten everything you've thrown at us so far," Oliver said without turning back. "If I were making a bet, it would be on us at this point."

Ellie pushed the front door open and they stepped through, then looked back at where Wormwood stood in the middle of the living room, his fists clenched, his face contorted with rage and what might have been fear.

Savage pleasure bolted through Ellie. *Now you know how it feels.*

"I'm fast," the demon seethed. "I'll follow you."

"Let me make it perfectly clear," Oliver said. "If you come after us again, you will get another round of this, and you will end up humiliated and abandoned, just like you are now. You'll be at worst a mild inconvenience. And if you *dare* turn solid ..." A snarl entered Oliver's tone. "Well, you've been in my head. You know what I can do."

Wormwood said nothing. Oliver looked at him for a second longer, his expression turning faintly disgusted. "How's it feel to be the deer, Wormwood?"

Without waiting for a reply, he closed the door.

Ellie took his hand. "Are you ready?"

Oliver looked down at her and smiled his real, beautiful smile. "I am. Let's go bet on ourselves, Ellie."

Epilogue

*W*ormwood stayed in the cabin. *"I can't go after them."* He whispered the words aloud, even though he knew Death didn't need his voice in order to hear him.

"Can't, or won't?" Death asked.

"I... I can't." Wormwood's resolve hardened. There were other prey out there. If there was one thing in this world as common as human villainy, it was human shame. *"I won't."*

Silence greeted Wormwood's words. He waited, growing more sure of his course every second. In all his short time Awakened, he'd never been without an overseer. Other demons weren't so unlucky. They could be free, figure things out on their own. By some cruel twist of fate, he'd never had that, and he wanted it.

"I see," Death said. His voice was so low Wormwood had to strain to hear it, even in his own mind. *"Well, Wormwood, the good news is that there are other ways you can be useful."*

"Nah. Not to you. I'll make my own way to the gate and fight there, but that's all you'll get out of me."

"Is it?" Death's voice had become a slither. *"I'm hungry, Wormwood. I'm in a very small town with very few available options."* For a moment, Death's consciousness fuzzed and Wormwood felt a blinding rush of energy. Then, the other demon returned. *"Though I suppose it'll have to do."*

"That's not my ... problem ... anymore ..."

Death's thoughts blurred again, then again, then again. Wormwood frowned. *"How many are you killing?"*

Another ecstatic blur, then a moment of clarity. *"All of them."*

"Why?"

"For power."

Wormwood fought down a scoff. "You're out of control. If you kill them all, there will be none left, and then what will we eat?"

The blurs subsided; it seemed like Death had killed fifteen or more in the space of less than two minutes. It was the most reckless, wanton display Wormwood had ever seen.

"But contrary to what you believe, it isn't needless," Death purred.

"You idiot. Killing a whole town gives fuel to Oliver's story. The Seldovians are simple, not stupid. If they see this in the news—"

"That's no longer your concern, Wormwood."

"Of course it's my concern—"

"No, my dear Wormwood. It is not."

Then power the likes of which Wormwood had never known overwhelmed him; he was pinned in place, trapped in his body by a strength he couldn't believe existed.

"WITNESS THIS." Death's voice boomed in his mind. "WITNESS WHAT COMES TO THOSE WHO WILL NOT OBEY ME."

And then Wormwood was incandescent. He was writhing, screaming as Death burrowed into his very essence, devouring, consuming, splitting his every seam and edge, he was pain,

pain

PAIN

PAIN! Darien screamed and jerked upright, struggling to get out of the grasp of the monster that was killing her but it was all around her, twisting her silk shift across her midriff, clasping at her legs and arms. She thrashed her arms free and started beating at it, *tearing* at it—

"Darien! *Darien!*" Strong hands caught hers. "You're safe! Everything's okay. Stop before you hurt yourself!"

Awareness returned to Darien. She was gasping, and so soaked in sweat that she might as well have just crawled out of the ocean. Sam's face swam into view, inches from her own.

"Sam." She threw her arms around him and buried her face in his chest.

He rocked her back and forth. "I've got you, Dar. I've always got you." Gently, his fingers stroked through the tangled ends of her hair, brushing over the skin between her shoulder blades.

"That was the worst nightmare I've ever had," she said hoarsely.

"Do you want to talk about it?"

"I ... I was in a cabin and so angry. *So* angry. And then something ... something *ate* my mind from the inside out. It was awful, it was ..." Darien shuddered and Sam held her more tightly.

"It'll be okay," he said. "It wasn't real."

"I hope not. No one deserves to die like that."

Sam held her until the shudders subsided and long after. When they finally lay down again, he pulled her back against his chest and curved his massive, strong body around her. She shrank against him, burrowing into the security of his protection. There was no place in the world better than this.

"I've been awake most of the night so far," he whispered, his breath tickling the shell of her ear.

Darien frowned. "I thought we agreed we didn't have to do that anymore. Ankle Tickler's nice now."

"It's not because of him. I just ... can't sleep."

"You need to, though."

"I'd like to, believe me."

Darien sighed. "Have you heard anything from our little friend?"

"No. I'm sure he's around, though ..."

But Darien didn't hear the rest of Sam's sentence. The strangest feeling had come over her, as if another mind was brushing against hers, soft as cat fur. It was so curious, so hungry, and so ... *alien*.

"He's here. He's under the couch, watching us."

Sam pulled back. "How do you know?"

"I feel ..." Darien nearly choked. "I can feel his *mind*, Sam."

"*What?*"

But there was something else. Another mind, one much closer and much more ... *like* her. It was so simple it was barely a mind at all, but it exuded peace and comfort and rest. And *warmth,* the warmth of lounging in a hot bath, or being in the arms of a loved one, or ...

Or both.

Darien gasped and started to tremble again. "Sam ..."

He came up on one elbow, his face inches from hers, eyes so worried they were nearly frantic. "What is it?"

Darien looked up into those eyes that had captivated her since they'd first twinkled at her from across their classroom. "I can hear our baby."

Get Your Free Demon Fighting Playlist!

Sign up for Caitee's email list and get instant access to the Demon Fighting Playlist – over three hours of doubt-killing, fear-smashing music that's there to lift you up whenever you need it. Fun fact: it's also a *living* playlist, meaning music is being added all the time at the request of readers all over the world. (If you have a suggestion, send it to caiteecooper@gmail.com)

Go to caiteecooper.com to sign up!

If you enjoyed *The Dark Lady*, please consider leaving a review (or rating) on Amazon or Goodreads. Reviews help both authors and other readers, so you'd be doing everyone a huge favor. Thanks so much for your support!

Acknowledgements

If you read the acknowledgments section of any author's second novel, you'll notice a common theme: writing book two sucks. Seriously. Maybe it's because people are actually *watching* now. Maybe it's because you've been knocked off the top of Mount Stupid and are now painfully aware of how much you don't know. Maybe it's because it's the first experience with finishing something momentous ... and then having to start aaaaalll over again.

But who cares? We did it! And by "we," I really mean "we." I've been blessed with the most extraordinary team an author could have. Let me introduce you to them.

I owe my first and forever thank you to my Heavenly Father. As hard as writing The Dark Lady was, it was downright breezy compared to a lot of the other battles I fought during the six months I was actively writing it. I'm grateful for the little nudges of inspiration that came right when I needed them, for the lessons this book taught me about people, and for what I learned about myself while writing it. *Therefore have I set my face like a flint, and I know that I shall not be ashamed. (Isaiah 50:7)*

Second, to Dallin, who is truly my other half. Thanks for all the conversations, encouragement, feedback, icon designs, and yes, all the holes you poked in the plot. I love you, and I love that you can do that, even if I'm rolling my eyes in the moment. And second-and-a-half, thank you to Evan and Levi for your all your help, giggles, love, and patience. I'm lucky to be your mother!

Third, to my editorial team and beta readers: to Kayla Jackson for her sharp proofreading eye, to the incomparable Chris Chinchilla, (who may be the best beta reader on the face of this planet), and to Nikki B., Kate E., and Rebecca G. for your excellent feedback. Thank you to Laura Brotherson and her team for their expert opinions on a few key sections of this novel, and to Uncle Donny for your guidance on my portrayal of Hawaiian culture. And certainly not least, thank you to my Alpha team: Mom, Dad, Clara, Shelby, Jaxon, Alice, and Kari. I can't overstate how much each of you matters, both to me personally and to these books. Thank you for your time, thoughts, and especially for the deep, thought-provoking conversations that editing this one sparked. (Let me also throw in an additional thank-you to my parents, and to Dallin's parents. I loved and appreciated you before, but now that I'm a parent, I *get* it, and I can't thank you enough!)

Finally, a shout-out for all those who backed The Lady's Kickstarter: Brandon Adair, Clan McDonald, Jackie Kilby, Nichole Lavender-Booth, Nick Choate, Brandon B. Taylor, Rachel J, Shane Lobaugh, Rachel Meier, Steve & Kari Cooper, Ryan Scott James, Laura Oler, Meghan Wirick, Bud E. Cox, Anna L, Brandon and Lexi Thompson, Alexia, Shay, Mary, Neese, Cilla Graupmann, Samantha Newberry, Andrew Herrick, Kay Ross, my bestie Elinor Smith, Elizabeth W., Katherine Shipman, RLGoodell, Pamela M Smith, Michelle and Perry Swenson, Krystina Roupe, Katie Young, J.S. Baehr, Darian Hallsten, Emily Saunders, Karen P., Shannon J., Megan Peterson, Theresa Sorrell, Shane & Loree Cox, Amanda Dees, Keri Lindstrom, Amy W. Boyer, Rykki Neale, Aurora Winter, StarbuckApolloFemshepKaidanAliCole, Tori & Rhett Muchmore, Tina Jordan, Christy Dorrity, Annie, Matthew Wood, Stephen Wills, Lauren O'Byrne, Jenni D. Strand, Debbi and Jeff Anderson, Amanda Batta, Rachel J. Rapp, David & Wendy Pratt, Hannah McCort, Jeff Siegersma, Donna C. Morgan, Becky Condie, Jessica, and Morgan G.

It's always a humbling experience for an artist when people step up and support their work. I'd write in a vacuum, but it's so much more fulfilling when I can share my art with people (and I think, across mediums, most artists would agree.) Thank YOU for picking up this book, for taking a chance on an unknown, unproven indie author. I can only hope I delivered a book worthy of you all!

About The Author

Caitee Cooper grew up in Laramie, Wyoming, where she enjoyed all things outdoorsy, musical, and bookish. She went to college at the University of Wyoming, where she earned a B.S in Psychology, and met her husband, Dallin. They went on to start several businesses and have many adventures. Caitee currently lives in Casper, Wyoming with her husband, their two boys, and a half-feral barn cat.